More Early Praise for The Outsider

"For starters, The Outsider is a suspenseful yarn about brilliant, charming and cunning businessman-politician. But co-authors Marvin and Jamie McIntyre have more in mind than just suspense. They bring an insider's perspective to the world of financial economics, embellished by provocative writing set against a political backdrop grabbed from today's headlines. The result is a highly entertaining tale that's both authentic and informative. If you're into public policy - even if, like me, you don't embrace the protagonist's entire platform - just relax and enjoy a clever plot, intriguing and unpredictable characters, a dose of political philosophy and page-turning fun."

Robert A. Levy
Chairman of The Cato Institute

* * *

"After writing a number of unauthorized biographies (Jackie Kennedy, Frank Sinatra, Nancy Reagan}, I know what it's like to be The Outsider with insider knowledge. The McIntyres' prescriptive thriller will have you screaming at your television this election season."

Kitty Kelley
New York Times Best Selling Author

* * *

"What happens when a brilliant investor, with no regard for political correctness or rules of fair play, decides that he is anointed to "Fix America"? The Outsider has a plot that would have been considered impossible prior to this election cycle. With impeccable logic and page-turning action, the authors' have created a battle between an outsider and the establishment that requires your investment."

Bill Miller
Legendary Fund Manager

The Outsider

Marvin McIntyre and Jamie McIntyre

GraMac Press

Published by Dog Ear Publishing
4011 Vincennes Rd
Indianapolis, IN 46268
www.dogearpublishing.net

ISBN: 978-1-4575-5010-2

This is a work of fiction. All of the characters, names, incidents, organizations, and dialogue in this novel are either the products of the author's imagination or are used fictitiously.

Because of the dynamic nature of the Internet, any web addresses or links contained in this book may have changed since publication and may no longer be valid.

This book is printed on acid-free paper.

Printed in the United States of America

Dedication

IN JUNE OF 2014, I lost my best friend, Rick Sharp, to early onset Alzheimer's disease. We'd been friends for over 40 years; our families grew up together. Well, everyone but Rick and me; outside of business we remained infantile and immature.

Rick's business career was legendary: CEO and then chairman of Circuit City when the stock made its miraculous rise; CEO and then chairman of CarMax; and then chairman of Crocs. Even in his last years, Rick was arguably the smartest guy in the room.

In my first novel, *Insiders*, the character Rod Stanton was based on my friend. At the time the book was released, it was difficult for Rick to read, so we sat down on a sunny day and I read him the chapters about him. I'd made sure to make him a formidable personality, because he might not have been able to remember everything, but he would have remembered to pummel me.

The Outsider, a political thriller, was inspired by over two hundred walks in which my friend and I spent countless hours debating political absurdities. It is with honor and appreciation that my son and I have pledged all proceeds from our book to the Rick Sharp Alzheimer's Foundation.

PROLOGUE

July 4, 2018

THE SOLDIER LOOKED DOWN AT his hands, tanned and calloused. He held them out straight from his body: no movement. Training and experience assured that. Except this time was different.

On his knuckles were the symbols of his life's work — an eye for an eye. He felt that it was his Christian duty to place a cross on each victim and ask God to grant that person forgiveness and asylum in heaven. It was fitting that today he wore the collar of the cloth above his black shirt and accompanying pants. Normally, this outfit could attract undue attention. Today, as he mingled among the close to 800,000 people of all races, genders, and diverse discernment on what was appropriate attire for this historic event, it was clear that he blended in just fine.

Trained to be immune to weather or any external obstacles, he nevertheless felt the burn of the hot sun on the back of his neck. He could not escape the thought that the intense heat was the accusing finger of God.

The soldier never asked himself the logical questions: *Why would a man choose to become a lethal weapon for his government? How could a man of faith allow himself to break the Sixth Commandment, even when so ordered?* Or, in contemplating his personal idiosyncrasy, *Does my final act justify the taking of a life?*

His reflexes: still razor sharp. The equivalent of a third-degree black belt martial artist (his training did not believe in ceremony), he was able to use his 6 foot 1 inch frame to take down multiple opponents of much greater size. The foundation of his training was in jujutsu, which taught him that resisting a more powerful opponent will result in defeat. That instead, you adjust to your opponent's attack, using his aggressive momentum to propel him off balance, reducing his power. Only then can you defeat him.

Now, here he was, with a second chance to complete the only mission that he had failed, the only mission that had been unauthorized. The steadiness, the certainty that had guided him all his life, was gone. Now he was powerless, off balance, his mind a whirling dervish of regret and recrimination. He had been outmaneuvered, and his target's revenge would be eternal.

Sweat rolled off his chin. With the back of his left hand, he wiped his brow. Humidity in the nation's capital in July was omnipresent, cloying, suffocating. His right hand reflexively pulsed around the ceramic weapon in his pocket, tightening and untightening his fingers in concert with his resolve. He lifted the silver cross worn around his neck and pressed it to his lips.

This soldier never questions his orders. Duty's requirement is absolute. Deviation is not an option. His orders were specific and could not be countermanded. It did not matter that execution of the mission could be fatal to the soldier. It did not matter that execution of the order was treason.

PART I

CHAPTER 1

November 1, 2012

SHE AWOKE WITH A START. The luminous dial of the clock showed 2:07 a.m. She was disoriented, but adrenaline kicked her into full alert. Someone was pounding on her hotel room door. This was the Hay-Adams, right across from the White House. Hotels didn't get any more secure. Bomb? Fire? Her mind accelerated through a progression of the possibilities. Why wasn't there a siren or some sort of alert? Was the house phone out?

An involuntary shiver of fear ran through her. She swung her legs over the edge of the bed. She exhaled and considered more benign possibilities. Mischievous kids, a drunk who couldn't find his own room?

Her cell phone dinged. Text message. She grabbed the phone and squinted in the still-dark room:

No emergency. Package = present, yes or no by 2:45. You have first option. CC

She reread the message, took a breath. "CC" were the initials for "Concerned Citizen." It used to be a code just for her, but now the whole word knew. She reached out and turned on the bedside lamp. Whoever had been at her door was either gone or waiting for her to open it. Nice choice. The safest route would be to call the desk and ask someone to come to her room and check the package. She looked at the clock again: 2:11. No time.

She looked down at the oversized frayed Georgetown tee shirt that barely covered her backside. In moments of nostalgia, she would reflect that this was her former fiancé's favorite. She'd even imagine that his scent lingered in the soft cotton. A casualty of her job. He had wanted to domesticate her, have her step out of the limelight. So when he left, the faded tee shirt became her favorite and a sign of her independence. Nobody puts Baby in the corner.

Screw it. Calling for help was not her style. If someone was waiting, they'd get an eyeful. She looked around for a weapon in case she had to defend herself. The best she could come up with was the hair dryer from the bathroom.

Feeling ridiculous, but still apprehensive, she poked her head out the door. The hallway was empty. She quickly picked up the envelope, then closed and locked the door. She tore open the envelope and breathed a sigh of relief when she saw what it contained. In her business, a black thumb drive was not a sign of danger; it was a sign of opportunity. She opened her laptop and plugged the drive into the USB slot. As she opened the file, her screen went black with a small white line that undulated with a digitally altered voice. It sounded like hostage demands:

Friday, November 2, a Signature Air flight will leave at 10:00 a.m. from Washington Dulles Airport. You will be sedated en route. Lunch with subject at destination. Interview at 2:00 p.m. Return flight to Dulles at 4:00 p.m. You will be sedated. You will guarantee one half-hour special to be aired Sunday, November 4, at 8:00 p.m. No mention of subject to be interviewed. Absolute secrecy required. Reply by 2:45 a.m.

What the hell was this? She ran her hand through her thick, ash blond hair. Why didn't she just wear a sign around her neck that said, "Please abduct me?" Sedated ? Give me a break! Did she have the juice to call New York and tell them she would have an interview worthy of a primetime slot? *Yes.*

Who would watch an impromptu special if the subject of the interview was a mystery? She let that thought linger and again answered her own question.

Everyone.

CHAPTER 2

THE MIRROR HAD NOT BEEN kind this morning. At 61, Mac McGregor felt like he wasn't at the age yet where he was supposed to feel old, so that didn't enter his mind. His short brown hair was sprinkled with flecks of gray, but he preferred to think that made him look distinguished. From an appearance standpoint, in a dark suit, starched white shirt, and perfectly knotted blue silk tie, he might get away with that look. If by accident he was in a totally serious mode, a bystander in his native Washington, D.C, could easily mistake him for a congressman, a lawyer, or a television personality. The answer was (d) none of the above.

Mac was a financial advisor, or wealth advisor, whatever former stockbrokers were called these days. Deadly serious about his business and his clients, that is where the similarity ended with his professional appearance. A strong fiscal conservative, Mac was passionate about his politics, but had claimed "too many skeletons" when friends made offhand suggestions about his running for political office. Before getting a real job, he had considered going to law school, knowing that he would love the Perry Mason part. His impatience to start a career forced him to table that idea. However, had the opportunity presented itself to be a television personality or an actor, there would have been no hesitation.

The primary reason for the mirror's painful reflection was that Mac had received a phone call at midnight last night and after answering, his mind started running a marathon. As improbable as it seemed, Mac felt like he knew the crank caller.

Grace, Mac's wife of thirty plus years, had not been in the mood to discuss it in the wee hours of the morning, and before he left for work, she not so kindly offered a dab of make-up for the suitcases under his eyes. He declined.

Mac heard his young partner R.J. Brooks enter the office, but his eyes remained focused on his computer. Receiving over 250 emails a day ensured that his to-do list was never ending. Until two years ago, it had been a race to see whether Mac or R.J. got to the office first. Now it wasn't a contest, but it came with a caveat. Five days a week R.J. hit the Metropolitan Club for what could be described as an extreme workout. As a result, he could now legitimately be classified as a lean, mean financial machine.

R.J.'s first job out of college was with the regional brokerage firm of Johnston Wellons in their D.C office on Pennsylvania Avenue. Only 21, he was too young to apply for an advisor trainee position, but he was determined to learn the business. He was armed with a facile mind, as evidenced by his 4.0 GPA from the University of Maryland; an exceptional, if often strange, vocabulary; and a quick, but respectful wit. He was hired as a gopher/administrator, and his work, while not challenging, was noticeably error free.

However, it was not the quality of his work that caused him to be taken on by the office's top producer, Mac McGregor. R.J. could make people laugh. In many businesses, that attribute might not be a prerequisite for success, but in Mac's world, while not required, it was definitely an asset. If Mac had to choose between a keen analytical mind and likeability, he'd opt for likeability every time. To Mac, boredom was an unappreciated form of torture .

When he first started working with Mac, R.J. had dark, thick hair and was of average height and above-average weight. (That phrase seemed less depressing than the odious "plump," "overweight" or "fat.") A great smile was accentuated by deep dimples and gray eyes that found amusement in everything. Clients loved him. He was thorough, caring, and had a talent for saying the right thing.

On his own R.J. decided to study to become a Chartered Financial Analyst (CFA), and he easily passed the arduous three-year certification course. When he joined Mac in client meetings, he took copious notes, and he appeared sheepish when his boss assured the client that any losses endured by the client would indeed be R.J.'s fault. After every meeting, he would ask Mac what he did wrong and how he could improve. R.J. was a sponge, so Mac enjoyed mentoring him, particularly since he never had to couch his critiques.

Now, twenty years later, it was a bit of a different story. While R.J.'s hair had remained thick, the black was a distant memory, replaced almost entirely by gray. Without any scientific substantiation, R.J. attributed the color shift to working so closely with his mentor. It was a fair trade; Mac still blamed R.J. for any less than optimum investment outcomes.

Both men were comfortable in their own skins and rational enough to realize that you never stop learning to share critiques. R.J. had proven himself in sales, and his lovely wife, Janice, was a testament to his world-class sales ability. The bond between the two men, while forged with integrity and commitment to a clients-first philosophy, still left room for healthy competition and constant banter.

"I need to test a theory out on you," said Mac as R.J. approached his desk.

"Is it a theory based on fact or, as per your usual, blatant speculation?"

Narrowing his eyes, Mac asked, "Do these eyes look like they are seeking your banalities or your opinion?"

"Frankly, they look like they could use a cold compress and about eight hours of sleep."

Mac shrugged and motioned for R.J. to follow him into the conference room.

They sat down, and Mac winced. "Are you okay?" R.J. asked with concern.

"Yeah, no physical pain, just a dose of anguish. I got a call last night at midnight. It was a three-word message, and then the caller hung up."

"Is everyone all right? "

"Yeah, sorry, it's not a family thing. I'm just trying to sort it out. The caller said, 'Trick or treat.'"

"So it was a crank call?"

"That's the obvious assumption. The question is, who was the crank?" asked Mac. He paused and looked defiantly at his friend. He knew his assertion would be challenged as well as ridiculed. "I think the caller was Jeremy Lyons."

CHAPTER 3

ONE OF THE MANY INEQUITIES of life is that fear is lessened in the presence of either attractive or harmless-looking people. In reality, many serial killers have been pleasant looking, well-mannered individuals.

As stipulated, the private aircraft was waiting for Jackie Mayfield, Fox News's most popular anchor. A diminutive, beautiful Asian woman greeted her at the open door and ushered her into the plane. After she was belted in, the woman gave her a pill and a very apologetic look. The next thing she knew, Jackie was gently awakened.

Walking down the stairs, she naturally looked around. Her reporter's instincts had kicked in. Tropical climate, air moistened with a summer breeze. The Asian woman touched her arm. She was smiling, but the smile failed to reach her eyes. "His privacy is sacrosanct," she said.

Jackie nodded and meekly followed her to their destination. The entire process had the unmistakable precision of a military operation.

Well, at least I'm wherever-the-heck-I-am safely. If my suspicions are wrong, the network will take me to the woodshed. The time is reserved, promos have begun, and here I am without any communication equipment or backup. She even confiscated my cell. I guess I'm lucky I wasn't strip searched.

Media insiders believed that Jackie Mayfield would have walked naked over burning coals to get this particular interview. In a kinetic world, where news is over-covered and over-analyzed, and the audience's attention span is nonexistent, the interview that stops time is the Holy Grail.

She thought it was just a saying, but when Jackie saw him, her heart actually skipped a beat. Adrenaline coursed through her body. She took deep breaths to calm herself. Then she began.

"I have so many questions, Mr. Lyons, and I don't know how much time you'll give me. But first I have to say how wonderful it is to see you." Jackie's words poured out with obvious sincerity. No one had been more important to her career than Jeremy Lyons. Her impassioned face and wrinkled nose gave her a look of childlike urgency.

Lyons smiled in a paternal way and nodded. The lighting was ideal. As he had expected, his associate, Alegria, had learned videographer skills quickly. She manned the camera, and she had attached and tested the lavaliere microphones. Of course, Lyons would be in control of the editing.

Jackie took a few deep breaths and asked her host the first question. "How are you feeling?"

"I'm doing well, Jackie. Thank you."

"The whole country's been wondering about you. You were in that terrible accident, and then you just vanished. There are so many gaps in your story that I don't really know where to begin."

"Allow me to explain," said Lyons with a welcoming smile. "After the cowardly assassination attempt, I was in a coma for three months. My representatives knew that I would be uncomfortable recuperating in the public eye, so they arranged for me to be transferred to a private facility."

"And the bulk of your treatment has been here, in this facility?" Jackie pointed around her, but the camera stayed fixed on her. "What was the extent of your injuries?"

"Concussion, fractured ribs, ruptured spleen, lung collapsed for a bit, and assorted bruises. But as I am sure you will agree, I suffered no neurological impairment."

Jackie nodded enthusiastically and moved on. "Why did you disappear?"

"Well, unlike some politicians, I tend not to make decisions while I am comatose."

Her laugh was as contagious as a yawn. "Can you tell us who made the decisions for you?"

"I'd rather not," he answered in a non-negotiable manner.

"Do you remember anything about the attack?"

Lyons's words were spoken mechanically. "I left a meeting with the president and was walking the short distance from the White House to the restaurant. There was very little traffic on the street. My last cogent thought was that a black SUV was barreling towards me, and I had to leap out of the way. I was unsuccessful."

Jackie swallowed before asking her next question. "Do you suspect any government involvement?"

"No."

"So you believe that the driver purposely hit you, and that the conspiracy theories are invalid."

"That is correct."

Unconsciously canting her head, she asked, "Do you have any idea why someone would want to kill you?"

Lyons paused. "It's difficult to achieve success without making some enemies. The United States is the most successful country in the world. We are not aggressors, and yet we have many enemies that try to destroy us." He looked earnestly into the camera. "I cannot think of any individual or organization that I have maligned to the extent that they would want to kill me." He paused. "I would caution them not to try again."

As the professional she was, Jackie let his statement linger. "Can we cut on that for commercial?" she asked both Lyons and Alegria.

When they resumed, Lyons said, "Three days ago I woke from the coma, and you were the first person I contacted."

"I'm flattered, but why me?"

"I still intend to win the senate election."

Her eyes widened. Instinctively, she waited a beat to let her audience digest his declaration.

"I've heard of an October surprise, but never a November one," said Jackie. Regardless of the legitimacy of the reasons, you have not been in the public view for three months. No one knew whether you were dead or alive. Senator Smathers has run a positive campaign, he has an excellent senatorial record, and in essence, he has been running unopposed. Wouldn't it make more sense to wait until '14?"

"Those are all logical assumptions, Jackie. However, I don't think that the country can wait to have a strong, *independent* voice in Congress. I am unencumbered by party loyalties, beholden to no one, and immune to political correctness."

"I can certainly agree with your freedom from party pressure or special interests, but can you elaborate on how you are immune to political correctness? By the way, I apologize if it sounded like I was campaigning for your opponent."

Lyons ignored her apology. "The people are well aware that political correctness has metastasized into every nook and cranny of our society. It is a straightjacket for our legislators. One wrong word, one gaffe, and that becomes the story rather than the substance of their beliefs or actions. We spend half our time apologizing for being human. I won't be a prisoner to the polls or afraid to speak my mind."

"That *would* be refreshing. Before the accident..."

"It was not an accident." His jaw clenched.

"Sorry," Jackie said, raising her hand. "Before the assassination attack, you had campaigned for the Florida senate. I know you described your platform then, and you really haven't had time to make many revisions, but could you outline to our viewers why Floridians should vote for you?"

"Finally, a softball question." Lyons smiled. "People are tired of politics as usual. Lying has become acceptable to the point that blatant, knowing fabrications have no consequences. We allow gridlock, and worse, our elected officials can make character attacks rather than debating an issue. I represent the anti-politician. Congress does not want me to be part of their elite group, because I can't be bought or manipulated. The people have seen my resolve, and now they need to see that I am their best advocate."

"Mr. Lyons, you had a close brush with death," Jackie said into the camera with a look of concern, "and I'm not sure you have any idea how many people were praying for you. Since no one could reach you," now she had a wide-eyed look, "they sent cards and notes to *me* at the station! We ran out of room!"

"I'm very grateful." Lyons said, lowering his head.

"You mentioned off camera that if the hit-and-run driver had succeeded, your biggest regret would have been that you were unable to fulfill your promise to America."

Jackie turned to instruct their audience. "For the record, Mr. Lyons has no speech writer, no notes, and no teleprompter. I am asking him to tell us, all of us, about his vision for America. His voice will be the last voice you will hear in this interview. Mr. Lyons?"

"Thank you, Jackie, for coming to see me and for your kind words. This country has been fed the Kool-Aid of apathy and despair for too long. As a result, we are at war. It is not a war of armament; it is worse. It is a war of the soul.

"In the Revolutionary War, we fought for our independence. We did not want to be under another's control. We did not want to be beholden to anyone!

"Why do we allow it now? Is there a flicker of pride that remains in a once-proud nation? Or have the cancer of low expectations, the altered perception that it is better to receive than to give, and the enemies of incentive extinguished our flame of self-respect forever? Can we once again walk upright, with our heads held high, and look ourselves and other nations in the eye? Can we change from a dependent nation and become an independent nation again? Or is it too late?

"I will help America win this war. I believe our citizens want to succeed, to be educated, inspired, and given an opportunity to contribute. The adage 'Give a man a fish and you feed him for a day; teach a man to fish and you feed him for life' is still viable today. Economic and social revolution is possible if we have the will.

"Is this a nation that should kowtow to terrorists, apologize to countries that exist because of our generosity, or be intimidated by the threats of lesser nations?"

Lyons paused, looked down, and then looked back at the camera with humble purpose. He spoke softly and built to a muted, but intense crescendo. "I cannot be influenced by special interests. I cannot be intimidated by authority." He gave a fatherly smile. "As you can see, I cannot be easily eliminated. Neither can the American spirit. We *can* control our destiny!"

He took a breath, then closed his eyes for a moment as if in prayer, and closed by saying, "Thank you, and may God bless America."

The interview ended. Jackie sat stunned, mesmerized by his passion. After an awkward moment of immobility, she stood up, reached over, and shook his hand. "May I give you a hug?" she asked.

Lyons nodded, and she leaned down and hugged him.

Alegria took her by the arm, and they walked out of the room. Jackie was flushed with excitement; this was pure gold.

She turned back around one last time to thank the man who would most likely be Florida's first Independent senator. When he spoke of what he wanted to accomplish, it was as if it were a decree, or a proclamation. She had no doubt that he would succeed. Jackie Mayfield had already witnessed amazing things from him; she would never bet against him.

Jackie watched as the most beautiful African-American woman she had ever seen helped Lyons from the room. He was still the most commanding figure she had ever met. And just as with Franklin Delano Roosevelt, the wheelchair did not diminish his power.

CHAPTER 4

SENATOR ALAN SMATHERS'S FACE COULD have been a recruitment poster for the United States Marines. His square jaw was locked in place, his eyes laser-focused straight ahead at the now dark flat screen in his office. For the past five minutes he had remained motionless, leaning forward in his chair, his forearms planted on his muscular thighs. From all appearances, the man was experiencing the first stages of rigor mortis.

The other two spectators in the room also appeared to be transfixed. Both Richard Orth, the senator's Chief of Staff, who had served alongside him in the Marines, and Cindy Smathers, the senator's wife, instinctively waited for Alan Smathers to sort it out.

Orth didn't need for his friend to talk to know what he was feeling. Six months ago, unbeknownst to Cindy, the senator had received a package from an anonymous source. Inside were nude pictures of Cindy with an equally nude beautiful African-American woman draped over her. Without question, Smathers's wife had been drugged, and the pictures were staged. Nevertheless, the threat of exposure was enough to keep Smathers from using any of the negative information that his team had assembled on Jeremy Lyons.

When Lyons called him to suggest that they both agree not to use negative advertising and television spots, Smathers was forced to comply. After Lyons disappeared, even though the strategy was coerced, it made it look like the senator had taken the high road by choice. Now, with Lyons's almost mystical reappearance, coupled with the man's obvious and sympathy-gathering disability, Smathers had no cards left to play.

Alan Smathers was an extremely ethical man. The fact that evil might now triumph over good was breaking his heart.

Finally, Orth turned and looked questioningly at Cindy. Her concerned look did not diminish, but she reluctantly took two steps toward her husband. Taking a breath, she gently placed a hand on his back. After a few moments, she leaned down to look at his face and gauge his reaction. Only barely perceptible movements in Smathers's chest indicated that he was even alive.

Cindy's hand remained where it was, unmoving for long minutes. More than anything she wanted to wrap her arms around him, press her swollen belly against his back, and make his pain go away.

Tears sprang from Cindy's eyes as she waited for her husband to react. This was supposed to be their time. Alan was a great senator who was going to be reelected, and after five years of trying, Cindy Smathers was finally pregnant.

Smathers blinked. It was as if he finally felt the warmth of Cindy's hand, and he spoke. His voice halting, dispirited, sounded like it came from a tunnel. "In combat, you understand the risks. You're not going to win every battle; you just can't lose the war. Well, I lost the war. I failed in my mission."

"How the hell could you predict..." Orth interjected.

Smathers's right hand shot up to cut him off. His eyes were still fixed on the dark screen as he continued his monologue. "I fought so hard, pulled ahead of the fucking ghost in the polls, and now..." He stopped as if dumbstruck.

Again, Orth and Cindy looked at each other to see who should make the next move.

Then, without looking at either of them, Smathers stood slowly and walked over to the wall TV. He examined it, stepped back, and launched a side kick at the lower left corner. The flat screen flew off the wall and crashed to the floor. He spun around to the two people who knew him better than he knew himself. "And now," he said, his face red with fury, "I'm going to lose an election to Lazarus!"

CHAPTER 5

IT WAS RIDICULOUS. WITHOUT EVER discussing it, Mac knew that he had to be careful about showing unusual interest in the Florida senatorial race. Both he and Grace were on the same page when it came to presidential preferences, but their votes rarely counted in the bright blue state of Maryland.

The McGregors were watching the Fox broadcast of the election results. Mac would have preferred channel surfing when commentary got boring, but part of the remote negotiations was that he had to pick a channel and stay there. When it became obvious that the incumbent president would be granted a second term, Grace rose from the couch and announced, "I'm going to bed."

Mac had a quick internal debate, trying to decide whether he should follow her or wait until all the senate returns were decided. "Do you mind if I join you and keep the TV on low? I need to be assured that we win the senate.."

Her eyes were flat. "It's your house," she said as she turned and walked up the back stairway. *"Yours, too,"* he wanted to say in a singsong voice, but thirty years of marriage conditioned him to know better. He followed her up the stairs.

Grace had two types of nightgowns: the "come cuddle me" ones and, the "don't even think about it" ones. Mac was sufficiently astute to know what her choice would be tonight. *How convenient to have a marital traffic sign.*

Couples who have been married at least a decade tend to have designated sides of the bed. This does not vary in hotels or when staying at a friend's home. In the McGregors' case, Grace was on the left side of the king-sized bed, and Mac was on the right, farther from the bathroom. It was a typical tradeoff; the phone was on her nightstand.

Floss, brush teeth, rinse with mouthwash, use the bathroom. The routine didn't vary. Even before Mac clicked on the television, Grace had opened her Kindle and begun reading. The room temperature was the usual setting, but it sure felt chilly to Mac. It was like two fighters had gone to their separate corners, and the bell to start the fight had not rung.

Ten minutes later, Grace closed her Kindle, and turned on her side away from Mac. Twenty minutes later, the election results were finalized, and Mac was straining to hear Jeremy Lyons's acceptance speech.

"I am honored to be chosen to represent Florida. I am grateful, and I approach the challenge with optimism and resolve." He paused. "I would be remiss if I did not acknowledge the great work that Alan Smathers did as your senator. He is a fine man, a patriot, and I assure you that his career in politics and his service to this country are not over."

That's a bit over the top, thought Mac.

Lyons continued, "Fellow Floridians, I make but one promise: you will not regret having voted for me. Thank you."

Short but sweet. Clicking off the TV, Mac turned and placed the remote on the nightstand to his right. He propped himself up on his pillows and closed his eyes.

Without turning, Grace said, "Are you happy your psycho friend won?"

Mac waited a beat before answering. "He's not my friend."

Grace rolled over, facing him. "Oh, come on. You've been like a kid waiting for his first taste of an ice cream cone!"

"What's your problem?"

She sat up in bed now, her face contorted in anger. "*My* problem? Was it *my* friend who was run over and killed by Lyons's henchman? Was it just *my* daughter who was terrorized by the same maniac when he showed up at our church? And let's not forget the lovely inscription on his narcissistic manifesto. It might as well have said,

'You're next.' Maybe you forgot that you asked me if you could bring a weapon into the house."

"Are you through?" Mac asked, trying unsuccessfully to keep the edge out of his voice.

"I might as well be. I know that past performance doesn't guarantee future results in your world; but the same caveat doesn't apply to people. If you think being a senator changes Jeremy Lyons, you are a fool."

"Would you like me to sleep elsewhere," he challenged, "now that I know that curiosity is a cardinal sin."

"Not necessary," she answered, grabbing her pillow and storming out of the room. She slammed the door with such force that the picture frame on her nightstand wavered and then fell to the floor before Mac could reach it.

Mac wondered if the crack he heard when the glass front of the frame broke was a sign. He picked it up, and in the ambient light of the bathroom nightlight, he gazed at their wedding photo with longing.

CHAPTER 6

DAVID GRANT'S REFLECTION IN HIS bathroom mirror was not forgiving. In the last six months he had suffered an unwanted loss of twenty pounds. His gray eyes looked like the life had been bleached out of them. The dark circles under them made him a candidate for the raccoon family. Not only was the mirror a brutal reminder, it had no answers.

* * *

Unwrapping the cream-colored bath towel from around his waist, he used it to scrub his close-cropped hair. Then he walked over and hung it perfectly spread out on the towel rack. At least his sense of order was intact, even though last night's dance with Jack Daniels still hung with him.

When he was at work, David went through the motions. He knew that he was letting his team down; they expected more and deserved it. Mac had tried to talk to him, but he had avoided any in-depth conversation, especially *that* conversation.

* * *

He chose an older, dark gray suit with thin chalk stripes. He refused to have any of his suits altered, even though the trousers were beginning to look like clown pants. This was out of character, but so was the rest of his life.

David had been comfortable in combat, where the lines of demarcation were clearer. Here's the enemy: kill or be killed. Today, clinicians even identified PTSD and were working toward solutions. But to have those symptoms more than a decade after service? A therapist would tell him that he needed clarity to have closure. Easy to get. He could just pull out his iPad, email Blake Stone, and say, "Hey dude, did you try to do me a solid and run down Jeremy Lyons?"

His laugh echoed inside his empty bedroom.

David sleepwalked his way in to work. It was 8:45, and while he wasn't technically late, it was not his normal routine. By now he should have read the *Wall Street Journal*, gotten his black coffee from the Keurig, and at least answered a few emails. Instead he was squatting at Starbucks staring out into space. *Senator Lyons!*

He stood, crushed the coffee cup, and tossed it in the trash.

"David, join me in the conference room."

Mac's request felt like a punch in the gut. Like a prisoner walking the last mile, David opened the closet and hung his raincoat over the wooden hanger. With hunched shoulders, he followed Mac into the room.

Still standing, David asked, "Did *Senator* Lyons really call you before his November surprise?" Bitterness cloaked every word.

"Halloween night. A strangled, 'Trick or treat.' It was a blocked number."

"Why?" His tone was accusing.

"Maybe he wanted to find out if we had any candy left. How the hell do I know?"

"Sorry," said David, coloring. "It's not your fault."

"No, it's Florida's fault. And I liked Smathers. I thought he was doing a good job. But I didn't call you in here to talk about the elections or about politics. We're here to talk about you."

"Mac, I..."

"Have a seat," Mac instructed.

David sat down across from him, but failed to meet his eyes.

"Do you think Blake Stone ran down Jeremy Lyons?" asked Mac.

David's face went white, his lips trembled, and his eyes turned cold.

"If there's another reason for you walking around like a zombie, please let me know."

As Mac expected, there was no rebuttal, so he forged on. "Let's review the bidding. Lyons admitted that he had your dad killed. You wanted revenge – hell, *I* wanted revenge! Your dad was a great friend of mine."

David began visibly shaking, clenching and unclenching his fists.

"These are irrefutable facts," said Mac, leaning into the fury. "Lyons hired someone to kill your dad for profit. I know damn well that you didn't hire someone to kill Lyons. There's no eye for an eye in David Grant." He paused. "If your dad could see this self-inflicted cancer eating you alive, how would he feel?"

Mac's brutal question had the desired result. The anger in David's face changed to remorse. A bitter tear ran down his flushed cheek.

"Have you contacted Blake in the last six months?" asked Mac, pushing further.

David shook his head.

"I didn't think so. Listen, I've had to work through a few demons here, too."

David looked up, tears rimming his eyes.

"Yeah. I had a heart-to-heart with your Black Ops friend. I fanned the flame. I told him that I would've loved to have someone kick Lyons's ass, and there were times when I felt like I could pull the trigger myself."

"Really?" asked David.

"I'm not just trying to make you feel better. I've prayed on it. I was relieved when I found out he was alive. But David, neither you nor I intentionally tried to kill Jeremy Lyons, nor did we wish him dead."

The two friends stared at each other. Then David nodded. "You're right. I hated Lyons, and I'm furious that he was not prosecuted for his crime. But I didn't want vigilante justice."

"Neither did I," agreed Mac. "But if we're correct in our assumption, and it's only an assumption, it seems like Blake sees the world through a different lens."

David nodded again. "I haven't called him, because what if he said, 'Yeah. You're welcome.'"

"Do you think Blake would admit it?"

"I don't know. More than likely he would tell me that I don't have a need to know."

Mac waited, letting David's comment linger. Then he asked an uncomfortable question. "If we think Blake was responsible, do you need to tell him not to try to finish the job?"

"No," said David quickly. "Blake would believe that if Lyons didn't die, God didn't want him to die."

Mac sat back, reflecting on the comment. "In a strange way, it's enviable," he said quietly, "to have the belief that you're a messenger from God."

CHAPTER 7

It was supposed to be a cakewalk. No one votes for a candidate presumed dead. I know how to lose, as long as it's a fair fight. When that bastard sent me compromising pictures of my wife, which he created by drugging her, and then asked me to play nice, I should have just told him to fuck off and taken the consequences.

Alan Smathers sighed. He knew that he would never do anything to compromise his family. Closing his eyes, he rubbed his forehead with three fingers of his right hand. His wife, Cindy, stood nearby, as did his right-hand man, Richard Orth. Still, he was alone with his thoughts as he waited for the television cameras.

I know why I lost. Lyons single-handedly broke up a deadly drug ring and then stopped a terrorist attack. Then, he mysteriously appears after surviving an assassination attempt, and he is paralyzed from the waist down. Nobody beats a tragic superhero. So why am I wallowing? My life's not over; we're going to have a baby.

"In 3, 2, 1," said the cameraman.

Smathers's posture was firm, his eyes resolute. *Humorous, self-deprecating, end strong.* He looked amused. "Can someone tell me what happened?" he said as he made eye contact with his followers. The room broke into applause. "A week ago, I had a very powerful speech written that detailed the progress that we'd make during my term and outlining the pro-growth proposals that I wanted to share for Florida's future. I guess the good news is that this speech will be a lot shorter."

The laughter was comforting.

"I am humbled that you allowed me to serve as your senator and that I was able to make so many friends who were like minded in our pursuit of fiscal responsibility. But tonight is not about me. It's about a new direction for Florida. As an Independent, Jeremy Lyons will be beholden to no party affiliation or special interests." His smile was wan. "We know he didn't need help in financing his campaign.

"It is my fervent hope that your new senator will be your strongest advocate, and while he's at it, raise some hell in Congress! Thank you for your loyalty and support. I love you all."

CHAPTER 8

JOHN WESLEY REMEMBERED IT LIKE it was yesterday. That didn't make him special. Most people can recall the moment that changed their life.

He was the son of an evangelical father and a mousy mother. Wesley wasn't sure of the statistics on how kids with preachers as fathers turned out, but he suspected they weren't locks to become model citizens.

His father was the prototype fire and brimstone Holy Roller. No one dared to leave his services early, even though his bombastic sermons regularly ran over the allotted time. In his small suburb outside of Knoxville, Tennessee, the Reverend Charles Wesley was God. Unfortunately, the Bible thumping preacher's favorite line of scripture was also the one he practiced regularly: Spare the rod and spoil the child. John still had the scars to prove it.

On that fateful night, John's best friend, Steve Chin, was spending the night. The 15-year-olds were sleeping in John's bunk beds with John, of course, on the top, because it was his house. On this Saturday night, his father had been leading a revival meeting, and he and John's mother were expected home around midnight.

Previously, the boys had spent time together, and that had led to what they felt was harmless experimenting. Fondling each other was about as far as it went. Tonight was different. Steve had smuggled some vodka into the house, and they had both forced it down. Teasing, wrestling, giggling, Steve had climbed up to the top bunk. Touching led to heavy breathing, and Steve took young Wesley in his mouth.

At 10:10, Wesley never forgot the time, the Right Reverend Charles Wesley slammed his door open. "Soddomites!" he screamed, and nothing was ever the same again.

It took the Chin family three months to move to another city. It took John Wesley three years to memorize and recite scripture on demand.

CHAPTER 9

THE ASPEN HOUSE IN ALEXANDRIA, Virginia, is a nondescript, rarely full, high rise that has survived numerous refurbishings from its heyday back in the early 60s. Two tones of tan cause all sixteen floors of the monolith to blend into the background of the impersonal D.C. suburb. Reasonably priced rental apartments located fifteen minutes from Reagan National, and neighbors who kept to themselves, made it the perfect spot for John Wesley.

In truth, the man's given name was irrelevant. In his line of business, it was never used. Wesley's one-bedroom apartment was registered under one of his favorite aliases, Peter Van Horn. Some collectors prefer baseball cards or old *Playboy* magazines. Wesley collected identities.

His feet were stretched out, resting on a brown Formica-topped coffee table. Four fingers of his left hand were tucked inside the waist of his jeans as he flipped between channels to catch both NFL games. The knock on the door startled him.

Frowning, he stared at the door, assuming the knock had been a mistake. In the three months he had been a resident, he hadn't so much as nodded at anyone. This time the knocking was more persistent. Wesley unfolded, got up, and walked slowly to the door.

He turned the lock but didn't release the chain. He opened it warily, protecting against someone kicking the door in his face. Standing with her hands on her hips was a stunning African-American woman. Since she was in tight jeans and a Georgetown sweatshirt, he doubted that she had a concealed weapon.

"What do you want?" Wesley's tone was far from welcoming.

"May I come in, or would you prefer to meet me in a public place?"

"Lady, you have the wrong apartment." He started to close the door.

"I don't think you want to have this conversation through the door, Mr. Wesley."

Wesley fumbled with the chain, opened the door, and yanked her inside.

Instead of staggering by the force of his actions, she landed on the balls of her feet like an athlete. "I'll allow that one impetuous move," she said, "but if you touch me again, your life as you know it will be over."

"My name's Van Horn, not Wesley," he said, like a six-year-old denying he was in the cookie jar.

"We can save a lot of time, John, may I call you John? If you would like to deny my intel, why don't you wait until I tell you what I *do* know about you?"

"Why don't I just kill you, and then everything will remain a mystery?"

She took his vitriol and volleyed it back. "First, it would be the fight of your life, and in the unlikely event you were successful, you would be hunted, caught, and tortured beyond your imagination." She looked at his threadbare, puke-green couch. "I'm going to sit down."

Wesley walked toward the couch and stood within six inches of her. His fists were clenched, and the right one shook with anger.

"My name is Sabine. Your given name is John Wesley. You have no driver's license, no Social Security number, and impressively, no fingerprints on file anywhere. You are a consummate actor, and a master of disguise. You are invisible, which I why I want to hire you."

"Are you wearing a wire?"

"Don't be ridiculous. If the government had any knowledge of your existence, I wouldn't be interested in you. Your identity has not been compromised."

Instinctively, Wesley knew he had to change his tone. He tamped down his temper. "I'd feel better if I could pat you down myself."

"I'm sure you would. That's not happening."

"If you know everything, you should know I'm on a job."

Sabine waved her hand dismissively. "Seriously? You get a $25,000 fee to seduce a trophy wife so that your odious client can trigger the adultery clause and void his pre-nup. You're better than that." Her look was pitying. "I'm giving you the opportunity to work to your potential."

"I should be finished with the job by next week."

"No need to finish. I took the liberty of canceling it for you."

Wesley took a deep breath. "Lady, you better be offering the moon."

"You will receive a monthly retainer of $100,000 wired to your Swiss bank account."

Wesley threw up his hands. If she knew about his bank account, he was out of options.

"How long would I be retained?"

"A minimum of two years, a maximum of five."

"And I'm working only for you?"

"Yes."

"Who do I have to kill?"

"Only the audiences, with your performances."

Wesley looked her up and down, "Proverbs 6:25 states 'Do no desire her beauty in your heart, nor let her capture you with her eyelids.' Lady, you had me at $100,000."

CHAPTER 10

"ARE YOU SURE THAT I'M the right man for the job?" asked Steve Cannon with obvious incredulity. "I'm just a Washington lawyer who's only nibbled around the fringe of politics."

Lyons and Alegria Lopez, his brilliant researcher, appraised their guest. Ironically, the 60-year-old man looked more senatorial than most of the men currently in office. Cannon moved with the languid confidence usually reserved for natural athletes. His unflappable demeanor was nonthreatening and carried not a whiff of arrogance. His humor and authenticity assured that he was both well liked and well regarded in a town where trust and solid friendships were as rare as bipartisan agreement.

Physically, his longish gray hair, swept back on the sides, framed an attractive, strong face. His hazel eyes and noticeable laugh lines put him in the enviable category of pleasant looking without being a pretty boy.

Cannon had taken the request to arrive in Naples, Florida, in very casual attire to heart. A lemon-colored, long-sleeved shirt hung over his tan cargo shorts. On his sockless feet were a pair of electric-blue Crocs.

"We may have to take care of some wardrobe malfunctions," Lyons said to his guest as he looked at the man's unsubtle footwear, "but you are the right man for the job."

Cannon smiled a disarming smile, crossed his legs, and folded his hands on his lap. "Would you be kind enough to share your reasoning, sir?"

Lyons nodded. "You've done more than dance around the fringe of politics, Mr. Cannon; you are a Washington insider, a veteran. Yet, you are an anomaly: you are well-liked by both sides. Not only is the position that I am offering you financially rewarding to your two-man firm, it also has the potential to give you national recognition."

Cannon gave an acknowledging nod.

"Your older daughter is a staunch Republican, whereas your wife and younger daughter are liberals. Thus, your family is an amalgamated Independent."

Cannon smiled in response.

"The skeletons in your closet, such as past marijuana use and an isolated affair, are modest by D.C. standards."

Cannon appeared to remain unflappable, but the slight reddening of his ears was a definite tell.

Lyons paused. "And finally, the fact that you didn't correct my assertions or challenge my facts demonstrates your ability to remain cool under fire. That is just a short synopsis. We have extensive detail we can share if you so desire." Lyons sat back.

"Not necessary." Cannon raised his hands. "I knew that you performed at least a cursory level of due diligence on me, but you drilled a little deeper than I'd expected," he added dryly. He cocked his head to the side and asked, "Will I be required to color outside the lines while in your employ?"

"Your job will be to spin a web of gold," Lyons answered, "but I will only give you nuggets. You may be asked to cajole other politicians or the media, but I am well equipped to do the heavy lifting."

"I'll bet you are, sir," said Cannon, exhaling. "Well, I'm not sure that I ever dreamed of growing up to be a senator's chief of staff; but your offer certainly is lucrative."

Cannon looked hard at Lyons and then shifted to Alegria. "Miss, are you always going to monopolize the conversation in these meetings?"

She smiled. "My job is strictly analytical, Mr. Cannon. I was the one who recommended you to the senator."

Cannon raised his eyebrows. "Well, sorry, ma'am. I'll make sure that I fire no shots in your direction."

The room quieted. Cannon reached up and scratched his head. "Well, I guess it's safe to say I'll never be bored."

* * *

After Cannon left for his return trip to Washington, Lyons checked for reactions, "What do you think?"

Sabine had taken a seat next to Alegria. "He's very likeable, cute, in a strange way. He will not ruffle easily and is smarter than he acts."

"I agree" said Alegria.

"You don't get to weigh in, Alegria; you recommended him," said Lyons with a smile. "Next on the list is someone who can be more persuasive if it becomes necessary."

Sabine nodded and looked at Alegria. "His name is John Wesley, or at least that's what he says his name is. Excellent at disguise, he is fit and possesses excellent martial arts skills. When he wants to be, he can be charming and convincing."

"But?" asked Lyons. Sabine let out a breath. "Alegria did a great job dissecting the man and his past, but in person, he feels a little off."

"Explain."

Talking with her hands, she said, "I think he would perform any assignment with precision. I also think he would follow instructions and not take the persuasion to extremes. But, instead of throwing out pick-up lines, he threw out scripture."

Lyons raised an eyebrow. "Hopefully, that's not a sign of unbalance."

"It is if he spits out proverbs like a curse," she said.

Lyons rolled his chair to the wall of glass that looked out over the gulf. Both women watched as he continued to stare out at the darkening sky. They knew not to interrupt. Prior to his injuries, it had seemed like Lyons's decisions were almost instantaneous, as if his mind computed faster than the minds of mere mortals.

His voice was decisive and firm. "As his first assignment, have him work with Alegria and put a laser on the man who tried to kill me. That man must be neutralized."

CHAPTER 11

THE PAIN FROM THE SLAP brushed away the first layer of cobwebs. "Hey!" shouted David Grant as a second slap followed.

"Stop it!"

Whap! This time on the other cheek.

"What the fuck are you doing?" David asked, tears stinging his eyes.

"This is your wakeup call," the man standing over him answered in a bored voice. "Drunks rarely respond to the gentle approach."

"I'm not ..."

"Oh, really? So you voluntarily shackled your hands to the bed frame?"

David turned his head quickly and winced at the pain and the recognition. He frantically searched his brain to replay the past few hours. Vague images of an argument with the bartender and then nothing but fog - an all too familiar feeling as of late. His eyes spun like pinwheels. Straining against the cuffs, he stretched his neck and vomited violently onto the bed.

The intruder stepped back and mused, "I'd say that's a combination of clams casino with a hint of Cheetos... and more than a few maraschino cherries. Manhattans tonight?"

"Who are you and why are you here?"

"There it is! The inevitable question. Unfortunately, you are the one that's shackled, which puts me in the position to ask you the questions: Who killed your father?"

"What?"

The man leaned forward and slapped David once with his right hand and then once with his left. "Yes, I'm ambidextrous, if that was your next question."

"No," said David fighting to find defiance. "My next question was going to be why the hell do you keep slapping me?"

The stranger gave him a thoughtful look. "That one has some merit, and I'm not sure if it's because it's critical that you focus or ..." he smiled, "... because I enjoy it."

An involuntary shudder ran through David's body.

"As I said," the man continued, "I'm not here to answer your questions. You need to answer mine, succinctly, but above all, truthfully. It sounds rather melodramatic, but I'm afraid your life *does* depend on it."

David glared at him. The man's short brown hair barely exceeded a military cut, but his casual manner and focused demeanor reeked of training and efficiency. His dark brown eyes ran the gamut from amused to tense, and David doubted the man ever lost control. In between the vicious slaps, he burned the man's image into his brain. Highly chiseled cheekbones were remarkable by the fact that seemingly identical diagonal scars were on each. It was as if he had taken part in a bizarre ritual of disfigurement. However, the most threatening thing about the man was that he did nothing to disguise his appearance.

"Last chance. Who killed your father?"

"Max Parnavich, an assassin hired by Jeremy Lyons."

The man nodded. "See, that wasn't so hard. And who tried to kill Senator Lyons?"

"I don't ..."

Slap! Slap! Slap! Slap! Like a fighter on a punching bag, the man relentlessly pummeled both sides of David's face in a frenzied, yet stridently rhythmic, cadence. He paused and stepped back, studying his work like a painter evaluating a portrait. Then he looked at his blood-streaked and vomit-spattered latex gloves.

"Distasteful," he said as he wrinkled his nose. He raised a gloved index finger. "Therefore, we do not lose heart. Even though our outward man is perishing, yet the inward man is being renewed day by day."

"What the hell does that mean?" groaned David.

"I like to sprinkle my encounters with a bit of scripture. It tends to add solace to what is often an uncomfortable situation....for the victim, that is."

"I need to tidy up," the man said, as if he needed to explain his leaving the room. "Blood does carry disease, you know."

David's eyes were hollow, resigned. Tears mingled with the blood on his battered face.

A few minutes later, the stranger walked over, leaned down, and inserted the key into the handcuffs on David's wrists. David's arms fell limply to the bed.

"The next time I ask you that question," the man whispered, "you will give me the correct answer. Otherwise, my next house call will be in Bethany Beach."

"I will fucking kill you..." David lunged from the bed at his attacker, who deftly stepped to the side. David's momentum carried him to the floor, where his threats were choked out by a second, cleansing heave from his stomach. Just before he passed out, he heard the click of his apartment door.

CHAPTER 12

Eli Steiner looked like a possum. Small black eyes, so deep set they appeared to have been hammered into his face, framed what could only be described as a snout. A thin, cruel mouth that only smiled when he inflicted emotional pain was almost lost between sunken, acne-scarred cheeks.

Yet, this was the face of power in the Republican party. Not overt power, of course, as this repulsive man could not be front and center. Instead, Eli Steiner, a man unhindered by morality and afflicted with an obscene amount of wealth, simply pulled the strings.

A politician's currency determines influence. Steiner, a brilliant, manipulative, ruthless demagogue, dealt both favors and destruction from his stacked deck. His outrage over the Republican party's impotence had not diminished over the following six months. In fact, the internal divisiveness and lack of a competitive platform had whipped him into a frenzy. He was a perfect target for Senator Jeremy Lyons.

> ... I would love the opportunity to pick your brain, and I hope that you will accept my offer. I am happy to meet in your office or send my plane and have you meet me at my home in Naples.
> Best regards,
> Jeremy Lyons

Eli Steiner's smile widened as he held the embossed letter. Lyons was the one man with power whose fortune allegedly eclipsed his own. And regardless of the lack of evidence, there was no question that Lyons's wealth was the result of ill-gotten gains. That made him more interesting: a rich politician who owed no one and made his own rules. Steiner felt that an Independent was a fence-sitter afraid to take a stand, but he doubted that label would fit Senator Lyons.

Unlike many men of obscene wealth, as the current president called them unless they were major contributors to the Democratic Party, Lyons had earned his fortune. The man's success was a statistical aberration. Luck and skill may have played a part, but his access to inside information had to be unparalleled.

Steiner's hand went to his pointed chin. Why hadn't *he* been asked to invest? After considering a few possible reasons, he settled on the one most acceptable to his ego. Lyons did not want investors with his level of sophistication.

Refusing the man's invitation was not an option. There was too much influence at stake. If Steiner had reached out to Lyons (the thought that his offer might have been rejected never occurred to him), it would have been a sign of desperation or need.

He mulled over the choice of venue. Underlings always met him in his office. No fear of recording devices, as they were scanned before entering. Plus, it added to the intimidation factor. From everything he'd seen, Lyons could not be intimidated. Steiner surveyed his surroundings. Antique furniture, priceless art — it was a showcase of grandeur. What if Lyons dismissed his collective treasures?

There was a bit of chill in the air. Besides, he would like to compare Lyons's plane with his, and it was rumored that Lyons had a stable of extraordinary women on site.

* * *

"Welcome, Mr. Steiner," said the beautiful Asian woman with a warm smile. "I hope your flight was pleasant."

Steiner nodded, looking at her rather hungrily.

"May I take your coat and perhaps your tie?" she asked timidly.

Steiner recoiled mentally. He had worn his undertaker's suit: black with a white shirt and blood-red tie. He was not comfortable in casual clothes, and this was his signature uniform.

"Of course," he said reluctantly, as he gave her his coat and loosened his tie. "You are going to let me keep my pants, aren't you?" he added with a leer.

"Well, if you insist," she said teasingly, as she hung his coat in the hall closet. "Please walk this way. Mr. Lyons is anxious to meet you."

Steiner followed willingly, not only appreciating the rear view, but pleased that his host obviously did not refer to himself as Senator Lyons. Unlike his brethren, it must not give him an orgasm to be called "Senator."

The woman walked Steiner into a massive great room, which was bathed in sunlight from an entire wall of glass framing the Gulf of Mexico. Steiner glanced quickly at the majestic view to his left, then walked over to Jeremy Lyons, who smiled comfortably from his gleaming wheelchair.

In contrast to Steiner, Lyons had on cream-colored linen trousers with a black silk, short-sleeved shirt, which he wore untucked. "Thank you for accepting my invitation, Mr. Steiner," Lyons said after the handshake. "Please have a seat." He motioned to a dark tan leather chair about four feet from his wheelchair.

"It's Eli," offered the guest. "And may I assume our conversation is not being recorded?"

"Of course," said Lyons easily. "Only adversarial conversations require that extra measure of protection. And please," he added with a smile, "call me Jeremy."

Steiner nodded. "Okay," he said, eschewing any opportunity for small talk. "What do you want from me?"

Lyons sat back in his chair. "Your reputation is accurate. Social niceties do not increase net worth. Let me begin with a question. You have not achieved your enviable financial success and power without performing extensive due diligence. What are your thoughts about me?"

"Until I met you," Steiner answered quickly, "you were simply another politician. However, I do like the way you orchestrated your rise to power, and you probably broke every law in the process." He gave Lyons a challenging look.

Lyons looked skyward. "I may have to check. It is conceivable that I missed a few."

Empowered, Steiner continued. "In some ways, we're the same. The ends justify the means, and we both have overcome handicaps. Mine is that I am ugly, ugly to the point that people look away. But that does not define me. I use it to my advantage. It fuels me."

He pointed to Lyons. "You were handsome, charismatic; women would throw themselves at you. But now," he paused, pointing at him, "you're a cripple. From a perfect physical specimen to a cripple; it would destroy most men. It fuels you." Steiner sat back with a look of satisfaction.

Lyons waited a moment to respond. "You're refreshingly candid, Eli. I appreciate the rare individual who does not tap dance around my disability."

"Now," said Steiner, leaning forward again, "I'll ask again: What do you want from me? Are you ready to join my party?"

Lyons leaned forward and matched his guest's intensity. "On the contrary, I intend to destroy your party."

CHAPTER 13

In contrast to his animal look-a-like, the Possum was not feigning sleep. Eli Steiner leapt to his feet and twitched around the room like he was trying to extract an electric anal probe.

"This is your grand idea? You want to blow up the Republican party?" He threw his hands up in the air. He walked around in tight circles, his agitation increasing every second that Lyons failed to respond. "They told me you were smart. You're an idiot! Can you spell Armageddon?" he sneered.

Lyons sat impassively in his chair, fingers relaxed and resting comfortably in his lap.

"What a waste of my time!" shouted Steiner, venting frustration. "You're not only a physical cripple, you're a mental one!" He turned on his heel to leave.

"Before you leave," Lyons offered, "perhaps you'd like to see the Eighth Wonder of the World."

Steiner turned, his pale face still flushed and angry.

Lyons pushed a button on his chair, and Sabine walked into the room wearing a black thong bikini. She smiled and looked at Lyons.

"Our guest prefers histrionics to polite conversation. Perhaps you can get him to change his mind," he suggested.

Steiner stood transfixed. This was without a doubt the most beautiful woman he had ever seen. Her long, dark hair was braided and accentuated her high cheekbones. Almond-shaped eyes the color of milk chocolate with flecks of gold stared at him.

Steiner's eyes traveled up and down Sabine's exquisite body, drinking in its sculpted perfection. In response, her full lips offered an easy and suggestive smile.

Sabine glided over to Steiner and asked in a soft voice, "Are you sure I can't convince you to stay and have a relaxed conversation?"

Steiner glanced furtively at Lyons, as if asking for permission. *Maybe he's a voyeur*, he thought, as Lyons still appeared nonplussed.

Steiner looked hungrily into Sabine's eyes, certain that no chemical enhancement would be required with this woman. He leered just short of a full drool. "Let's find out," he said, as he reached his hands out, crablike, to touch her enticing breasts.

In one unhurried motion, Sabine snatched Steiner's hands out of the air and bent his wrists backward. Steiner dropped painfully to his knees.

"Ow!" he cried. Tears immediately flew from his eyes like rats from a sinking ship. "Ow! Stop! You're killing me – owwww!"

She stood over him, her magnificent breasts inches from his head. "You will be quiet, or I will hurt you beyond your imagination."

Steiner tried to roll onto his back like a dead bug to relieve some of the pressure on his wrists. Effortlessly, Sabine held his hands in place.

"Let me up!" he pleaded. "I'll do whatever you want!"

"I doubt that," Sabine replied. "I ask you to have a polite conversation, and you respond by trying to assault me."

"But I thought..." he whimpered.

"You didn't *think*, you vermin," Sabine said, "or you would have listened to a man who is granting you the opportunity for political immortality."

She released his hands, and he collapsed in a heap. but his relief was short lived. Sabine dropped to the floor. Her right arm grabbed his neck, while her left arm went around the backs of his legs. She clasped her hands together, crushing him into a painful cradle. "When you came in here," she said over his moans, "I know your head was in your ass. I may be able to reinsert it for you."

"Nooo!"

"If you ever call Senator Lyons a cripple again, the only working part of your body that will not be destroyed will be your brain."

Steiner's screeches increased as Sabine tightened her grip on his protesting body. Almost like a kiss, she leaned down and whispered in his ear, "The only reason I'll let you keep your brain is to remember this pain."

CHAPTER 14

"DAVID, A DOCTOR MARK'S ON the line for you."

David held up his index finger, signaling to the associate that he was wrapping up a call.

"David Grant," he said moments later as he picked up the line.

"Last chance," the voice said smoothly. "Who tried to kill Senator Lyons?"

"It was sanctioned by the administration," whispered David.

There was an almost imperceptible pause. It was enough to cause David a tight smile.

The caller sighed heavily. "That was the first interview I conducted. I assure you, the order did not originate at the White House."

"Doctor Mark," David interrupted, "I don't envy you your job. I can't even imagine how many people your boss has pissed off. You've got your work cut out for you."

"Interesting choice of words," the caller mused. A few moments of silence passed, and David wondered if he had put his adversary off balance.

"Senator Lyons is not my boss," the man said in a matter-of-fact tone. "In fact, I've never met him. You can simply think of me as an apostle for truth. Hmm, I think the apostle Mark has a more pleasant ring than Dr. Mark, which is so pedestrian."

"Listen, you sick fuck," said David, whispering into the phone. "The next time you see me, I won't be defenseless."

"You're not a very good listener. The next close dance will be with your mother."

David's body began to shake; his fingers were white as he gripped the receiver. "LEAVE HER ALONE, YOU COWARD!"

"It's only because we had a moment that you're getting a second warning. Now, write down this number and text me with the information I require." Before David could reply, the man recited a ten-digit number and disconnected.

* * *

"I've heard nothing from this guy for two weeks, and then he calls as the apostle Mark."

Mac finished chewing a bite of his lunch salad and wiped his chin with a paper napkin. He gave David a smile that matched his concern. "Were you really that balls-out with this freak? Or did you color your conversation so that I might adjust my impression of your overall wimpiness?"

David returned the smile.

Mac pointed at his friend's face and said enthusiastically, "An honest-to-goodness grin! Two weeks ago that wasn't possible. You've come a long way, baby."

"Thanks," David said, expanding his grin. "If I knew that all it would take for me to shape up would be to have someone slap me around, I would've asked for your help."

"My slaps are always verbal," said Mac, holding up his hands for display. "And they are as gentle as a soft rain."

David raised an eyebrow, but elected not to debate whether his boss's sometimes sharp tongue could leave a mark.

Although David acted like he had handled the call and wasn't worried, acting wasn't his strong suit.

"What's your level of concern?" Mac inquired into the heart of the matter.

"I have zero personal concerns. Unless he can walk through walls, he won't appear in my bedroom," David assured him.

"I know that you have a carry license."

"That's my second line of defense."

Mac nodded. "And if he goes after your mom?"

"Right after he hung up, I called Mom and asked her to host a houseguest, a friend of mine."

"Not Blake?" Mac asked with alarm.

"No," David assured him. "Believe it or not, I do have other friends from the Army. One of them needed a job. Mom's eighty-one and would be highly incensed if I suggested she might need some help."

"Is your friend with your mom yet?"

"He's driving from Texas and should be there by this weekend."

"What happens if the guy decides to move on her sooner. I hate to be throwing out that scenario," said Mac.

"That should be covered," said David confidently. "Sheriff Steele is a tough as nails 70-year-old who has been a family friend for years. He promised to keep a patrol car in her development."

Mac nodded. He had met the man and agreed with David's assessment. "So how'd you sell your mom on the visitor staying with her?"

David smiled. "I told her that Steven is a terrific cook and needed a job. Mom pays him, he stays with her, and she hosts dinner parties for her friends at the beach."

"Ahem."

"Yes, I'll make sure at least Grace is on the invite list."

"When does your mom go to Florida?" Mac asked.

"A couple of weeks. She's in a gated community there, so I'm not worried about her there."

"Will your friend go with her?"

"Who knows? She will like him, and she does love to host dinner parties."

"Is there any chance your assailant is working alone?" Mac asked, changing the subject.

"Maybe. You know Lyons and I don't, but would a senator hire someone to assault a private citizen?"

"I would not underestimate Lyons's capacity for animus," Mac responded.

"Apostle Mark was emphatic in denying that he had any connection to the good senator."

"Do you believe him?"

David threw up his hands. "Who else would give a shit? Actually, I agree. But would Lyons hire someone that I could identify and trace back to him?"

"No. Lyons thinks he's Teflon, but he wouldn't make such an elementary mistake." Mac paused and gave his friend a serious look. "However, if your apostle is a wild card *and* a religious fanatic, he may be more dangerous as a solo act."

CHAPTER 15

LIKE RIDING A BICYCLE, BEING acutely aware of your surroundings is second nature to a former Special Forces officer. When he rode the elevator to his apartment that night, David stood in the back. If it had been crowded, he would have waited for another. As he exited the elevator, his eyes looked up and down the empty hallway. Coming home at seven definitely cut down on the apartment traffic.

He opened the double locks on his door and walked into the foyer. The ringing landline surprised him, but he hurried over before it went to voicemail. "Hello?"

"David?" It was his mom's voice, in obvious distress. "He is going to ... cut me. Please ... tell ... him." The words were broken, spread out like a message pasted together for ransom.

"Mom!" he shouted into the phone. The dial tone was like a bullet, heading straight for his heart.

A preternatural calm came over David. He walked purposefully to his dresser and picked up his cell. He texted the number he had been given and typed in the only two words necessary.

He closed his eyes and rubbed them, then squeezed the bridge of his nose as he fought against the sudden wave of exhaustion. David Grant understood war. His mom should be safe now. Hurting her would put a bounty on Senator Lyons. Besides, David had paid the ransom: he had betrayed his best friend.

David texted one more person, then grabbed his pistol and shoved it into his pants. A rain jacket hid the weapon. He punched the elevator button repeatedly as he dialed his mother's cell. Voicemail. There was no percentage in hurting her unless the assailant thought that David had lied. But she'd be shaken up, scared even after the man who terrorized her had left. David needed to be there. He needed to be there now.

As his car peeled out of the garage, a sheet of rain engulfed it. He cursed, beat his hands on the steering wheel, and tried his mom's cell again. Voicemail. What if the man hadn't left? He stashed his gun under the seat and prayed that a cop wouldn't stop him. Twice on Route 50, he skidded; the last time brought his heart to his throat. His head was pounding.

His cell rang, and he picked it up like a drowning man grabbing a life preserver. "Hello!"

"You rang?"

"Blake, shit."

"Are you okay?"

"No. It's a long story, and not a pretty one. I'm driving to Bethany Beach in a fucking monsoon. Some bastard was with my mom."

"I can be there in 24 hours."

"No. She's probably all right. He used her to get me to give him your name." A knife-like pain shot through David's gut. He shook off the pain and uttered the words that would forever haunt him. "I betrayed you." David held his breath.

"First, you saved my life, Benedict Grant. Nothing you could ever do takes that away. Second, who did you give my name to and why did he want it?"

"Hold on. If I don't slow down going over the Bay Bridge, I'm going to be swimming with the fishes."

David released a breath. "This is not fun and games, Blake. This guy roughed me up once before, trying to get me to tell him who I thought went after Jeremy Lyons."

"And I was your first choice?"

"Yeah. You were my only choice. Man, I'm sorry. I'll do anything to make it up. Right now I have to be with my mom, but I've made you a target."

After a moment of silence, Blake gave an amused chuckle. "You always were a brilliant tactician."

David squeezed his eyes shut for a second. Part of him had hoped he was wrong.

"You need to concentrate on your driving, pal. You're not very good even when you are calm, cool, and collected. By the way, that is never. And if you have even a sliver of guilt over giving me up to save your mom, I promise that I will kick your ass. If you knew the size of the bounty that the really bad guys have on my head, you'd know that no matter how tough this dude is, he's only in the minors. Hang up the phone. Call your mom again, and text me the situation. If you need me, I'm there."

David wiped his eyes with the back of his hand. "Semper Fi, my brother."

"Wrong service, bro."

"Yeah, but right sentiment."

* * *

David pulled into a gas station, inserted his credit card, and started pumping. It seemed futile, but he reached inside the car and hit **redial** on his cell phone. His mom answered on the second ring. "Hi, honey. I just got back from bridge club and saw you called. I was just about to call you. You know that the girls don't let us have our cell phones on when we play."

David pressed his eyes closed and put his head on the steering wheel. His mind raced back to the phone message. It had been disjointed, like words pasted on cardboard as a ransom demand. The relief that flooded through his body washed away quickly as anger forced its way back in.

"Are you still there, honey?" Mildred Grant asked.

"Yeah, Mom. I, uh, thought I might stop by for a short visit if that's all right."

"Well, of course it is, honey, but it's the middle of the week!"

David smiled weakly. "I know, Mom, but as we discussed, I have a friend coming down, and I thought I'd surprise him when he gets there."

"How wonderful! I will have two handsome men in my house. Think of how jealous the neighbor ladies will be."

"I'm in Denton, now, so I won't be long. DO NOT wait up for me. I'll hit the code and sneak up to my room."

"Do you remember that you changed the codes? And I put on the alarm every night, even though I think it's silly. This is the 'quiet resort" after all. Do you want me to tell you the new code?"

"Not over the cell, Mom. Just put the key in our special place." David ran his hands through his wet hair. His stomach still churned.

"Okay, sweetie, I'll see you tomorrow. Love you."

"Love you too, Mom."

CHAPTER 16

AT PRECISELY 6:29 P.M., ELI Steiner shuffled into the great room of Jeremy Lyons's opulent apartment. His head swiveled on his thin neck, and his furtive glances made him looked like a junkie in a precinct.

"Please have a seat, Eli," Lyons said pleasantly, as he extended his hand toward the black leather swivel chair. "You look quite nice."

When Steiner had managed to crawl out of the shower and pull himself upright, a new dark suit, identical to the one he'd soiled, was laid out for him. It fit better than his own clothes. A starched white shirt with his initials on the breast pocket, dark socks, and clean underwear completed the picture. Steiner was too disconcerted to try to figure out how this had been accomplished.

Steiner nodded warily and sat down gingerly. Mia entered the room and offered a silver tray with a frosted martini glass to their guest. Steiner looked at Lyons and reached out tentatively to grab the glass. Grey Goose with a whisper of vermouth and three olives.

"Did we get it right?" Lyons asked.

Steiner nodded.

Lyons raised his drink, clinked Steiner's glass, and toasted, "To a new beginning, Eli."

For a moment, Steiner's eyes flared. " She…"

I know, I know," said Lyons, waving his hands dismissively. "But you did reach for her breasts." He waved an admonishing finger. "And that's unacceptable."

Steiner sucked down the martini, put down the glass, and folded his arms over his chest.

"Eli," Lyons said forcefully, "you and I are not prisoners of our pasts. We are men who determine the future."

Steiner sat back like a deflated tire. Mia magically appeared and refilled his glass from a silver cocktail shaker. Steiner took two large, greedy swallows. He had no leverage, no recourse. He had been brutalized by a woman and outmaneuvered by a man. The vanquished had to find the road to victory. Steiner asked quietly, "What do you need from me?"

Lyons nodded sagely, as if a student had asked an intelligent question. "It was a difficult hurdle for me to overcome," he began, "but the absence of arrogance makes a much more productive conversation. I regret our initial misunderstanding," he said softly. With a grimace he added, "Forced compliance is a last resort for necessary dialogue."

Absent a response, Lyons leaned forward. "Are you familiar with the differences between the large brokerage firms and Registered Investment Advisors who are not affiliated with financial institutions?"

"Yes," answered Steiner.

"Rather than remain at Johnston Wellons, which was an excellent regional firm, as you know, I struck out on my own. That allowed me freedom from many of the legal burdens of the brokerage firms and enabled me to operate under the radar. If they pass the requisite tests, anyone without a criminal record can declare themselves an RIA, whereas an individual must be hired to join a brokerage firm.

"Let's use you as an example, Eli. I believe that you have accounts in numerous firms." He waited until Steiner acknowledged this truth. "And that you pit one against the other. Is that correct?"

Steiner blinked. Did this man know when he took a crap?

"That's a questionable strategy," Lyons stated pedantically. "But that's a discussion for another time. The operative question is: Would the average investor feel more comfortable with an affiliated advisor or an independent advisor?"

Steiner considered. "Well, when you put it that way, I guess an independent advisor sounds more objective."

"Exactly." Lyons smiled. "Although the independents have fewer resources, significantly less regulatory oversight, and rarely a deep pocket behind them, they did choose the best name."

"What does that ..."

"Patience," said Lyons, holding up a hand.

Inwardly, Steiner bristled, but he maintained a placid demeanor.

"How has the media portrayed the Republican party?"

"Those bastards!"

"Agreed. But tell me what I'm missing: dysfunctional, rich, greedy, prejudicial, uncooperative, sexist?" Lyons paused. "Is that sufficient?"

"It's all bullshit!" spat Steiner, like a petulant child.

"Is it?" asked Lyons. "Let's examine. In our last election, one of the primary reasons for the challenger's defeat was his offhand comment that 47 per cent of the country wouldn't vote for him."

"Because they're on the fucking dole!" interjected Steiner spitefully.

"The reason is irrelevant. The administration easily used the comment to reinforce the media's depiction. Greedy, rich Republicans don't care about the little people. Note that we have in the candidate's own words evidentiary proof of three of my labels."

Steiner simmered.

"Dysfunctional? Too easy. The factions within the party can't agree on which hand they should use to wipe their collective asses."

"We will have a consensus before the mid-term elections," Steiner said resolutely, his face red with rage.

"Really? Who will capitulate? The moderates? The Tea Party? Will this be before or after you force a government shutdown over debt limits? Did you get your red line or here's my line in the sand strategy from our president?"

"May I speak?" Steiner asked evenly.

"Of course."

"I've been attacked physically, and my party has been attacked verbally. How about I ask you some questions?"

Lyons nodded.

"Do you believe in the Constitution?"

"Every word of it."

"Do you agree with our current foreign policy?"

"Absolutely not."

"Do you believe that government is bloated and inefficient?"

"Of course."

"Do you think Obamacare should be repealed?"

"Without a reasonable alternative, it is a waste of time and influence to try."

Steiner sat back with a sly smile. "Sounds to me like you're a closet Republican, Senator Lyons."

Lyons let the silence marinate. "Did I answer all your questions, Eli?"

"Oh, I have a bunch more I could give you; but I know the answers."

Lyons nodded. "I believe there are a few more that you should add to your list. "Do you believe that eleven million illegals should have a path to citizenship? Do you believe in gay marriage? Do you believe a voter ID card should be required? These are just a few of the many questions that may sound noble on the surface, but their only intent is to influence voters."

Before he spoke again, he noted Steiner's reactions. "Let me ask you what may appear to be an unrelated question. Have you ever used a weapon?"

Steiner wrinkled his face and answered defensively, "No."

Lyons looked at him thoughtfully, then reached under his chair and whipped out a .38-caliber pistol.

Steiner shrank back, instinctively throwing up his hands.

"Eli," Lyons said soothingly, "my pistol is for illustrative purposes only. It is to demonstrate that I am prepared for any contingency. Also," he held the weapon lovingly in his hand, but pointed at the ground, "it is a metaphor. It's loaded, I'm an excellent shot, and I wouldn't hesitate to use it."

Steiner had recovered enough to mutter, "I guess that answers the Second Amendment question."

Lyons laughed. "I like that side of you, Eli. Perhaps we need a more appropriate analogy. Have you ever played poker?"

"Yes."

"Would you ever lose to a player who bluffed on every hand?"

"No."

Lyons leaned forward and spoke with strength. "Your party has bluffed in every instance over raising the debt limit. You wave your pistol in the air, but you've shot your load, and therefore your credibility, before the battle begins."

"So what would your strategy be to stop this out-of-control spending?" challenged Steiner.

"You can't stop it. It's a runaway train, an avalanche of fiscal malfeasance."

"So we should just give up?" shouted Steiner.

"On your ideals, your goals, of course not. But the Republican party has cancer. You and I both know it." He looked at Steiner. As he expected, the man offered no rebuttal. "You think it's curable; I know it's terminal."

* * *

Eli Steiner finished one of the best meals of his life. A Caesar salad made at the table was followed by a perfectly grilled fillet of Kobe beef, sautéed mushrooms, summer corn, and grilled asparagus. For dessert, he'd wolfed down an exquisite chocolate soufflé. On the other hand, his host ate only vegetables. It was further confirmation that the two men were vastly different.

Still, the best part of the meal was that the black goddess of death was nowhere to be seen.

Sipping a magnificent brandy, Steiner threw out another volley. "Where do you get the sexist charge?"

"From President George H. W. Bush."

"What!?"

"In Bush's campaign against Clinton, James Carville brilliantly boxed the president into a political quagmire."

The fine wine and brandy had quelled Steiner's combativeness, so he just listened.

"The operative question is: Should women be allowed to choose?"

"That's not fair. What about the rights of the unborn child, the right to life?"

Lyons shook his head. "To many people, the moral answer to the question is simple. In this case, it's how the opposition has framed the question that damns you. Would any right-minded citizen really believe that your party has a war on women? Ultimately, you have to decide. Is that a question of government or a question of religion?"

"Both," said Steiner, pursing his lips.

"Maybe," Lyons conceded. "But certainly not now. Personally, I don't think the majority of people will ever be in favor of overturning *Roe versus Wade*. But it's a frivolous argument, regardless."

"How can a determination of where life begins be frivolous?" asked Steiner.

"If I didn't know better, Eli, I would think you were a closet Christian. My point is that any discussion of these views in a political campaign is suicide."

Steiner gave him a sullen stare.

"What is the goal of the Republican party?" Lyons asked.

"Limited government, ..."

"No," interrupted Lyons. "That is a platform. Your only goal is to be elected. Your own numbers tell you that the takers outnumber the givers. If you have unwinnable positions, why can't you just change them?"

"We can't change our core values and beliefs! Our constituents would desert us!" Steiner retorted heatedly.

Lyons sat back in his chair, backed away from the table, and moved forward until he was facing the gulf. A few minutes of silence passed before he turned his chair toward Steiner.

"In the last election, four million Republicans did not vote. Less of your party voted for Romney than for McCain in the '08 election. As a result, income taxes were raised, as were taxes on capital gains and dividends. And of course, the national debt skyrocketed." Lyons shook his head. "These are just the short-term repercussions of a party too polarized or too disinterested to vote.

"Eli, you're the quintessential powerbroker. As smart as you are, you're boxed in by the guidelines for the Tea Party. With your bickering and your trumpeting of the social issues, you have alienated the real majority in this country."

"The *real* majority?"

"Women. They vote for who resonates with them, who focuses on their issues. They are smarter than men. We just haven't figured that out. You lose the female vote, and you're waiting outside the club, and even your money can't get you in the door."

"And you have the answer?"

"It is time to shape the platforms of the party with one purpose: to win. You can join me and be an architect of the new order ..." he paused, "or you can be a victim of your party's inevitable demise."

CHAPTER 17

"THAT WAS TRULY A DISGUSTING man," said Alegria.

Lyons gave her a curious look. It was the first time he'd ever heard her make a negative comment about anyone. "Are you referring to his appearance?" he asked.

"No," she said, shaking her head. "I would never criticize someone for their appearance."

That made sense. Lyons had never met a woman who cared less about her appearance than Alegria. Her infrequently washed black hair fell in tangles around her face, and she had a total of three outfits and two pairs of sandals, which she alternated when she couldn't find the ones she wore last.

Still, he looked at her with the affection a father has for his child. Of Cuban descent, both of Alegria's parents had died as political prisoners. In the face of many competing offers for this young prodigy, Lyons had plucked her from academia and installed her as his head of technology. She went from a love affair with patterns and algorithms to being an integral part of his family. She was a savant, and she was devoted to him.

He smiled as said, "Please enlighten me with your observations."

Sabine, wearing a sheer, light blue cover-up over her black bikini, smiled as she watched the two interact.

Alegria proceeded to explain as if she were lecturing a biophysics class. "He slobbered over both Mia and Sabine; he's the prototype letch. He's rude, opinionated, arrogant, and truculent. He's used to bullying people, demeaning those that he considers his inferiors, which is everyone, by the way, and buying people. I'm sorry, but he is simply odious."

"You got all of that from seeing him for a few minutes?" asked Sabine.

"Well that, plus seeing you hugging him in the video." She cocked her head at her friend in an unusual display of humor.

Sabine burst out laughing.

"You are in rare form tonight, Alegria," Lyons said. She had the most brilliant mind he had ever encountered, but she was not judgmental, and she rarely engaged in assessments of people. With statistics, probability charts, and accessing any computer, she had no peer.

"I want to know, Jeremy, if you've ever seen a better take-down?" Sabine stood with her hands on her hips.

"When I first met Max Parnavich, he used similar moves on two men in a bar."

"Who was better?" she demanded.

"You are certainly more pleasurable to watch, my dear." She did not look satisfied. "And you have one quality that poor Max never learned."

"What is that?"

"Restraint."

Slightly mollified she changed the subject. "Do you really want to destroy the Republican party?"

"My preference would be to destroy both parties. In this instance, I had to come in hard to accomplish the goal and make him think that he eventually secured a victory. I want to destroy the party's elitism, the holier-than-thou attitude. If you are a centrist during the election, you can be whatever you want if you win. If they don't settle on a less charged platform, they will destroy themselves. They have to dictate the narrative."

"What's your goal in 2014?" asked Sabine.

"I want a Republican majority in both the Senate and the House. Because of my passion for fiscal solvency and limited government, they will consider me more of a Republican than a Democrat. Consequently, it will be easier to get them on board. But if Steiner were allowed to go unchecked, he could marshal the far right and make my quest more difficult."

"And if the Democrats keep the senate?"

"Then I will have failed."

CHAPTER 18

"LAW OFFICES."

"May I speak to Senator Smathers, please?"

"May I tell him who's calling?"

"Jeremy Lyons."

The long pause was not unexpected.

"Senator Lyons?" the receptionist asked.

"Yes."

"One moment, sir."

Approximately a minute later, an angry voice said, "Not funny. Who the hell is this?"

"I don't imagine you expected to hear from me, sir," Lyons replied.

"You've got some nerve. Have you found another way to screw with me?"

"Actually, just the opposite, Senator."

"I'm just a country lawyer now. Some son of a bitch stole my title."

"If I apologize for my methodology, would it do any good?"

"Nope."

"Then we will dispense with the recriminations and move forward. I would like to make you an offer."

"I don't want anything from you except to never hear from you again."

The decisiveness in the last statement would have been more effective if the phone had been disconnected. But curiosity is an enticing mistress.

Lyons waited a moment to make sure he would have Smathers's attention. "As I stated publicly, I believe that you were an excellent senator. The fact that it was you who were in my way instead of one of the many undeserving in the chamber was unfortunate."

"Yeah, I'm sure your eyes are rimmed with tears."

"You can continue playing the victim, or you can allow me to explain the purpose of my call."

"Speak. I can't wait."

"I would like you to run against Bill Sessions in 2014."

"Why? So you can bet on him to win? It's too late. He has too much money behind him, he is a four-term incumbent, and he won 62 per cent of the vote last time. You may know how to get what you want, but you're no political analyst." Embedded anger and derision colored his words.

"You're correct, Senator. I have no reelection experience. But I do have considerable experience in winning. I will fund your campaign up to a hundred million dollars. I would advise you to concentrate on positive ads. In addition, at a critical juncture, I will endorse you."

Alan Smathers's head was spinning. The man who had blackmailed him and neutered his 2012 campaign now wanted to finance a new campaign for him? As tempting as it was, you make a deal with the devil, you lose your soul.

"What's your pound of flesh?" asked Smathers.

"My first requirement is nonnegotiable. I need you to run as an Independent."

"You really are nuts. I believe in my platform. I won't compromise my integrity for anyone or anything."

"The Republican platform is a trap door. What is the biggest risk facing our country?"

"Our lack of fiscal sanity, but you know that."

"Examine the straightjacket of your party. As a Republican, you are forced to defend the 'war on women.' Forced to answer to income inequality. Forced to try to reason with the splinter groups of your party, and forced to be beholden to your base."

Lyons paused to let Smathers reflect on his words.

"As an Independent, you speak and vote only what you truly believe. There are no party lines. You will owe no one, not even me."

Another minute of silence passed before Smathers spoke. "And the second requirement?"

"There is none. In my short tenure, I have found the decay in the moral fiber of our elected officials to be worse than I had envisioned. We need people who care more about their country than themselves. We need men and women of integrity to change the rancid status quo. After you are elected, all I will ask of you is to keep an open mind about my mission."

"You sound like you're going to war."

"We are."

CHAPTER 19

"Mac, it's Senator Lyons on Line 1."

Mac threw his hands up in disgust. Although they worked only through Alegria, Mac's team managed significant assets for Lyons's charitable trust. It wasn't like he could ignore the man. He snatched at the receiver like it was the phone's fault.

"To what do I owe this honor, Senator?" Mac asked in a tone soaked in sarcasm.

"I called to apologize."

Mac resisted the temptation to respond.

"My near-death experience and a life confined to a wheelchair tend to offer time for painful introspective thought," Lyons continued. "I hope you will accept my apology."

Mac wished he could see Lyons's face, read his body language. His words sounded sincere and contrite. Yet, the prickles of apprehension that had become almost a reflex with this man would not dissipate easily.

"I appreciate your call," Mac said kindly, "and I'm sorry for what you've endured."

Lyons sighed audibly. "But you can't forgive the bastard who tormented you for the past five years."

"It's not easy," Mac admitted. "My whole family has lived in fear of you. Neither one of us can change the past." He paused. "But I've been your cat toy. We were never friends. You don't need me. You're filthy rich. Now you're a senator. Perversely, I admire your political positions, but I'm aware that you're a chameleon."

"I knew you would agree with my platform," said Lyons, purposely focusing on the only positive comment from Mac. "I also cherish your candor in a world where dialogue is clothed with what people want to hear."

The word 'cherish' seemed out of place to Mac. He continued to listen.

"Your insider's knowledge of our financial warts gives you a similar passion and sense of urgency."

Lyons's point was well taken, but Mac was not looking for collaboration or a compliment. "Seriously," he asked, "what would we gain by a Kumbayah moment? I am a realist. I know that at some point every friend I have will hurt my feelings or piss me off. I'll let it go for the sake of that friendship. But I don't have *any* friends who have tormented me. Besides, you're not really looking to be my friend."

"Actually, I am. I realize it's a lengthy process. I know the odds are against me," Lyons admitted. "I am a realist, too, and I hope that we can discuss issues affecting our country. I am certain that you will pull no punches. It would be extremely helpful if you would share your insights. Yes men or women are of no help to me; however, an acerbic critic would be quite valuable."

Mac didn't know what to say. The man twisted him in more knots than a contortionist.

When he did not respond, Lyons added, "Besides, the ninth step of AA is to make direct amends to people you have harmed. Although I am not a member of Alcoholics Anonymous, you would no doubt consider me a charter member of Assholes Anonymous. I believe their program is the same."

Mac smiled in spite of himself. "I see why you were so successful in your brief tenure at Johnston Wellons."

"Life certainly would have been different if I had stayed, but I had many demons to exorcise. I should get to the main purpose of my call. In addition to an overdue apology, I wondered if I could entice you and your wife or you and R.J. Brooks to have dinner with me in Naples. I will send my plane and make reservations for you at the Ritz or any other hotel you might prefer."

Mac was shocked into silence. If any other large client had made the offer, he'd have accepted in a heartbeat. *No hope of Grace,* he thought, *but it would be an experience to have R.J. in the Lyons Den.* "Of all the conversations I might imagine having with you, this is the most bizarre," he said.

"There is no urgency to respond," Lyons replied. "If you will excuse the analogy, it must feel like your unwelcome stalker just called and asked you for a date. However, when the cold north winds begin to blow, or the hot winds from 1600 Pennsylvania Avenue become too intolerable, please consider my offer."

Mac again was silent as he mulled over the conversation.

"Are you there? Lyons asked.

Mac let out a breath. "Recently, my partner got the crap beaten out of him in his own home. The attacker was looking for the guy who tried to kill you. It doesn't sound like much has changed, Senator."

"Mac, it was not me. If you like, I'd be happy to look into it."

"Not necessary." Mac replied and hung up the phone.

CHAPTER 20

THE RECOMMENDED STRATEGY FOR BREAKING up with a significant other is to invite him or her to dinner at an upscale restaurant. At the appropriate moment, the dumper should gently break the bad news. In theory, in such opulent surroundings the dumpee does not make a scene. Mac McGregor had never tested that theory, but thought that the concept made sense. He needed to have what might be a difficult conversation with his wife, and he thought that he would be safer if there were witnesses.

Accordingly, he was driving their white Honda minivan down scenic McArthur Boulevard to one of the couple's favorite restaurants, Old Angler's Inn. After 33 years of marriage, an impromptu, middle-of-the-week romantic dinner was a bit out of the norm, but so far Mac had pulled it off without raising suspicion.

Parking was just a few steps from the restaurant, and they lingered by the huge outdoor bonfire, warming themselves against the chilly evening. The outdoor seating area was lovely even in its emptiness, as if it were just waiting for spring's arrival. The heavy stone façade and dark wooden door made visitors feel like they were stepping into another century.

Regulars at this quaint restaurant, nestled across from the picturesque C & O Canal, knew to ask for downstairs seating, preferably next to the wood-burning fire. Otherwise, diners need to ascend a winding staircase to the upper levels, or main seating. The McGregors were definitely regulars.

The dinner conversation was innocuous and pleasant, and it wasn't until Grace's second glass of wine was delivered that Mac broached the subject. "I got a call from a United States Senator today."

Adding the title did not soften the blow. Grace's ice-blue eyes went to half-mast, and her fork, which held a delicious scallop, stopped in mid air.

"He called to apologize. I was skeptical and tried to poke holes in it, but he sounded contrite and sincere. It's possible that he has actually changed." Parsing the information wasn't going to work.

Calmly, Grace brought the scallop to her mouth, chewed it slowly, and then placed her fork on her plate. "It is also possible that you're an idiot. What did this creature want from you?"

"You do remember that he's a client," Mac said through gritted teeth.

"You use that client bullshit as if it says a blessing over everything you do. You do remember that he terrorized our family."

For a moment, Mac felt like he was talking to someone he didn't know. "I don't need a history lesson," he said evenly.

Grace leaned forward, folded her hands on the table, and gave him the look she gave their children when she demanded an explanation for their behavior. "What did he *want*, Mac?"

"He wanted ideas from R.J. and me about how to jump start our economy?" Mac hated being on the defensive.

Grace shrugged. "That's good; appeal to your vanity. I can just picture the three of you in the senate dining room solving the problems of the world."

Like many husbands, Mac's poker skills disappeared when he was in a contentious discussion with his wife. Still, he didn't want a counterpunch that would wound. "I don't care where the venue is. I plan to meet with him."

"Keep your voice down," Grace admonished.

Mac's jaw tightened as he looked around the room. "We'll continue this when we get home."

"No we won't."

"Even better."

CHAPTER 21

THE THRILL THAT INEVITABLY ACCOMPANIED a newly elected senator was absent in Jeremy Lyons. Attending the daily sessions of this dysfunctional body was, in fact, repellant to him. As a result, Lyons chose his spots, preferring to attend only sessions where there was at least a possibility that something meaningful might happen. As he had expected, this left him open to whispered, and even outspoken, criticism.

He was a curiosity: a troublemaker who had had the temerity to promise to serve for only one term; an Independent with no ties or allegiance to any party; a powerful man who might try to change the status quo. And the old guard were quite comfortable with the status quo.

Like the house of representatives, the senate meets in the United States Capitol in Washington, D.C. One hundred desks are arranged in a chamber in a semicircular pattern and are divided by a wide, circular aisle. By tradition, Republicans sit to the right of the center aisle and Democrats sit to the left, both facing the presiding officer.

By custom, the leader of each party sits in the front row along the center aisle. Without asking anyone, freshman Senator Jeremy Lyons powered his chair between the senate's two most powerful men. As if it were required, both leaders stood and shook his hand.

Today's session was open, which meant that it was televised live on C-SPAN2. Although the vice president has the authority to preside over the senate, he rarely does. Mostly, it's on ceremonial occasions. The fact that the vice president was in attendance now was because he had presidential aspirations.

Although he had not publicly stated his intentions, Lyons had previously determined that he would not attend sessions unless a vote was required or if he felt that the senate was in the last inning of a substantive debate. Before Lyons's injury, he had been vocal in declaring his intention to set the country on a different course. He had been critical of the body to which he was not yet a member, and it was suspected that the tradition, protocol, and seniority principles of this august group would not be respected by a man such as himself.

Perhaps the one thing his fellow senators did not expect was that Lyons would keep to himself, offer little in the way of criticism (constructive or otherwise), and appear passive on most issues. Like a good poker player, he kept his cards close to his vest.

He did not try to make friends, and merely graced those who approached him with a handshake and a tight smile. At first it was disconcerting for the members, like waiting for a bomb to explode; however, Lyons's continued lack of involvement gave them a sense of superiority. The murmurs were quite similar: "I knew he'd be all talk and no action," or "He's an Independent, all right - independent of any opinions."

During his first few months, the only sound bite Lyons gave reporters was his opinion that the senate spends too much time on protocol and not enough time on progress. Since the Liberals had renamed themselves Progressives, they pushed this comment to the media, which gave it about a two-day shelf life.

The reason that most newly elected senators feel a thrill when they first walk onto the senate floor is because they've achieved their goal: pension and healthcare for life; prestige; guaranteed employment after the senate. It is to them a dream come true.

To Senator Jeremy Lyons, his time in the senate was more of a nightmare: a torturous period of enduring banalities and listening to pompous windbags. Yet, it was a necessary evil, with its only consolation being that it was a way station.

CHAPTER 22

THE WEEK AFTER MEMORIAL DAY is primarily locals only in Bethany Beach, Delaware. It is the eye of the hurricane for this lovely seaside resort. The onslaught from the holiday weekend is almost forgotten as merchants prepare for the school year to end and restaurants gear up to compete for hiring college kids and exchange students. The beaches adjacent to the town carry an unwritten warning to mark your spot early.

By Thursday, the weekend weather outlook was so promising that Mac McGregor decided to make a spontaneous escape from work. He called Grace as soon as he got to the office and said, "Pick me up at the Metro at 2:30. I have a lunch meeting, and then you and I are off for an impromptu weekend of sun and mind-blowing sex."

"I'm up for at least half of that," she said. "Did you check the weather forecast for Bethany?"

"Yes. We are golden."

"Well, okay. Let's rock 'n' roll, you rebel, you."

* * *

Mac's cell phone jarred him awake. To him, sleeping with the windows open in the salt air, accompanied by the rhythmic roll of the waves, felt like sleeping on clouds. Invariably, he woke up smiling, refreshed, and not the least bit groggy. The clock on his nightstand read a surprising 8:30, and Grace was long gone. Articles on sleep indicated that it wasn't possible to really catch up on sleep, but at the moment he disputed that conclusion.

"Hello?"

"Hey, boss, it's David. I hope I didn't wake you guys up."

"Well, as you would expect, Grace is still lounging in bed. After another day of eating bon bons and being catered to, she needs her rest."

"Doesn't she drive you to the beach?"

"Another nasty rumor. She naps while I drive."

"Well, now everything makes more sense, Mac. You do everything around the house, and that's why everyone caters to *you* at work. You must be exhausted."

Mac had let the nonsense run its course. "So, fellow beach bum, how's your mom?"

"I can't keep up with her. I think she's going to be crowned the queen of Bethany. She's like a little kid when I come to see her."

Mac laughed. "Please tell her I love her. We managed to squeeze in a dinner with her last year, but she is a party animal."

"Is there a chance I could pick your brain for a little while today?" David asked. "Mom is hosting her bridge club, and I may be too tempting to some of her friends."

"She must have desperate friends. Let me check with Grace to see what she's got planned, and I'll either text you or call you back."

"I don't want to intrude."

"I get on her nerves after a day or two. Shouldn't be a problem."

Grace wanted to spend some time with a high school friend who lived in Ocean City, Maryland, so she suggested that the two men have dinner together. Rather than eat at a restaurant, Mac had picked up two salmon meals from Northeast Seafood Kitchen, and he and David were eating outside on Mac's screened porch.

"Hard to imagine it's this nice in early June," said Mac. He held up a large Turvis tumbler with a Redskins logo. It was chock full of ice, a shot of Mount Gay rum, caffeine-free Diet Coke, and two limes. He clicked glasses with David's Diet Coke.

"You don't drink at all anymore?" Mac asked.

"Nope," said David resolutely. "I don't intend to ever be vulnerable again."

Mac nodded his approval.

"By the way, said David, "this salmon is great. I love the maple flavor with the baked beans and frizzled onions. But you weren't supposed to buy food. I asked for this meeting."

"I bask in being called a rebel."

David smiled and then cocked his head towards the wall.

"Who's who?" he asked, pointing to the sign on the gray siding of the house.

"Isn't it obvious?" Mac raised an eyebrow. The sign read, "Me and My Old Crab Live Here." A picture of a large, hard-shell crab hung below it.

"I guess so…," answered David. "I just didn't expect Grace to dis you like that publicly."

"Look at you, Eagle Scout, mixin' in a little street talk."

David smiled.

"That's a good look on you," said Mac, acknowledging his friend's smile. "You should wear it more often."

David took a deep breath. "Yeah, you're right." He bit his lower lip, looked hard at Mac, and grimaced. "I … uh … didn't tell you the whole story about giving up Blake to that psycho."

Mac put down his fork, placed his elbows on the table, and interlaced his fingers.

"If I gave you the full version, you would really think I'm an idiot."

"I've heard enough to know that you got professionally conned. The guy's good," Mac said calmly. "Knows your weak spot. Tails your mom, records her conversations, and then splices together the fake hostage tape." He paused. "We might not know anything about who he is, but we know something about his capabilities."

David looked up.

"He broke into your apartment and expertly subdued you," Mac went on.

"Not hard to overpower a drunk," David interrupted.

"Bullshit. He's still got to be a cat burglar to not wake you, and he's undoubtedly competent in hand-to-hand combat. You didn't see a weapon, did you?"

"No."

"Next, he had the time and expertise to set up a situation with your mom. Maybe the good senator has changed, but this operation feels like his fingerprints were all over it."

Mac picked up his fork and started waving it for emphasis. "It's an unforgivable sin for a person to not recognize Jeremy Lyons's greatness or his historical significance. Then try to kill him? End up crippling him? And then roam free? He tried to play it off when I confronted him, but I'm not convinced. I don't think Lyons will rest until his attempted assassin is found and killed."

"You confronted him? You asked a United States Senator if he hired someone to assault me?" David's eyes were wide open.

Mac raised both hands and waved him off. "Don't act like I'm your hero; it just came up."

"That's crap. But tell me what he said."

"He said that he did not hire anyone to find out who tried to kill him."

"But you didn't believe him."

Mac reached up and scratched his head. "I don't know. Lyons sounded sincere, but he can make people believe anything he wants them to...."

"Still, Mac," said David, as he reached over and squeezed his friend's shoulder, " I appreciate your standing up for me."

Feeling a little uncomfortable with the praise, Mac changed the subject. "How did Blake react to your fingering him as Lyons's assassin?"

David shook his head. "Unfazed. He took the news unemotionally, as if I'd told him that the market dropped two points."

Mac shrugged. "You damn near worried yourself into a rehab facility with guilt, and yet your relationship with Blake is not compromised in any way. There is a lesson there."

David's smile was tight. "Point taken. In fact, his exact words were, 'Half of the Mideast has a price on my head. Tell this jerk-off to wait in line."

"I think my money would be on Blake."

David slid the baked beans around the plate with his half-eaten salmon for a moment. then looked up.

"He did make a request."

Mac gave him a quizzical look.

"Give me the GPS on that asshole who bitch slapped you; only *I'm* allowed to do that to my boy."

CHAPTER 23

GRACE MCGREGOR WOKE AT 4:00 A.M. from a bad dream. It's often a defense mechanism for mothers with multiple children to imagine the worst. It's nature's way of allowing them to cope and solve any of the family's lesser problems.

She felt a sense of relief that the frightening scenario was just a dream. She forced her mind to focus on the lulling sounds of the waves washing to shore. She knew if she fell right back to sleep, there was a strong probability that her nightmare could go into a second act. She did a half scoot to her right and reached over to cuddle Mac. A middle-of-the-night spoon was better than a sleeping pill.

She stretched out farther. Reluctantly, she opened one eye. A sliver of moonlight provided her illumination. His side of the bed was empty. Grace sighed, turned back to her side of the bed, then sat up and put her feet on the floor. She knew where she would find him.

It was quite a picture: Underneath the ratty bathrobe that Grace had threatened to burn, Mac had on boxer shorts, a sweatshirt, and a beach towel wrapped around his waist and worn like a skirt. From the back, his hair looked like a teepee. Bent over with his arms resting on his knees, he was staring out at the moon and the still, dark ocean.

Grace opened the heavy glass French doors. Mac didn't turn to acknowledge her. She leaned down and gently touched his back. "Scoot down," she whispered.

Still without turning, he moved forward on the chaise to allow her to straddle it and sit behind him. She wrapped her arms around him. Neither spoke as they absorbed the night. Grace knew that he would talk when he was ready.

"I'm sorry," he said softly.

She hugged him tighter.

"We're not us," he said in the same resigned voice. "I spend my life giving people answers, and above all, I never wanted this kind of distance between us. Jeremy Lyons seems to infect our lives even when he may be doing the right thing." He turned to look at her and took her shoulders in his hands.

"I realize that I don't have an explanation or a reason that you or any sane person could understand as to why I would voluntarily get involved with him. It's not about danger any more. And it sounds almost deluded if I say that it's about something much bigger."

"Maybe it's about ego," she said, but not unkindly.

Mac let out a breath. "Thinking that maybe I could contribute and make the world a better place....you may not be far off."

"Mac, I've never tried to tell you what to do…"

His severely arched eyebrow stopped her.

"Okay," she said. "But stand up straight, pick up your clothes, put your dishes in the sink doesn't count. It's my job to make you look good. If *anyone* tells you that you have to do something, every hair on your head stands up, and your first instinct is to fight back." She sighed. "But if you expect me to be happy about you slow dancing with a murderer, it's not going to happen. I'll respect your choices, but I don't have to agree with them or approve of them."

"So what do we do?" he asked, his brown eyes plaintive and pained.

She held his gaze for a moment, then stood up and motioned for him to stand also. "As usual, I have to think of everything. We start by having some of that world-class sex you promised."

CHAPTER 24

IT WAS THE CHEEKS. RAISED and slightly puffy, like they might be filled with marshmallows, they gave the illusion that Joe Carvel was always happy. When you are an anchor on CNBC, America's go-to source for financial news, you need to be able to see a little sunshine regardless of the situation.

In a nanosecond world where buy-and-hold investors have morphed into high-frequency traders whose average holding period for stocks is three seconds, our guide through the morass of financial jargon must possess keen intellect, an unwavering gaze, and the ability to appeal to both the sophisticate and the novice. Brown, wavy hair that boasted the never-need-to-comb look and pale blue eyes that were perpetually crinkled as if waiting to unload a humorous dig combined to make Joe Carvel the people's choice. The only certainty in the stock market is that stock prices will fluctuate between euphoria and the mortuary. Without a guide, investors would undoubtedly become schizophrenic.

One of the reasons that CNBC has emerged as the premier source of financial information is its pull-no-punches interviews. Commentators often stop just short of hostile when questioning corporate CEOs, mutual fund managers, economists, or politicians. Because Carvel was armed with the industry's quickest wit and an engaging demeanor, he could probe into the psyche of an interviewee like a surgeon.

Today's interview had been eagerly anticipated. It had been heavily promoted by the station, and Carvel's instructions had been to "go deep or go down." He was ready.

"Senator Lyons," Carvel said with a large, infectious grin, "I was offered a year's pay by someone who wanted take my place today." Play time had begun. A smile can anesthetize even the most closed subject.

"That could make a serious dent in the national debt," quipped the laconic guest.

The camera was still kind to Jeremy Lyons, even though he was now 60 years of age and had been through a trauma that would have killed most men. His blinding white dress shirt highlighted his flaw-less tan, and his black silk jacket hung perfectly on his broad shoulders. With his bronzed bald head, piercing dark eyes, and strong jaw line, his presence alone commanded attention and respect. The required camera angles did not reveal that the senator was in a wheelchair, but even that would not have lessened the charisma of this man.

Carvel turned and addressed his fellow commentators, who looked like hungry wolves as they leaned forward in anticipation. "I'm loving this guy already."

His aside completed, Carvel turned quickly back to the senator. "I'm not going to spar with you, sir. I know when I'm outmatched."

It was an obvious feint, and Lyons ignored it.

"We are truly grateful to have you here today to weigh in on these important issues," Carvel added, getting down to business.

Lyons shrugged nonchalantly, and Carvel pounced on it.

"You don't think a government shutdown and the possibility that the United States might default on its debt are serious issues?" Carvel asked, his face a mask of disbelief.

"I think it's theater. The strategy is flawed. The process is ridiculous. And regrettably, the actors fail to rise to the level of mediocrity."

"So you're in the camp that believes this will be settled?"

"I am in no one's camp. But yes, every play has an ending."

"Who blinks?"

"Who cares? Neither party appears concerned about putting our country first. If our politicians were corporate officers in a public company, they'd all be fired."

Carvel, a life-long Republican, probed quickly. "And the CEO of that corporation?"

"Replaced," was the definitive response.

Carvel ran his hand through his hair as he digested his guest's words. "Your candor is refreshing and appreciated."

Lyons acknowledged his comment with a small nod.

Carvel changed direction. "I know that discussing the attempted assassination is off limits," he said easily.

Lyons's flat eyes reinforced that fact, and Carvel moved on quickly.

"But I do believe that all America is perplexed that you have been relatively quiet since your election. Quite frankly, we expected you to create much more of a ruckus." The interviewer added a boy-next-door smile.

Lyons turned to the camera. "Precipitous action in politics, like we are currently witnessing, as in investing, is rarely rewarding. A critical ingredient of investment success is exhaustive research and due diligence. Acting before fully analyzing a situation would be like signing a bill before reading it."

Carvel's eyes lit up like a kid's at Christmas. "You sound like a Republican. Are you sure you're not one of us in disguise?"

Lyons gave a tight smile and replied, "Politicians are owned by their donors, PACs, and their constituency. I can assure you that no one owns me."

Carvel started to speak, and Lyons held up a cautionary finger. "Governance is not something that should be left to a legislator's staff or to a lobbyist."

"Your staff is the smallest on Capitol Hill."

Lyons flashed a wry smile. "Consider it the first step in reducing a bloated government."

Carvel's smile was genuine as he chuckled in response.

"The people that I employ are analytical, not afraid to speak their minds, and loyal. I prefer quality over quantity," said Lyons.

"So other than bolster the Florida economy, and it appears your tweaks have accelerated that process, what is the mission for you and your elite team?"

Again Lyons turned to the camera. "To bring reason to our nation's economy and integrity to our government."

"Specifically, what are you referring to when you question the lack of integrity?"

"I am referring to the lack of integrity of our elected officials."

Carvel attacked. "Sir, politicians from both chambers are going to question how a man who was a fugitive from the FBI and was threatened with indictment over insider trading is calling out all of the legislators over lack of integrity!" Carvel knew that he might have pushed too far. He also instinctively knew that the man in the wheelchair could snap him like a twig, but Lyons had lit the fuse. Carvel was just fanning the flames.

Instead of anger, Lyons showed a flicker of amusement. Carvel felt like a fly who had just walked into a spider's web.

"The IRS targets Tea Party Republicans. The NSA listens to all of our pillow talk." Lyons waved his hands out to the viewers. "Character assassination and baseless accusations have been a weapon of our government long before any of us were born."

He leaned into the camera like a preacher making the point of his sermon. "How have we allowed governing bodies to pass self-serving legislation? Legislators routinely engage in political blackmail to pander to their special interests, and above all to ensure that they stay in office. I have said that I will only govern for one term; that is self-imposed term limits. Do politicians want to vote themselves out of a job? They can already impose rules on *you* that *they* do not have to follow."

Carvel cocked his head. "Senator, the fact that you were elected is one for the record books. Your competition was a popular and productive incumbent. It was the most civilized campaign in modern history: no negative advertising, no spurious accusations. Your qualifications seemed to be that you ran a covert, highly successful hedge fund for the ultra-rich and that you were a modern day James Bond. Seems to me that your background, or lack of background, would have been a lightning rod for an aggressive opponent such as Senator Smathers. Yet he never even asked why there is really no biographical information about you. Why do you think that is?"

"As we have witnessed on the presidential level, privacy does not preclude victory."

Carvel gave a prompting nod, wanting more.

"On a more serious note," Lyons went on, "campaigns have become bloodbaths. National embarrassments. They have denigrated the office and the voting public. If Senator Smathers lost because he chose not to lie, distort, or throw out innuendos, then that is a tragedy. He governed with character and passion. His life in politics is not over."

Carvel studied him for a long moment. He was about to say something that was designed to be controversial. "You were elected because you're a hero who awoke just in time," he said softly. "And you're a born-again Christian."

Lyons nodded.

"Do you think that God wants you to govern?" The question was asked with complete sincerity.

Before he responded, Lyons looked straight into his host's eyes, extending the moment. "Yes," he said with conviction, "I do."

Always the pro, Carvel looked into the camera, raised his eyebrows slightly, and nodded. It was as if he silently communicated to his audience that they had heard the same thing. Senator Jeremy Lyons believed that God chose him to govern.

Carvel exhaled and turned back to Lyons, still looking a little befuddled. "Last question, Senator. You're an Independent, not aligned with either party. In fact, you have called out both parties and the president! How do you get anything done? How are you going to make a difference?"

Lyons regarded him carefully, as if the two were sitting across from each other at a chessboard. Dead space is death on air, and seconds seem like hours. Finally, Lyons smiled confidently. "I guess I'm going to have to change the playing field...."

CHAPTER 25

I⊤ MAY NOT HAVE BEEN Super Bowl numbers, but for nine o'clock on a Wednesday morning, eighteen million viewers was an unbelievable number. Among the curious and interested were all members of the High Net Worth Group of Johnston Wellons who were not on phone calls. Mac McGregor turned off the TV and left the commentators' post mortems for the rest of the audience.

Lena Brady, Mac's highly efficient right hand, made the first comment. Although she might make five feet in heels, she nevertheless struck fear in the whole team. *"The New York Times* will rip him a new one. The politicians will have to wait in line to spout their collective indignities."

R.J. Brooks voiced a different opinion. "They used to call Slick Willie the 'Teflon Man.' Then Bush was like a magnet for the ills of the world. The press never cut him a break. Now if we criticize the current king, we are labeled racists." His summation was simple. "I think Jeremy Lyons is bulletproof."

The ever irreverent Lena turned to their senior partner. "Mac Attack, you've been bunking with the dude, for like, forever. What's your take?"

Everyone waited for a response, but the usual instant rejoinder didn't come. Mac's eyes were focused at the now dark flat screen, and he seemed lost in thought. He cocked his head and said. "I think the man is mesmerizing. He calculates everything; we may never see a misstep from him. I agree, he is bulletproof. The media is paralyzed. How do you hammer a disabled hero? Any grumbling and blustering from our elected officials will be behind closed doors. The last thing they want to do is give this story legs."

Mac paused, leaned back in his chair, and swung his legs onto his desk. He stared at his friends and spoke in a hollow voice. "He is the only politician in modern times to be a true fiscal conservative. He does not spend his time worrying about political correctness; he says what he thinks. If I had never been involved with Jeremy Lyons, I would be a disciple, pure and simple. I would lead his troops up a hill. However, it's very difficult to reconcile his apparent patriotism with my previous assertion that he was the most dangerous man on the planet."

In a rare moment of public empathy, Lena patted her boss on the shoulder. "At least he's not your problem anymore."

* * *

Another interested party watching CNBC's Jeremy Lyons interview was Fox News superstar Jackie Mayfield.

Eddie Richter, her longtime cameraman, roused her from her reverie. "Uh-oh, Jackie's boyfriend is cheatin' on her."

"What?" She reddened slightly. "That's ridiculous. He's a financial genius. Of course he's going to be interviewed by CNBC."

"Ah, baby," said Eddie consolingly, "I've told you before that the only guy you can count on is good ol' Eddie."

Jackie shook her head derisively at the 62-year-old Buenos Aires native who had worked with her for the last 12 years. They had such a rapport that his teasing was as easy to take as Sunday morning. "I never expected to be Jeremy Lyons's exclusive interviewer," she said patiently.

Eddie cocked his head. "You've been his advocate, his friend, been in his corner since the beginning. It's not right. He coulda' called you and told you first, so you coulda' made it look like he discussed it with you."

Jackie smiled sweetly. She loved Eddie's protective nature. "I'll only say this to you," she whispered, "but it does make me feel a little jealous." She paused. "And maybe a little sad. He's made my career, so I could never turn against him unless he did something truly reprehensible."

She leaned over and gave him a kiss on the cheek. "You've been in this business longer than I have, Eddie, and you know how cut-throat it can be. When you have a fabulous source or a famous celebrity that uses only you, it's nirvana. But it's not the real world. It doesn't last forever."

"Loyalty should last forever," said Eddie stubbornly.

"What am I going to do with you?" she asked, giving him a look of mock frustration.

"Marry me!" Eddie responded brightly.

Jackie laughed. Still trying to convince him, she added, "CNBC appeals to anyone who has money or wants to have money. That's a large group." She whispered again, "Even liberals watch CNBC, and they wouldn't watch me even if I did the news in the nude."

Eddie's head bobbed up and down like a fishing lure with the big one on the line. "*Everybody* would watch if you did the news in the nude!"

CHAPTER 26

New York Times   October 4, 2013

THE GOSPEL OF GREED by Seth Goldfarb
   I can't take it anymore. Cross my name off the list of syco-phants. The self-proclaimed messiah of money, Jeremy Lyons, tells us how it is and how it should be. He scolds us and schools us, and we better pay attention. The avenging angel is omni-scient, omnipresent, and thus we wait breathlessly for his every proclamation.

   I recommend that every parent save his interview. When you want to demonstrate to your children how offensive arrogance is, you'll have the perfect example. "I guess I'll have to change the play-ing field?" This man was elected senator for Florida because he woke from a coma three days before the election. He's been MIA in the senate, and seems to prefer his own company to that of any of his more experienced peers.

   Imagine a world glued to CNBC to hear Jeremy. He should have been convicted, yet he instructs us on integrity. For all of the right-wing protestations about President Obama's sealed college records, where is the uproar over Senator Jeremy Lyons's sealed life?

   What do we know? He amassed an obscene fortune mak-ing the richest people in the world even richer. Every brilliant investment move was done in secrecy. He was suspected of insider trading, extortion, and ... oh, yes, murder. He was never brought to trial, and the witnesses probably died of natural causes. And the shootout with the FBI? I'm sure that was just a case of mistaken identity.

Because reporters are by nature curious, I am waiting for one solid fact about Senator Lyons's family, upbringing, or education. More information is available on a CIA operative. He claims to be an Independent. I think that means that he's just independently wealthy. He does not agree on health care for everyone, and nothing in his sparse record indicates any thought to anyone other than his precious one-tenth of one percent.

Underneath his self-assured demeanor, which often comes off as smug, the answer man wants to save us. Perhaps he will eliminate all of the federal programs that help the poor and disadvantaged. Remember, he did write a bestselling book entitled Survival of the Fittest. *Not to worry, though. Jeremy Lyons is a financial genius, so his next book will be* I Survived, Sorry You Didn't.

We need to wake up. This is not a sneak attack on our moral values and our way of life. If he wants to rule the state of Florida with an iron fist, let's give him that playground. When it comes to the United States of America, however, I will trust our body of vetted elected officials, no matter how dysfunctional they are.

I would be remiss in not showing compassion for a man who has helped protect our country and was struck down in the prime of his life. Saddled to a wheelchair, he is a heroic figure. We should salute him for his contribution, and sympathize with his disability. Yet, even though he declares he was ordained by God to govern, let us not crown him the Savior.

Anger. A familiar feeling. Control it! Corrosive, explosive. It doesn't dissipate just because it's unleashed. It is the most seductive and addictive of human emotions. His strong hands crumpled the paper, grinding it into a smaller and smaller ball. Impulse is the enemy, and he felt his control dissipating. Not now. Not yet.

He squeezed his eyes shut, concentrated on his breathing. This blasphemy must be punished. Immediate or delayed? An almost imperceptible skip in his synapse infuriated him, and if he had allowed it, would have frightened him. He grabbed his phone and hit speed dial.

CHAPTER 27

R.J. Brooks had the fresh-scrubbed appearance of a man who had just showered after a vigorous workout. His face was flushed, and his eyes sparkled with the satisfaction of completion.

It did not take any special deductive powers for Mac McGregor to reach this conclusion. In fact, although the dark-green plastic lid was closed, Mac knew that R.J.'s carryout breakfast from the Metropolitan Club was scrambled egg whites with spinach, and mixed berries.

"Hey, Six-Pack," Mac called out as he approached R.J.'s desk.

A slightly raised eyebrow was his response. In spite of R.J.'s weight loss and conversion from what could have been referred to kindly as flab to muscle, a six-pack was still far, far in the distance.

"Yeah," came the delayed response. R.J. had the ability to combine sustained boredom and why-are-you-bothering-me in one short face.

"Thanks for sending me the Goldfarb article."

"Since you refuse to ever read any *New York Times* article unless I send you the link, I had no choice," R.J. said wryly.

"I've told you before, those leftist columns can be contagious. Goldfarb really ripped Lyons. If I were him, I'd beef up security."

"You don't really think Lyons would retaliate physically."

"I put nothing past him."

"Did you see his interview with Jackie Mayfield?" asked R.J.. "I read about it, but didn't see it."

"Because you were too busy reading the *Times*. It was short, but interesting. When she asked him about Goldfarb's hatchet job, he said, 'Apparently, the man has a vendetta toward me. It's rather sad, actually.' He made Goldfarb sound like a tragic figure, showed no animus."

"And he didn't back away from the 'God made me do it' comment," said R.J.

"Nope, he doubled down. He said, 'Christians believe that God has a purpose for every life. After my beginning, the fact that I'm here means that I'm supposed to be here. I won't apologize for that. We should never apologize for our beliefs.'"

R.J. thought for a minute before responding. "So the question is, does Jeremy Lyons walk with the angels, or is he just the silver-tongued devil?"

CHAPTER 28

ON HIS WAY BACK FROM the bathroom, Mac stopped in front of R.J.'s desk. His partner was portioning a fistful of vitamins, but looked up to acknowledge him. "Do you have some Vitamin D3 in amongst your plethora of pills?" Mac asked.

"I do. Would you like one?"

"Nope. I have a better way for both of us to get our sunshine."

R.J. looked at him curiously. "Are you going to enlighten me, or is this just another of your cryptic comments?"

"Okay, now my feelings are hurt," said Mac as he started walking back to his desk. "I'll get somebody else to go with me."

Every fiber in his body screamed at R.J. to ignore the last remark and not pursue it. But this was why he never played poker. With a sigh, he pushed his ergonomic black chair back, stood up, and walked over to Mac's desk. "The futures are down a hundred points," he said. "The market is in the toilet. Is it possible to just fast-forward your torture?"

Mac picked up his telephone receiver and banged it on the desk. "Hear that?" he asked.

"Of course."

"That's opportunity knocking. When winter comes, how would you like a little tropical vacation?"

R.J. raised an eyebrow.

"Go see a very wealthy person and stay at a Ritz Carlton on the beach."

R.J. nodded and lowered the eyebrow of suspicion. "Proceed."

"We would fly private."

Finally, a small smile curled onto R.J.'s lips. "Who's the prospect?"

"A United States Senator."

R.J.'s face turned white. "I pass."

"You can't pass. Senator Lyons asked for you by name."

"Tell me you're playing, or better yet, tell me that you told him no. I want nothing to do with him, and I'm really unhappy that the psycho even knows my name."

"Listen. He called to apologize."

"And you bought it?"

Mac reached up and rubbed his forehead. "Yeah, I sort of did. Maybe I'm a sucker for someone who asks for my forgiveness, but I really don't think there is any physical danger for me or my family in meeting him."

R.J. shook his head from side to side, distrust all over his face.

"You do remember that Lyons has a sizable account with us?"

"So now this is about getting more business?"

"I have no idea what it's about. He said that he wanted to pick our brains."

"From our lifeless bodies," R.J. muttered.

"Forget it," Mac said. "I'll make it a solo flight."

"Do you want to know what I think?" asked R.J.

"Sure," said Mac with a disinterested shrug.

"If you can get a permission slip from Grace, I'm in."

CHAPTER 29

"You actually got Eli Steiner to buy into your program?" asked Steve Cannon. Accentuating his disbelief, the last word of the question ended about an octave higher than the first.

"You do remember that my previous job was in sales," Lyons said with a smile.

"But," Cannon continued, "Steiner is hard core, an arrogant asshole whose weapons of mass destruction are money and influence. He needs power like a vampire needs blood. You sure he won't try to screw you?"

"Perhaps once," Lyons reflected.

Cannon sat back. "Like I said, I don't have a need to know how you persuaded him."

"I prefer to keep your hands clean," Lyons responded.

Cannon rubbed his chin. "What do I tell people my job is with you?" he asked. "You pay me way too much money to be your chief of staff. Government regulations don't give even *you* that type of leverage."

"Do you require a title?"

"It's what *you* want, Jeremy. Some sort of title gives me gravitas and more attention from folks you want me to influence. But," his gaze shifted almost involuntarily to Sabine, who had just changed her position, "I can be a shadow dancer if that's your call."

"If you looked like her, a title would be superfluous," Lyons said easily. "What if I make you my chief investment officer?"

"Aside from the fact that I have absolutely no financial acumen," Cannon said with a smile, "it makes total sense."

"If you were my chief investment officer, wouldn't that remove you from governmental scrutiny and reporters' questions?"

"Yes it would, but nothing's changed from my first comment, Senator. I didn't get any smarter with money."

"I'm well aware of that. In fact, with the money that your wife allows you to divert from her antique purchases, I would suggest you consult an advisor friend of mine. Your portfolio is not properly aligned."

Cannon stood abruptly and threw his hands in the air. "I don't think I'm the right man for this job. I'm a private person, and I don't like anyone going through my finances. It's bad enough that you rummaged through my dirty laundry. NSA is an amateur compared to you." Heat rose on the back of his neck. "I'm just a country boy. I'm not used to somebody knowing everything about me." His hands dropped to his hips.

Lyons waited until he sensed that Cannon felt awkward standing there and then gave him an exit ramp. "Would you mind sitting, Steve? I feel intimidated when a man stands over me."

"Ha!" said Cannon, with anything but a laugh. "A frigging firing squad couldn't intimidate you!" He shook his head and returned to his chair.

"You are the right man for the job, or I would not have chosen you," Lyons said quietly. "In order for you to be most effective in your position, you need to know that our resources are unlimited. If you understand that, it gives you more confidence in any conversation. Money is power, access is power, influence is power, politics is power. Do you believe that being a senator from Florida is my aspirational nirvana?"

Cannon studied him while digesting the question. "No," he said.

"I want you to share my destiny."

"How about we share your financials instead?"

"Of course. I'll buzz for Alegria. "

"No," said Cannon, waving him off. "I don't want to see your financials; it would just depress me." He reached up and rubbed his forehead with his left hand, his face in a grimace. "I'm stuck now. I'm too damn curious to pack it in."

Lyons smiled. "Politics is just like the stock market, Steve. The great ones always reach new highs. But they are both roller coaster rides, and the only ones who get hurt are those who jump off.

"All politicians can be influenced," Lyons said in a professorial tone. "Our job is simply to find the most effective method. You need to set the table: gain access, explain our strategy, appeal to their patriotism and pragmatism, and then move on to the next target. If you plant the seed, we will make it grow."

"Do I offer them any inducements, promise something vague down the road?" Cannon asked.

"That is for our more experienced operatives," answered Lyons.

"Operative? Is that what I am?"

"Not really. You're more of an opening act."

"Really? I'm paid big bucks to be a warm-up? I'm the guy at the bar that buys the pretty girl drinks all night and she goes home with someone else?"

"It's my job to assess the talents of my key associates and allow them to operate in their most effective roles," said Lyons. "In addition, it is essential to keep your reputation unsullied."

"How could I step in it by just trying to get some of these clowns to do the right thing?"

"Politicians are influenced in one of four ways." Lyons sounded like he was reading a textbook to a bored class. "Bullied, bought, blackmailed or bribed — the four Bs. Which of these strategies would you like to pursue?"

Cannon smiled sheepishly. "I guess I'll stay on the high road."

CHAPTER 30

IN STEVE CANNON'S OPINION, PATIENCE was an acquired virtue. Since they are normally paid by the hour, attorneys can be very patient when waiting for an appointment, as long as the money clock is running. Cannon wasn't billing by the hour, but if he were, he would require a huge bonus to wait for Eli Steiner.

Cannon ran through the messages on his phone, checked the stock market, and then texted his wife. Finally, he was led into Steiner's office. Instead of offering his hand, Steiner waved to a seat in front of his desk. Everything about this man reeked of condescension.

Cannon declined the offer to sit, hoping it would lessen the time he had to be in the man's presence. Looking at Steiner, he tried not to wrinkle his nose in disgust. Sabine was right. Eli Steiner *did* look like a possum. However, he wasn't sure that Jeremy Lyons was right. Cannon did not believe the man would ever be a reliable ally.

Yes, Steiner had introduced him to the Far Right Libertarian types, but his lack of enthusiasm was not disguised. Steiner was way too self-absorbed to want to advance any cause other than his own.

The intent was for congressmen and congresswomen to feel the weight of Steiner's wallet when Cannon met with them. Instead, it felt forced, like they were spending required time with a constituent.

Cannon's delivery varied with the different personalities, but as per his instructions, his message was always the same: If you don't want your government messing with the Second Amendment, you damn well better win an election. If you want to secure our borders, you've got to *win* first. Fiscal responsibility will not happen in a country run by

Democrats. Your taxes will continue to rise under a socialist government. Without a majority, you are pissing in the wind. Victory can only be assured by a new, more palatable, logical platform.

Softening the lines of political hardliners would definitely take more than well-spoken rhetoric. Cannon wasn't sure why Lyons had him focus so much on Republicans. In his mind, the Democrats were equally screwed up. Yet the longer he worked with Lyons, the less pressing his need to know.

After only half listening to Steiner's nasal rasp, Cannon challenged him. "You're 100 per cent with us, aren't you, Mr. Steiner?"

The long beat before his response was all Cannon needed for confirmation.

"Of course, Mr. Cannon," Steiner replied, grabbing Cannon's arm to usher him into the next office. "Come with me. The congresswoman is anxious to meet you."

After another meeting of polite indifference, Cannon left without acknowledging Steiner. Maybe it would get better, but for now, it was a shit job, and he felt like he was wasting his time. After each meeting, Lyons wanted him to give a post mortem.

It made no sense to Cannon, but it wasn't his money. He felt like an NBA star collecting six mil a year and sitting on the bench. The difference was that he wasn't interested in increasing his playing time with this team.

CHAPTER 31

"THIS IS A REALLY BAD idea!" said R.J. as he drove past Washington Dulles International Airport and turned right at the sign that said "Signature Flight Support."

"Really?" said Mac with an edge. His partner had been a broken record ever since Mac had insisted that he accompany him to Jeremy Lyons's lair.

"Let's do the math, Sir Whine-a-Lot." Pointing to the dashboard, he said, "Time: one fifty; temperature: eighteen degrees. In five minutes, we'll be on board a private plane sipping Arnold Palmers. When we arrive in Naples, Florida, in two hours and fifteen minutes, it will be approximately seventy-eight degrees. As per our host's request, we are dressed casually: no starched white shirts, no ties choking our necks. Tonight, after a sumptuous dinner and scintillating conversation, we will be driven to the Ritz-Carlton, which is on the beach. The math tomorrow is that we leave whenever the sun goes down, and then we, the conquering heroes, arrive home and are embraced by our adoring wives."

"Do all of your fantasies have happily ever after written into them?" asked R.J. "Is this one of those times when you need a disclaimer that says, 'Past performance is no guarantee of future performance?'"

"Now, that was clever," said Mac as he opened the car door. "Run like the wind to our private plane."

* * *

R.J. had to admit that the first part of Mac's fantasy had gone as scripted. It felt a little funny for him and Mac to be the only passengers in a super-luxury airplane with twelve seats. The employees of Signature treated them as if they were big deals, and he had parked right at the terminal. The hostess, who had greeted them by name, was a beautiful Asian woman with a bright smile and gentle eyes. When she offered him a toasted bagel that had to have come from a New York deli, he tried to dispel the thought of a prisoner's last meal.

On the surface, Mac seemed comfortable with the fact that Jeremy Lyons was at least a born-again senator; but there were miles to go before this man could earn his trust.

On the other hand, R.J. wasn't comfortable with the fact that Lyons even knew his name. If he found out that his presence had not been requested and that Mac had, in fact, asked if it was okay to have R.J. accompany him, then regardless of the age difference and his respect for the man, R.J. would have to hurt him.

Apparently, the gorgeous Asian woman went with the décor, because she rode with them to Lyons's compound and walked with them to the gleaming elevators. Two security-type bookends allowed them to pass without a second look.

The elevator doors opened directly into Lyons's suite. Like a magnet, the huge expanse of blue sky and white clouds visible through the open doors made everything else an afterthought.

They were met by a Latina woman who transformed her plain visage with a warm smile. "Greetings, gentlemen. I am Alegria." Both Mac and R.J. echoed her warm greeting. Alegria had power of attorney on Lyons's accounts with them, and although they had spoken often, they had never met her.

"We're delighted you could join us," she said. "I hope the flight was comfortable."

"We feel really spoiled," said Mac. "This could become habit forming."

"Well, we hope that visiting us becomes habit forming, also," said Alegria. As she turned to leave them, Mac and R.J. exchanged glances.

* * *

"Sunset at 6:02," said Lyons, "and it is a Florida ritual to celebrate another day of God's blessings. Won't you join me?" He wheeled his chair out onto the balcony.

Leaving their drinks by their matching leather chairs, Mac and R.J. followed him. In the almost two hours they'd been there, there had been no substantive conversation. Lyons had asked their opinions of the markets, admitted that he continued to suffer withdrawal symptoms from not managing money, and totally avoided any reference to the past. A bystander would see the three men lined up on the rail — R.J., then Lyons, then Mac — and assume they were longtime friends.

Silently, Lyons moved his wheelchair closer to R.J., who was transfixed looking out at the sunset. He touched R.J.'s leg and said, "It looks like the rumors are true: you *have* been working out."

It was an innocent enough gesture, but R.J. jumped straight up, and his fingers grabbed the railing with a death grip.

"Sorry if I startled you," said Lyons with a sly grin. Meanwhile, Mac was biting the inside of his cheek to keep from cracking up.

"No problem," said R.J., as he composed himself and looked at the senator. "I should be used to inappropriate gropes from my elders by now."

"Ha!" laughed Lyons. "I knew that I wanted you to join us. Come inside, and let's see if I have the dinner orders correct."

He turned to Mac. "You're the crab encrusted local grouper over a lemon risotto." Mac nodded. "And, R.J.," he said with the same sly grin, "We have a roasted vegetable ratatouille with a side of the house's Lyonnaise potatoes."

After what was undoubtedly the best dinner either Mac or R.J. had ever eaten, Lyons opened the conversation. "First, I can't tell you how enjoyable it is to be around smart people with a sense of humor. That is a senatorial oxymoron, but I did have a purpose other than to begin to make amends to Mac." As Lyons leaned forward, both Mac and R.J. did the same, as if they were sharing an amazing secret.

CHAPTER 32

"I NEED YOUR HELP TO save our country." Jeremy Lyons's dark eyes were so intense, hypnotizing, that the silence after his words felt required. He continued staring at his two guests until Mac spoke.

"Senator, all you've got here are two schmucks who manage money for folks. If you need our help, you're in a world of hurt."

Lyons sat back and folded his hands in his lap. "I'm open to suggestions. Should I turn to members of congress? Economists? Right- or left-wing think tanks?" He looked directly at Mac. "I would come up empty. Objectivity is an elusive quality. Everyone has an agenda. Why wouldn't people who care for small business people and their families have valuable insights?"

Mac lowered his head and squeezed his eyes shut. He was mentally wrestling with himself. "I'm sorry," he said, throwing up his hands. "The same guy who forced me to have a weekly call with him, hired an assassin who threatened my daughter, and after he left the country in exile sent me his book, *Survival of the Fittest*, with a threatening inscription — stop me if you've heard this. I'm just hitting the high points to save us all a hell of a lot of time." Mac took a breath. "That same guy now wants me to help him save our country?"

R.J. recognized his friend's venting, the frustration pouring out of him like water from a broken fire hydrant. He stepped into the awkward silence, pointed at Mac and said, "What he said."

"R.J., was your presence today coerced?" asked Lyons, focusing on him.

"Yes, it was. You were not on my list of must-meet celebrities. And I have no basis to trust you."

Lyons nodded. "Yet, here you are."

R.J. again pointed to Mac. "I *do* trust *him*."

"If a client of yours asked you for ideas to fix the economy and gave you reasonable time to respond, would you honor that request?"

Realizing the trap that had just been set, R.J. grew sullen and gave the only answer he could: "Yes."

"I thought so," said Lyons as he shifted his gaze to Mac.

"As improbable as it may be, I am a U.S. Senator. Mac, when we were young, that meant something. Now, in most cases, it just means you've been purchased. For the sake of your children, that must be changed."

Mac looked him straight in the eye. "So as a condition for us to continue managing your money . . ."

"No!" said Lyons sharply. "Just for today, reserve judgment. At least consider the possibility of authenticity. Don't look around every corner for an ulterior motive.

"Alegria," he called.

When she entered the room, Lyons spoke to her. "Please prepare a check for one hundred million dollars to add to our account at Johnston Wellons. These gentlemen have done an excellent job, and they deserve it." She nodded and left the room.

Chastened, Mac said, "That's not necessary."

"It is," Lyons replied. "Your continued management of my assets is due to your philosophy, your strategy and your performance. It is not contingent on your cooperation with my mission to help this country."

He let out a breath and sat back. "I appreciate the fact that you both accepted my invitation, and I'm sorry that I cannot rewrite my past." Another lengthy silence ensued.

Mac broke it. "I get the fact that we talk with a large cross-section of clients. But there are advisors who would kill — sorry, bad choice of words — to have an audience with you. So why are our thoughts important?"

Lyons stretched out his long fingers and lifted each one in sync with his points: "One, you have experience and insight, and you care about our country. You have not been reticent about expressing your views.

"Two, you have a cadre of economically savvy clients and investment professionals with different political views. Discussing with them ways to better supervise markets and strengthen the economy would be second nature for you. I would ask you to consider all their thoughts and discard the illogical and impractical.

"Three, you will be doing this for the right reasons, not to gain new business."

His little finger rose slowly. "Four, you are competitive. You will want ideas superior to my own." He added a challenging smile.

Lyons raised his thumb. "Finally," he cocked his head, and his smile became ingratiating, "what could be more objective than an analysis from someone who still holds a residue of hate for me?"

Mac shook his head as if he were trying to escape the hypnotic power of this man. Almost under his breath, he said, "Hate is a wasted emotion." He looked Lyons in the eye. "As a Christian, I have to give you the latitude to believe that you have changed. I'm in no position to judge anyone."

He wrestled with the request a little longer, then spoke again. "If I can't dissuade you, and you won't ridicule our recommendations, we'll give it a run, but first I need an answer from you."

Lyons's face tensed.

"Why did I get the 'trick or treat' call?" Mac asked.

There was a long pause, and then Lyons seemed to gather himself. "I don't have friends. Never did. No family. I've only had employees and clients, who never met me." His voice strengthened. "I needed to call someone to prove I was alive." He laughed a mirthless laugh. "Believe it or not, you're closest thing I have to a friend."

The chill that ran down Mac's spine had nothing to do with the temperature in the room.

CHAPTER 33

"WHAT ARE YOUR PLANS FOR TOMORROW?" asked Lyons as Mac and R.J. stood at the door.

Mac looked at R.J. He made a quick decision. "Would it be possible to head back this evening?"

"Of course," said Lyons. "The plane is at your disposal."

"I haven't discussed this with R.J.," Mac said, looking at his friend, "but I'd feel better if I could go in to work tomorrow."

"Ah, dedication. As a client, I have to approve."

* * *

The plane touched down shortly after 11 p.m. Both men had called their wives before take-off, but the spouses' reactions were markedly different. Grace's "Thanks for letting me know" didn't sit particularly well with Mac.

Conversation on the plane had been minimal, with reading and intermittent napping being the order of the evening. It wasn't until they had hustled to R.J.'s car and cranked up the heater that they discussed the meeting.

"I'm sorry I pushed for an early exit and cost you a relaxing day in the sun," said Mac.

"I tan so easily, I would have only needed 30 minutes to be a twin to our favorite senator," R.J. replied.

"So that occasional blotch of pink on your face is considered a tan?" asked Mac. "It must be makeup that hides the golden brown after you return from the beach."

"You don't have to apologize," said R.J. "Grace couldn't have been happy that you made the trip."

"As improbable as it seems, even America's couple doesn't always agree on everything."

"The fact that the weight of the evidence is on her side probably makes her position even tougher to swallow. Besides, women tend to have better instincts about people then we do."

"I don't disagree. However, I don't think she ever met Jeremy when he was with the firm. Her opinion was colored by the fact that I thought he was an asshole, but she figures if I feel that strongly about something, the odds are that I'm right."

"Yeah. There is probably a very short list of people you think are jerks."

"You're excluding politicians and team members?" Mac did not have to cut his eyes to check the eye roll.

Turning serious, R.J. said, "I'm not sure that I ever truly appreciated the power of that man. You were forced to mentally grapple with him, and I'm sure it often felt like a fight to the death. He looks at you with the intensity of a convert. I would imagine it's similar to witnessing an evangelical preacher giving you a call to arms. He fixes you with that stare, and it's like an electric current comes out of his eyes, demanding attention and causing your pulse to race."

"I just felt like I had to get out of there, as far away from him as I could." Mac let out a breath. "When I used to wrestle, getting pinned was not the worst feeling. In most cases, if I got pinned, it was because my opponent was just better than me. No; to me the worst feeling was when I got reversed. I was on top, winning, and suddenly I was flipped over, and my opponent was in control. That's what tonight felt like."

"Mac, this guy has a PhD in manipulation. I was certainly predisposed to discount everything he'd say, and what happens? My head ends up bobbing up and down like a sycophant." He cut his eyes sharply at Mac. "And do not derail this conversation with a sophomoric reference to my head bobbing up and down."

Mac smiled. "Too easy."

"I also hate to say it, because it makes me feel dirty," said R.J., "but a check for 100 million dollars does sort of buy my love."

"Does it also buy the head bob?"

CHAPTER 34

EDDIE RECTOR SHOT THE STATION'S bread and butter a suspicious look. "You've got something up your sleeve, don't you, kiddo?"

"Why, Eddie," Jackie Mayfield said playfully to the cameraman, "it's an equal playing field. Fair and balanced could never have one up on the monarchs of media."

Eddie gave her the high-pitched giggle she was looking for. "I knew it. Cat ate the canary again."

"In 5 ... 4 ... 3 ... 2 ... 1 ..." said the technician.

Jackie's beautiful smile hit the airwaves. "According to most of the media and political analysts, the senatorial elections of 2014 were the result of a normal changing of the guard during the lame duck session of a president. We at Fox News have a slightly different take. We agree that the result wasn't a Republican mandate, in spite of their advantage of campaigning against the president's agenda. And surprisingly, the Tea Party's influence and rhetoric seems to have diminished. In 2012, candidates who were thought to be moderate Republicans and derisively called RINOs, or Republicans in name only, were replaced by staunch conservatives. However, gridlock continued, and what was supposed to be a more ideological party was simply steamrolled by the president's initiatives."

"On the other side of this chasm, the Democrats tried to put as much distance between themselves and the president's performance as humanly possible. They were not entirely successful. It also was not a coincidence that the Democratic senators who had been among the Affordable Care Act's most vocal supporters lost their seats. As we said at the time, the president's declaration that all of his policies were on the ballot did not benefit his party."

She paused and added a practiced offering of humility. "I apologize if it sounds like we are high-fiving, but having the Republicans hold both houses does not guarantee anything." She smiled broadly.

"Are we witnessing the start of a trend?" Jackie asked the viewers. Her provocative teasing was evidence of her ability to keep her audience interested. "Stay tuned to our interview after the break."

* * *

"Here is an exclusive clip from my interview with the surprise winner in Florida, a former Republican senator who lost to Jeremy Lyons two years earlier. Alan Smathers ran this year as an Independent and narrowly beat the popular Democratic incumbent, Bill Sessions."

Jackie winked at her cameraman, who had not been aware of the clip. He, in return, wagged a finger and gave her a full-toothed grin.

"Senator Smathers, first let me add my congratulations."

"Thank you, Jackie," Alan Smathers replied.

"Why did you campaign as an Independent? Is this Jeremy Lyons's influence?"

Smathers smiled. "Party affiliation had become a straitjacket. If you don't vote with your party, you become a pariah. I wanted to be able to vote my beliefs."

"Did you have backing from your former Republican supporters?" Jackie asked.

"After I explained my position, most of them did support my campaign."

"I guess it costs less to win an election when you're not spending money on negative ads about your opponent."

"It does. But I'm also seeing a lot of young people who are turned off by the politics-as-usual practices. They energized our campaign and at times wore us out."

Jackie laughed. "I'll take that with a grain of salt, Senator. You Marines are always in shape. How does it feel to be part of history? Never before have both senators from a state been Independents."

Alan Smathers answered in a solemn tone. "I think it's our time, Jackie. I think it's America's time."

CHAPTER 35

THE MODESTLY SIZED DINING ROOM tucked into the east flank of the U.S. Capitol building is old-school formal, with a stained-glass image of George Washington on horseback overlooking the room. If the odds makers in Vegas made book on it, the last place they would expect to see Senator Jeremy Lyons would be in the senate dining room. Years ago, there was a small private dining room adjacent to the senate dining room where powerful senators would roll up their sleeves and actually try to forge compromise. Contrast that to today's bombastic rhetoric, pandering to the respective bases, where gridlock is the inevitable and expected outcome.

"Congratulations, Senator," said Lyons with a smile to the new Independent senator from Florida joining him at the table. "You have considerably more history here than I do."

Alan Smathers shook Lyons's hand as he sat down opposite him. "You're a hard one to figure," Smathers said, returning the smile. "If you can predict the stock market like you predicted my election, we're both wasting time here." He glanced quickly around the room, then leaned across the table and whispered. "Please call me Alan. You financed my campaign, got me to run as an Independent, and thanks to your associate, have seen pictures of my wife naked. I think we can be on a first-name basis."

Lyons smiled. Smathers's statement confirmed his belief that he had chosen well. "Fair enough. Call me Jeremy."

"Why did you want to meet here?" asked Smathers. "It doesn't seem like your style."

"It's not," Lyons agreed. "It's tactical. Watch."

Within minutes, senators from both parties came over to the table to welcome Smathers back and to covertly gawk at Lyons, who was more myth than man.

"Good to have you back, Alan. Let's have lunch soon."

"Nice to see you here, Senator Lyons."

Lyons had estimated that within fifteen minutes, the curious would descend upon Florida's two Independent senators, who were dining together. He'd overestimated; it was less than five.

From the twinkle in Lyons's eyes, Smathers could feel the approach before it happened. Former Senate Majority Leader Everett Leeds, the epicenter of political power, put his hand on Smathers's shoulder. Ostensibly, it may have been to prevent the newly elected senator from rising to greet him; but if that was the case, it wasn't necessary.

"You two fellows made quite a stir," said Leeds, grinning widely. He held up a pudgy hand, the thumb and forefinger about a half-inch apart. "You beat Sessions by *this* much. Must be nice to have a billionaire as a bedmate."

"Not as nice as it is to have a private lunch with a man of principle," countered Smathers.

Leeds ignored the shot and raised an eyebrow at Lyons. "Rare to see you here, Senator. Actually, it's rare to see you anywhere other than on television. Maybe we can even get a vote out of you sometime."

"I hereby promise to vote on every piece of logical, streamlined legislation," responded Lyons, holding up his first three fingers like the Boy Scout salute.

Leeds moved around so that he was standing between the two senators. He turned his attention to Smathers. "So, Alan, it was an impressive victory. And you're really an Independent now? Well, if you ever want to caucus with the folks who actually care about the country, let me know."

"Independents tend to caucus with that rare breed that are not owned by special interests," said Smathers easily.

Leeds pursed his lips. "Is that like the conscientious objectors of politics?"

"No," said Lyons, his voice matter of fact. "It's more like the *conscience* of politics. I think that you've worn out your welcome here, Mr. *Minority.*"

Red blotches sprang out on Leeds's neck and pale face. He leaned aggressively down into Lyons's face, his back purposely shielding Smathers from view as he whispered, "It's a good thing you're not running for reelection in 2016; the rigors of this job would *cripple* you."

Leeds stood up abruptly, spittle resting on the corners of his mouth. "Don't bother getting up, Senator, I can let myself out."

Smathers instinctively started to stand, but Lyons's firm grip on his arm stopped him. "Alan," Lyons said calmly, " I love it when a plan comes together."

"Did you know that would happen?" asked Smathers between slurps of his senate bean soup.

Lyons shrugged. "I've played the odds all of my life; it was a good bet."

"I just got this suit back from the cleaners," said Smathers, brushing off his shoulder. "Now I've got to send it back again."

Lyons smiled.

"You know it would have been my distinct pleasure to accidentally give him a forearm shiver. So what's that pompous bastard's next play?" asked Smathers.

"First, he tried to intimidate. Next, he will try to ingratiate himself to you. Abject apologies, perhaps even with a story about how I had previously wounded him."

"Have you?"

"Not yet," Lyons answered lightly. "Unless you are engaged in battle, there is no need to inflict pain upon the enemy. Leeds hates being out of control, a footnote in the news. Do not underestimate him."

Smathers put down his soup spoon, picked up his white linen napkin, and wiped his mouth. He put the napkin down, then crossed his arms. "It doesn't seem like you're concerned. You wanted him to explode. You baited him."

Lyons looked at the younger man for a long moment. "The best way to assess a man's weakness is to entice a confrontation. As I suspected, Everett Leeds is entirely ego driven."

"How does that help? A thirty-second conversation would have given you the same information."

"You are correct; however, it would not have given me the same amusement."

CHAPTER 36

MAC WONDERED HOW MANY ADVISORS spent time thinking about the frailties of the markets or the economy. It might help them gain perspective, but there was no real possibility that an advisor could effect change.

He remembered back in 1986, when computer programs were operating at a speed that could cause a hundred-point drop in the New York Stock Exchange in less than a minute. Mac wrote a letter to the SEC and told them he felt that this was a dangerous situation, and particularly frightening for main street investors. As he expected, he did not receive a reply, and he felt no vindication when on October 19, 1987, the stock market dropped 23 per cent in one day.

When his firm got to ring the opening bell on the exchange, Mac was honored to be the lone advisor from Johnston Wellons included in the management group. He remembered meeting Dick Grasso and marveling not only at his history (he had risen from being a stock boy), but also at the way the president of the exchange listened intently to whoever asked a question. Yet when Grasso mentioned that the NYSE was considering going to 24-hour trading, Mac thought his heart would stop. Thankfully, that never happened.

Now, by sheer chance, a person who was not only powerful, but was also a forceful, fiscally enlightened leader wanted Mac's opinion. The allure of actually being heard after 30 plus years in the business far overrode the conflicting emotions of communicating with his former tormentor. In the worst case, Jeremy Lyons would dismiss the ideas put forth by Mac and R.J. as naïve or unworkable. In the best case, the chance that an idea might gain traction was incredibly seductive to this dreamer.

Mac rationalized that there was no reason for Lyons to ask them to make recommendations if he wasn't going to seriously consider their thoughts. Mac wondered if he should test whether Lyons read all their ideas and gave them a fair evaluation. All he had to do was add a final idea: "Turn yourself in and confess your crimes."

Now all Mac had to do was convince R.J. that they had no choice but to give it their best shot.

CHAPTER 37

"Do we need additional collaborators?"

Mac gave R.J. a shocked look and pointed to him and then back to himself. "Is there some reason you don't feel there is sufficient intellectual wattage inside this conference room to handle this?"

"It is not a question of talent; it is a question of perspective," answered R.J.

"So is it our objectivity or our creativity that you doubt?"

"Perhaps I should not have been so obtuse in the beginning. You and I, for all intents and purposes, are politically aligned. If we are responding to the great Jeremy Lyons on operation 'Save the World,' shouldn't we have input from someone with a more, uh 'progressive' view?"

Mac considered the question. "The progressive view has been rammed down our throats for the past six years; consequently, a plan to save the world is necessary. 'Save the World' is a bit too trite for our mission. Let's refer to it as 'Restore Fiscal Sanity.'"

"How could I ever doubt your objectivity?"

Turning serious, Mac said, "For some unknown reason, Lyons wanted our thoughts. I don't have the hubris to think that we have any practical answers. Part of me wants to confer with appropriate clients, but I am not confident enough in Lyons to trust that this isn't a trap."

"And egg goes better in the mouth than on the face."

"I don't want to make this a bigger deal than it is. These are *our* ideas, and if he laughs them away, we can handle the fallout. Lyons was right when he said that we are privy to varying opinions from some really smart people and that our friends are comfortable expressing them. We also know that the ideas have to walk the line between economically practical and socially acceptable." He shrugged. "So we'll give him our best advice."

"What risks do you see?" asked R.J.

"I don't for a second forget how duplicitous the man has been to me," Mac answered. "Potential embarrassments from the charity scam and his dropping my name in a speech didn't cause any damage, but the threat doesn't disappear. So, for example, even if we believed it would help, and we were morally okay with it, we couldn't advocate legalizing drugs."

"We're safe there."

"Well, we just have to remember that if we suggest a course of action and it's implemented and doesn't work, we could become the authors of the legislation."

"We?"

"You're in the big leagues now, pal"

R.J.'s look of concern was almost comical. "Letter or email?" he asked despondently.

"Email." Mac smiled shyly. "On the off chance that he uses one of our ideas and our clients like it."

R.J. wrinkled his face in thought. "Tell me again why we're doing this."

"Because rookies like us rarely get a chance to play in the 'bigs.'"

CHAPTER 38

EARLY SUMMER RAIN WAS PELTING the floor-to-ceiling glass windows of Jeremy Lyons's great room. A jagged streak of lighting pierced the sky, followed instantly by a loud thunderclap. Lyons reflexively diverted his attention from the hard copy of the email that he held in his hands.

Unlike most young children, he had never been frightened, but instead had been fascinated by powerful storms, and especially by lightning. The absence of any adult supervision allowed him at the age of six to walk outside in the face of a storm and challenge its power.

Lyons often revisited the moment in his mind. The hard rain soaking his body, his hair matted to his face, and the six-year-old standing transfixed, looking at the sky, blinking away raindrops. In a magical moment, a bolt of lightning struck a large tree three feet in front of him. In slow motion, he watched the top half of the tree come crashing down, missing him by inches. The ground shook as the top branches fell across his feet. He hadn't screamed or cried out. Somehow he knew that his power was greater than the storm's.

The experience created an aura of invincibility that became a part of his core. Just as lightning couldn't kill him, an assassin couldn't cripple him.

Reluctantly, Lyons tore his attention from the light show and returned his eyes to the email. Afternoon summer storms in Naples were a regular occurrence, so he would have ample opportunity to witness a storm's majesty. He touched the intercom and asked Alegria to join him.

Childless by design, or, more accurately, because he hadn't met Sabine earlier, Lyons was forced to consider who would preserve his legacy. Sabine had the operational skills. He knew that she resented being removed from his day-to-day operations, but there had been a short media frenzy with pictures of her when she arrived at the scene of the hit and run. She'd been exposed. Lyons had continued to get her input on strategy, but he did not want Sabine in the field.

On the other hand, Alegria Lopez, with her brilliant, analytical mind, was the perfect person to direct the financial issues of his empire. Fiercely loyal, with a hermit mentality, her passion was to help him. While he was in a coma, Alegria ran his operations flawlessly. She lived and breathed Jeremy Lyons.

Lyons looked up when Alegria entered. Unwashed black hair framed a face devoid of makeup. A faded green sweatshirt, which looked like it had fallen off of a Goodwill truck, hung over her well-worn jeans. Her personal appearance was, at best, an afterthought. She was the polar opposite of Sabine.

"You're going to want to read this," Lyons said as he smiled and handed her the email.

Alegria sat on the edge of the leather divan nearest him and began reading.

Our Two Cents

A sound economic policy should promote growth, provide the proper incentives, be sustainable long term, be pragmatic and evidence based, rather than ideological and rigid, while providing adequate support to the least fortunate.

In our opinion, most of the economic problems we face are the result of policies that allocate the country's resources according to political power or popularity, but lack economic merit. A perfect example of this misuse and a significant problem is the tax code. Established over a hundred years ago, it is idiotically complex and counterproductive. It is the embodiment of political power trumping economic sense. In 2014, Warren Buffet stated in his annual report to shareholders of Berkshire Hathaway that their federal tax return was 23,000 pages. In the same year, General Electric's return was 57,000 pages.

The first step in fixing the tax code is to lower the corporate tax. It only accounts for 10% of the tax paid and is the highest tax rate in the world. Due to a myriad of loopholes, many companies pay little or no tax anyway, and the man-hours saved would be enormous. Since the world generally operates on a territorial tax system, where companies pay whatever the going rate is in countries where they operate, this would mean a competitive tax rate on operations in the United States. Obviously, this would lead to an enormous shift of facilities and operations to the U.S. and virtually eliminate unemployment.

In order to pay for this, the following actions could be taken:

1. Eliminate all deductions except for charities, and have a single rate of 20% for all income from wages, dividends, and capital gains. If Congress wants to add deductions, they must find a way to pay for them.

2. Decentralize health care and put the burden of cost control at the individual level. States should determine the type of health care required.

3. Do not tax consumption; it never gets traction. This is a logical step and does not thwart entrepreneurialism.

4. Tax wealth, not just income. A tax of just 1% per year on household net worth would yield almost 900 billion dollars, which is significantly more than the revenue currently received from corporate taxes.

5. In the event that (4) is too controversial, consider a tax that the vast majority would support. Levy a one cent tax per share on any transaction held less than 24 hours. Your former peers and high-frequency traders would pitch a fit, but the stock market was created for capital formation.

6. Devise a safety net that will provide both a guaranteed income and an incentive to work. This could be augmented by vouchers for necessities such as food, clothing, and shelter.

7. All government entitlement programs should be means tested, with the benefits taxed or capped for people beyond a certain level of income or wealth.

Some of these ideas are retreads, are admittedly radical, or may even be ideas you have discussed and discarded. Please remember that any idea you might try that does not work was solely the creation of R.J. Brooks.

Best regards,

Mac

Alegria looked up from the email with raised eyebrows. "There's some interesting content," she said.

Lyons knew that was high praise coming from his protégé. "Any specific reflections?"

"Not that we needed confirmation, but he agrees with our decision to first focus on lowering the corporate tax rate. There are also some innovative and even radical ideas," she mused, "and a wealth tax would appease the Democrats. All in all, I think he is an excellent strategic thinker."

"Anything else?"

Alegria thought for a moment. "Yes. He is funny."

* * *

After a quiet dinner with Sabine, Lyons handed the email to her.

When she finished reading it, her first reaction was to laugh. "I see why you enjoy playing with him. He's smart, too. What are you going to do with this?"

"Seriously consider implementing some at the appropriate time."

She smiled at his inference. "And what are you going to do with him?"

Lyons leaned his head back and placed his hand on his chin. He remained in that position, his dark eyes staring upward. Finally, after what seemed like an unusually long period of reflection, he spoke. "Perhaps I will make him famous."

* * *

"Mac, it's Senator Lyons on line two."

As Mac reached to click on his headset, he smiled, thinking that his stomach didn't clench in response to his associate's announcement. "Are you calling to deride our attempts to restart the economy?" Mac asked, taking the offense in case Lyons was going to give him a shot.

"To the contrary. Your ideas were well thought out and demonstrated some original thinking."

"But?"

"Sorry to disappoint you, Mac, but there is nothing but gratitude in my call. I have shown your ideas to my team, and all were suitably impressed."

Mac looked over at R.J., who had heard that the senator was on the phone and was intently listening to Mac's side of the conversation. "So, Senator, you were disappointed in R.J.'s input, but you thought that my ideas were brilliant?"

Lyons laughed, and R.J. completed the motion by shaking his head in disgust.

"On that note, Mac, I would like the opportunity to visit with you when I am in D.C. and discuss some thoughts I have about current events. I would like to get your perspective."

"Was the pronoun on purpose?"

"Yes. I do appreciate your friend, but I believe we can have a more candid conversation one on one."

"Do you have a particular time in mind?"

"Not at the moment. I have a few things that I need to put in place before I strategize with you. I just wanted to be sure that you would be amenable to having breakfast with me."

"The commute won't be as upscale, and I still think you are giving me more credit for wisdom than is warranted."

"Great. I will give you sufficient advance notice so you won't have to scramble your schedule. It won't be in the Senate Office Building. I will secure a more private venue. Not many legislators carry their own chairs with them, so I'm rather easily recognized."

"Anywhere is fine with me, Senator. Just let me know."

"I will, and thanks again to both you and R.J. for your well-thought-out ideas."

Lyons turned to Sabine and Alegria, who were listening to his call. He nodded and flashed a tight smile. "Now it begins."

CHAPTER 39

F̲ascinated̲, S̲abine̲ watched as a sequence of nods moved towards its inevitable conclusion: Jeremy Lyons's head fell to his chest. His reading glasses were still affixed to his face; his hardback book lay open across his knees. His custom-designed wheelchair was still in the upright position. On a rainy Sunday afternoon it would not be unusual for a 60-year-old U.S. Senator to fall asleep reading ... unless it was Jeremy Lyons.

Silently, Sabine rose from the black leather armchair, placed her Kindle on the small marble coffee table, and left Jeremy in the study. She walked to the dining room and opened the glass doors onto the massive deck overlooking the Gulf of Mexico. In Naples, Florida, the majority of rain showers in the winter are short lived. She watched the late-afternoon sun struggle to peek through the dark gray clouds.

The drizzle had almost stopped, so Sabine walked over to the linen cupboard and removed a plush beach towel. She went outside, wiped the moisture off the chaise, and sat down.

The euphoria that she had felt when Jeremy awoke from his coma had not dissipated, but the changes in him required some adjustment. Jeremy had never been a good patient. Rarely had Sabine seen him physically ill, but on those occasions he had rejected medicine, relying only on his force of will.

However, since the assassination attempt, his mood swings were frequent and sometimes irrational. He was not adjusting well. His initial reaction to the doctors' determination that he was a paraplegic was disdainful dismissal. Quickly it had progressed to rage.

Now it consumed him. His public persona was that he was not defined by his disability. That was an illusion. If Jeremy accepted his permanent confinement to a wheelchair, he would wither and die.

CHAPTER 40

WHEN SOMETHING APPEARS TO BE too good to be true, it probably is. That admonition kept running through Dr. Adam Pollack's mind. He didn't try to shut off the thought, because it was preferable to assessing his current situation.

One of the foremost neuroscience experts in the world, the bespectacled, diminutive man had published more books on paraplegic care than any of his peers. A frequent lecturer, he was confident in his ability to offer counsel without offering false hope. Certain individuals had challenged his prognoses, but as of yet, no one that he had confirmed as paraplegic had ever walked again.

Pollack had been asked to review the x-rays and tests, fly on a G4 to Naples, Florida, personally examine Senator Jeremy Lyons in his high-rise mansion, collect $100,000, pass GO, and enjoy the ride back.

After he examined the patient, Pollack was escorted to a two-level waiting room. He had been instructed to wait just inside the doorway on the lower level. The second level was about two-and-a-half feet above the entry level, and the polished wood formed a U shape around the first level. The only pieces of furniture in the room were two mahogany rocking chairs and a small, black, onyx coffee table set between them. It was not a large room.

Because there appeared to be no other entrance into the room, Pollack assumed that his host would enter from behind him. Thus, he was turned at a 90-degree angle to the room while he waited. Suddenly, Lyons's voice came from the back of the room, directly opposite the entrance.

Pollack turned and saw Jeremy Lyons in his wheelchair, arms folded and jaw clenched. For the first time in his life, Adam Pollack felt claustrophobic. He was on the floor of the Coliseum, and the lion had just been let loose.

With rapid strokes, Lyons manually sped the wheelchair down the upper level until he stopped exactly at its edge. He lowered his face to less than twelve inches from the doctor's and glared down at him. Reflexively, Pollack took a step back.

"You're not trying to run away, are you?" challenged Lyons.

"No! No, sir."

"Well?" Lyons demanded.

"Uh, did you read my report, sir?"

"Yes."

"I wanted to mention again that whoever ordered the injection of methoprednisolone was spot on. If it is not administered within two hours of the trauma, then…"

"I said I read the report."

"Yes, yes, then you're aware that even though the drug prevented a complete severing of the spinal cord, even a partial lesion theoretically allows only a *possibility* of regaining function…"

"When possibility acquires indomitable will, it becomes certainty."

Pollack winced. "I regret to tell you that the prognosis…"

"Then don't. Never for an instant consider a negative outcome when you are discussing my case."

Pollack felt like he was pleading for his life. "Did, did the other doctors disagree with me?"

"No. The fools all agreed with you."

A shudder of relief went through Pollack's body. He asked plaintively, "May I sit down, sir?"

With even more bite in his words, the steely-eyed senator responded. "No. Are you willing to stake your life on your prognosis?"

Pollack blinked rapidly as he considered his answer. Sweat ran down his back, and his short-sleeved white shirt clung to his chest. He felt his body involuntarily shiver.

"No... uh, no, sir," stuttered the doctor, shifting his weight from foot to foot. "There are things..."

"What 'things'?" spat Lyons. "Are you going to tell me about Ekso Bionics? Are you going to tell me there's a bionic suit that will allow me to stand?"

"There have been – there have been strides," Pollack said in a panicked voice.

"I know all about 'strides.'" Lyons lowered his voice. "You need to take this challenge very seriously."

He froze the man with his dark eyes and withering gaze. "Two other alleged 'specialists,'" he said derisively, "have submitted their proposed treatment plans. Whoever's routine I deem to be the most helpful will be handsomely rewarded. The other two? Well...," he motioned to his wheelchair, "I shall bequeath them my wheelchair."

After a very pregnant pause, Lyons continued. "What do you advise?"

The doctor's breathing had become ragged. "The National Rehabilitation Hospital in Washington, D.C., is working on some possible solutions. In a few years..."

"Neither of us has a few years. What are the experimental therapies? My body is structurally and muscularly sound. It can accept any treatment."

Pollack spoke quickly. "Plasma-enriched platelets treatment won't work for you. It won't mend the nervous tissue within the cord."

Lyons grabbed the small man by his lapels and lifted him bodily into the air. "What will work, doctor? You are the foremost expert in the field. You have conferred with the doctors at Rutgers who are proponents of curative surgeries. Do you believe there is merit in their research?"

"Not really." The doctor's voice rose another octave as the words spilled out of his mouth. "The Chinese research was previously so secretive, and their theories..." Lyons was holding him aloft as easily as someone would hold an infant.

"'Not really' will suffice, doctor. Have you studied the China SCINET Phase II trials held in Kumming, China?"

Pollack was stunned. This man was more versed in spinal cord injury treatments than the majority of Pollack's peers. He nodded dumbly.

Cords stood out on Lyons's neck. "Then what is your recommendation!" he screamed.

"I don't know! Some day stem cells may be a part of the protocol. They assume the identity of whatever they latch onto. They may be able to bridge the chasm. Please don't hurt me."

Lyons released the man, who struggled to regain his footing.

"It is logical that you have fantasized about the perfect combination of therapies that would enable a man in my situation to walk. For someone like you, it would mean a Nobel prize. You have undoubtedly put hours of study into this potential solution. If another doctor made this discovery, you would become a mere footnote in history."

Pollack seemed to stagger with each sentence. He opened his mouth to speak, but Lyons held up a warning finger.

"In your studies, you've analyzed combinations of stem cell injections, regenerative drug cocktails, and extreme physical rehabilitation."

"That's pie in the sky," screeched the doctor. "None of the experimental drugs have been tried on humans. They may well be toxic. You could die!"

Lyons leaned forward like a praying mantis. "I could have died when a cowardly assassin struck me with a moving vehicle traveling in excess of 40 miles an hour, but I didn't. That is not my destiny.

"So here is what will happen, doctor. Stem cells from umbilical cord blood will be injected into my damaged spine. In addition, lithium will be used to regenerate my damaged neural fibers. You have thirty days to design the combination of experimental drugs that will accelerate the healing. Prepare this cocktail as if your life depended upon its success. Oh, and don't be concerned. I will formulate my own exercise regime. Pray for success, doctor.......for both of our sakes."

CHAPTER 41

ALL THREE REPORTERS WERE BEYOND being impressed. After visiting with heads of foreign governments and being privy to off-the-record conversations in the Oval Office, neither celebrities nor icons elevated their collective heartbeats. Yet as they exchanged nervous glances while waiting in the opulent lobby of Jeremy Lyons's compound, a current of excitement connected them.

Of the three, Tom Hessel, from *The Washington Post*, was the most surprised by the invitation. Three years ago, with significant background from his friend Mac McGregor, he had written a scathing exposé on his host.

Betsy Pakenas, from *The Wall Street Journal*, understood the invitation as soon as she saw her two liberal colleagues. As an Independent, Senator Lyons wanted at least one point of view from a fiscal conservative.

Sheldon Green knew why he had been invited. Seth Goldfarb, the only other *New York Times* senior reporter, was DOA with the Lyons camp, and if the *Times* had not been invited to the party, it would not be news.

"Gentlemen and Betsy, I appreciate your cooperation in adhering to my conditions. Before dinner, all questions and answers are fair game, but our dinner conversation is off the record." Lyons sealed the agreement by making eye contact with each reporter.

"Splendid. Your drinks have been ordered. While we wait for them and a few hors d'oeuvres, will you accompany me to the balcony, where you can witness a beautiful Florida sunset?"

Following their host's wheelchair, the reporters walked out onto a balcony that felt like a football field. Instead of sitting, each walked to the gleaming white railing and looked out at the pristine white beach.

Hessel, a frustrated beach bum, felt a pull akin to acrophobia as he looked below. The sun seemed to dim as if its energy were waning. He watched, fascinated, as it slowly, methodically receded into the dark waters streaked with blue. As if commanded by their host, the cloudless sky provided a canvas for the finale with bright shades of red, orange, and yellow. Hessel blinked twice. The others had returned to Lyons's great room. He really did need to spend some time at the beach.

"Help yourselves to the stone crabs," offered Lyons. "They are a Florida delicacy. Who has the first question?"

"Senator, you weren't in favor of the Tea Party's government shutdown," said Sheldon Green, stepping into the breach. "And I'm sure my readers would like to know your opinion of that group."

"Are you sure?" Lyons asked with a smile. "It's similar to my opinion of the far left."

"Yes?" replied Green with a frown.

"They're fighting a losing battle."

Green gave him a smug smile.

"Not because of their beliefs, but because of their tactics. Betsy, what are their impediments to success?" Lyons asked, turning to her.

"I thought *we* were asking the questions," she answered wryly.

"Fair enough. First, they were in the minority. Ultimatums never work unless you have the votes. Second," he turned towards Green, "the majority of the media would ridicule any idea they had, regardless of merit."

"If you intend to disparage the media, why did you invite us?" asked Green.

"That's a fair question, Sheldon. I believe that you three are among our country's finest political minds."

Lyons's remark was met with a synchronized look conveying that the reporters believed they were being fed an hors 'd oeuvre of patronization before the main course of bullshit.

"You have combined experience of over 55 years in finding the grains of intent in the political fodder dumped on our country every day." Lyons continued. "This requires an intense analytical mind and a thorough understanding of the issues our country faces.   As an Independent, I need to embrace issues important to both Democrats and Republicans. You three have your fingers directly on the pulse of the people.   You serve as the direct conduit and voice that they are solely missing."

Green's posture noticeability softened.

"Senator, why did you invite me?" asked   Hessel.   "My article about you was certainly not flattering."

Lyons nodded. "No, it wasn't. And Tom, you obviously ignored your mother's advice: 'If you can't say something nice about some-one, say nothing at all.'"   He looked hard at the reporter, who was smiling nervously.   "You wrote what you believed.   We could argue over whether you were right or wrong.   If after tonight you still feel I am totally off base..." he held up his tanned right arm and flexed his bicep, "we could arm-wrestle."

The reporters all smiled, and Pakenas asked, "Can Obamacare be fixed?"

"I believe anything can be fixed with intellect and integrity, but this law was jammed through, and it's tragically flawed. Forget the technology; the math is wrong. Redistricting, immigration reform, entitlement expansion. Are all these grand ideas because we want a perfect world and everybody happy, or do both sides just pander and prostitute for votes?"

This profound statement was met with silence.

* * *

Over dessert of key lime pie and fresh raspberries, Lyons asked the group, "If your financial advisor were consistently able to make you money and never lose your money, would you ever dispute his or her financial advice?" He raised his hand. "Assume legitimacy."

They looked at each other. Green spoke first. "No."

The others nodded.

"Without the legitimacy assumption, your first thought would have been Ponzi, correct?"

This time their heads flopped up and down.

"Academicians may disagree on global warming, but one cannot disagree about the fiscal fragility of our country. Every member of the house and senate knows that the entitlements will destroy our economy if left unchecked."

"And Obamacare is the nail in the coffin," interjected Pakenas. Green gave her a glare.

"If my assertion is correct," said Lyons, ignoring Pakenas's comment, "why don't the legislators get together to fix it?"

Green spoke. "I'm not sure your premise is accur..."

"I would not have spoken the words if they lacked accuracy," said Lyons, interrupting him. He whirled his head toward the *Post* reporter. "Tom, why is there not a bipartisan discussion on these critical matters?"

Hessel shrugged. "Everyone wants to get re-elected."

Lyons nodded. "Exactly. I'm sure that you agree with that premise, don't you, Sheldon?" He softened his words with a smile.

"This must change," he said with conviction. He looked at each reporter. "You are men and women of vision. The media in this country has become ideologically imprisoned. Conservative talk shows view everything through the same lens. The liberals fail to hold the president accountable; ink instead is dumped on hapless Republican missteps. In the next iteration of news, the public will demand objectivity. The spin masters will fall from their lofty positions, and the merchants of truth will ascend. It will be a new order."

"That is a pretty radical prognostication," said Green, still unhappy about being interrupted.

"Imagine the intellectual freedom you would have," Lyons continued, unfazed. "No editorial red pens for going against party affiliations. Political correctness would become secondary to factual correctness. Imagine the power of a truly informed electorate. This information revolution will happen. I would like the three of you not just to be part of it, but to lead it."

Uncharacteristically, the reporters were at a loss for words.

Lyons continued. "I don't expect you to agree with everything I support." He smiled. "This is only our first date, after all. But you three will also have access to discuss anything I propose that you disapprove of or, be still my heart, anything that you agree with."

They nodded in concert with his conviviality.

"When I call on you," Lyons continued, changing tone, "I will ask you to take a stand. Do you want to heal your country?" He leaned forward and spoke in a low voice filled with passion. "You can be known as the men and woman of courage who helped save the United States of America."

CHAPTER 42

WITH UNCHARACTERISTIC NEATNESS, MAC PILED *The Washington Post* on top of *The New York Times* and *The Wall Street Journal*. He attached his headset and punched in a familiar number.

Tom Hessel picked up his phone with a feeling of foreboding.

"Congratulations, Tom Terrific! I'm so proud of you."

"Uh-oh."

"Seriously, my main man, you got this interview even without Deep Throat."

"I should've called?"

"If you had, you wouldn't have gotten the award."

Hessel sighed. "I'll bite, Mac Attack. What award?"

"Why, they named a street after you: One Way."

"Okay, listen. I've got deadlines, research..."

"Hold my calls," Mac interrupted and called out to his team. "I've got my pal Tom Hessel on the line and don't want to be interrupted."

Hessel laughed. "You can be a brutal son of a bitch. I'm sorry. I should've called you. You're the ultimate Jeremy Lyons source."

Slightly mollified, Mac said, "If Lyons invited you, it must be because he thought your article was a puff piece."

"I was afraid to make it much tougher. As it was, you got your ass kicked by a girl because of it."

"How did –"

"You're the financial wizard. I'm the investigative wizard."

"And you saved that tidbit?"

"On the off chance that I stepped on my dick with you."

Mac laughed. "That's definitely anatomically absurd. Okay, what did he tell you that you didn't print?"

Hessel paused.

"Give," Mac said.

"I'll call you back."

* * *

When Mac saw Hessel's number on the caller ID, he grabbed the receiver.

"Sorry," the reporter said. "I wanted to make sure this was private."

"Really?"

"Hey, I know our new owner is a technology whiz. I've heard he's a Republican, too."

"Thank God."

Hessel paused again. "I felt like we were with the Godfather. There was nothing particularly revelatory in our interviews; but when we were off the record, it felt like he was planning a palace coup. By the way, this needs to be off the record with us."

"No problem. Did he make you an offer you couldn't refuse?"

"Maybe. He's got a major hard-on about the financial Armageddon that only he can stop. When the time is right, he will contact each of us and ask for our support."

"Support for what?"

"Not stipulated. The three of us speculated – oh, by the way, you don't *have* to tell me how much better my piece was than those of the other two hacks. Anyway, we figure that Lyons is going to make some country-saving proposal, and he'll want us to beat the drums for it."

"But you don't know any specifics: when? context?"

"Nope. But I got the feeling that Lyons plans way ahead of anybody else."

"What would your inducement be?"

"That's a tougher question. Listen, there were three reporters there, all with disparate politics. Yet for just a moment, he made us feel like we were a band of brothers. You know me. It takes more than a beautiful sunset and a gourmet meal to get in my knickers. Don't quote me, Mac Attack, but your BFF may be the real deal."

CHAPTER 43

DREAMS AND ASPIRATIONS RIDE THE *powerful steed of Hope. Without tunnel vision, they will never outdistance Hope's nemesis....Fear. For Fear cannot exist in a vacuum. It requires an invitation to enter the psyche. Fear is unrelenting, crippling. When allowed to linger, to fester, Fear will introduce its bastard child, Failure.*

Fear is vigilant, omnipresent. Its weapons are doubt, the inevitable chorus of naysayers, and often simply reality. Missteps and random uncontrollable events fuel it. And if Failure ever becomes an identity instead of an episode, then Fear consumes the soul.

Jeremy Lyons exhaled and dropped his pen on the small writing desk. In contrast to the rest of his luxurious compound, his writing room was small, sparsely furnished, and private. It was here that he had written his record-breaking book, *Survival of the Fittest.* In retrospect, he had been too candid in his prose, and that would become an issue. His purpose had been to educate, but the sensationalism of his reality overwhelmed the instructional value.

His mistake was not in the content; it was in the fact that his vision was not fully formed, and thus his lessons were premature. His solace was in the fact that he never indicated whether the book was fiction or truth. Regrets were a waste of time; it is only the present and perhaps the future that can be controlled.

It was here where he could reflect, map and revise strategies. Lyons was not adverse to input from his team, but only *he* knew all the facts. He glanced again at his words. Writing was his defense against his demons. Doubt could be crumpled and disposed of if it was found in his written words. It was only in this room where he allowed thoughts of failure to enter his mind. *Would his mind and body cooperate for the duration of the mission?*

Wealth and power no longer mattered. Jeremy Lyons had confessed his sins and been forgiven. It was not enough. Retribution was required.

His planning was meticulous. His followers were both talented and committed. He had analyzed the enemy's weaknesses. He understood the magnitude of his quest.

Lyons shivered. He reached down and rubbed his bare arms. The temperature in his room remained a constant 68 degrees. It was not the cold that caused the shivering; it was the fear of failure.

CHAPTER 44

IN A VOICE THAT WAS strangely coquettish, Sabine asked, "Do you remember anything from that time?"

Lyons looked up from his writing pad, puzzled by both the interruption and the question.

She picked up a bleached-wood dining chair and placed it in front of his wheelchair. She sat down and smiled. "While you were in a coma, I ministered to you, developed a routine of familiarity. I just wondered if you had any memories from that time."

Lyons laid his writing pad and Montblanc pen down on the adjacent white wicker end table. Before answering, he luxuriated in this woman, who had devoted her life to him. Beautiful women were like grains of sand to him. They had become faceless, nameless, simply bodies to use and discard. Sabine was different. To Lyons, love was an illusion, a distraction. But Sabine, with her flawless beauty, animal-like sensuality, cunning mind, and unquestionable loyalty, had become his only lover, his closest confidant. Even the absence of intimacy since he had regained consciousness had not dimmed her love for him. Sex would return, but it would be on *his* terms.

"*Recollections of a Comatose Icon* sounds like a good title for my next book," Lyons mused.

Sabine's smile broadened. "No ducking the question," she said, reaching over to squeeze his arm. "I may be asked to write a sister novel: *How to Wake a Sexy Man from a Coma*."

The tease fell harmlessly. "As long as you don't try a proof of concept study with any other patients," he admonished playfully, adding an arched eyebrow.

"Do you remember anything?" she asked hopefully.

His expression tightened. "There are reasons that we haven't discussed the specifics of your protocol or treatment of me." He raised his right hand and cupped his chin, resting his elbow on the arm of his chair. "My gift is clarity. Life is a chessboard: I strive to be three moves ahead, with countermoves prepared for any setbacks. I plan everything, remember everything ... except for that period. Excerpts, impressions, conversational snippets, vague memories," his hands flew straight out, "I don't want them!"

Sabine rose from her chair and walked behind him. She touched his back, pushed him gently forward, and began massaging his neck and shoulders. Lyons initially resisted, then exhaled and allowed her strong hands to work.

"Remembering out of context is worse than remembering nothing," he said, his residual anger starting to dissipate.

When she felt Lyons's body relax, Sabine leaned down and pressed her soft breasts into the back of his neck. "Would you like me to recreate my nightly ritual with you?" she asked seductively.

His eyes were closed. She waited. His breathing slowed as a guttural "Yes!" escaped his lips.

CHAPTER 45

THE PALE GREEN SHEET WAS cool on Jeremy Lyons's hairless body. He was propped up on the bed at slightly less than a 90-degree angle, and only his waist and hips were covered. Otherwise, he was naked.

As he looked at Sabine, Lyons wondered if any man could resist her. With each movement, the fine silk of her teddy lightly touched and then moved away from her glorious breasts. It was like the fabric was designed to pay homage. Her erect nipples were magnets. Her long, superbly toned ebony legs were perfectly formed, even to the slender ankles. Yet it was her eyes, now enlarged from desire, that gave a shot of electricity to Lyons's loins.

Sabine leaned over, smiled sweetly, and plumped his pillows. Her breasts were inches from his lips. She smelled of lavender. As she lay there next to him, the sweet musk of her body filled his senses.

She looked at him expectantly. "Are you ready?" she whispered. "My video is especially made for your eyes only."

For a moment, the urge to grab her and pull her on top of him was overpowering. His body shook. It was not time. He repeated that to himself. Although men are born with the talent to excuse their weaknesses, he would not succumb to a morning-after rationalization. This goddess deserved a whole man. However, lust is a drug more powerful than heroin, and as Lyons devoured her with his eyes, he felt his resolve crumbling. "Yes," he said through strangled breath.

She pointed the remote at the flat screen, and Lyons's stomach tightened as the images appeared. He saw his powerful body, immobile on crisp white sheets. Helpless.

"First, I want to show you my routine of sensual massage. Don't assume that these are services on command," she added coyly.

Lyons's breathing became labored as he watched her hands lovingly caress every inch of his naked body. She anointed him. No one had ever ministered to him like that. Her beauty was visceral, and her hands were as gentle as an angel's. He felt a warmth he'd never experienced. Her love was unconditional.

He was broken. He reached for her. Sabine rolled into his arms and hungrily kissed him, her hands kneading his strong shoulders.

Breathless, she tried to pull away. "Wait. First you must see the finale."

Lyons held her tightly; his loins were on fire.

Laughing, she twisted away just enough to hit the remote and advance to the next sequence. The scene shifted. With the sun barely rising above the azure waters of the gulf, a solitary swimmer advanced towards the underwater camera with powerful strokes.

Lyons struggled to make sense of what he was seeing while knowing at a primal level that something was dramatically wrong. With each stroke the swimmer advanced towards the lens and the person behind it. It was like watching an inevitable car crash as the brakes squealed, leaving a portion of their rubber hide on the pavement. Time expanded. His senses fired at seemingly five times normal speed. Lyons sat bolt upright in the bed as recognition forced adrenaline through his veins, crushing his libido.

On the screen was Margo Savino, his first true love and his greatest regret. Not only had she supplicated herself to him physically, she had been instrumental in helping him build his empire. As his fortune amassed, so did his narcissistic arrogance. His cheeks flushed, remembering how, in the end, he had treated his lover like mere chattel. When Margo disobeyed him, he'd let his thug, Max Parnavich, literally brand her to remind her that she would always belong to Lyons. He wasn't proud of that, nor was he immune to his own foibles. But at the time, his mantra was 'discipline is absolute,' and it was necessary to ensure loyalty and secrecy.

As if a horror movie were approaching its inevitable climactic scene, a wrist camera turned inward, revealing a black-clad SCUBA diver awaiting the swimmer. The smile in Sabine's eyes was unmistakable through the mask.

"Stop!" screamed Lyons.

Sabine looked at him with a shocked expression. "It's Margo. She betrayed you."

"I KNOW WHO IT IS!"

"This is your surprise." The words rushed from her mouth. "It was a perfectly executed mission. I left no evidence."

He whirled on her. "It was an *unauthorized* mission! She was no threat!" Lyons moaned as if in pain. He had never wanted Margo hurt. When Mac McGregor told him that Margo had died, presumably at the hands of an assassin, he'd been legitimately shocked. For the first time in his life, he'd felt a genuine loss. He couldn't imagine that someone would kill her.

"But, I..."

His venom was like a viper strike. "Leave me."

"I'm not going to leave you," protested Sabine.

"Get out!" he snarled. "You could have ruined everything. Every mission, every action that happens is meticulously planned. I thought you, of all people, knew that. I thought you were different."

"I am different," she said as a tear of hurt crossed her cheek.

His eyes flashed. "No! You are a rogue operator! It was not Margo who betrayed me; it was you!"

Sabine grabbed her robe and ran from the room.

Lyons remained upright and slick with perspiration, his eyes boring into the closed door with the intensity of a laser. If Margo hadn't told her story to McGregor, Lyons would've still been manipulating both men and the markets to continue amassing his fortune. He would have never had the impetus to search inward and ultimately upwards, shining light on a more meaningful path. He would never have set out to achieve his true destiny.

Regret for his treatment of Margo, long compartmentalized, now ripped through his every fiber like molten lava. He could have confided in Sabine, but instead he had suppressed his barbaric past. He could have saved Margo. *Father, please forgive me.*

CHAPTER 46

THERE'S NOT ENOUGH MONEY IN the world....The refrain kept running through Dr. Adam Pollack's brain like an annoying subliminal advertising loop. On the surface, he knew that his peers would kill for his assignment: personal physician to one of the most powerful people on the planet. No problem — devise a never-before-attempted protocol; create a miracle, nonfatal drug cocktail; and drop by every quarter to draw blood and analyze the results. Yet they had no concept of the risk. He was being paid an enormous amount of money to administer a potentially lethal concoction to a United States Senator.

He had no choice. Pollack had no way to determine the risk to his patient's central nervous system. Lyons dismissed every warning of severe complications from the drugs. When Pollack tried to discuss the slight deterioration indicated in the latest blood samples, Lyons ignored his cautions. Contrary to the majority of doctor/patient relationships, where the patient complained of every ailment, Lyons's stoicism was impenetrable. Pollack's last conversation with him had been less than satisfying.

"If I notice a major change in my circumstances, would that cause you to alter the cocktail?" Lyons had asked.

"Not really..."

"If I acknowledge pain, if I recognize a weakness, then it exists."

This was said matter-of-factly and acted as the slamming of the door. *It was like arguing with a child,* Pollack had thought.

From a legal perspective, Pollack was covered. A court of law would rule him blameless for any adverse side effects of the experimental drugs. He had not wanted to administer them, he had warned the patient in writing of the likely adverse side effects, and he'd received an airtight indemnification from Jeremy Lyons.

What if I killed him? It was hard to imagine that Pollack could be accused of assisted suicide. No; his lawyers swore that there would be no criminal liability, no matter what. But how about the court of public opinion? Lyons was a hero. Pollack was pretty sure that he'd be convicted in the peoples' court, and there wouldn't even be a trial.

The doctor looked down at his hands. When he held them out straight, the movement was becoming more noticeable. Thank God the tremors appeared only occasionally. In fact, they appeared only when he was going to meet with Jeremy Lyons.

It had taken Pollack three months to design, order, and implement the construction of Lyons's exercise and therapy room. It was his responsibility to oversee every aspect of what ultimately was reminiscent of a medieval torture chamber. The doctor's reluctance to participate in every aspect of the unconventional and dangerous treatment had been smothered by money and a justified fear of refusing.

Even in this arena Pollack's admonitions had fallen on deaf ears. Lyons had been warned to never exercise alone. A professional trainer should always accompany him. In response, the senator allowed no one except Pollack to enter his inner sanctum. It was the doctor's job to administer the stem cells and lithium in combination with his experimental drug cocktail. Pollack collaborated and helped establish Lyons's rigorous, bordering on inhuman, physical therapy with the faint hope that it would cause Lyons to abandon his impossible goal.

For most patients, the exhausting, repetitious, physical rigors of the therapy would be overwhelming and despised. For Lyons, wearing the exoskeleton bionic suit from Ekso Bionics was his albatross. Intended for medically supervised use, the wearable bionic suit enabled him to walk with a natural, full-weight-bearing, reciprocal gait. Walking is achieved by the user's weight shifts, which activate sensors in the device that initiate steps. Battery-powered motors drive the legs, replacing deficient neuromuscular functions.

In Pollack's opinion, the less than one per cent chance of the man regaining the use of his legs went to zero without this device. The one time that the doctor entered the inner sanctum unannounced and the patient was ensconced in the bionic suit, the fury he saw in Lyons's face staggered him. He quickly hurried from the room.

The confrontation was never discussed. Pollack knew that as much as Lyons despised this aspect of the therapy, it did not deter the man. Every day Lyons would struggle into the robotic suit by himself and walk for hours.

Pollack's desire for self-preservation far outweighed his desire to continue trying to convince his patient of the futility of his pursuit. Never again would he tell Jeremy Lyons that he would not walk again.

* * *

Lyons's hands, slick with sweat, gripped the bar. His face contorted in rage, he ignored the perspiration dripping into his eyes. His legs, a shadowy memory of their former power, stretched down from his torso, possessing the rigidity of a snail.

Breathing deeply, Lyons girded his body for the final lap. At the end were a dry towel, cold water, and release. His shoulders ached from hanging suspended on the singular bar. His fingers were white from the exertion of holding his weight with soaking wet hands.

He swung his useless torso to gain momentum, sucked in another breath, and grabbed the next bar with his left hand. Forcing the pain and exhaustion from his body, he gripped that bar and reached quickly for the one after it. As his left hand slid off the bar, he grasped air and fell crashing to the floor. A soft, involuntary moan of pain followed him.

Eyes closed, he mechanically felt his upper body for possible breaks. The cushioned floor was of little solace to his tender ribs. He exhaled and held the breath. No biting pain. He felt his head with his right hand and found a lump already beginning to form. He'd stayed conscious. No concussion. *What if I'd been seriously hurt? Would Sabine call Pollack to get the combination to the room? How long before anyone knew I was hurt?* He slammed his fist on the floor, driving these thoughts from his mind. Nothing would stop his destiny.

He forced his mind elsewhere, But doubt was no longer a visitor. It had taken up permanent residence.

CHAPTER 47

MAC MCGREGOR COULDN'T DECIDE WHETHER he was annoyed or indignant. It was not an unfamiliar feeling when it came to analyzing Jeremy Lyons. For Mac, like most people in his industry, a quick read, honed by meeting and working with a client, was sufficient to form a concrete opinion. His emotional roller coaster with Lyons ended up being more volatile than the stock market.

Years ago, when Lyons was working at Johnston Wellons, their minimal contact convinced Mac that the man was arrogant with an unmistakable air of superiority. Looking back, Mac's assessment was correct. Yet it was of little solace and offered no absolution for Mac's subsequent actions. How many times had he asked himself, "If only I hadn't...."

After his friend, and head of the then-president's task force, asked him to help find Lyons, Mac reluctantly agreed to make some entreaties. Although he had little confidence that he could find the advisor-turned-hedge-fund-manager, Mac ended up being successful. Any thrill of victory was dashed when Mac's family ended up in the crosshairs of Lyons's henchman.

During the period when it appeared that he was hiding form the authorities, Lyons disappeared from Mac's life. The logical assumption was that Mac's involvement with the man was over. Lyons's re-emergence into society and subsequent election shocked Mac and left him with conflicting emotions. He felt that Lyons was bereft of conscience, lacked a moral compass, and played only by *his* rules. Yet, he was a born leader and a tactical genius. Had he really changed? In a world desperate for a leader, the richest man ever to hold public office found a way to relate to the common man.

Mac believed that Lyons's passion and intensity were genuine. Lyons's beliefs were not influenced by polls or a political party. Intellectually, he had the ability to dissect a financial system and accurately pinpoint the fault lines. Mac believed that he would be relentless and unequivocal in the pursuit of his agenda to fix America.

The people loved him and stood in awe of his bravado. Negative articles were conspicuously scarce for such a high-profile figure, and when they did emerge, they were usually dismissed.

Grace was probably right when she accused Mac of obsessing over Jeremy Lyons. When a man goes from what feels like a mortal enemy to a client, and in the process becomes a U.S. Senator, he deserves more than a passing thought. A powerful adversary who had admitted privately to Mac that he once had a man killed to increase his bottom line was now a born-again Christian and a charismatic leader.

At least, that was what he was selling to the America people. But Mac McGregor would need a lot more convincing before he was "all in."

CHAPTER 48

DURING THE LATE AFTERNOON, THE senator's driver made his way from his offices on the Hill through the early rush hour traffic to Sixteenth Street, where he turned right. He followed the street past the Mayflower Hotel to Rhode Island Avenue, where he made a left. He proceeded slowly past the YMCA, and a few yards later made a right into a small alley adjacent to St. Matthew's Cathedral.

The black town car stopped a few feet later in front of a small side door of the massive red brick cathedral. Access into the sacred place was easiest for the senator's wheelchair from this door, and the solitary alley isolated him from public recognition.

The inner space of the cathedral was strikingly different from the plain red brick that formed the facade. Inside there were towering, multicolored marble walls, and iconic images of saints and angels looked down from the vaulted ceiling. All senses were engaged. The absence of clatter emphasized the other-worldliness of this space when contrasted with the cacophony of Connecticut Avenue a few yards away. And almost imperceptibly, the nose caught the faint aftermath of incense.

At this time of day the cathedral was usually empty, but open for observant men and women to come and do what Catholics call "make a visit."

The marble floors absorbed the sound of the senator's rubber wheels as they gently rolled toward the rear of the massive space. The senator was anxious. It was imperative that the meeting be private, and privacy was elusive for him. He was here to meet one person, and he was not disappointed. Sitting on a wooden chair in a side chapel, that person was waiting, almost as if he were there to go to confession. In reality, however, it was the senator who needed absolution.

"I always thought that if I ever had a truly clandestine meeting, it would be with Jennifer Aniston," the man said by way of greeting, "but I never pictured it in *this* venue."

"Jennifer Aniston?"

"Yes," replied Mac McGregor. "Grace has given me permission that if Jennifer Aniston ever tries to seduce me, I am allowed to succumb."

"Very generous of her."

"Not as much as you might think. She makes sure that we are never in the same place. So, Senator, instead of me asking why you wanted us to meet and why in such secretive fashion, perhaps you could enlighten me."

Jeremy Lyons nodded. "I have discussed a number of strategies with my team, and frankly, I'm not convinced that I am on the right path."

"Has lack of certainty been a problem with you before? You give the impression that your path is predetermined and that you never equivocate or are in doubt. One of my father's favorite sayings was that he was occasionally wrong, but never in doubt."

"Certain events have added new levels of complexity and importance."

"Are you referring to 'Mr. Executive Order?'" asked Mac.

"As you would expect, my people are intelligent and will not just tell me what I want to hear, but I need additional perspective."

"And it was necessary for us to sequester ourselves in this magnificent cathedral for you to glean whatever color I might add to the situation?"

"Contrary to what you might believe, I am very comfortable being seen with you in public. If my plan were formed to my satisfaction and implementation had begun, we would be meeting in the senate dining room."

"So whatever *plan* you have, you're not prepared to launch."

"Precisely."

"Your estimation of my potential contributions far exceeds my own valuation, but how can I help?"

"Thank you. Mostly it concerns timing. I intended to begin an initiative in the fall of this year. That would result in a year's exposure, which is about eleven months and 29 days more than I would like, but waiting too long may seem too contrived and like I am hiding something."

"You're going to run for president?" asked Mac with astonishment.

"I'm sorry. I thought that was clear," replied Lyons. "I would rather walk across live coals than spend any more time than is necessary in congress."

"And you would run as an Independent?"

"Of course. There is no possibility of straightening out this mess if you are beholden to a party."

"I assume this conversation is off the record."

"I am your client, Mac. Anything we say is confidential."

Mac smiled. "Good point." He ran his hands through his hair. "Well, it now makes a lot more sense why you wanted this meeting to be under the radar. I feel like you just gave me some inside information, and now I can't buy the stock."

"Here are my concerns." said Lyons. "One, could the next president lead from a position of strength? I'm concerned that our defense is underfunded, undermanned, and uncoordinated.

"Two, do I need to form a coalition and pass legislation now in order to substantiate that I understand politics? As you stated in your email, the easiest area to attack is the corporate tax rate, which is an abomination.

"Three, because I believe in a strong defense and fiscal sanity I will be perceived as a Republican. What issues can I support that are Democratic issues that will substantiate that I am not aligned to a party, only to my country?"

Mac had interlocked his fingers and rested his chin on them. He thought for a few minutes before responding. "I still don't get it, Jeremy. There are thousands of political strategists more qualified to answer your questions. Why me?"

"Because, Mac, you are my only friend."

Mac looked for a smile, a tell that told him that Lyons was playing with him. He saw only sincerity, which was frightening. "I, I don't know what you want from me," he said.

"I want your thoughts, your reactions, your truth," said Lyons angrily. "No one else knows my skeletons, my unforgiveable past. Do you think I should be president?"

Mac pondered the question. He could cut this uncomfortable meeting short if he just said no. "Maybe. I don't know. You're asking me for absolutes. If your past was an open book, wouldn't that disqualify you to be the leader of the free world?"

"Now," said Lyons. as he sat back in his chair, "that's what I want. Provoke me, confront me, tell me all the reasons I'm not qualified. You've reviled me, feared me, and now we are in the same room discussing my run for the presidency. Doesn't that indicate that I have some redeeming qualities?"

"It means that you are a persuasive son-of-a-bitch," answered Mac. "Okay. Not that it will come out, but how do you reconcile the fact that you authorized someone to kill David Grant's father?"

"It can't be reconciled, and it can't be forgiven by man, but God can forgive, and He also forgets...wipes the slate clean. King David was an adulterer and a murderer, yet he was allowed to lead a nation. Why do you think I want to do this?" His voice rose. "It's not for money or power. It's not to wipe my slate clean with man. It's because I believe my country is on the edge of an abyss, and it will take a ruthless, persuasive son-of-a bitch to save it."

"That's the hook with me, and you know it," Mac said softly. "I'm still afraid you are playing me. I don't know why you want me invested in you, and that troubles me. I'm not a politician, I have no power, and you don't need me to contribute to your campaign. Probably the scariest thing you said was that I was your only friend. That makes me sad, but it also makes me feel like I have to be your friend."

He let out an audible breath. "Faith is another weapon against me. I can't judge your degree of commitment, nor can I question whether you have been saved. I can only trust that God put me here, so maybe I do have a part to play."

"I would be most grateful."

Mac looked at him for a long moment and blew out a breath. "You can't wait until the last minute to announce. Assuming it was not contrived, you effectively entered the senatorial race at the last minute. You were a novelty, a fresh face, a hero, and a survivor. Could you wait until the early caucuses are out of the way? Yes, but the later you enter, the more thrust you will need out of the gate. Without saying it, the public could feel like you entered because you could no longer endure the infighting, negative campaigning, and empty promises.

"I think that your instincts will tell the right time to announce. In the interim, you need to do something to demonstrate that you are not yesterday's news. I agree that you need to at least propose some legislation that would be popular. One of the positives of our current situation is that patriotism has had a comeback. Anything to help our servicemen and women could work.

"I believe that the American people are very concerned about the direction of our foreign policy. They do not want to go to war, but they want a stronger leader. I think that you need to begin to establish your beliefs in a simple, and I hate to say it, but a sound-bite manner. Go on *60 Minutes* and illustrate the benefits to the country of lowering the corporate tax. That should be a cakewalk for you. Don't schedule it during the NFL season.

"I don't know what else." Mac threw up his hands. "What are your views on immigration?"

"Secure the borders, a path to citizenship, one and done if they commit a felony. They shouldn't clutter our jails."

Mac shook his head. "You really are a closet Republican."

Lyons shrugged. "I could care less about gay marriage, and I believe in a woman's right to choose, but those should not be presidential issues. This country needs to focus on defense and the economy."

"I agree that they should not be issues for governance," said Mac, "but if you don't want to be pounded by the liberals, you need to embrace one of their issues. You could emphasize the ignored elephant in congress and at least mention that it's not only the country's deficit, it's the size of the debt that matters.

"Maybe propose means testing for Social Security while you're at it. Programs that Americans have relied on should be there when they need them, but the operative word is need. I believe that the one per cent wouldn't mind paying more if they knew that the money would be used appropriately. You could also mention abolishing pork. Explain it in plain English, and that will help your approval. I'm just rambling, and nothing I've said is well thought out, but I don't mind spending some time thinking of more substantive ideas."

"This is an excellent start, Mac, and I appreciate your candor as well as your thoughts."

The two men were quiet, each absorbed in his own thoughts. "Jeremy," Mac said, "do you really think you have the patience to campaign? I've never thought of you as the kissing babies type. You would have to weather a mountain of bullshit. Do you have the stamina, and quite frankly, the endurance to fight for eighteen months?"

"I have no choice," said Lyons somberly.

"And you really think you could win?"

Lyons purposefully took a slow visual tour of the lovely chapel, then turned to look into Mac's eyes. "I think I've passed the toughest test today."

CHAPTER 49

It had been the worst three weeks of her life. Jeremy had deteriorated right before her eyes. As much as she resented his private therapy room, the fact that he had stopped his rigorous workouts for over a week after that horrible night was alarming. He'd become reclusive and unfocused, refusing to attend any meetings. Twice she had tried to approach him, and both times he would not look at her or acknowledge her words. She was invisible to him.

Like a splinter under the skin, Sabine knew that allowing Jeremy's anger and hurt to fester would be mutually destructive. And if he deviated from his mission, he would lose the will to live. She had to lance the wound.

She stopped as she heard voices coming from Alegria's office.

"But sir, congress is in session. If you are not attending, I need to give them a reason." Alegria's concern masked her obvious frustration.

"Congress is a collection of predators and pedophiles. Tell them they can fuck off."

Sabine heard Alegria's intake of breath, almost like a muffled sob. She stepped into the room. Jeremy glared up at her and angrily wheeled out of the room.

* * *

His wheelchair was out on the balcony, and he had been staring at the gulf waters for over thirty minutes. It was not like him to zone out. Sabine knew that he had been fuming. She stepped into the breach.

"I need to talk to you," she said. "Could you please come inside?"

Jeremy's shoulders rose slightly and then lowered at the sound of Sabine's voice. He didn't move, turn around, or react. She stood inside the balcony doors and waited. Then he turned the chair around, moved into the great room, and motored to within two feet of her. She pulled over a soft leather ottoman and sat so that she was looking up at him.

"I'm sorry. Really sorry." She closed her eyes. "I thought that you'd be proud of my initiative. I was wrong, so wrong." She paused, opened her eyes, and looked at him. "You know that I would rather die than compromise a mission."

Tears of regret dropped from the corners of her eyes. She reached over and took his hands. Jeremy flinched, but did not pull them away. Sabine exhaled.

"We've never discussed what I did when Stone tried to kill you. I ran down the street to the scene and took control. I had the Secret Service medevac you to Bethesda Naval Hospital, and then our private service flew you to your own hospital and rehab center. All of this was done under total secrecy.

"You saw how I ministered to you every day during your recovery. Did you know that the great majority of patients who are in a coma for three months are quadriplegics? Anything less than perfect for you is not acceptable to either one of us, but the doctors were amazed that your upper body was totally functional. Maybe it was divine intervention or luck, but I'd like to think that you were aware, because for three months I never left your side." She stifled a sob.

" I will do whatever you want. Please let me in; I can't live without you!"

Sabine's hands slipped from his. She dropped her head into her hands and sobbed. Time seemed to move in slow motion. Her sobs became ragged. Jeremy sat immobile, watching her. Finally, she shook her head slowly in despair and reluctantly raised her eyes to him.

After an excruciating period, when it seemed time stood still, Jeremy nodded. He reached out and took her hands. "Come," he said softly. "We have work to do."

CHAPTER 50

GOVERNOR MARY BETH JUSTICE WAS a statuesque woman. She stood 5′ 9″ in her stocking feet, and her high cheekbones, olive skin, and dark, penetrating eyes highlighted an appearance that was considered attractive, bordering on sexy. A gym rat, she was the physical equal to most men she met and intellectually superior to all but a few.

At 46, she hovered on the cusp of electability: old enough to be experienced, young enough to not be irrevocably tainted by the political system. A two-term Republican conservative governor of the blue state of New Jersey, Justice nevertheless rode her Republican bona fides as a badge of honor. Naturally comfortable in almost any situation, her red-faced, defiant look belied her history.

"You *summoned* me?" Justice said, biting the words out as if she were addressing an incompetent subordinate.

Her host assessed her indignation. "Would you like to sit down?" he asked in an uninterested voice.

"Are you sure that I don't have to kneel?"

"I have more gifted options for that role," Senator Jeremy Lyons countered dryly.

Justice looked around his office to be sure they were alone. Satisfied, she took four quick strides until she was hovering over his wheelchair. Lowering her face to within six inches of his, she snarled, "I did what you asked. It's been six years! My debt is paid. You didn't ask me to come see you. I was fucking *ordered*!"

A fleck of spittle landed on Lyons's cheek. With cobra-like speed, his right hand shot out, grabbed a fist full of dark auburn hair, and yanked her head down to his lap. Justice stumbled and fell forward, her hands just managing to grab the arms of his chair. "Perhaps I should reconsider your offer," he whispered into her ear.

Her wail was muffled by Lyons's linen trousers.

Still holding her hair, Lyons pulled her head back, smiled into her tearing eyes, then slammed her face into his knee. "Quiet!" he hissed.

Justice shrieked in pain as blood spurted from her nose and spread over Lyons's pants. In one fluid motion, he pushed her off his lap. She fell backwards, landing awkwardly on the carpeted floor.

"Do *not* bleed on my floor! You have already ruined my pants!" Lyons removed a white handkerchief from the pocket of his navy blue blazer and tossed it at the beaten woman.

Justice tilted her head back, trying to muffle sobs, and pressed the cloth beneath her nose.

Lyons waited patiently until the bleeding slowed. When she looked up at him, he motioned for her to sit in a nearby chair. She rose and sat heavily in the offered seat. Through her tear-filled eyes, she glared at him with utter contempt. "I guess a power play wasn't the right move with you." Her words were defiant and distinct, though filtered through the bloody handkerchief.

Lyons emitted a short laugh. "But you tried. And that is why I have chosen you."

"Chosen me?" she sputtered. "As what, your fucking punching bag?"

"I do love your spirit," Lyons said pedantically, "but the temper still needs work."

"Give me a break, Jeremy."

"I may have," he said, interrupting.

Her eyes flashed. "I get a call from your aide, telling me that you expect me in your Florida office in four hours. No advance notice, no concern for my schedule or flight arrangements; just get your ass here."

"That sounds right." He smiled evilly. "I'm glad that you could get your *affairs* in order."

"Fuck you," Justice said in a defeated tone.

"Language also needs to be upgraded."

"Jeremy, you smashed my face! How do I explain that?" she argued weakly. He watched as resistance seemed to drain from her body.

"You don't. You don't explain; you don't complain. This unfortunate incident could have been avoided if you had demonstrated the proper amount of respect for a United States Senator. What you will do is listen closely to everything I am about to say. When I finish speaking, you will do exactly as I have instructed. There may be a statute of limitations on your transgressions in of the eyes of the law, but there is none in the arena of public opinion. Do we understand each other?"

"Yes, you bastard."

Lyons studied her. "You still have a residue of antagonism. Why don't you regurgitate all of the bile that is souring your stomach and clouding your reasoning? Do tell me what is on your mind." He sat back in the wheelchair.

"You *know* what's on my mind. You blackmailed me. Yes, I had an affair with a younger man. I was exhausted from campaigning, and I know, put me in the same class as that serial sex addict, he was an intern!" She hung her head. "And it happened more than once," she said with regret.

Her head snapped up and her eyes were defiant. "When I found out how old he really was, I broke it off immediately. How you fucking found out about it, I'll never know."

She stopped, gathered herself, and returned with even more vitriol. "I paid my dues, damnit. I don't want to be linked to you in any way. In my mind, any man who manhandles a woman like you did me should be locked up. A prime example of why this country is so fucked up is that a brutal crook like you could get elected to the U.S. Senate! You may beat the shit out of me for saying this, but I'd have been happier if the hit and run had succeeded."

Lyons folded his hands in his lap and continued to scrutinize her like a scientist observing an experiment. Content in his silence, he waited for her to speak again.

"What the hell are you doing?" Justice asked. "Sizing me up for a coffin? If you're waiting for me to take back what I said, it's not happening."

"You are very astute," Lyons complimented. "I am appraising, evaluating, analyzing probabilities. Assessments in the abstract leave much to be desired. Face to face meetings or, in your case, face to knee meetings provide much superior metrics."

"In addition to being the most ruthless bastard in politics, and that is not easily achievable, you are also the most fucking obtuse! What the hell do you want from me?" Justice asked with weary exasperation.

Lyons crooked a finger and motioned for her to approach him.

Justice gritted her teeth, stood up, and walked over to him, all the while maintaining eye contact.

Lyons's face softened. "I assure you that I will never strike you or physically assault you again. It was an extreme measure, possibly poorly chosen, but I needed to test your mettle."

"You mean the *great* Jeremy Lyons might have made a mistake? Damn right you did, you asshole!" She shook her head angrily, and a residue of blood fell to the carpet. "For the last time, what do you want from me?"

He nodded, motioned for her to lean down.

She exhaled and complied. Her fists, held at her sides, were clenched tightly.

"It is not what I want *of* you, Mary Beth Justice, it is what I want *for* you." He waited for her curiosity to build. Like a rash, red crept up her neck to her face. Her lips were pressed together, locking the door on the words fighting to come out.

"You will be our country's first woman president."

Her harsh laugh emboldened her. "You are so full of shit. Like I would have any chance of beating Jean Carlyle."

"Your assessment is correct. You could not beat her now. You will win the election of 2020, when you are more seasoned."

Justice's eyes widened. "If you think that she will step down after one term..." She paused. "If Carlyle wins, how could I be the first female? Do you know something about her sexuality that I don't know?" Her last comment was overdosed with sarcasm.

"She will not be the president in 2016," Lyons said with assurance.

"Then who the fuck will, Carnac?"

"I will."

CHAPTER 51

"MIA," LYONS BECKONED TO HIS Asian assistant, "could you please bring us a white linen napkin and a bucket of ice? It seems that in her enthusiasm over seeing me again, the good governor stumbled and fell."

When Mia returned, Justice took the cold compress, her eyes daring Mia to ask a question. She held it to her nose and glared at Lyons.

"What are you smoking?" she asked, hoping to hear his statement again.

Lyons smiled. "A peace pipe." He returned her look and added skepticism. "However, you may not be up to it."

Justice took a seat across from him and stared combatively into his eyes. "You wouldn't have offered if you didn't think I could win. Apparently, my indiscretion is not an impediment to your ambition."

He gave her a self-deprecating smile. "I have already demonstrated that winning public office is achievable in spite of what might be seen as a rather sordid past."

Justice didn't respond, so he continued.

"We have witnessed with our current president that winning can be a powerful aphrodisiac. It can make you think you are omnipotent, omniscient. Power is the most addictive drug. However, men, or in your case, women, make mistakes. The confidence of victory extends to the delusion that you, and you alone, know what is right for the country. Yet only God is infallible. Being able to govern to the extent that meaningful accomplishments can be made requires guidance, cooperation, and humility."

Justice nodded. "Is that how you would govern?" she asked, pointedly holding the cold compress to her nose as water dripped from it.

"Do not confuse my methodology with my patriotism. If you accept my conditions, I would expect the same passion and commitment to purpose."

"If anyone else in the universe told me that he was going to be president, not seek a second term, and give me a red carpet into the Oval Office four years later…." Her voice trailed off.

"If you follow my precise instructions, that is exactly what will happen."

Justice narrowed her eyes. "What happens to me for the four years you are in office?"

Lyons smiled. "You get the opportunity for extraordinary on-the-job training."

"Huh?"

He extended his hand with a flourish. "I have chosen you to be my vice president."

CHAPTER 52

IT SHOULD HAVE BEEN EASY. John Wesley was a born actor. Still, walking into Sabine's office and attempting to maintain a disinterested facade took method acting to a new level.

Instead of a desk, she sat behind a glass table, which was bare except for a computer with two 24-inch monitors and a manila envelope. A silky, light blue top was tied below her breasts, and her white shorts ended inches from her pubic area. Her beauty was not a distraction; but she seemed unaware of the effect she had on men.

Looking up, Sabine said, "I have an interesting assignment for you." She motioned for him to take a seat across from her. "Elise Franklin is a powerful, liberal Democrat. She believes she is invincible. Consequently, that self-assurance enables her to bully other legislators to the point where she can become a modern-day pied piper."

"What do you want me to do?" asked Wesley.

"She needs to become an apostle."

He raised his eyebrows, hoping to mask that he had been staring at her legs. "Isn't she entrenched with her constituents and her party?"

Sabine's look was patronizing. "Of course, John, otherwise we would handle this ourselves." She picked up the folder on her desk and handed it to him.

"This took some digging, but Alegria has some interesting research that should be helpful to you." She smiled. "Please leave out no details when you tell me how you accomplished your mission."

Wesley opened the folder, then closed it and said, "Just so I am clear, this is more than getting her to vote on a specific bill. She needs to be converted, not only to someone you can count on to support you, but to someone who will lead others down that path."

Now Sabine looked impressed. He had summarized the assignment perfectly and made no excuses about the difficulty of the task. "You're a quick study, John. I think we'll work well together."

CHAPTER 53

As she had been instructed, Mary Beth Justice called Jeremy Lyons on her unregistered phone. He had assured her that his private line was encrypted and could not be monitored. After she met Alegria, his assurances were not necessary.

The email she had received just asked her to call. Other than that it was benign.

After listening to Lyons's offer and hearing his plan, Justice had spent time analyzing the likelihood of his success. Of course she wanted to be President of the United States. No matter what they say, every politician would like to be the top dog. Her resume, at least what could be divined by anyone other than Lyons, was impeccable. As Governor of New Jersey, even her missteps had ended up working.

With the Democrats, anyone with charisma and sound bites could get the nomination. On the other hand, in the Republican party, it seemed like you had to wait your turn. So regardless of her qualifications, how could she get the funding to launch the required billion dollar campaign? With Lyons, she at least had the chance to leapfrog the competition.

In reality, in spite of Lyons's passion and presence, the chance of anyone running as an Independent and winning the presidency seemed remote. So her next step was to figure out the down side of jumping into bed with him.

Did she risk being splattered with any evidence that cropped up exposing his more questionable business practices? Not really. She would claim that the country vetted him in his senatorial bid, and all she knew was that he was totally committed to making our country stronger. If the Lyons/Justice ticket lost badly, would that paint her with the brush of being a loser? No. She would shine in the debates, her name would become recognizable, and if Jean Carlyle won and miraculously did a good job, Mary Beth was still young enough to be the second woman president.

"It is I, your faithful servant, at your beck and call, O Fearless Leader." Justice was annoyed that Lyons had not followed up on their previous conversations.

"Excellent. It seems that absence does make the heart grow fonder."

"Let's be clear," said Justice, emboldened by the distance between them. "I was not a one and done governor. If I do become president, I may not be content with setting my own term limit."

"Actually, your career ambitions have nothing to do with the purpose of this call, but when you are president, you are in charge," said Lyons. "I have no intention of dictating the terms of your presidency."

Mollified, Justice waited for Lyons to continue.

"I am considering a segment on *60 Minutes* in which I will outline a proposal to lower the corporate income tax rate."

"Both sides agree that it needs to be done, but no one wants to step up to the plate," Justice responded.

"I intend to structure my comments to appeal to both your side and the liberals. The objective is obviously to present the idea in an understandable manner so that the public will weigh in on the issue."

"I hope you know how to do that. Getting them involved in anything that doesn't have 'free' in front of it is next to impossible."

"Nevertheless," Lyons went on, "that is my charge. I need you to reach out to a handful of your Republican friends in the Senate and the House and tell them that you would appreciate their support. You can tell them that I asked for it. They know that I helped Smathers win his race, so they will ask you if that means a contribution to their campaigns. You can intimate whatever you want, but give them no solid promises. Let me know who you can count on and your degree of certainty, and I may or may not reach out to them after the show airs."

"I'm pretty sure I understand why you're doing this now, but lay it out for me."

"My opinions on anything involving money will be respected. Even if the legislation fails, I will be seen as a man of action rather than a do-nothing legislator."

"We're seeing how well that works," Justice said. "So it shouldn't be hard to get some Republican backing, but how will you get *any* of the Democrats to support you?"

"Why, exactly how I enticed you to join me, my dear, with charm and a gentle touch."

CHAPTER 54

ELISE FRANKLIN WAS AN AGING baby boomer masquerading as a mid-forties cougar. From a distance it was not a difficult sale, but up close and personal was a different story. A helmet of white-blond hair, touched up weekly, was hurricane proof. Her face was stretched so tightly you could bounce a quarter on it and it would trampoline back to you. A similar experience was likely with her best-that-money-can-buy perky breasts. It seemed that regardless of the talent of the world-class Hollywood surgeon, the patient would ultimately resemble a wide-mouthed frog.

These undisputable facts were nevertheless ignored by the senior senator from California. It was Elise Franklin's conviction that age would not *dare* to diminish her. There was absolutely not a molecule of insecurity in her as she addressed her young, very handsome guest. She stepped closer, purposefully invading his space.

"Peter," she said softly. "Your name just rolls off my lips."

Peter Van Horn smiled tentatively in response, but stood his ground. "Is there a place where we might talk, Senator?"

"What about?" she asked, raising her eyebrows in a parody of innocence.

"I hold you in very high esteem, and I would like to discuss matters important to our county."

"You would, would you? And how did you get past my security to get an audience with me?"

"Senator, I promise you they vetted me very carefully. I am here on a vital mission."

"Okay, boy scout, who are you representing?"

"I am sorry ma'am, but I'm not at liberty to say."

Franklin threw her head back and laughed. She leaned down so that her full lips were inches from the young man's throat. "Do you think your handler thought that you would compromise me?" she whispered.

"No," Van Horn said quickly, his face reddening. "I have complete knowledge of the facts, and she felt that I could make a strong case for your cooperation."

"Cooperation?" A slow smile spread as she licked her lips. "You have a lot to learn, *Peter*. The only senator desperate for my support and crafty enough to send a young Adonis is Jeremy Lyons. I'm sure that he's aware of my predilection for handsome young men, as well as the oft-rumored stories of my sexual prowess.

"Look at you," she continued as she placed her manicured hands on his shoulders. "Wavy brown hair that is begging for my fingers, chocolate brown eyes that should never be out of a bedroom, and a hard body that's only considered soft when compared with your cock."

Van Horn did not flinch when her hand grabbed his genitals. "Senator, this makes me very uncomfortable."

Franklin laughed harshly and spun away. When she turned back to him, the façade of civility had faded. "Don't tell me that you weren't told what your real assignment was. Your boss wants you to soften me up so that I'll support him on some crappy legislation he's behind. If you missed her message, then you probably are great in bed, because that's all you'd be good for. For God's sake, Peter, you allowed yourself to be blindfolded and driven to my secret lair! What did you expect? Tea and crumpets?"

"Please, will you just let me explain?"

"Of course," she answered. She grabbed his hand and led him into her bedroom. The sheets had been pulled down in the king-sized bed, and bottle of champagne was chilling in an ice bucket. On a muted flat screen was frozen a picture of a younger and gloriously naked Elise Franklin fellating a man who looked like a male model. His head was thrown back in ecstasy.

"It is possible that you are wearing a wire, so please disrobe," she said.

"I'm not wearing a wire," he protested.

"I will listen to whatever you say," Franklin told him. "I will answer any questions that you might have, but I always have the upper hand. If this discussion is to take place, only one of us will be dressed. It's your choice," she said, throwing her hand out.

Van Horn winced, squeezed his eyes together, and slowly began to undress. When he finished, he looked at her. "May I at least sit on a corner of the bed?"

"Of course," she said with a confident smile. "Now, what it the purpose of this urgent meeting, Peter?"

CHAPTER 55

WITHOUT A VISUAL ON THE scene, it would be assumed that Senator Franklin was holding a press conference. Gone was the predatory tone. Her answers were responsive and polite.

"May I ask you a few questions now, Mr. Van Horn?" Franklin began.

"Of course," answered Van Horn, still obviously uncomfortable having a discussion while sitting naked on the edge of the senator's bed.

His questions had been perfunctory, easily answered. Each request was summarily dismissed. During the entire conversation, her gaze was riveted to his crotch.

"You are quite a competent young man," she said as her hands made a sweeping motion emphasizing his nakedness. "Why are you wasting your time attaching yourself to Lyons's wheelchair? He has no gravitas. He's a flash in the pan. Did

he really think you'd be able to seduce me into abandoning my principles?"

"I'm not sure of his intentions," said Van Horn in a confident tone. "I'm not in Senator Lyons's employ."

"What?" It was the first time that the senator felt like she was not in total control. She held up her left arm and placed a finger on her bracelet. "If I punch this button, my security comes through that front door and tosses you out on your ass."

"I'm aware of that," he said calmly, as he reached over and picked up his powder-blue boxers.

"Then what are you doing?"

"First, I will give you some advice."

"Advice! Did you forget who the fuck you're talking to?"

As if he had not heard her, he said, "Clothe yourself with humility towards one another, for God is opposed to the proud; but gives grace to the humble." He smiled, "Scripture is good for the soul. "

"That's it, choir boy, I am calling for security," she threatened.

"I'm getting dressed, Elise. This game has become tiresome. I have some information that you need to know. It's about Jacob."

"Who the fuck are you?" Her face was contorted in rage. "How dare you bring up his name?"

"I'm a man on a mission," he replied, smiling easily as he continued dressing. "I was curious to see if you lived up to your reputation for depravity."

"Get out!" she shouted.

"If you insist," he said breezily. "No one knows I'm here, but what I know could be hazardous to your wealth. Oh, and it would also destroy your career."

"You are a nobody, a gnat on my windshield." Franklin eyes blazed at him; contempt dripped off every word.

Leaning into her rage Van Horn said, "Do you really think I'm stupid enough to walk weaponless into your spider's web?"

"What do you want?" Her clenched lips were white.

"Don't you think I should first tell you everything I know?" Van Horn asked.

Teeth bared, she controlled her fury and remained silent as he finished dressing.

Van Horn moved back to the bed, lay down on his back, interlocked his fingers behind his head and rested on the pillow. "Once you know the full extent of my knowledge, you'll be more inclined to follow my instructions precisely."

In an attempt at composure, Franklin checked her watch and said, "You have three minutes, Mr. Enquirer, and then I'm calling security."

"Fair enough, Senator," he said. "I was in your son Jacob's class at Harvard. He hated the school, by the way. You really shouldn't have made him go."

Her eyes showed surprise and then fear.

"He was very sensitive," Van Horn said with compassion. "And at that time, society wasn't quite as progressive as it is today. I would be remiss if I didn't thank you for your efforts, by the way. It has taken a long time for even the partial acceptance of today."

Franklin couldn't breathe

"Trying to hide your sexuality has always been difficult, but being forced to do so because your mother refuses to have sired a 'fag' ..." he said the word like he had just tasted the vilest food on the planet... "well, it's like the ultimate betrayal."

He paused.

Franklin's face was white. Her eyes threatened to roll back in her head.

"Should I continue?" Van Horn asked, not unkindly.

She nodded woodenly.

"A politician gets a great deal of sympathy when her only child commits suicide." He stopped and gave her a long, accusatory look. "Unless it's determined that his mother drove him to it."

"You can't prove anything!"

"*Au contraire*, bitch," he said forcefully. He moved quickly from the bed until he towered over her. "I'm afraid I can. You see, I was Jacob's lover."

CHAPTER 56

JOHN WESLEY LEARNED ABOUT HIS second assignment in a more plea-surable setting. The temperature was in the high 70s, it was early evening, and he was stretched out on a chaise drinking a gin and tonic. From an adjoining chaise, Sabine raised her wine glass to him. She'd tried not to laugh when he'd described how he compromised Elise Franklin.

"If she weren't so anal about security, you could have made a video, popped it on YouTube, and retired," said Sabine. "Well done."

"Thanks. She is one scary broad; but she'll have no choice. She will stand up when called."

"Your next assignment will require more than your acting skills. Again, the methodology is entirely up to you. Like the last time, if you're caught, you're on your own."

"I'm used to taking care of myself," said Wesley.

"I know, but I never want any confusion on our responsibility."

"Is that why I haven't met the man?"

"He is not involved in my business," Sabine said decisively.

She looked out at the gulf waters as she sipped her wine. "Everett Leeds is a different kind of bully. The former Senate Majority Leader does not acknowledge any loss of power. He runs roughshod over people. Blackmail and intimidation are legitimate political tools to him. I doubt that our objective can be accomplished in one visit."

"And he needs to become an apostle also?"

"Not necessarily. He's powerful, but he's despised and feared. Franklin derived her power with her 'most popular girl in school' shtick. Women need to follow her to be popular. On the other hand, Leeds is the schoolyard bully. Everyone is afraid to challenge him. It's imperative that he never filibusters against Senator Lyons."

CHAPTER 57

Senate Minority Leader Everett Leeds's mottled, speckled arms stretched painfully over his head in a classic victory pose. When his red-veined, white, fleshy legs were included, the composite picture of the naked man's tightly secured arms and bulbous legs formed an unappetizing X.

The pleasant-looking man sitting in a nearby chair alternated between watching his captive and reading his Bible. As Leeds began to stir, his abductor put the finishing touches on his observations: the senator's spread-eagled body bore an uncanny resemblance to three-day-old cottage cheese.

Predictably, the first movements from the shackled senator were to try to lower his arms. The wrought-iron rails that supported the wooden headboard of the room's single bed clanged like a discordant dinner bell as Leeds's handcuffs banged against them. In response, the man in the chair raised his eyes from the good book, noted Leeds's movement, and then resumed reading.

Fighting through the blur of his drug-induced sleep, the senator rolled his head to the right towards the room's sole illumination. A single lamp stood in the center of a small Formica-topped table. Leeds recognized the occupant of the straight-backed, black chair as the man who had approached him at the bar.

Focusing on the man, Leeds waited for acknowledgement. "Hey!" he called out. The man known to Leeds as Luke Graham did not respond. "Hey, asshole, are you deaf?" The man raised his index finger, but his eyes never left his Bible. "You crazy bastard, close the fucking book!" screamed Leeds.

Graham sighed, finished what he was reading, and gently closed his Bible. Tucking it under his arm, he rose from the chair and walked over to the bed. Angry red blotches flared on the senator's cheeks as Graham approached. Graham leaned down so that his face was inches from Leeds. With a mother's touch, he reached over and smoothed the senator's sweat-stained white hair out of his eyes. He put his lips next to the senator's ear and whispered, "I'm sure your vision was impaired." He held the Bible before Leeds's eyes.

"Excuse me, Father Graham, or whatever the hell your name is," Leeds said through clenched teeth. "If I've offended you, maybe you should just ask me to leave."

Graham gave him a puzzled look and shook his head. "That would be illogical."

"Really? Please enlighten me on what is logical about a member of a fellow senator's staff drugging, abducting, and stripping the minority leader of the United States Senate?"

"Did you ever notice that when elected officials want to make a point, they use the entire name of their title? May I ask your opinion on a brief quote from scripture?" the man asked with childlike enthusiasm.

"Sure, you have my permission," said Leeds sarcastically.

"We find so many truths in the Bible. Listen to this: 'They promise them freedom, while they themselves, are slaves of depravity.....for people are slaves to whatever has mastered them.' Isn't that just a perfect description of a politician?"

"What the hell do you want, preacher man?"

"I'll make you a deal. If you allow me to filibuster – it's always been a dream," he added pleasantly, "I will tell you all that you need to know."

"Need to know?" spat out the irate politician.

"You prefer to break protocol? The other option is that I take my Bible, go out and get a bite, and perhaps come back later."

"No, no. I'll listen," the senator answered quickly.

"Splendid." Graham's hands joined to clutch his Bible between them. His beatific smile was disarming. "I should begin by confessing a few untruths." Smiling conspiratorially at the senator, he added, "You, of all people, should appreciate the power of a well-told lie."

Graham held up an index finger. "First, the official documents that you glanced at for approximately three seconds at the bar were an expert forgery. I must admit that I was a bit offended at your cursory peek. In the future you may want to be a bit more circumspect. Second," he held up his middle finger next to the first. "I was not sent by Senator Lyons. In fact, I don't even know the man. However, I would love to meet him. I'm a big fan."

The straight line of Leeds's thin lips twitched, but he said nothing.

"Third, the drug that knocked you out is my own creation and has no side effects." He bowed. "You're welcome."

Leeds's body stiffened as the man called Graham looked at him.

"I'm afraid you're a bit odoriferous," said Graham, wrinkling his nose. Would you mind if I returned to my chair and continued my tell-almost-all?"

Still scowling, Leeds nodded.

When he was seated again in the chair, Graham reached inside his jacket pocket and pulled out a switchblade. Snapping it open, he waved it at Leeds. "You really need to be more careful. If I were the violent type, I would have stabbed you before you had your third drink." He examined his fingernails, frowned, and began to clean them with the blade.

"You're probably wondering why I brought you here." He stopped and smiled a happy smile. "I've actually always wanted to say that."

Leaning forward, he placed his forearms at his sides. "I believe we're all here on this planet to make a difference. I believe that one man can make a difference, don't you? The knife moved through the air, accentuating his words. Leeds started to respond.

Graham frowned and waved the knife from side to side. "Well, I hope you believe that, because I'm actually that man." He smiled, raising his hands straight above his head like he had hit a three-point basket.

He laid the blade down on the table and folded his hands angelically. "And the good news for you, Senate Minority Leader Everett Ryan Leeds, is that I have chosen you to help me."

Leeds's arms ached. He had to piss so badly that he was ready to soak the bed. It was cold. He felt like his ass was going to get bed sores, even though he couldn't have been in this position more than a couple of hours. Meanwhile, the nutcase just sat there smiling. It was time to tighten his scrawny ass up and get out of this hellhole.

"Are you finished?" Leeds asked.

Graham nodded.

"It's customary when you finish a filibuster that you publicly cede the floor. You mind telling me how I'm supposed to help you?"

"Of course not. I'm going to get the government working again, really working. I know," he continued, raising a hand. "Politicians have been promising that since the beginning of time. But I am not a politician; I am a crusader."

"A crusader! God give me strength," muttered Leeds

"Aha! We may have something in common after all."

"I seriously fucking doubt it."

"Well, perhaps not, but let's find out. Can I count on your coop-eration?"

"Yeah, if you need me to testify at your parole hearing."

Graham laughed, a high-pitched rather feminine laugh.

Tired of the ambiguity, Leeds asked, "So what exactly do you want from me? How about some specifics instead of banalities."

"Of course. You will begin by assuming more moderate posi-tions. Your liberal left ideas, as well as the far right platform, are not helping the financial underpinnings of our country."

"Shocker! The abducting crusader is a political junkie."

"Thank you, Senator. I do take my politics seriously," said Gra-ham, whose face actually looked like he thought he had received a compliment.

"Well, what is your game plan, Karl Rove?"

"It's really quite simple. If you cut off the head, the body fol-lows."

Leeds swallowed, but persevered. "Meaning?"

"In your case, and yes, I admit this is somewhat Godfatherish," he said apologetically, "I may call on you to do a favor for our coun-try. Since we have sort of bonded," he pointed to Leeds's restraints, "I needed to know that I could count on you. I'm a man of God, but you probably already figured that out. It certainly can't hurt to bring Him back into our country's psyche. Still, I can't really ask the Almighty to do *everything* "

"What I figured out," Leeds said, raising his head, his face crimson with rage, "is that you're a goddamn criminal and a phony-ass man of God who's also a goddamn charlatan."

THWACK!!

With a flick of the wrist, Graham's forgotten switchblade was now embedded in the wooden headboard two inches above the senator's head. Before the gasp fully emerged from Leeds's throat, Graham was on him. He wrenched the knife from the headboard and jabbed it under Leeds's chin. Graham's eyes bulged with a madman's intensity. "NEVER use the Lord's name in vain in my presence!"

Graham closed his eyes, tilted his head back, and took a number of deep breaths. He looked down at Leeds and wrinkled his nose when he saw that the esteemed senator had pissed himself. "I believe you are known as the king of pork. Is that correct?"

The defiance in Leeds's eyes had dimmed to a flicker. He nodded.

"And I believe you are proud of that fact. No bill passes without your insertion of a little friendly pork."

Leeds did not respond.

"So think of the favor," Graham's voice rose with excitement, "that I could do for the public by carving the pork right out of you!" The flat of his knife smacked first the left and then the right side of the senator's trembling belly.

CHAPTER 58

Everett Leeds sat heavily on the urine-stained bed, his legs hanging over the sides. A threadbare white towel covered his genitals. He rubbed his face with both hands, then scowled.

"What now?" he asked angrily.

The man called Luke Graham sighed. "Sorry. I was mentally castigating myself for not being better prepared." He looked away. "I believe a beach towel would have been more appropriate."

"Yeah, you're clever, and you hold all the cards. I know you can stop me from walking out of here, so let's cut the crap. Tell me what you want, so I can get dressed and leave." Now that he was freed from restraints, Leeds's combative nature returned.

"I want my country back."

"Christ! Of course you do. Another Patrick Henry." Leeds rolled his eyes in an exaggerated manner.

"Please pay attention, Mr. Leeds," Graham said with quiet menace. "It will prevent confusion in the future. Or," he paused, "noncompliance.

"These are your requirements: One, you will follow my instructions to the letter. Two, your shifts in position will be gradual. This will create the illusion that the change is due to your conscience rather than coercion. I admit that is illogical; you lack the integrity, but we'll make it work. Three, you will use your legendary powers of persuasion to convert other extremists to your new positions." Graham smiled. "You will be my apostle."

Leeds sat, his hands on his knees, his overlapping belly covering the towel, and glared.

"When I contact you," the instructions continued, "you will respond quickly from a burner phone. I am sure you understand that any mention of me or our arrangement, or any attempts to record conversations, will result in termination." Graham folded his hands together and looked pleasantly at Leeds.

Leeds turned his head to the side. "Termination? Like you'd kill me?"

Graham looked at him like he was a slow student. "'Your life is like a mist. You can see it for a short time, but then it goes away.' John 4:14. This really isn't that complicated," he said, wrinkling his brow. "Without your cooperation, you become just another impediment to remove." He smiled. "Besides, all God's children live but one final breath from their own funeral. You are one of God's children, aren't you?"

"Oh sure, absolutely. I'm a former altar boy," said Leeds. He shook his white mane as if he were trying to dislodge a bug in his hair. "I get it," he continued, stepping onto the floor and tossing the towel back on the bed. "Give me my clothes, and I'll get the fuck out of your way."

"A slight adjustment to that plan," said Graham, as he also stood.

Leeds put his hands on his hips, unfazed by his nakedness, and stared at the man in disbelief. "I got it preacher-man. I'll do what you want."

"A few precautions are necessary, I'm afraid." Graham replied. "It's not that I doubt your sincerity." His left hand rose and rubbed his chin as he studied the unappetizing sight before him.

"The first order of business is to get you dressed. Afterwards," he smiled, "you will get a final taste of my elixir of dreams. When you awake, you will be comfortably stretched out on your own bed in your apartment." His smile broadened.

"There's no other way?" asked Leeds.

Graham shook his head.

Leeds pushed his shoulders back and gave Graham a searing look. "I can get dressed by myself, but you may want to think real hard about pushing me, that is, if you intend on keeping those brass balls."

CHAPTER 59

"Sir, what happened? Are you all right?" Russell Tomlinson stammered nervously. If the senator's chief of staff were objectively evaluated, he would be praised for his efficiency, his work ethic, and his loyalty. The son of a Yale professor of history, Tomlinson followed in his father's academic footsteps. Although he'd been accepted into Yale's law school, he simply could not wait any longer to enter government service.

A slight, fastidious man, his obsession since youth was to help make policy. Highly respected by his peers, Tomlinson nevertheless must have possessed latent masochistic tendencies to remain in the employ of the towel-snapping bully, Senator Everett Leeds.

"Overslept," Leeds snapped as he walked into his office. "Where's my fuckin' coffee?"

"Right away, sir," said Tomlinson as he scurried away.

Leeds sat down heavily in his custom black leather office chair and threw his five-hundred-dollar Allen Edmonds wingtip black shoes onto his massive desk. In the car he had debated whether he'd bring Tomlinson in on this. The man was the best computer guru in the whole damn government, but the little priss was scared of his own shadow.

Tomlinson appeared in the doorway, the large black cup emblazoned with the word "Leader" held securely in both hands.

"Don't pirouette. Get your ass over here."

Tomlinson hurried over and placed the cup gently on a napkin in front of his boss. Impeccably dressed, he was Leeds's testament to his presumptive respect for gays. Unfortunately, Leeds's public support for gay marriage and equality did not act as a deterrent for his frequent slurs.

Leeds eyed Tomlinson, seeing the man's concerned look. His prolonged stare caused Tomlinson's Adam's apple to twitch, and as a result, his burgundy and blue bow tie bobbed up and down.

"I need to find a man," Leeds said through clenched teeth. "Get a sketch artist in here. After he draws the man I describe, I want that man found!"

Tomlinson spun on his heel, as if he had received a military command, and left the room.

While he sipped his coffee and fumed, waiting for Tomlinson to carry out his orders, Leeds tried to calm himself by visualizing particularly inventive forms of retribution. This Billy Graham wannabe had made the wrong enemy.

* * *

In spite of his superb hacking skills, Tomlinson was unable to match the sketch with any known data base. With the senator's access, he was able to run the image through every law enforcement agency, but to no avail.

Now Tomlinson walked into the room like a dog expecting to be beaten.

Everett Leeds ripped the blood-pressure cuff from his arm and threw it at his chief of staff. Tomlinson ducked and winced, prepared for the torrent of invective.

"My pressure's through the roof. Whose fault is that?"

Tomlinson knew better than to respond.

Leeds held up a meaty finger. "You were supposed to send this everywhere. You're a computer savant who knows every other nerd in the system. And none of your girlfriends has a clue to his whereabouts? Do you think I just imagined that some evangelical psycho kidnapped me and chained me to a bed?"

Spittle flew from his mouth. "If I have a heart attack in this chair, just pin a note on my chest: 'It's Russell's fault.'"

Regardless of how many times his boss had verbally assaulted him, Tomlinson felt each blow. His head hung on his chest as his eyes welled with tears.

CHAPTER 60

BARNARD COLLEGE IS A PRESTIGIOUS women's liberal arts college that was established in 1889. Since 1900, the college has been affiliated with Columbia University. Located in the Morningside Heights neighborhood in the borough of Manhattan in New York, Barnard has a student population of approximately 2400. For former senator Jean Carlyle, the women's champion, it was a perfect launching pad.

With fingers-crossed faith in the weather forecasters, the dean of Barnard had agreed that the commencement proceedings would be held out of doors. The weather, like the students, faculty, and alumnae, knew better than to disappoint Dean Crosswhite

The sun kissed Carlyle's upturned face as she let the dean's words wash over her like a soothing balm. In genuine pleasure, her smile was fixed as the words seemed to flow into her bloodstream.

It's my time, she thought. *The country is waiting for me.* Her mind wandered. *What if I told these bright, young women the truth. This country is on the precipice. Why? Because of incompetent, preening men whose only objective is to get reelected or to create a legacy of illusion.* The increase in volume in the dean's voice brought Carlyle back to reality.

"A woman of vison and indomitable will. For the past ten years, our commencement speaker was voted the most admired woman in America. She's not only burst through the glass ceiling, she's reached back and brought us along with her." Dean Crosswhite's robe-covered arms rose with her passion. "We tell the world that our students are bold, brilliant, and inspiring. They change the world and the way we think about it. Ladies and gentlemen, I submit to you that Jean Carlyle is the epitome of this promise."

Crosswhite smiled coyly. "My only question is how she could do this without a Barnard education." The crowd burst into laughter. When it died down, the dean proudly concluded. "I now introduce to you the next president of the United States, Jean Holland Carlyle.

Carlyle gave the dean an "I'm going to get you" smile. "Although it's true that I've been educationally disadvantaged," she began, "Dean Crosswhite has been kind enough to give me some needed tutoring." The women in the crowd roared their approval.

When the laughter subsided, she asked a question. "Why would anyone want to be president of the United States? You graduates are too young to remember when the office of the presidency was revered. You might disagree with his policies, or even dislike the man, but publically disparaging the leader of the free world was blasphemy." She shook her carefully coiffed blond hair.

"George W. Bush was called stupid and a liar. Now, he and I weren't close, but how disrespectful to attach those labels to our president. The current president? Don't get me started: over his head; born in Kenya; a narcissist; incompetent. If you want the entire list, you'll need to contact the Tea Party directly.

"So why would someone who served in the United States Senate for four terms and has also been an advisor to presidents, even granting my substandard education, want to run for this office and end up being the target for four or eight years of abuse?" She waited as hands rose tentatively.

"It may not be what you think," she said softly. "It's *not* that I have a burning desire to be the first women president. It's *not* that I need to be part of history to feel like my life has had meaning." She paused, and her smile was winsome.

"I want to be the next president of the United States because I will make a difference. I will represent those that cannot represent themselves. The first thing I will do when I am president is to ask, "Why? Why does the richest nation in the world still have fifteen per cent of its citizens living in poverty? Why are banks lending money to rich people at two per cent while some student loans, to our future leaders of America, are charged interest at more than six per cent?" Carlyle had to wait as the crowd cheered.

"Why are we still discussing gay marriage? And why, over forty years later, are Republican men still trying to tell us what we can do with our bodies?" Her hands went to her hips; she was the picture of defiance.

"I've told you why I want to be president. Now I want to tell you why America will want me to be president. Our enemies will know there is an experienced leader in the Oval Office. Our allies will know they can trust me. Our middle class will realize that they have a president who cares…" She gazed lovingly at her audience.

Carlyle's smile was genuine, warm. "Now, let's talk about you. We are in the early stages of a feminine revolution. You don't have to be a part of it," she teased, "but it's going to be exciting."

"The gender gap?" She held her hands straight out from her body about six inches apart. "I AM COUNTING ON EACH ONE OF YOU EXTRAORDINARY YOUNG WOMEN TO SLAM IT SHUT WITH SUCH A VENGENANCE THAT MEN WILL HAVE TO FIGHT TO BE EQUAL WITH US!"

When she clapped her hands together, the students stood in unison, clapping and screaming with joy. The applause ran through Carlyle's veins like electricity. She looked skyward.

"Do you believe we are the weaker sex?"

"Noooo!" cried the students.

"Are our possibilities limited?"

"Noooo!"

"Look up with me." She waited a beat. "Do any of you see a glass ceiling?"

The shouts of "No" could be heard in nearby neighborhoods.

"You are the future leaders of America. I don't say that cavalierly; I believe it. It is your responsibility, your moral obligation to use your exceptional education to change the world. I want you to soar above the clouds, above all ceilings!"

Into the cheering, which lasted over five minutes, she added her closing. "I need you to do me a favor. If anyone asks you why Jean Carlyle should be president of the United States and you want to give them a one-sentence answer, just tell them this: 'Because she is one bad-ass bitch.'"

CHAPTER 61

Jackie Mayfield was not happy. An interview with CNBC was one thing; it was logical. But going on *60 Minutes*, well, that was a direct competitor, a slap in the face. When Fox's top national reporter was frustrated, she paced around the studio like an angry leopard. Everyone, including long-time cameraman and friend Eddie Richter, stayed out of her way.

It was a slow news night, but Jackie had ninety seconds before she was on camera. At the last possible second, she slammed herself down in her chair, squared her shoulders, gave her long hair a decisive toss, and plastered on her award-winning smile. "Good evening, and welcome to Fox News. I'm going to go off script tonight, and if the producers cut me off," she leaned in to the camera and spoke in a stage whisper, "I want you to call the station and raise heck." Unless she went completely off the rails, the chances of her being taken off the air were zero.

"I feel like a jilted lover." Her pout was classic. "My friend and favorite politician is going to offer a solution for America. And can you believe he is doing it on *another* network! I can't ever tell you to watch another network or I'd lose my job; but I will say that if Senator Lyons says he has a solution that will help our country, I would agree with him. Still," she put on a frowny face, "*we* would have given him *61* minutes." She paused. "In other news...."

* * *

Sitting on their living room couch, a large L-shaped sofa that was nicknamed the "giving couch," because every family member's birthday celebration was held at their home, Mac turned to Grace and said,

"That is the epitome of the high road. No other newscaster could get away with that."

Grace reached over and removed his arm, which had been around her shoulders. "You are a bit too enamored with Jackie Mayfield," she said playfully, "and if I am ever the jilted lover, don't even think about me taking the high road."

* * *

Sitting up straight on the chaise, Sabine reached over to the adjacent small table and picked up her mint iced tea. She closed her eyes as she sipped it and let the sun kiss her face. She brought her chin to her chest. An ice cube that had been captured by her tongue rolled over her lips, began a slow descent down her chin, and dropped squarely between her naked breasts. She smiled as she picked up her iPad and read aloud:

"*60 Minutes* is the oldest and most watched news magazine on television. From its inception, the program has used a unique style of reporter-centered investigation. In 2002, the show was ranked sixth in *TV Guide's* ranking of the 50 greatest shows of all time. *The New York Times* called it 'One of the most esteemed news magazines on American television.'"

As Sabine read the description, she scoffed, "The *Times* accolade has the appearance of high praise, because the implication is that it is one out of hundreds. If they wanted to really own the network, they should have just said that *60 Minutes* is the *most* esteemed."

"Why engage in hyperbole when you already own the network?" asked Lyons in a droll manner.

"I love it when you talk in multi-syllabics," Sabine teased.

"The TV appearance is the fuse. The show is simulcast on several CBS radio stations. Audio versions sans commercials are distributed via podcast to iTunes. Streaming is available several hours after broadcast, and there is a *60 Minutes* mobile app. You know what happens next."

Sabine nodded. "Alegria takes social media to a new level."

Lyons was shirtless, his wheelchair tilted back, dark glasses shielding his eyes. Beads of sweat ran down his sculpted chest. The gulf breeze was sufficient to make the 90-degree Naples day tolerable, but not enough to make it pleasant.

Sabine leaned over and ran her hand lovingly down his right arm. " I know you're not, but I'm really nervous about this."

He turned to her, removing his glasses. "Why is that?"

"You are going into hostile territory. Fox would give you all the time you need, and you know they wouldn't do anything underhanded and try to trip you up."

"You are correct," he said. "What are your specific concerns?"

She threw up her hands. "What if they bribe a former client of yours to discuss the requirements for becoming one of your clients? What if someone exposes your surveillance protocols? What if someone testifies that your previous persuasion techniques were extreme? Let's face it, there are plenty of legitimate skeletons, and an adversarial network may not be above fabricating a few more."

Sabine felt his assuring nod was patronizing and amped up the volume. "Investigative reporters make their careers by exposing scandals. Are you sure you're comfortable with the risk?"

With his left hand, Jeremy caught her hand and squeezed it. "The only way to get acclimated to the fire is to step into the flames. I need the exposure," he said in a soft voice, "and I need the risk."

"You promise you have a contingency plan if things get ugly?" Her face showed her continuing worry.

"Always. Will it make you more comfortable if I take out a little insurance against the possibility of a nasty surprise?"

"Yes!" she said excitedly. "What is it?"

"Sorry, my dear, that's between me and the leader of the free world."

CHAPTER 62

OFTEN THE REASON THAT BATTLES are lost is not lack of preparation or because the opposition is better armed or trained. It is the lack of analysis around the "what ifs?" Where are the fault lines and the unanticipated weaknesses of the battle plan?

This is even more vital in the political arena, where one gaffe, one unlikely surprise can discredit a plan and marginalize the proposer. In the battleground of politics, it is necessary to diffuse potential unfriendly forces before combat.

"Mr. President, thank you for taking my call."

"Of course, Senator. My door is always open to you."

"That's very gracious of you, sir," Lyons said respectfully, "and I appreciate that we can talk on a secure line."

"After six and a half years in this office, I can pretty much tell when someone is going to waste my time or need an unlikely favor from me. I don't place you in either category."

Lyons knew that the president had used this line many times before; it had the feel of well-worn shoes. This statement would make most callers question their request, or at least knock them off balance. "You are correct, sir. There is just a situation where I believe it's important to give you a heads-up."

"I'm listening."

"As you are aware, I am being interviewed on *60 Minutes* this Sunday. I will have the opportunity to discuss a legislative agenda that you have previously advocated. As you have correctly maintained, it is an exercise in futility to try to get meaningful legislation through our dysfunctional congress."

"We do share common ground there," interjected the president with a polite chuckle. "However, I'm not sure where else we agree, Senator. I believe that you've been a pretty harsh critic of my health bill."

"Your intention was honorable, Mr. President; in fact, you accomplished what the Clintons could not." Lyons paused to let the flattery marinate. "On the other hand, the implementation and some of the unintended consequences were unfortunate. Therefore, the humanitarian positives of the concept have been tainted by the execution of the law. In my mind, the law needs to be sanded down, not blown up."

"So what is the specific issue you will discuss?" asked the president.

"Lowering the corporate tax rate."

"And you are seeking my endorsement?"

"No, sir. You were correct in your assertion that I was not seeking a favor. It will ultimately be up to you to determine the outcome of my proposal, and I just wanted to be sure that you were prepared."

"What specifically will you propose?"

"We are dealing with hypotheticals here, because I'm not sure that I will have the opportunity to be specific. I just want a discussion and hopefully to light a fire under a recalcitrant congress."

"Good luck with that."

"Sir, the only thing I would ask of you is that you not discuss our conversation with any of your advisors until after the program has aired."

Lyons's request was greeted with a purposeful silence. "Why is that important to you, Senator?"

"I would like to have an open dialogue with you, Mr. President. As an Independent and a one-term senator, I have no party obligations, so I need a forward thinker in my corner. If this rather harmless conversation remains confidential, it demonstrates to me that you respect my thoughts and that perhaps there will be items in your agenda for America that I could champion for you."

"So if play ball with you, then I can count on you in the future?"

Lyons smiled into the phone. Even though he was only asking that the president keep their conversation private, the man turned it around that he was doing him a favor. "That's a reasonable assurance, sir."

"Okay, good luck. If the response is positive, you'll remember my endorsing it."

"Of course, sir. Oh, one more thought. I've agreed that the reporters can ask me personal questions before I propose the agenda. You know those folks better than I do. Do you think they'd try to sabotage me?"

Lyons waited out the silence.

"I believe I can guarantee that they won't," said the president.

"Thank you, Mr. President. I appreciate your time."

CHAPTER 63

THE PRODUCERS OF *60 MINUTES* had not seriously considered interviewing Senator Jeremy Lyons in their studio in New York City. When you have the opportunity to film a segment in a billionaire's natural habitat, that becomes the only option. Lesley Simmons, a popular, seasoned reporter, had been chosen for this plum assignment.

The network had rebuffed lobbying from their prominent male anchor, believing that Lesley had the skills to make incisive, surgical cuts while flashing an "I'm sorry I have to do this" smile. The unspoken reason was that the optics of a man asking extremely uncomfortable questions to a disabled hero left more room for criticism.

Before anyone spoke, the camera danced a slow panorama of Lyons's great room and massive balcony. It was a Sunday evening, the Florida sun was shining brightly, a gentle ocean breeze flowed through the open doors with reverence, and it was prime time.

Lesley Simmons, in a light turquoise pants suit with a white shell underneath, began with the pleasantries. "Senator, it's so nice of you to invite us into your home." She looked around and smiled. "So this is how the rich and famous live."

Lyons returned the smile, as expected. "I am wealthy, Lesley, but as you know, fame is fleeting."

"I'm not so sure it is for you, Senator," she joked.

Eschewing his normal casual attire, Lyons wore a navy suit and starched white shirt, but no tie. "That probably depends on how invasive your interview is."

The reporter smiled, enjoying the banter. "You know we always treat our political leaders with kid gloves," she said. "Let me state the ground rules for our audience, and then we can begin the interview in earnest."

She turned to face the camera. "Normally, if *60 Minutes* is interviewing a politician other than the president, it is because of a misstep, a critical situation, or a scandal. In the case of Senator Lyons, it is none of the above. He called and asked us to give him the opportunity to present a legislative initiative to the public *before* he introduced it to congress. This is unprecedented.

"That in itself would likely have been sufficient to earn a segment on our show. However, we wanted more from our subject. This man has been shrouded in secrecy. He is a public servant, and we believe that our audience shares our curiosity about a man who by many is considered to be a hero. A man struck down in an attempted assassination, then sequestered in an unknown location, who woke from a coma just in time to become the first Independent senator from the state of Florida."

Lesley smiled coyly into the camera. "Maybe you already know the answers to these questions, but if not, stay with us after the break."

* * *

"Senator Lyons, tell us about your family."

"No siblings. My father was a brilliant scientist who was furious that I hadn't been aborted."

The reporter blinked.

"My mother tried to protect me, but she was powerless against his disdain and silence."

"Did he abuse you?" asked Lesley.

"Not unless you consider his never acknowledging my existence."

The finality of his statement caused her to shift slightly. "Is either of your parents still living?"

"No."

"What about your educational background?"

"After my mother died, my father sent me to Fork Union Military Academy in Virginia."

"And from there?"

"No further scholastic education. I graduated with high honors from the academy, and the proctors advised me to apply for a scholarship to college."

"Why didn't you?"

"I preferred an education in the real world. I concentrated on finance. I am a voracious reader. I also studied human behavior."

"So what did you do before you joined the brokerage firm of Johnston Wellons?"

"We can follow this path as long as you like, Lesley, but one of the reasons that I have not divulged my past is that it is uninteresting. High school graduates can't intern at brokerage firms, so I was a gopher at a couple of smaller firms, just trying to learn the language, and in most cases, learning what not to do."

"Okay, I might disagree that your background is uninteresting, but let's go in another direction. Senator, you were instrumental in stopping the manufacture of the deadly drug Euphoria and its distribution in our schools. In addition, it was your information that stopped a terrorist attack on the National Cathedral. Apparently you accomplished what our government could not."

"Your words, not mine, Lesley."

"Nevertheless, the results were extraordinary. If you don't mind, let's start with how you uncovered the source of the drug ring and notified the authorities."

"Of course, although it was probably more luck than skill. One of the advantages of wealth it that it affords access to information. My researchers are trained to look for anomalies in investments. As a result of their in-depth analyses, they may uncover irregular patterns or data that seem out of sync."

"It has to be more than happenstance. The DEA, CIA, FBI, none of these agencies was able to find where Euphoria was being manufactured."

"My computer experts are quite gifted," said Lyons. "As soon as we discovered the fatal side effects of this drug and that it was targeting our schools, we stopped everything else and focused on probabilities. As I said, we got lucky. I'm sure the authorities would have arrived at the same conclusions a day or two later."

She gave him a tight smile and pressed on. "One incredible discovery is remarkable, and I don't really buy that your researchers just stumbled on it."

"Then give me another scenario," said Lyons, interjecting and breaking her rhythm.

"I don't have one," she admitted, "but I'll give you a chance to make me a believer when you give me an explanation on how you broke up a terrorist plot."

"It's rather detailed, but I am happy to break it down for you. As you are aware, I managed money for high-profile individuals. One of those individuals was a congressman who had been acting strangely."

"Will you tell us who that was?"

"No. The identity of our clients remains sacrosanct."

"Even though you're no longer managing money for individuals?"

"Confidentiality does not have an expiration date. Our privacy agreements went both ways. If any clients mentioned that we were managing money for them, we would terminate the relationship."

Lesley cocked her head. "Wouldn't you want more clients, more money to manage? Why so secretive? That doesn't make sense."

"I can see where it could be confusing. Most money managers publish their track records, particularly when they beat their indices. Then new money pours into their coffers, and invariably results suffer. In managing money, often the more you have, the more difficult it is to outperform. Our methods were proprietary. If they had been revealed, we would have lost our competitive advantage. Consequently, we controlled every aspect of the relationships."

Lesley attacked. "Isn't it true that all of your clients were centers of influence? CEOs of public companies, influential politicians? Weren't there allegations that your methods involved squeezing information from your high-profile clients?"

"We sought individuals with means, and equally as important, discretion," Lyons answered evenly. "There were never any charges filed against us for using non-public information in our investment decisions." He sighed. "Any time someone has a superior record of success, it doesn't mean that they compromised their values. Lesley, you are aware that the SEC examined all of our records. Frankly, I'm surprised that you would rehash the baseless accusations."

"Senator, it's natural to want to know the secrets to your financial success," she said, reluctant to back down.

"In order to outperform the markets, you need to have a competitive edge. The three types of evaluation are informational, analytical, and behavioral. No one gathered more information; no one did a deeper dive into the fundamentals; and I continue to be an ardent student of human behavior."

Her pursed lips showed no signs of agreement.

Lyons considered adding another rebuke, but instead asked her a question. "Lesley, do you manage your own assets?"

"Senator, I'm not the one being interviewed."

Lyons smiled at her combativeness. "I was merely trying to determine your level of sophistication." He paused. "The best indicator of the future success of a company is the quality of its management. If we can determine that through a friendship, rather than observations of others, it is helpful in our decision making."

"So you did include only individuals who could help your results."

"That is posed much better as a question than a statement. It is an unsubstantiated leap. Besides, as I previously stated, our client list will never be public information. In retrospect, we obviously should have sent you an invitation to invest with us." The comment was playful and gave her no opening.

The camera panned to show Lyons looking straight ahead, but massaging his thighs with his hands.

Masking her frustration, Lesley said, "Sorry to get you off track, Senator. Let's get back to the near attack on the National Cathedral. So a congressman is acting strangely. How does that translate to his being involved in a terrorist plot?"

"A key provision of the confidentiality agreement that our clients signed with us was that we had the authority to monitor their behavior."

"Monitor? Like you were allowed to *spy* on them?" Her face was a combination of disbelief and outrage.

"That's correct," said Lyons.

"Why on earth would anyone submit to that?" Lesley asked. "And why would you want to spy on your investors?"

"The answer to the first question," replied Lyons in his easy, unruffled manner, "is that elite management has certain requirements for admittance. No one was coerced to invest with us; in fact, each new client not only had to sign the agreement, but their legal counsel also had to sign. The answer to your second question is that another essential condition was that our investors never divulge their relationship with our firm. In order to ensure compliance, surveillance was often necessary."

In spite of her experience, Lesley Simmons's mouth hung wide open. "I can't.... Folks, I don't know about you, but I need a commercial break. We'll be right back."

CHAPTER 64

A LITTLE MAKEUP ON HER cheeks, hair freshly brushed, Lesley had regained her composure. "I won't interrupt again, Senator. Please tell us how your investigation enabled you to uncover a terrorist plot."

"I think it was a combination of our due diligence, a suspicious nature, and mostly because of the grace of God. If someone you know — family, friend, or business associate — starts acting irrationally, the first thing you do is try to identify the cause. Is it illness, alcohol, drugs, sex? In this case, simple surveillance revealed that it was sex.

"The object of his affection was a woman with no apparent ties, no job, and no past. Again, this wouldn't be our concern, except that this particular congressman had access to top secret information. I can't be any more specific, but if he revealed classified information during pillow talk, it could be disastrous for our country. Fortunately, we determined her true identity and were able to alert the authorities before the plan could be executed."

Lesley had been hanging on every word. "Do we want to know how you discovered her true identity?" she asked.

"Technology opens many doors that were previously closed."

"Technology?" she said with heavy sarcasm. There was no question in her mind that they had tortured this information out of the woman. It was outrageous. "So you have no regrets about your process?" she asked with a bite.

He leaned towards her. "All I cared about was the protecting the lives of Christians on their high holy day."

Lesley nodded and gave him a tight shot. She was out of time and out of bullets. "Senator, we appreciate your candor in answering our questions. Now it's your turn. If you have legislation you want congress to pass, why would you not take the normal route and propose it on the senate floor?"

"Allow me to briefly review what happens to a bill in the senate," he began. "After the bill is introduced, it goes to committee. The committee votes if it should go further. If that action is taken, the majority leader then decides *when* the senate will consider the bill.

"The next step is debate; amendments may be added; then, finally, it may be sent to the house of representatives. No matter how much sense a proposed bill may make, amendments that are totally unrelated to the good of the nation are invariably tacked on. Lobbying, horse trading, bullying, bartering, all are part of the process of getting legislation passed. This process is antiquated, and patently unfair to the American people."

"But you won't be able to end-run that established legal process."

"Not yet," Lyons said with an innocent smile, "but I think I can expedite the process and, as a result, end up with a clean bill."

"Please explain," said Lesley with a welcoming arm wave.

"The real power in this country is not in the hallowed halls of the senate or the house. The real power is in the internet." Lyons held up his iPhone 6. "It's in your phone, on your tablet or your laptop, or on your wrist. It's time the people had a say in the way this country is run.

"I want to start with a proposition that the president has endorsed, as have the majority of Democrats and Republicans. However, in spite of this common belief, nothing has been done. Our corporate tax rate is the highest in the world. Rather than admonish companies that take jobs out of the United States because it saves them money, let's entice them to keep the jobs here. In fact, let's give these companies an incentive to bring jobs *back* to America.

"Even though the maximum rate is 39.4 per cent, the average tax paid by the richest corporations is only 13 per cent. Those corporations that can't afford the high-priced lawyers or accountants, well, they pay the maximum. Who are these companies? They are small businesses, the backbone of our country. Is that fair?"

Lyons waited to let the question sink in. He lowered his voice. "No more loopholes, no more benefits for the fat cats. Everybody pays 15 per cent. Real simple. It makes us competitive. Companies will want to do business here. Since 1986, we have lost over half of our corporations due to the combination of the world's highest tax rate and onerous, voluminous regulations. Lesley, I know that you are an advocate of leveling the playing field."

Not willing to agree with him, she simply acted as if he had not addressed her personally. "That's certainly a unique concept, Senator, but how does alerting the public to your intentions help you achieve your goal?"

"The 26th Amendment, granting the right to vote to 18-year-olds, took only three months and eight days to be ratified. Why? The people demanded it. Lesley, this was in 1971, before computers, email, or cell phones."

Lyons stared into the camera with a fierce intensity. "Tonight is the beginning. We are going to *unleash* the power of the people. I believe that social media will accept the challenge and make politicians listen. Our citizens deserve clean bills, without pork or special interest input.

"Today, every one of the 1.5 million small companies currently paying more than their fair share has a web page, a Facebook page, and a Twitter account. If one-tenth of these companies indicate what #oneflatrate would mean for their business, their families, and new jobs, then the outcome is assured. Your elected officials, your representatives may struggle to hear your individual voice. They can not deny your collective one."

Lyons reached into this coat pocket and brought out a single sheet of paper folded lengthwise. With his iPhone, he snapped a picture and touched a few buttons. "This is the bill that I will present to congress. If you go to my Instagram account, you can read it in its entirety."

Lesley tried to mask the fact that she had lost control of the interview as Lyons said, "If we can change the process, we can change the world."

* * *

Grace McGregor turned to face her husband, her blue eyes questioning. "Could he do that?"

"I thought you didn't like politics," teased Mac.

"I don't," she replied, wrinkling her nose, "and a good reason is that it is so complicated and so easily influenced by special interests."

"You hit the nail on the head. Lyons's idea to circumvent the process is unconventional, probably unconstitutional, and from anyone else, ridiculous. Lowering corporate taxes makes all the sense in the world, but he's right. The process takes forever, and special interest groups all want their pound of flesh."

"So nothing will happen?"

"I didn't say that. I've learned never to bet against Jeremy Lyons."

CHAPTER 65

MAC CLICKED THE TV ON in the kitchen as he was preparing his breakfast. "... started on the senator's feed. The '#oneflatrate' phenomenon has over 300 million mentions and climbing."

Mac placed the carton of organic skim milk on the counter and unlocked his iPad. Like hundreds of thousands of people this morning, his social media feeds were blanketed with comments and shares about Senator Lyons's historic proposal. *Now this feels pretty cool,* Mac thought to himself. *I've got no real claim of authorship, but it still feels like being a part of history.*

* * *

Alegria Lopez's legs were bouncing as she sat perched on the edge of her seat behind the bank of 4K screens. Her bare feet were tucked under the chair and nervously rubbed against each other. Cans of Red Bull stood like soldiers surrounded by the paper coverings of half-eaten energy bars. She had been glued to her post since initiating the onslaught at the end of Jeremy's interview.

She didn't hear the door open as Sabine entered the room.

"Impressive."

Several of the empty cans fell to the floor as Alegria whirled around toward the intrusion. Her face went white. "I .. I'm trying to slow it down. I was just trying to goose the numbers a bit, but it's out of my control."

"How can I help?" Sabine asked coolly.

"I shut down the bots, quit auto-liking the feeds, and I've completely cut off the click-farm activities."

"Click-farm?"

"Thousands of people in Indonesia that I contracted through a third party and paid to comment and share any of the mentions related to #oneflatrate and the bill. I just wanted to do my part in making this happen!"

"So what happened?"

"Honestly? I don't know. Even after I shut everything off, it keeps spreading like wildfire. It seems like people really want the change."

Sabine stared at the screens for a few minutes. She wasn't really interested in understanding the stream of information; she was just buying time to process. "Alegria, you know Jeremy thinks the world of you, and he would not be a senator without you. We have achieved a lot as a well-honed team. I need you to communicate with me before acting on something so important. We can't risk even the suspicion of voter manipulation."

"I completely understand," Alegria said, casting her eyes downward.

"This is new territory for everyone. Jeremy can run cover with some more press appearances. Best for you to step away and get some sleep."

CHAPTER 66

AVID READERS OF THE SUNDAY edition of *The New York Times* tend to be a fiercely loyal group. Liberal fodder emanating from this venerable newspaper is like chum to sharks for these aficionados. It is often ritualistic and a source of pride to devour the sacred words over coffee.

Yet on this Sunday morning, the gentleman unwrapping the newspaper with the reverence usually reserved for a fine Cuban cigar was the antithesis of the normal reader. Eli Steiner despised *The New York Times*. To him, the *Times* was the poster child for liberal ideology, bulletproofed by a likeminded Socialist president.

Steiner went immediately to Seth Goldfarb's column. Entitled "Pick a Card, Any Card," the article was a predictable rant about the glaring lack of any redeeming qualities among the numerous announced candidates for the presidency. Accordingly, the bulk of the article was not on Steiner's approved reading list. It wasn't until the last paragraph that his frown turned upside down. He read that paragraph with the excitement that he experienced when he first opened a *Playboy* magazine. He read the words slowly, savoring the criticism. Then he read them again.

Just so my faithful readers don't label me as anti-Republican, I will offer sound advice to the winner of the "who is the most fanatical" scrum. If the Republican candidate wants any chance against an experienced, proven political servant like Jean Carlyle, he or she needs to hire the perfect campaign manager. Who better than the most confident man in politics? Jeremy Lyons could fund the campaign out of pocket change, and if recent history is a guide, somehow convince every citizen to vote... at least once.

Remember, whenever this snake-oil senator doesn't like the rules of law, why, he'll just change the playing field.

The Ritz-Carlton on 23rd Street in Washington, D.C., served as Eli Steiner's home and office. He had combined a four-bedroom, four-bath condominium with a three-bedroom, three-bath one to give him over six thousand square feet. A designer had helped configure the rooms to his specifications so that his office did not resemble a bedroom. When Steiner was in town, both his secretary and his chef lived in the residence. To avoid unnecessary complications, the two attractive young women were a lesbian couple. The Ritz-Carlton staff obviated Steiner's need for security, and because they were generously compensated, the staff provided him with any services he might require.

This Sunday Steiner was alone. He'd just finished his breakfast when the doorbell rang. Annoyed, he looked up from the paper. Although he had not issued a "Do Not Disturb" notice, it had to be either someone in his employ or someone on the hotel staff.

He frowned, pushed the paper aside, pulled his scarlet silk bathrobe around himself, and walked to the door. Not thinking clearly, he unlocked the chain and opened the door about six inches.

"Who the hell are you?" he demanded, wrinkling his face in undisguised distaste.

The man at the door looked to be at least 80. Thin, white hair curled around his ears. His bloodshot eyes and red-veined nose made him look like a homeless drunk. His dark suit was wrinkled and two sizes too big for his hunched-over body. "I have priceless art," the old man whispered.

"I don't care if you have a Rembrandt. Make an appointment."

As Steiner moved to close the door, it was slammed back into his face. With a cry, he fell back onto the hardwood floor, and blood erupted from his nose. Steiner's eyes went wide as his hands flew to his face.

"You must learn to be more hospitable," said the man in a dispassionate voice as he closed and locked the door. The contradiction between the aged face and the firm demeanor was predictably frightening. He reached into his pocket and pulled out a roll of duct tape. "Must I?" he asked.

Steiner shook his head frantically, blood now spewing through his fingers.

"Okay. Then let's have a civilized conversation." The old man, now standing perfectly erect, grabbed Steiner by the back of his robe and dragged him over to the kitchen table. With one hand, he lifted him and sat him down on the same chair from which Steiner had earlier eaten his breakfast.

"Did you save me some breakfast?" the man asked the terrified Steiner. "I'm a tad hungry, and violence makes me ravenous."

"How did you...?" blubbered Steiner, his tears now mixing with the blood.

"Why am I always asked that question: 'How did you get in here?' How did I convince the Ritz to allow me to come upstairs unannounced? Okay. That one I'll answer." The old man reached into his pocket and pulled out his driver's license: Abraham Steiner. He threw out his arms. "Happy birthday, son!"

The stranger laughed at Steiner's stricken face while he pulled a dish towel off the rack and tossed it to the bleeding man. "Hold your head back and press this to your nose," he commanded. "If there's a need to talk to me, you may call me James."

He reached over and picked up the newspaper, still open to the Seth Goldfarb column. "What we have here is a failure to communicate."

When Steiner gave him a confused look, James shook his head in dismay. "Okay," he said. "I'll add a visual aid." In one motion, he grabbed Steiner's left hand and wrenched his index finger back until it snapped.

"Ooow!" wailed the shocked victim. Steiner's eyes rolled back in his head, and James slapped him to prevent him from fainting. As Steiner's anguished cries intensified, James jammed the dish towel over his mouth.

"I know your home is soundproof, but I'll bind and gag you just for the fun of it if you're not super quiet."

Steiner's eyes pleaded compliance as his mouth held the dish towel like a golden retriever with a prize.

"Take that out of your mouth, hold it under your nose, and give me your other hand," James commanded.

Steiner began to wail, "No, no, no!" Then he scooched his chair back.

"I'm not going to hurt you anymore, Eli. You'd have to really be dense not to have gotten the message. Now, come back to the table."

Slowly, tentatively, Steiner maneuvered the chair back to the table. When James took his trembling right hand, he held it gently. "Raise your index finger, please."

Steiner's head was shaking, and the look of terror in his eyes made it appear that he was teetering on the edge of sanity. James tapped Steiner's index finger on Seth Goldfarb's column. "This man would not have written that last paragraph without an inducement. Don't try to deny it." He took Steiner's finger and wagged it at him.

James released Steiner's hand and sat back. "I don't know what to do with you," he said, cocking his head left, then right. "One option is to assume for the second time that you got the message. I wasn't *told* you were dense." He continued to scrutinize the sniffling man.

"You can't be half pregnant, Eli. It's like Texas Hold 'Em. You either go all in or you fold; those are your only choices. You can't act like you're with the program and then hire a verbal assassin to slander it. If you want to be part of the new order, you need to use your money and your influence to help us. Is that so hard?" he asked.

"No, no!" said Steiner.

"Well, the other option," James continued, "is to sever the relationship. Some of the team think that might be the safest route with you," he added in a reluctant voice. "Though it might get messy, and I'd hate to think your estate plan wasn't in order."

"No, please!"

"I must admit that it was pretty ingenuous of you to pimp a dyed-in-the-wool liberal to do your dirty work. I mean, you being on the farthest feather of the right wing and all," mused James. "Maybe you're too smart for us," His look of contemplation caused Steiner's eyeballs to dart around like they were pinballs.

"You could turn into a real liability. Maybe we should just –"

WHAM! James's hand came down on the table with such force that the wood cracked. "— cut it off right here," he whispered.

Steiner stumbled onto the floor and got on his knees. He clasped his good hand and the one with the bent finger together as if in prayer.

"Ah, Eli," said James as he reached over and tousled the man's thin, black comb-over. "I'm always a sucker for God."

James got up, walked to the door, and then turned back to the trembling, beaten wreck of a man. "Just so we're clear: One more misstep, and you'll need all three — the Father, the Son *and* the Holy Ghost — to save your sorry ass."

CHAPTER 67

Tuesday, March 17, 9:00 a.m.

R.J. BROOKS APPROACHED HIS SENIOR partner's desk brandishing a copy of *The Washington Post*. Holding out the paper for Mac to see, he raised and lowered his eyebrows. "Is there a ghost writer in the house?" he asked. Now both hands held the paper open to Tom Hessel's column.

"Do you think that I would opine on anything without prior approval of our compliance department?" asked Mac.

"You invented the concept of begging for forgiveness," replied R.J.

"I do have to admit," said Mac with a sense of wonder, "that my boy Hessel is not only a brilliant writer and a celebrated columnist, but also an unequaled political analyst. If I ever doubted Lyons's powers of persuasion," he pointed to the column, "the fact that he's converted Hessel solidifies it."

"That answers the rhetorical question. Are you following the social media avalanche on this?"

"Not as much as you, I'm sure. Fill me in."

"Just like Lyons predicted, #oneflatrate is blowing up. The bandwagon is overflowing with supporters. Small corporations see this as a path to fairness; individuals are sharing stories about how the high corporate tax and excessive regulations put them out of business; and companies are pledging jobs if the bill is enacted *in its original form.*"

"He couldn't have scripted this any better," said Mac thoughtfully.

"*The Journal* floated an interesting idea that a media spotlight should shine on any attempt to insert a special interest provision into any bill," said R.J. He read farther. "The best way to stop legislative perversion is to make sure the public is aware of it. It was not the first time that readers had been advised to visit the website, Openthebooks.com. Their slogan was, 'Join the transparency revolution.'"

Mac nodded, agreeing with their conclusions.

"A website has popped up with totals on the pledge information," added R.J.

Silence between the two friends was rarely awkward. In this case, both were contemplating the ramifications of this information. R..J spoke first. "If this actually works..."

"We could actually have a government for the people, by the people," said Mac. "Getting people engaged, fired up about positive changes in the economy is better than sex."

"Maybe at *your* age..."

The shot bounced harmlessly off Mac as he continued his thought pattern. "Why couldn't the same strategy be used..."

CHAPTER 68

"L<small>IVE IN</small> 3-2-1…" V<small>ETERAN CAMERAMAN</small> Eddie Richter couldn't hide his enthusiasm as he counted down the numbers.

"Senator, we're delighted to have you back with us." Jackie Mayfield, Fox News's top-ranked news anchor, exhibited only slightly less enthusiasm.

"Does absence truly make the heart grow fonder?" Jeremy Lyons asked with a wry smile.

She laughed. "Nothing could make us love you more. But it's no fair charming me. I have some serious questions to ask you."

"I promise to be responsive and droll."

"So here's what everyone's talking about. Both the pundits and the computer experts were astonished at how your sites received 150 million responses in the first hour!"

"Were they astonished, Jackie, or skeptical?"

"Both. The numbers seemed unreal! It was like everyone who responded thought they had a shot at the mega lottery."

"I believe that if congress passes the bill to reduce the corporate tax, then the economy may feel like it won the lottery."

It was a clever response, but Jackie wasn't going to let it go. "There are approximately 320 million United States citizens. Yet at last count, you had over 290 million hits on the five links designated to support your proposal to lower the corporate tax rate." She threw her hands in the air. "What gives?"

Lyons waited a few moments before responding. Jackie's inquisitive look and frozen, tight smile did not falter. "People outside of the United States were also affected by the high rate. We all know small businesses that are not owned by U.S. citizens, so global support is not unusual when we consider that fact. It's not surprising that the rallying cry for equality has been universal."

"Still, it is amazing that so many people seem to *care* about this issue. It's like more people are interested in this legislation than in the Super Bowl. Can you explain how this groundswell happened?"

"There could be a number of reasons," said Lyons. "First: the Super Bowl is almost eleven months away. Second: it may be that their March Madness bracket is already busted."

He waited until her infectious laugh subsided.

"Third: don't you think that people are tired of the status quo? Not too long ago, Everett Leeds, the former senate majority leader, commented that when *U.S. News and World Report* issued its annual ranking of the top 'porkers'"... He paused to let the phrase resonate. "He was upset that *he* wasn't in the top three. Apparently, he thought it was amusing to put one over on the American people. I think that our citizens agree that it's time for congress to pass legislation that benefits the country, not just one state, one city, or one county."

Jackie had been listening intently. "So what is your next step, Senator?"

"Congress should have heard the will of the people. Our job is to serve the people. The next step is to introduce the bill in the house of representatives. My friend, Congressman Floyd Caldwell, has volunteered to lead the charge."

"And you really think this will work? The house and senate will follow your lead?"

Lyons shook his head from side to side. "No. They will follow the people's lead. Millions of concerned citizens have spoken. Much has been written about dysfunction and the partisan factions. Gridlock has been the rule rather than the exception. But just as no nation should ever underestimate America's resolve, we should have confidence that our elected officials will do the right thing."

"And if they don't?"

Lyons shrugged. "Then we need new leaders. This bill will put more people to work in better jobs It will restore our competitiveness in the world."

"Will your name be on the legislation?"

"No. I am a one-term senator. I am not seeking glory. I just want to make our country better."

"Last question, Senator. How many hits will you get before the bill is introduced?"

"The sites will be taken down at the conclusion of this show. Our legislators have gotten the message. Any more would be redundant and a distraction. I have every confidence in our elected officials."

Jackie turned to face the camera. "Ladies and gentlemen, Fox News is pleased to have had the opportunity to broadcast this special discussion with Senator Jeremy Lyons. We will return you now to your regular programming."

* * *

It was later that day that Russell Tomlinson had a reason to approach his boss without being summoned.

Everett Leeds was sitting behind his desk, his shirt unbuttoned at the collar, and his tie askew. His socked feet were on the desk. He had a shot glass in his hand full of 20-year-old scotch, and his eyes looked like it was not his first. It was four o'clock in the afternoon. "What the hell do you want?" growled Leeds. "Can't you see I'm busy?"

"Sir, I have an email for you." Tomlinson held out a piece of paper.

Leeds shook his head in disgust. "*Before* you give me this earth-shattering information, let me ask you a question. Why is this country in the shitter?"

Tomlinson was too seasoned to venture a guess.

"I'll tell you. When upstart, know-nothing senators can propose a bill on the damn television, and the dumb-ass public pound their cell phones like they were a piece of sweet ass, we are teetering on the edge of sanity." He narrowed his eyes and glared at his chief of staff. "Do you know how a bill is enacted and becomes law?"

"Yes, yes sir," said Tomlinson quickly.

Leeds nodded. "How many of those dumb sons-of-bitches who tweeted how much they *loved* Lyons's proposals know that?"

This time the senator expected an answer. "Probably very few, sir."

"No shit." Leeds took another swallow of his drink and swished it around in his mouth.

Remembering why Tomlinson was there, Leeds said, "Well, if it's so damn important, read it to me."

"It says, 'Support the corporate tax bill.'"

Leeds barked out a harsh laugh. "*That's* the news-flash, all-important email?"

"Sir, it's not what the email says, it's who sent it that's important. It came from someone calling himself 'Resisting Temptation.'"

"Who the fuck is that?"

"Sir, I believe it is from the man you're looking for."

Leeds furrowed his brow and sat up in the chair. "How did you arrive at that conclusion, genius?"

"Sir, the sender was untraceable."

Leeds leaned back and downed the last of his drink. He held his glass out. "Fill me up, boy."

Tomlinson hurried over and poured him another shot.

Leeds chewed over this information and then his face broke into a grin. "Amateurs, boy; I'm dealing with amateurs. No way this clown could be connected with Lyons. I'm a shadow warrior. I work behind the scenes. No one will know whether I support a bill or kill it. Besides, if Lyons was behind this, he'd know that nobody has the balls to go against the corporate tax cut after," he raised his sausage-like fingers and made quote signs, "the people have spoken."

Leeds let out a rolling burp. "You know what happens if you piss off the people, boy? All of a sudden you end up working for a living."

CHAPTER 69

Good Friday: 7:00 a.m.

WEATHER FORECASTS DETERMINE MOVEMENT FOR beach bums, particularly when the New York Stock Exchange is closed the next day. The McGregors left their Potomac home at seven o'clock the night before, after a quick dinner. Sunny and 60 degrees made the decision easy. They were in Bethany Beach shortly before ten.

At 6:55 Mac McGregor's mental alarm woke him. He slipped out of bed, grabbed his jeans, threw on a Maryland Terps sweatshirt, and left the bedroom. Before he opened the door to the lower level to head outside, he slipped into flip flops and secured his "Life Is Good" hat on his head.

Now he stood transfixed, facing the ocean. At seven in the morning, it was about 20 degrees shy of 60, but uncharacteristically, Mac didn't seem to notice. He was at church, and the service had begun.

The clouds on the horizon seemed to create a formidable barrier. The air was salty and tingly, as if it held great expectations. To the north, towards Dewey Beach and Rehoboth, scattered dog walkers allowed their unleashed canines the freedom of the morning. To the south, towards Fenwick Island and Ocean City, only a solitary couple sat on a blanket holding hands. Mac felt a flush of envy.

Grace would have joined him if he'd awakened her. But on this morning, he sought solitude. Mac thought of one of his favorite psalms: "Be still and know that I am God."

The first sign of illumination backlit the wall of clouds. Ever so slightly, the rheostat brightened. Twin streams of light, the consistency of a rainbow, reached for the sky. A gentle path escaped from beneath the clouds, forming stepping stones of light across the blue-green water. The path stopped, beckoning, right in front of Mac.

His eyes went back to the horizon as the streams of golden light from the top of the clouds stretched out like the opening arms of a child. The sun seemed to struggle to break the bondage of the tenacious clouds. On this sacred day, every feeling, every sensation was amplified by Mac's thoughts of the cross. As if drawn by a dark magic marker, an outline traced around the clouds. Mac let the crisp air fill his lungs. The sun began its inevitable ascent.

Almost defiantly, the sun continued its climb. As it shook off the shackles from the clouds and rose to the crystal blue sky, there was a sense of triumph. Mac's hand shielded his eyes. Then he closed his eyes and prayed. When he opened them, the clouds, like the Roman soldiers who tried so hard to discredit Jesus, had disappeared.

* * *

Mac heard the sliding glass door open, but he continued reading the *Washington Post*'s predictions of the upcoming NFL draft. When Grace smacked his shoulder, he turned around.

"Hey, child abuse!"

"Why didn't you wake me?" she asked as she sat on the adjacent white deck chair. She took a sip of her coffee as she awaited his response.

"You looked so angelic…" This was followed by his puppy dog look.

"You were just afraid I'd be yapping and distract you."

"How could you ever think that?" he asked with wide-eyed innocence. Wanting to change the subject, he asked, "Did you bring me something to drink?"

"Nope. It's obviously every man for himself today. Besides, you looked so angelic on your iPad."

Mac laughed and reached over for her hand. His eyes went between the houses in front of them to gaze at the ocean. "God had been very good to us, baby," he said quietly.

Grace squeezed his hand. "*Especially* to you," she said with a smile.

"Okay, genius, how did he do it?" Grace challenged. Mac was still planted on their deck. She handed him a cup of green tea with lemon.

He didn't need to ask who *he* was.

"And don't tell me you haven't thought about it or figured it out. Or maybe Lyons told you the big secret and you don't want to share. It's a *big* secret." Grace continued like she was talking to herself. "I can't believe I just asked you that. I wasn't going to give you the satisfaction of being interested and then have you give me that know-it-all look. So, consider this a warning. What's the answer?"

"Thanks for the tea." Mac stared out at the ocean. He wanted to wait a few minutes before answering, but he wasn't that brave. "You're half right. I have thought about how a zillion people apparently care about lowering corporate taxes. Unless the majority of respondents somehow think they are corporations, or that if these taxes are lowered then their taxes are next, the response was amazing. It is possible that if Lyons proposed mandatory celibacy it would pass, but you're right, the results are not logical. Even more intriguing to me, voting kept increasing until Lyons told them to stop voting."

Mac ran his hand through his uncombed hair. He looked over at Grace, and with his left hand took hold of hers. Raising three fingers of his right hand, he said, "About *how* he did it? Boy Scouts' honor, honey, I've got no frigging idea."

CHAPTER 70

THE TOP OF THE RECTANGULAR conference table in Mac McGregor's office is less than one inch thick. A frequently Windexed glass plate covers the black wood. Two sets of rubber coasters are positioned equidistant between the head of the table and the foot so that coffee cups or water glasses don't leave a mark. Six black leather office chairs with height adjustments surround the table, while the wall holds pictures of iconic clients who have agreed to be on display. To some, a brag wall is tacky; to Mac, who never calls attention to it, it is money.

The room serves many purposes. Mostly, it is a place where prospects tell their stories, and listening advisors formulate a strategy to help them realize their goals and dreams. Clients may meet in this room or the larger one, depending upon availability, but the new ones start in the showcase. In truth, the psychological advantage of smiling poses with celebrities has diminished over the years. Today, everything you always wanted to know is revealed on Google.

The conference room also works as a small lunch room for days when Mac needs to just fuel up and go. Another team member may use that time for a hopefully uninterrupted one on one. Finally, this room serves as a private place to discuss problems, new strategies, or minor subjects such as world peace.

On this hot summer day in June, Mac's thoughts were interrupted by his favorite sparring partner.

The Fair Corporate Tax bill passed both houses and was signed into law by the president in a record 37 days. Arguments had been few and simply cautionary about how this action could increase the national debt. The overwhelming response from social media, plus the fact that this would make it easier to punish the corporations who refused to bring facilities back to the U.S., made it an easy call.

Senator Lyons had tweeted his thanks to the people and to the White House for their unwavering support.

"Do you know what muted any protests over the way the Fair Corporate Tax bill was, as one reporter said, 'rammed through Congress'?" asked R.J. Brooks as he entered the conference room.

"Am I supposed to speculate or just wait until I hear your brilliant conclusion?" Mac countered..

For the uninitiated, this sort of male interplay is akin to tossing a football back and forth. In this case, R.J. asks a thoughtful question, obviously feeling that he has something to add. Without premeditation, his senior partner volleys it back with a thin coat of sarcasm. It's just another day in the financial trenches.

R.J. responded in his very patient voice. "I have not discovered a cure for cancer. I am simply reflecting on the futility of anyone complaining about the bill. I thought it might be an interesting conversation and possibly, as you are Lyons's love interest, you might have another take on it."

"You do remember that this is one of the ideas that we sent him. Our ideas were not required to be original. In fact, this idea was pilfered from our favorite conservative think tank. But maybe, just maybe reiterating the idea and reinforcing the logic contributed to the fact that this was Lyons's first initiative."

"Hmm. In that case, we should have insisted on naming rights."

Mac shook his head. *"Dumb and Dumber* has already been copyrighted. Okay, I'll bite. Why can't people complain that the rich just got another break?"

"The stock market is up eight per cent since it was announced. Unemployment has gone from 5.4 per cent to slightly under five per cent. The only ones pissed are the lawyers and accountants, and everyone likes it when they are angry."

"Okay, consider me enlightened. I didn't think about all those tax breaks keeping our attorney friends in thousand-dollar suits."

"Now that you have confirmed my thinking, I need to bring up another topic. It is juicy, so I will bring a bribe," said R.J. Raising a finger, he got up from his chair and walked out of the room.

As he got to the doorway, Mac said, "You do know the way to my heart."

A minute later R.J. returned with a small Tupperware container full of local blueberries. He held them out to Mac with a flourish. "It is after four, and you need some sustenance to answer my question."

"Thanks," said Mac as he gratefully picked up the container.

R.J. sat back down and then gave Mac his serious look. "So, there are no secrets between us, right?"

"Wrong," said Mac as he popped a blueberry into his mouth.

"Let me rephrase. When it comes to business opportunities, we share everything."

"I'll buy that." Mac tossed a blueberry in the air, moved his mouth under it, and caught it. "Ta-Da!"

"My gift should grant me your undivided attention," R.J. admonished.

Mac eye-rolled a response. "Okay, okay."

"Is Jeremy Lyons running for president?"

Mac coughed. A blueberry was halfway down. He grabbed his water bottle and swallowed quickly. "Where did that come from?"

"No deflections, verbal thrusts, or parries. Will the witness please answer the question."

"How would the answer affect our business?" asked Mac.

"I wouldn't take any money off the table if it's true. As it is, I was considering rebalancing some accounts, but if Lyons is running, I believe that would be a positive for stocks."

Even though Mac knew that the privileged information would be 100% secure with R.J., there is a risk when you share information with a partner that you won't share with your wife. Mac thought about his answer as he finished the blueberries.

R.J. spoke into the silence. "I would appreciate knowing the answer and whether it's inferred or actual. It's not fair that I'm involved in the uncomfortable episodes of your relationship with Lyons and not privy to the positive ramifications."

"You're right," admitted Mac as he leaned forward. He lowered his voice. "Right in your reasoning and your assumption. This can absolutely go no further."

R.J. let out a breath. "Are you okay with this?"

"Not my call, obviously, and I'll deny it under oath. But I think that Jeremy Lyons may be the *only* chance for our country."

CHAPTER 71

A SECRET IS A BOILING cauldron. More tempting than a seductress, more potent than the strongest aphrodisiac. No matter how well intentioned, the locks on the vault of a precious secret are flimsy. Eve took the apple; Pandora opened the box.

The power that comes from knowing the secret is fleeting. When it is revealed, if no one knows you knew the secret, it is worthless. So the dance begins with a knowing look. The next step might be an innocent shrug, a smug smile, or an unconvincing denial. Perhaps the lock remains in place, but others know that you hold the key. Enticing the two most powerful positions in congress with the secret that would change history would go a long way toward gaining their trust.

The United States Capitol building is located at the eastern end of the National Mall, and it is among the most architecturally impressive and important buildings in the world. The design was selected by George Washington in 1793. The capitol has been built, burnt, rebuilt, extended, and restored. It stands not only as a monument to its builders, but also to the American people and their government.

The building is divided into five levels. The second floor holds the chambers of the house of representatives and the senate, as well as the offices of the congressional leaders.

Based on the venerable political practice of rock, paper, scissors, a much more prestigious method than a coin flip, the venue was determined. The two most powerful Republicans in congress sat around a small, dark-wood conference table in House Speaker John Breedlove's private office. Rather reluctantly, Breedlove and his senate counterpart, J. Randolph Hunter, had agreed to meet with New Jersey Governor Mary Beth Justice at 2:00 p.m.

"Tell me again why we're doing this, John," said the recently appointed senate majority leader, who was still heady over the honor. Hunter was a staunch conservative, who easily wrapped himself in the cloak of a moderate on the rare occasions when it was required. The 64-year-old four-term Kentucky senator had been helped by his physical resemblance to the Kennedys and his ample supply of Southern charm. An attorney and former NCAA basketball star for his beloved Kentucky Wildcats, he kept his body as strong as his mind.

Breedlove, who looked like a college professor and was respected for his precise, logical explanations, leaned across the table and spoke in a low voice. "Because she's hot."

Hunter barked out a laugh. "That's sure as hell the way it used to be around here." His tone turned serious. "I hope she's not going to throw her hat in the ring."

"That would be awkward," said Breedlove, as he took a sip of his fourth cup of specially brewed coffee. "Even a battered Carlyle would demolish her."

"She does have some skills," mused Hunter. "She's kicked some ass in New Jersey, and she is quick witted and photogenic."

"Way too early," said Breedlove. "Plus, when it's woman versus woman, experience will always win. She might be a viable candidate in the future."

"I would have no problem getting *behind* her."

Now it was Breedlove who laughed. "We did vet her in 2012," he said thoughtfully, "and there were no major skeletons."

* * *

At precisely 2:00 p.m., Governor Justice was ushered into Breedlove's conference room. She was dressed in a navy pants suit with a white blouse, and her pearl earrings coordinated perfectly with her matching necklace. The woman was indeed striking.

The two men simultaneously pushed their chairs back and stood. Justice smiled with amusement at the discordant screeches of their chairs on the hardwood floor.   "Gentlemen," she said holding out her hand.

Breedlove took her hand in both of his. "Welcome, Mary Beth."

Hunter flashed his almost still boyish smile and stepped inside her outstretched hand.   "Kentuckians know it's a sin to shake hands with a beautiful woman," he said as he gave her a quick embrace.

Justice raised an eyebrow. "Did you learn that from the vice president?" she asked with teasing smile.

"No, no ma'am."   Hunter raised his hands and backed away quickly. "I'll be good."

"I'm sure you always are, Senator," she added a soft laugh.

"Please have a seat, Governor." Breedlove held out a black captain's chair and motioned for her to sit across from them.

As she took her seat, Justice said, "Thank you, and I do appreciate you gentlemen giving me a few minutes of your time." She paused, took a breath, and seemed to weigh what she would say next. "I must have your assurance that this conversation is off the record."

"Of course," said Breedlove dismissively.

Justice lowered her voice, and her eyes flashed. "I'm as serious as a heart attack.   No mention to your staff, other legislators, your spouse, or your mistress." She looked directly at Senator Hunter.

"Now wait a minute!" blustered Hunter.

"Would you like pictures, Senator?" she asked.   Her face was humorless.

The color that had risen in Hunter's cheeks started to pale. He sat back in his chair. He was pissed, but pragmatic.

"I need to ensure a cone of silence. If the information we discuss is leaked, it can only come from one of you. Then it would be out of my hands."

"Governor, that almost sounds like a threat," said Breedlove, his tone measured.

"I would rather have you think of it this way: After our conversation, you will both be privy to top secret information. Any breach of that could be detrimental to our country. I'm merely appealing to your patriotism."

The country's two most powerful politicians outside of the president exchanged glances. They knew that they were being hustled, but they were curious. Their faces remained stern, but they were willing to give this upstart woman some rope.

"Please enlighten us, Governor," said Breedlove, with an undercurrent of steel in his voice..

"Thank you. If the election were held today and you could choose any Republican candidate, could he or she beat Jean Carlyle?"

Both men were silent.

"I know the question is rhetorical. That's why I'm here. We have a year and a half before the election. Each candidate thinks he or she can unite the warring factions. They are all wrong. Do you disagree?"

Again, she received no response.

"We are running out of time to restore our country as a superpower. The morale of our troops is in the toilet. And I know it's not a news flash to our party, but America is bankrupt."

"We know that, Governor. We don't need a civics lesson," said Hunter impatiently.

Justice nodded and waited for a long moment. "Why don't you tell me what you do need, gentlemen, because unless I'm missing something, you have jack shit."

Hunter led out an insulting snort. "The reason we're in office is because we know how screwed up our country is. If you have some answers, we'd love to hear them. Otherwise, I don't know why the hell you're here." He folded his arms across his chest.

"I have two words for you . . . Jeremy Lyons."

"That's preposterous!" said Hunter. "He's not even a Republican."

"You already admitted that no Republican can beat Carlyle," Justice shot back. "Where is the corporate tax rate now? How many hits did Lyons get on social media?" She threw her hands in the air. "Who has the highest approval ratings of any politician in America? You don't take a dump without checking the polls."

"Now just a minute!" exclaimed Hunter, starting to rise.

Breedlove held out a placating hand. "We are speaking freely, so 'esteemed colleagues' is not necessary. However, it is also not necessary to insult us to make your point."

"I apologize."

"We seem to do that a lot in our party," said Breedlove with a forgiving smile. "But there are numerous, perhaps irreconcilable, differences between our platforms and beliefs and those of Senator Lyons."

"Desperate times call for desperate measures," said Justice quietly. "Without a fiscal conservative in the White House, our party is doomed. The demographics will kill us. The far right will never get the Hispanic vote, or the African-America vote, or sadly, even the youth vote."

"So you're suggesting that since the Republicans have *no* nominee, we all get in line and support an Independent candidate?" asked Breedlove. "That would set a terrible precedent."

"Or," Justice countered, "it could demonstrate that we are the party of compromise. Our legitimate candidates step down for the good of the country."

The politicians chewed on her answer.

"Who would be the veep?" asked Hunter.

"I would."

Breedlove looked to his senate counterpart. Hunter's face was skeptical, but not dismissive. "It might work," said Breedlove.

Justice pounced. "It will work. Lyons will stay for only one term. He won't care if he is popular. He also won't care if I publically disagree with him on issues that are important to our party. After losing for the second time, Carlyle won't run again." She flashed them a dazzling smile. "With your support, in 2020 I can win the presidency, and the decades old 'war on women' bullshit will be put to rest."

The lure was dancing in front of their eyes. All she needed was for them to take the bait. "I've saved the best for last," Justice said seductively. "Lyons won't need any of *our* money."

CHAPTER 72

SPRINGTIME IS A VALID REASON to never leave the Washington metropolitan area. The often unpredictable, but rarely disappointing, glorious cherry blossoms that line the streets, the preening red, pink, and white azalea bushes, and the delicate purity of the white dogwood flowers still took Washington native Mac McGregor's breath away.

As he walked the familiar path from his Pennsylvania Avenue office to the Hay Adams Hotel, his mind wandered to his mysterious breakfast companion. All of nature's scenery seemed to be beckoning, but instead of submitting to its lure, Mac focused on the strangeness of the call he had received. A woman with a slight accent had spoken with Lena Brady.

Her name was Simone LeGrand, and there was no profile on Google. Quoting a recent *Barron's* article, she said that she was sure she wanted to visit with Mac. In cases where a prospect does not come from a referral, normal procedure is always to schedule a meeting in the office. Lena had given that her best shot, but the woman insisted on a breakfast meeting.

For three reasons, Mac had agreed to the meeting without any information that could be confirmed. First, the woman had mentioned that she represented a ten-figure account. Second, the Hay Adams was a regular spot for client meetings for him. Third, the woman was buying.

Mac smiled as the doorman opened the door and greeted him. "Welcome back, Mr. McGregor."

"Thanks, Felix. Are you well and continuing to break women's hearts?"

"Yes, sir," came the enthusiastic reply.

Mac turned left and walked up the few stairs to the dining area. "Hi," he said to the hostess. "I'm about ten minutes early, but I'm expecting a Ms. Simone LeGrand to join me. Could you show her to my table?"

"She's already arrived, Mr. McGregor. Please follow me."

Eager, that's a good sign, thought Mac.

The woman sitting at the discreet corner table rose and gave him a dazzling smile.

Mac's feet stopped like he had walked into wet cement. The puppeteer pulled the string, and his mouth gaped open. She was a memory he couldn't repress, and his bitterness almost consumed him. On a cold morning last year, she had been running toward him on the canal. Purposefully, she slammed into him, knocked him to the ground, kicked him in the ribs, and then left. The threat had been delivered in a convincing manner.

"Mac, please come join me," she said motioning him to an adjacent chair.

Dumbfounded, he stepped tentatively forward and sat across from her.

"May I get you something to drink?" asked the waiter who had magically appeared.

In a voice a few octaves higher than usual, Mac replied, "Uh, I'll have an iced tea."

When the waiter left, Mac continued to stare. The woman's smile was hopeful, but fearful.

Regaining a semblance of composure, Mac said, "By the way, I'm not staring at your breasts." That had been the excuse she gave for attacking him.

Her head flinched like she'd been slapped. She said, "I know."

In a clipped tone, he added, "I wasn't being disrespectful to you on the canal, either."

Her face registered more pain. "I know that also. I'm so sorry." She reached her hands across the table, and he pulled back like she was contagious.

"Is Simone LeGrand your real name?" he asked

"No. I am Sabine."

"Only one name. Like Madonna or Cher?"

"Yes, except I am not famous. I never knew my parents."

Mac leaned across the table in an aggressive manner. "I'll bet you're a lot tougher than those other two." He shrugged and gave her a wide-eyed stare. "Or maybe they could beat me up, too."

"The reason I'm here…"

"Why should I care? Did Jeremy send you to make nice after you beat the snot out of me on the canal?"

"NO!" She was frightened now. "He does not know I'm here!"

He continued to pepper her with questions. "Do you really represent ten figures?"

"Well…"

Mac grabbed his iced tea and took a long swallow. "Thanks for the drink; can't remember when I had a better time." He stood up from the table.

"Please," she begged. "I am sorry, more sorry than you will ever know that I hurt you. I implore you to hear me out."

Mac felt rather than saw every eye in the restaurant on him. He was angry and about to walk away from arguably the most stunning woman any of the patrons had ever seen. Calculating quickly the danger of a rogue click of a cell phone camera, he sat back down. Regardless of his innocence, careers had been compromised for less. He studied her face for a tell, a trace of deception.

"Are you ready to order?" asked the waiter who had appeared between them.

Sabine's eyes beseeched him. Mac held her gaze for a long moment and without looking at the waiter, spoke. "I'll have the oatmeal, skim milk, and mixed berries. Thank you."

Her sigh of relief was audible. "I'll have the same," she said in a small voice.

When the waiter left, Mac put his elbows on the table and leaned on his interlocking fingers. "Speak."

Sabine began hesitantly. "I want to thank you. I was so afraid when you met with Jeremy that you would tell him about our … encounter."

"I don't normally advertise when a woman kicks my ass."

"I attacked you. It was totally unprovoked. I have no excuse."

"Why the hell did you jump me?"

She lowered her dark eyes and shook her head. "I thought you were harassing the man I love."

"Harassing? The man you love harassed me, intimidated me, and outright threatened me. I was the victim, not Jeremy."

"I understand everything now. Jeremy would have been furious if he knew what I had done." She paused, and a single tear leaked from her left eye. "He respects you so much. If Jeremy knew that I had betrayed him and hurt you, he would never forgive me."

"Do you swear that Jeremy never knew about the attack? "

"On my life," she said softly.

Mac's hands went to his face, and he rubbed his eyes. He felt like the biggest sucker in the world, but he believed her. Was it because she was beyond drop-dead gorgeous? That certainly didn't hurt. Still, she hadn't dressed provocatively or acted in a suggestive manner. It was like she wasn't trying to mask her scent. Was it because he wanted to believe that Jeremy had changed? Partially. But mostly, his gut told him that Sabine was truly remorseful and, as hard as it was to fathom, telling the truth.

"So was this just an apology tour, or was there more of an agenda?"

"The agenda was an apology, Mac. Now more than ever, Jeremy needs you by his side. I'll understand if you can't forgive me, but I want us to be friends. Or at the least, I don't want you to hate me."

The waiter had placed the oatmeal in front of them, and Mac silently added his berries, a pinch of brown sugar, and the skim milk. She followed his lead. They ate in silence for a few minutes, and then Mac laid down his spoon.

"Sabine, Christians try their best not to hate. It couldn't have been easy for you to come here today and really sort of beg the court for mercy. I felt wronged, but not entitled to that level of contrition. If I can't forgive you, then I am incapable of carrying out one of the most important tenets of my faith. I accept your apology; you are forgiven. We will never mention this again. However," he raised an admonishing finger, "you damn sure are picking up the check!"

CHAPTER 73

As Jeremy Lyons emerged from his newly constructed private therapy room, the pneumatic door closed behind him. His arms gleamed with sweat, his muscles still distended. Rivulets of sweat seemed to run angrily down his face.

Sabine stood before him, a picture of confrontation.

"What?" he asked with ragged breath.

She tossed him a white terrycloth towel, which he caught with one hand. His eyes remained on her.

Sabine's patience had worn thin. She challenged him with a one-word response: "Why?"

Jeremy's dark eyes burned into her until he calmed his breathing. He wiped himself down with the towel, then tossed it casually on the floor. "The African impala is one of the world's most powerful and graceful beasts," he said. "It can jump as high as ten feet and cover a distance of thirty feet in a single jump."

She kept her gaze level.

He clenched his hands and raised his powerful forearms. "But if you enclose these animals within a solid three-foot fence, they are trapped. They cannot see where their feet will land. They are paralyzed.

"The doctors have no vision. They cannot 'see' me walking." He looked at Sabine accusingly. "You cannot 'see' me walking."

She did not shrink from his gaze or his accusation.

He leaned forward. "Second Corinthians 5:7: 'For we walk by faith, not by sight.' I *will* walk again."

"Then let me help you!" she screamed.

His face closed like an executioner's. He wheeled past her without a word.

CHAPTER 74

Twenty years ago, if Jean Carlyle met an attractive single man in his suite at the Ritz Carlton, it could have conceivably caused a few tongues to wag. It wasn't like she wasn't still attractive at 67, it was simply that she was so focused on getting elected President of the United States that she would never allow a distraction such as a dalliance. Besides, she wasn't meeting with just any man, she was meeting with a kingmaker.

Gabe Hill, who was almost twenty years younger than the Democratic candidate, was a confirmed bachelor, and on those rare occasions when he was seen in public, it was with a much younger woman. A fastidious man of exacting routine, he never did anything that he didn't want to do.

The consensus was that each of the last two Democratic presidents owed their success to this brilliant political strategist. He was known by both his detractors and his admirers as the puppet master. After graduating at the top of his class from Georgetown Law, Hill worked for a preeminent private equity firm. At age 40 he had sufficient assets to support his lifestyle, and he set up a one-man shop.

Although it would have been accurate, it would have been a bit pretentious for Hill to advertise himself as a kingmaker. At the start, congressional candidates sought his advice. In less than an hour he would either tell them that he couldn't help them, or he would chart their path to election. The only requirement to remaining a client was that the candidate had to do everything Hill said. Any deviation resulted in Hill's firing the client. In spite of his aversion to publicity, his uncanny strategizing and the incredible success of his campaigns had made him a Washington legend.

Most consultants charge by the hour or are on retainer. Hill worked only for a success fee, which, because of the size of the fee, required that someone other than the candidate be his nominal client. The same billionaire liberal hedge fund operator who had contracted with him for the current president was also footing his bill this time.

In contrast to his client, who needed heavy makeup to hide the worry lines, Hill was unflappable. His five days a week, 60-minute workout in the Equinox gym from five in the morning until six removed any semblance of stress from his features. Jean Carlyle had gossiped with her husband that Hill was probably even nonplussed during sex.

"Are you sure we can't leak that you are shepherding my campaign?" asked Carlyle.

It wasn't the first time she had asked. Nevertheless, Hill repeated his previous answer. "If that happens, we can't work together," he said in a patient monotone. "In that case, I get my five-million-dollar cancellation fee, and you are on your own."

"It would really juice up the donors," she grumbled.

"Are you having trouble raising money?" He knew she was not.

She rolled her head back like an eleven-year-old who was told no. Big sigh. "There is no such thing as too much money, and it is just that if people know you're with me, they will *know* that I'll win."

"If everyone thinks you are going to win, no one will vote. Your job is to run the country, mine is to get you there. I don't want to have this discussion again."

She nodded, wishing again that she didn't need this arrogant prick.

Hill leaned forward, his dark eyes boring into her. "The next ninety days are crucial. It is my job to outline events that I believe will happen, to forewarn you, and to prepare you for every contingency. If you do not get ahead of events, you will lose."

"There is no way anyone in the clown car can beat me," she said derisively, adding a harsh laugh.

Hill sat back and folded his arms over his chest.

Carlyle stared at him and reddened. "Okay," she said, waving her hand, "I won't interrupt again."

He waited a full minute before speaking. "I'm not convinced that you'll be running against a Republican."

CHAPTER 75

I⊤ MAY NOT BE IN everyone's gene makeup, but a competitive spirit is a common thread among the American people. We are a nation that loves underdogs, applauds effort, and canonizes champions. We are passionate about our sports and our achievements, but only politics can generate lasting vitriol.

Competition exists in every product and every service. It is logical that the most searched questions on Google begin with the word "Best." If a candidate could get listed as the best potential president, he or she would win in a landslide.

Only in America could competition extend to which city has the best celebration for the birth of our nation. In a recent ranking, Macy's massive show was recognized as the biggest in the country, with 40,000 effects, and a 25-minute fireworks extravaganza viewed live by three million people. Boston, Las Vegas, Nashville, and San Diego all have amazing shows. However, the most patriotic Fourth of July celebration will always be in our nation's capital.

A *Capitol Fourth* is broadcast live on PBS and simulcast on NPR member stations nationwide. Via the American Forces Network, it can be heard live by American service members and their families stationed at bases in 145 countries, as well as 140 U.S. Navy ships at sea. The pyrotechnics are launched along both sides of the Lincoln Memorial and the Reflecting Pool, illuminating the National Mall and beyond. The broadcast is live from the west lawn of the United States Capitol, which is the perfect venue.

* * *

A heat wave had enveloped the Washington area for the last two weeks of June, sapping the energy from first-time tourists and even native Washingtonians. later in the month, a vicious thunderstorm had created mini floods, but it had washed the humidity away with it. A rarity for this city, the evening forecast for Independence Day was 75 degrees with a slight breeze. Couple that with an unprecedented array of country superstars scheduled to perform, and not only was it standing room only, but anyone who did not arrive at least three hours early was out of luck.

An anonymous donor had given PBS an extremely large check, secured the superstars, and outlined the night's agenda. Performers included Carrie Underwood, Brad Paisley, Blake Shelton, Miranda Lambert, Darius Rucker, and Garth Brooks.

When Lee Greenwood walked on the stage as the final performer, the entire audience, estimated at over 700,000, stood. Some struggled, some had to be helped, but there was no question which song he would sing. Flags were already waving before he hit the first note. In a semicircle around him, uniformed men and women of every service stood at attention. A wave of patriotism enveloped the crowd, and voices rose in unison to sing the final "God Bless the U.S.A."

The stage went dark. For thirty seconds, there were no sounds except for a few murmurs from the crowd. The television audience thought they had momentarily lost the feed. Suddenly, a bright spotlight lit the stage. Sitting in his wheelchair, Senator Jeremy Lyons flashed a tight smile and nodded. Dressed in a navy blazer accented with a red silk pocket square, he wore a blinding white shirt. Two small American flags protruded from the back of his chair.

"As we celebrate the birth of this great nation, let us remember the gift of freedom that our forefathers fought for and the wisdom they gave us on how to preserve that freedom." His powerful voice stilled the crowd.

"The battle still rages against our enemies both foreign and domestic, against poverty and discrimination, and against unfairness and apathy. All around us we can see evidence of individuals overcoming seemingly overwhelming odds to succeed. Soldiers who lose limbs in battle, cancer victims given a death sentence by their doctors, athletes who were told all their lives that they were not good enough, all fighting to prove the naysayers wrong. They believed that anything was possible. Now, in 2015, so must we.

"It is possible to better compensate and better equip our soldiers in battle." Lyons waited until the cheers and applause faded. "It is possible to ensure that our children get a quality education." Again he paused. "It is possible that every American who wants to work can have a job, and it is possible that the greatest nation in the world can once again be treated with respect by our friends." He lowered his voice. "And justifiably feared by our enemies."

The standing crowd cheered wildly. "Finally, it is not only possible, but mandatory, that your leaders tell you only the truth." Every person who was there that day felt as if Jeremy Lyons were talking only to him or her.

"Who among us is not frustrated with our political leaders?" He raised his arms and pantomimed giving the crowd an embrace. His passion was palpable as his voice soared. "I will not let us give up on the American dream, and I implore you to join me in that promise."

Lyons waited until the shouts of support subsided before he spoke. Now his voice was measured, its quiet sincerity causing people to lean into his words. "It is my promise that with your help I will make our country's possibilities our reality. I thank PBS for the opportunity tonight to allow me to announce my candidacy for the presidency of the United States."

He paused as the crowd went wild. "Thank you, my fellow Americans, and God bless America."

Again the stage went dark, and then the sky was bombarded with the colors and sounds of celebration. It was the longest and most spectacular display of fireworks in history.

PART II

CHAPTER 76

Sunday Morning, July 5th

"DAMN! HE WAS RIGHT," JEAN Carlyle said in an amazed voice. She was fighting off a summer cold, so she had ducked any Fourth of July celebration. The front page of *The Washington Post*, heralded the newsworthy aspect of Jeremy Lyons's announcement while criticizing the audacity of his interrupting the sacred holiday.

Her husband shrugged and added his little-boy smile that still managed to charm the ladies. He picked up his coffee cup and sipped. He was too smart to engage without an invitation.

Jean Carlyle had not showered or run a comb through her hair. She spent her life in the public view, and the times when the cameras were off were precious to her. "How the hell did Hill know that Lyons would enter the race? This changes everything."

Again her husband remained silent, though his eyes said, "I told you so."

"Now he's got my attention," she said, as if Hill's predictions were designed for that purpose. She put down her coffee cup and massaged her chin with her left hand. "Reynolds will shit a brick, and the other glory-seeking candidates have a few fitful nights ahead of them. I won't have to expose Lyons's underbelly. They'll do it for me." She laughed at her conclusions.

She raised her arms like she'd just scored a touchdown. "Everyone knows Lyons is a closet Republican," she said. "We'll just sit back and watch the other right wingers devour each other."

Her husband reached over and patted her arm. "It may be a mistake to underestimate Lyons," he said kindly. "Let's wait and see what Hill says."

CHAPTER 77

SOME DAYS ARE JUST NOT your days. Everett Leeds's typical July 4th holiday in the Hamptons had been ruined the minute that "limelight stealing cripple" had wheeled onto the stage. Only in America could some asshole buy the capital's Independence Day celebration.

He was still hung over the next morning when he returned to his office. An inadvertent miss with SPF 70 had left the back of his neck scarlet. There was no way he was wearing a tie. He plopped down in his office chair with a grunt.

"Coffee!" he screamed.

Moments later his chief of staff entered with a steaming cup held in both hands. His head was bowed, and when he handed Leeds the cup, his hands were shaking.

"What the hell is wrong with you?"

Russell Tomlinson stood with his head still lowered to his chest. He was unable to meet his boss's eyes.

Angered, Leeds leaned forward, and coffee sloshed over the rim of his cup and onto his walnut desk. "Shit! Now see what you made me do. Clean this up!"

Tomlinson quickly left the room.

"What a pussy," said Leeds, talking to himself. "No way Lyons is going to come in and dictate this election. Let him duke it out with Reynolds over whatever votes are left after I pump some more gas in Carlyle's campaign."

"Russell!" shouted Leeds. Tomlinson quivered into the room holding a handful of paper towels.

"After you clean up this mess, call Carlyle's people. Tell them to invite me to that Hollywood fundraiser, gratis, of course, and I'll endorse her." He narrowed his eyes. "You know we've got problems here. I can't have you go all twitchy on me."

Tomlinson looked up, his eyes filled with tears.

Leeds slammed his palm on his desk.

"What is it? It had better not be another," Leeds made air quotes with his hands and spoke in a falsetto voice, "he wasn't nice to me, or he cheated on me."

Now Tomlinson's face was as red as Leeds's neck. "No, no sir," he stammered, "It's not about me."

It didn't take long. Leeds's breakfast found the bottom of his trash can after only three photos of himself naked and smiling, his eyes closed in apparent bliss, with an equally naked man who called himself Graham draped over him.

CHAPTER 78

Jeremy Lyons was prepared, but he knew the risk of failure. This was a verbal battle to the death with a man whose wife was already mentally redecorating the interior of the White House. Preparation, irrefutable logic, and passion are necessary weapons, but convincing a proven winner that he is a dead man walking would take a miracle.

In any conversation that has the potential to be confrontational, venue is important. Privacy is critical, and whoever has the home court advantage tends to be the more comfortable. Accordingly, Lyons had asked for the meeting to be at 7:00 p.m. in Senator Bill Reynolds's office. At that time of night on the Monday following a holiday weekend, privacy in the Senate Office Building was guaranteed.

Reynolds was the Republican frontrunner and an experienced campaigner with an ample war chest. He looked at Lyons with undisguised skepticism.

"Senator Lyons, I've listened to your proposal with a combination of shock and, I'm afraid, amusement. I understand and admire your current popularity in the polls, and as a fiscal conservative, I grant that the maneuvering you did to get the corporate tax lowered was brilliant. The economy is already seeing the benefits. But I didn't throw my hat in the ring to lose. I have the support, the gravitas, and the integrity to be a good president."

"You not only have the qualifications to be a good chief executive, it is likely you would be a great one" responded Lyons. "Governor Romney was also exceptionally qualified and a good, moral man. It doesn't matter if you're a perfect Republican candidate. We need a maverick, someone who will defy convention, call out the political hacks and the flip-floppers. We need someone who has no fear of opinion polls or the media.

"Which of us would be a bigger threat to our enemies? It may seem naïve to appeal to your patriotism, but I will get things done that are impossible for a Republican president. You cannot escape your allegiance to the Republican party My allegiance is only to America."

In a familiar gesture, Reynolds ran a hand through his thick gray hair. It flopped back perfectly in place, which was enough to lose the follically challenged vote. "Senator," said Reynolds with forced patience, "you're a speechifying superstar. I admit that when you're whaling on politicians, I am riveted." His look was pained. "You seem to view my party with the same disdain as the press; but sir, I'm pretty proud of our values."

"I am pragmatic, Senator," responded Lyons. "In the last election, the Republicans could not have had a more qualified candidate. Yet, you lost. Until you clear out the clutter of false accusations and the self-imposed straightjacket of ideological purity, the country will not elect a Republican president."

"And you're the man who can get elected?"

"Who else can put the social issues on the back burner until we can bolster our defenses and restore fiscal sanity?"

Reynolds waited a beat before speaking. "Senator, you've got about the same legislative experience as our current president, and well, that hasn't worked out so well."

Lyons nodded, agreeing. "That is why I hope you'll play a significant role in my administration as my secretary of state. I will surround myself with only superbly qualified patriots. Party affiliation and diversity will not factor into the equation. My advisors will be the best of the best."

Reynolds responded with a full belly laugh. "Damn, you're good. How about I make you my treasury secretary instead?"

"You cannot beat Jean Carlyle."

Reynolds's face flushed. "You can't know that. We're damn near a year and a half away from the election."

"I do know that. No matter what you decide, I am running as an Independent." His tone was strident. "I will suck away votes from the Republican nominee like a vacuum cleaner on steroids."

Reynolds instinctively tried to stare him down. "I'm not sure I agree..."

"Senator, you know that I speak the truth. And if the Republican nominee came in third, the party would be irreparably damaged. Even in the event that you won and you still had the majority in the senate and the house, do you honestly believe you could cut entitlements?" Lyons asked.

"In that case, sir, we'd have a mandate," Reynolds said forcefully.

Lyons shook his head. "The Democrats would fight you tooth and nail, and your 'war on women' label would be secondary to your portrayal as a heartless bureaucrat intent on killing seniors and punishing the impoverished. We are not a proactive country, we are reactive. Our only hope is that someone will be able to restore fiscal sanity before the rest of the world figures out we are bankrupt. Do you really think a Republican president could get that done?" His voice had risen, and Reynolds was momentarily shaken by the man's passion.

Reynolds held the stare and then let out a breath. "No. The lobbyists are too damn entrenched. AARP, ACLU, every liberal blogger and media outlet will use every possible means to resist any cuts."

"And I will use every possible means to succeed. Four years," said Lyons, raising the fingers of his right hand, "and then it's a jump ball. Bill, we both know that a politician's promises are made of tissue paper, and you don't know me well enough to know that my word never wavers. Two of my nonnegotiable goals are to dramatically reduce our national debt, and...," he paused, "to loosen the chokehold of lobbyists."

"Senator, that's a tall order," said Reynolds, studying the man. He knew that Lyons was prepared to answer most of his objections, and he needed to throw him off stride. He issued a challenge. "If I knew everything about you that there was to know, would I want you to be my president?"

Lyons gave him a long, appraising look. The question was only relevant to a man of character. "It depends on whether virtue or accomplishment is your measuring stick."

"Why can't I have both?"

Lyons ratcheted up the intensity. "The end justifies the means. As a result, I will intimidate or humiliate anyone who stands in my way. For the last six and a half years, the chief executive has been very likeable. Do you think he has been an effective president, an honest one? The last adjective may be an oxymoron when it comes to describing presidents, but he has something that no other Republican, even an enormously qualified one, has. He has the Oval Office.

"Let me ask you a question. Do you believe that I would accommodate our country's enemies?"

"No."

"Do you believe that I can accomplish what I declare?"

Reynolds let out a long sigh. "You sure have big enough balls to do it."

"I know we may disagree on social issues," Lyons went on, "but as I said before, they need to take a back seat. We need to fix our country before it's too late. You know I am not exaggerating."

"What makes you so sure you can win?" asked Reynolds. "If you ran and lost, our 'sacrifice' for the good of the country, and I am assuming that you'll make the same case to the other viable candidates, would make us look foolish, and the party might be dead forever."

"I can make inroads into the African-American community, the Hispanics, even the LBGTQ community;" said Lyons. "Can you? I have senators and congressmen and women in both parties who will support me. I have neutralized my strongest opposition."

"How the hell did you do that?"

"Here is a case where plausible deniability works," Lyons said somberly. He waited as Reynolds digested his statement. "Your concern is genuine, but not valid. I will pledge one billion dollars to the Republican party in the event that I am defeated. If nothing else, that should convince you of the seriousness of my intentions."

Reynolds raised an eyebrow. "I don't doubt your intentions, nor do I believe that you want to be president for the wrong reasons." He considered his next words carefully. "I won't dismiss your proposal out of hand. I guess you won't consider being my vice president?"

"We would win," Lyons said easily, "but our administration would still be hamstrung." He paused. "You, sir, as well as the other candidates, are forced to be politicians. I am only required to do my duty."

* * *

As Bill Reynolds walked away from the meeting, he mentally organized his thoughts. *What were the pros and cons of Lyons's unprecedented proposal? If he runs as an Independent in a three-party race, good chance I'm bringing up the rear. That corporate tax victory gives him a hell of a tailwind. Lyons owns social media.*

His pace quickened as he weighed the possible outcomes. *Short term…am I labeled as a quitter and a loser? If I can't dictate the narrative….Damn, I hate that overused word…my political career could be in the toilet.*

He slowed down and had another thought. *The party's money men would go postal if I dropped out for Lyons. Not only does Lyons not have the conservative bone fides, but no way that pretentious prick Steiner owns him.*

Reynolds stopped, reached in the left breast pocket of his hand-tailored suit, and pulled out his iPhone. He smiled as he texted: ELI, NEED TO TALK TO YOU ABOUT A PROPOSAL I JUST RECEIVED.

CHAPTER 79

BILL REYNOLDS HAD HOPED TO get an immediate conversation with Eli Steiner, but his majesty had made him wait the obligatory 24 hours. One of the real downsides of being a Republican politician was having to occasionally kiss this misanthrope's ass. Oh well, the Democrats had the same problem with their super PACs. At least, he was meeting the man at eight o'clock and didn't have to have dinner with him.

"Hopefully, I am back within the hour," Reynolds told his driver. He waited for the protocol procedures that kept elite residences such as Steiner's well protected and then entered the elevator and punched the button for the penthouse. A lot of folks would be happy living in this elevator, thought Reynolds. Everything the Ritz did was first class.

Steiner had dismissed his staff and had given his scarlet silk bathrobe to Goodwill, taking a sizable deduction. It was cursed. Tonight the bathrobe was black, and the custom-made pajamas were emerald green. His facial expression indicated that this meeting was an imposition. Reynolds had never seen the man with any other expression, so he smiled humbly to acknowledge his eminence.

Rather than extend his hand, Steiner simply motioned to an antique, black, straight-backed chair. He knew the golden rules of power. Supplicants always come to you. It had been a mistake to go to Lyons's lair, but he blamed that on libido, not tactics. Always make them wait. Finally, never allow failure to attach itself to you.

After Reynolds took a seat, Steiner slowly lowered himself into his cream-colored, soft leather recliner. Hands folded judgmentally on his chest, he waited for Reynolds to speak.

"Asked me to drop out......Party can't win......Carlyle crushes us......."

With each word of Reynolds's recitation, Steiner sat up straighter in his chair. His blood pressure spiked, and his breathing become labored. "Who the fuck does he think he is?" The words came out like the hiss of a serpent.

Unfazed by the interruption, Reynolds continued his slightly modified rendition of his meeting with Lyons. "It was hard to hear, Eli." He looked down at the ground.

"Why didn't you stand up to him?" sputtered Steiner, spittle flying from his mouth.

"I didn't roll over," protested Reynolds adamantly. "But every word that Lyons said denigrated our party, slammed our morals."

"He's a convenient Christian," said Steiner, "a crook, and a world-class phony."

"I agree, but he threatened to enter the race as an Independent if I didn't bail."

This brought Steiner out of his chair. He was less than graceful as he stumbled and had to grab hold of the arm of the chair to steady himself. "He threatened that?" he raged. "He would guarantee a Carlyle victory?"

Reynolds was afraid the man would have a heart attack, but he continued ratcheting up the pressure. "The people think he's a hero, and he has an unlimited war chest."

"Does he think he's the only person who can raise money?" asked Steiner.

Bypassing the rhetorical question, Reynolds asked, "Have you met with Lyons, Eli?"

"Of course I've met with that charlatan. He begged me to come to his home for dinner, tried to ply me with liquor and women." He paused and stared angrily at Reynolds. "He had about as much chance of compromising me as Jean Carlyle would."

"I'm glad to hear that, Eli."

"I don't make deals with the devil," Steiner said emphatically, "and this ride-a-long wants to destroy our party!"

Reynolds winced inwardly at the man's description, but it was time to deliver the piece de resistance. "He said one more thing, Eli, and it was the worst thing he said. But, I, I'm uncomfortable repeating it."

"You have no choice," said Steiner menacingly.

Reynolds shrugged, winced, and spat out the words with palpable reluctance. "Eli, he called you out. Jeremy Lyons said you were a cancer on the party, and as long as you were involved, the party was terminal."

Instead of exploding, Steiner closed his eyes, and his head bobbed up and down. He opened his eyes, but they were narrowed, two furious slits. "I'm going to raise a shit pot of money for you. But first, I will appear on *The O'Reilly Factor* tomorrow night."

Reynolds was taken aback. "Eli, you tend to shy away from publicity. Are you sure?"

Steiner looked at him with disdain. "Set it up," he said.

CHAPTER 80

THROUGH FOUR CHILDREN AND NOW two young grandchildren, Caitlin Reynolds had been the chief executive of their household and the caretaker of their lovely Chevy Chase home. Before her husband, Bill, had literally swept her off her feet in a whirlwind romance, she had been the one of Washington D.C.'s top advertising executives. With the arrival of their first child, she found her true calling.

When Caitlin's husband walked through the door that night, the six members of his presidential exploration team trudged sheepishly behind him. The fact that he'd forgotten to call was evidence enough that it was not good news. She kissed away his pained expression of apology, and without asking, called the Pines of Rome and ordered white pizza with fontina cheese, along with both veal and eggplant parmigiana. Takeout Taxi was happy to deliver it.

Reynolds handled the drinks and added a log to the wood fire. With the black poker, he pushed the logs around while he gathered his thoughts. His team members gravitated to familiar seats, the soft couch and stuffed armchairs in a living room that was impervious to change. They sat in a loose semi-circle around their candidate, waiting for him to speak. They had received no information, just been told to follow him.

Reynolds turned to his entourage, flashed a tight smile and began speaking. "Two nights ago, Senator Jeremy Lyons came to my office. He had an unusual request...."

* * *

Eli Steiner was too focused to appreciate the obsequious staff that greeted him as he walked through the opulent lobby of the Ritz

Carlton. Normally, he would give a curt nod in response to their practiced smiles and obligatory, "Good evening, sir."

The doorman opened the rear door of the black town car, and Steiner slid into his seat. The driver silently moved the car forward.

Steiner's live interview with Bill O'Reilly was scheduled to air at 9:20, because the producers wanted to tease the audience. After all, Eli Steiner *was* the invisible power broker of the Republican party.

Even though the remote location for *The O'Reilly Factor* was only fifteen minutes from the Ritz at this time of night, Steiner had left his home at 8:30. He'd required a make-up artist, and he had specific instructions for the cameraman. He was unconcerned about his own performance; however, he had little faith in the performance of minions.

He smiled, revealing newly whitened teeth. *Tonight, Mr. Jeremy Lyons will feel the full weight of my power. I believe you call it a pre-emptive strike.*

* * *

"Obviously, I did not agree to his requests," said Reynolds, raising a comforting hand as a stop sign. "Instead," he sighed loudly, "I made the odious trip to see Steiner."

"What color pajamas did he have on?" asked Reynolds's chief of staff.

"Green, for money."

Everyone smiled.

"Most of you are too young to remember the phrase, 'he blew a gasket,'" said Reynolds, "but that's what happened. A nitpicker might suggest that I slightly colored my conversation with Lyons, but the good senator from Florida told me himself that he believed that the end justifies the means, so I was just following his lead."

"What are the chances that your refusal to bow out to Lyons causes him to run as a third-party candidate?" asked the newest female staffer.

"That's the 64-thousand-dollar question, but one that I believe will be answered by 9:30 tonight. Eli's tirade may not be enough to dissuade Lyons, but he'll know that he's in for a hell of a battle."

* * *

Eli Steiner was like a fighter talking to himself before a championship bout. "This will be the shot heard around the world. The cripple and the black bitch may try to retaliate, but I will have a fucking army around me. When I explain how the man tried to intimidate me, sending one of his henchmen to my home to torture me into supporting him, his political star will become a shooting star." He reached into the right breast pocket of his black suit and pulled out the picture of his broken finger.

The driver, who was a seasoned professional, did not react to his passenger's rants. He simply continued driving to their destination.

* * *

The excitement in the Reynolds living room was contagious. "So he claims that Senator Lyons sent someone to his home, and the man broke his finger?"

Reynolds nodded. "I find it rather preposterous, but whatever stirs Eli up, I'm for it."

Caitlin Reynolds had a doubtful look on her face. "I'm sorry, Bill, but I never pictured Eli Steiner as being brave. You really think he will give you a full endorsement tonight and not want something in return?"

"Oh, he'll want plenty in return, but he did not designate a quid pro quo. He promised me not only full endorsement, but also that he was going to take care of Lyons's third party threat. All we can do is wait and see."

* * *

As the driver pulled the car over and stopped, Steiner said irritably, "Are you sure this is the right spot?"

"Yes, sir. Google Maps confirmed it. I'll wait right here for your return."

Opening the car door, the driver reached to help Steiner out. "I can get out myself, idiot," said Steiner as he stepped out of the car. The man remained in Steiner's space. "Back away," Steiner commanded.

The driver's left arm went behind Steiner's back, holding him steady, and his right hand viciously grabbed Steiner's testicles.

Steiner's gasp of pain was muffled as he was pulled closer. "If you scream, I will twist and take them with me. It takes no more than thirty seconds. I've timed it."

Reflexively, Steiner tried to crumble to the ground, but he was held aloft. His moans of pain were inhuman.

The driver slightly released the pressure, and Steiner let out a breath. Just as quickly, the man squeezed again. "You were correct, sir. This isn't the right place. It's two blocks from here, but I thought we needed a more private chat."

"Pul...leese."

"Sorry, please and thank you don't work anymore." Like moving a joystick, the man maneuvered Steiner back into an alley. "I thought we had an understanding. Did you forget that I'm your daddy?"

He released Steiner's testicles and reached into his captive's right breast pocket.

Steiner let out a small cry as the picture was plucked from his pocket. "I must admit I do good work," said the driver. "Here. You must be hungry. Eat it!" He stuffed the picture into Steiner's mouth.

Steiner gagged.

"Do you think I'm playing games with you? You are vermin. Do you think anyone can protect you from me? I am relentless. Now, eat every bite. Daddy has to clean you up so that you can be on television." He abruptly positioned Steiner back in the vehicle and handed him a single sheet of paper. He clapped his hands. "And guess what, Daddy has even written your speech for you."

Fortunately, this time Steiner had not pissed himself. A stained crotch would be hard to explain to the producers. Steiner's regular driver was not quite as unsullied after being tased in a Ritz Carlton bathroom and given a finely honed injectable cocktail. The car pulled up to the station entrance.

"Stand up straight," said John Wesley to Steiner, who was staggering into the studio like a drunk on a bender. "Make Daddy proud."

* * *

By 9:19. Bill Reynold was chewing the inside of his cheek, eagerly awaiting the unleashing of Steiner on the airwaves. He wanted

Lyons's head on a platter for proposing that he drop out of the race. It was Reynolds's dream to lead the country out of the approaching financial Armageddon. He had raised the money, built the team, garnered support, cut the deals, and made his promises. The next ten minutes would secure an unfettered path to his seat in history.

* * *

The camera showed a frustrated Bill O'Reilly expecting fireworks from a guest who looked pale, confused, and sweaty, despite the caked-on foundation covering his face.

"Last night," Steiner began, "Bill Reynolds dropped by my home concerned about the sudden entry of a new player in the presidential race. Our conversation was brief. Our PAC's resources will be more meaningful to the country's future if focused on the senatorial and gubernatorial races instead of a presidential fight." The announcement was so far off script that O'Reilly fled to commercial and flailed his expletives off air as Steiner left the set.

* * *

"You lying asshole!" Reynolds's chief of staff shot straight up and yelled at the television as if Steiner could hear him.

Reynolds didn't move. The staffers looked at him in shock. He put both hands over his face and didn't say a word. Caitlin Reynolds nodded towards the door and helped the staffers gather laptops, purses and coats. They exited the house silently.

Finally, Reynolds raised his head and looked beseechingly at his wife.

She walked over to him and took both of his hands before she spoke. "You know that whatever you decide, I will support you. I would hate to see you lose," she paused, "and I would hate to see you win." She lowered her head. "If you drop out, I will know that God heard my prayers."

With a look of resignation, Reynolds reached for his phone.

CHAPTER 81

AFTER AN EARLY CLIENT LUNCH, Mac McGregor jumped on the Orange Line subway, exiting at the New Carrolton station. It was never prudent during the summer to leave for the beach on Friday afternoon, so if at all possible, Mac would head out early on Thursday.

He waited outside on the edge of the parking lot for ten minutes. The mid-afternoon heat was oppressive, and he was anxious to shed his coat and tie. He saw the white van pull into the lot and resisted the temptation to chide Grace. Her constant mantra was that he was habitually late. Right was on his side this time, but rubbing it in was not a wise marital strategy. Instead, he would nod patiently at her traffic excuses.

* * *

Now, it was quarter to six on Friday evening, and the wind was coming from the west, bringing with it the pesky flies. As a consequence, the beach in front of their development was almost deserted. An attractive, short-haired, blond woman was slinging a ball left handed to a golden retriever, who was the odds-on favorite to outlast her. Racing to get the ball, tail wagging like a propeller, on the sand, into the surf, the dog would not be denied.

Mac struggled out of the surf and wagged his head as if competing with the dog. He'd taken a quick dip after a thirty-minute walk/run, and he headed over to pluck his blue-and-white beach towel from his chair. Grace had declined the pleasure of his company and seemed perfectly content reading her Kindle.

He sat heavily in his chair, letting out a moan. "Are there really people who enjoy this kind of torture?"

She gave him a sideways glance. "Your dad died of a heart attack, if you gain five pounds you obsess about it, and you still eat every dessert you can get your hands on. Stop whining."

Mac reached down beside his chair and picked up his "Life Is Good" hat and sunglasses. "Did I say something to piss you off?" he asked.

She wiggled her legs to shoo off a persistent fly and sighed. "I'm sorry. Actually, I'm the one obsessing. Your eyes lit up Saturday night when Jeremy Lyons made his announcement. I'm really afraid that you'll get entangled in his web."

He reached over and took her hand. "This whole scenario is crack to a political junkie. There's no question that I will be immersed in the drama; and in truth, we've never seen a crazy candidate like Jeremy Lyons."

She yanked her hand away. "You're the one who's crazy. You don't have an excuse. You're not the uninformed public. You know the type of man he is."

Mac clenched his jaw, biting back a response. Grace's face was red, contorted in anger. He turned back to the ocean and breathed deeply of the salt air. He waited until the rhythmic rolling of the blue-green surf calmed him.

"I cannot envision a scenario where he could be harmful to me, our family, or frankly, our country. What kind of confidence do you have that any other candidate will do what they say? Empty promises are like the songs of the sixties. They never go away." He hesitated, searching for the right words.

Mac knew that it would sound like a stump speech, but he couldn't stop himself. "We need a strong, forceful leader, one who ignores the polls and will do whatever it takes to make our country stronger."

He took off his sunglasses and looked at her. He saw her arms folded, her lips pursed. He was getting nowhere. "I know discussing Lyons is like pulling off scabs for you, and I'm sorry. It's why I keep these thoughts to myself."

Realizing that he was not making a difference, Mac made a comment that he knew would end the discussion. "Don't build a wall between us about this, Grace. He's not worth it."

CHAPTER 82

Jeremy Lyons's camel-colored, soft leather recliner was in the upright position. His theater room hosted eleven more of the same chairs and a 104-inch screen. Flanking the most recently announced presidential candidate were four of his co-conspirators: Mary Beth Justice, Steve Cannon, Sabine, and Alegria. All were equally engaged.

At exactly 7:21 p.m. on Sunday, July 12, reporter Lesley Simmons of *60 Minutes* asked her first question.

"Senator Reynolds, were you surprised that Senator Lyons threw his hat in the ring last week?"

"I wasn't aware of the timing, Lesley, but I was aware of his intentions."

She raised an eyebrow. "Really? What are your thoughts?"

Looking very presidential in his custom-made, three-thousand-dollar, blue pin-striped suit, Bill Reynolds came across as confident and definitely in the know. "I've spent considerable time with Senator Lyons. I was impressed with his unconventional method of pushing for the corporate tax cut. The boost to our economy and the additional new jobs created as a result of that bill were expected, but still very welcome." He smiled to imply that he had been intimately involved in the process.

"Make no mistake," Reynolds continued, raising a hand. "The senator and I do not see eye to eye on a number of issues. However, on the most critical issues affecting our country we are perfectly aligned."

"And what are those issues?" asked Simmons, anxious to be involved.

"Protecting our citizens and making sure that we are not the next Greece."

"Isn't that an over-exaggeration used by your party?"

"It's the way families make a point, Lesley. We tell our children not to talk to strangers, because they could be abducted. The odds of that may be low, but we don't want to test the odds. Is it likely that we would sink to that level of economic chaos? No, but it is certain that at some point uncontrolled spending will make us a bankrupt nation. Any nonpartisan academic projection will substantiate that."

She nodded, unconvinced. "So, I will agree that Senator Lyons is a strong fiscal conservative, which puts him in the same boat as you and the other Republican candidates. He will obviously siphon votes from your side, and from my viewpoint, make Senator Carlyle our first woman president."

"Your viewpoint has been crystal clear for a long time, Lesley," Reynolds said with a smile. "And I do agree with your analysis."

Simmons was shocked. She had expected a rebuttal of her premise. "So what's the next step?" she asked tentatively.

"As long as I have been in public service, my goal has been to try to do what is right for the country." He cast his eyes downward and then looked back up to the camera. "I believe in my heart that I would be a strong leader and a president that could make Americans proud again. But I am not convinced that at this moment in time either I or Senator Carlyle can unify our country."

The reporter's eyes widened, and she started to interrupt, but Reynolds's sharp glance silenced her.

"The bickering, the vitriol, the snipes . . . our fellow Americans are sick and tired of the infighting. How else can you explain the popularity of a Donald Trump? We have some politicians who are wonderful talkers, but how many doers do we have?

"Over many discussions with Senator Lyons, and after extensive analysis by outside experts, I contend that it is imperative that our next president come to office without any outside influences or obligations, and with a simple mandate: Fix America. There are many who will say that we should just keep going, that the economy, the millennials, or maybe God will bail us out."

He nodded his head. "I think that it's time we helped ourselves. One term. Four years. That's not a long time in the history of our country. Isn't it time we had a warrior as our commander in chief? Isn't it time for the truth?"

"It sounds like you are Jeremy Lyons's campaign manager," said Simmons, not bothering to hide her outrage.

"I believe that I am still a United States Senator, Lesley," he said with steel in his voice.

"Of course you are, sir," she said backtracking. "But what do we really know about this man? Do you expect any of the other Republican candidates to just lie down?"

Reynolds turned to her. "That's a callous way to characterize patriotism. I have a moral obligation to do what I feel is best for our country. I cannot speak for the other Republican candidates, but I am stepping out of the race and throwing my support to a man who does not represent my party. He is a true Independent. Give Jeremy Lyons four years, and I believe we will get our country back."

* * *

Jeremy Lyons smiled at his friends and confidants. "He made a few changes to the script, but he delivered it well."

The only one not smiling was Mary Beth Justice. "Maybe too damn well."

CHAPTER 83

BILL REYNOLDS'S BAILOUT CHANGED EVERYTHING. It even prompted an impromptu meeting with the tightly scheduled Gabe Hill. Exactly three minutes after Reynolds's interview on *60 Minutes* ended, Jean Carlyle received a text: TOMORROW TEN O'CLOCK.

As upset as she was about Reynolds's exit, Carlyle could not resist a smile at the message. Perhaps Hill had a pulse after all. She typed: AGREED.

* * *

Carlyle searched Hill's face for signs of distress. Clearly he hadn't foreseen this turn of events. She was still an attractive woman with the blond hair that seemed required for prominent women in their late sixties. Always well groomed and alert for photo ops, she had a ready smile and the ability to reassure and put people at ease. When the camera was off, she could be a bitch on wheels, but that was partly attributable to the fact that she had no patience for fools or failure. At this moment in history she was, by all measures, the most powerful woman on the planet.

As if he were reciting scientific facts, Hill listed his assumptions in staccato fashion. "Reynolds knew. No leaks. Amazing." He seemed to pace in cadence with his proclamations. "Reynolds is either dirty or bought," he added, "Others will fall like dominoes soon. Reynolds knows he loses to you. Now he's all in on Lyons." He stopped and stared at her as if he'd just realized she was there. "Jump ball."

"What?" she said, raising her voice.

"Unlike normal competition, Lyons is smart, dynamic, and filthy rich. He will not have to pimp for funding."

"Neither will I," Carlyle said forcefully. "Liberals will attach themselves to me like leeches. Lyons will scare them to death."

Hill smiled at her. "It'll be interesting."

"I don't want interesting. I want a decisive victory, a mandate," she said, with steel in her words.

"So far he's ahead. Fired the first shot," said Hill with a faraway look in his eyes. "But he'll run out of surprises, and we'll have some of our own."

CHAPTER 84

THE BEST TIME OF THE year to navigate the commute from suburban Maryland to D.C. is in the summer, when schools are out and congress is in recess. Mac McGregor had opined that congress should be in a time out rather than in recess, but the idea had failed to get traction.

After 35 years in the business, Mac had given himself permission to relax what had previously been a regimented routine. For example, the top button of his starched, white shirt remained unbuttoned until there was a client sighting or he was outside of his building. His tie was tied, but positioned two inches below his Adam's apple. He had mastered the fake cough and close maneuver so that he could be presentable in less than five seconds.

Another variation from a three-and-a-half-decade regimen was that he no longer stayed in the office until 6:30 or 7:00 p.m. Whenever possible, he passed on meetings or dinners downtown. Not that he always succeeded, but the goal was to leave at five o'clock to beat some of the traffic.

Late Saturday Mac had emailed his team that their Monday meeting was canceled. Too many thoughts were pinballing around in his mind. Now, as he lingered over his cereal topped with fat, local blueberries, he decided that he'd make a leisurely trek into work. Yes, he was a rebel.

During his commute, Mac kept the radio off as he tried to sort out some things. Both his business and the stock market were on auto pilot, so his thoughts were solely concentrated on his second passion: politics.

* * *

As Mac walked by R.J.'s desk, R.J. stood and offered light applause. "I think you'll make a great vice president," he whispered. His eyes twinkled.

In contrast, Mac's eyes flashed angrily, and he made an abrupt motion for R.J. to follow him into the conference room. R.J. followed, a bewildered look on his face.

Mac tossed his black briefcase on the conference table, sat down, and glared at his friend. "How did you know?"

R.J.'s face lost all its color. "You're kidding me."

Mac's face hardened. "Do you think this is something that should be announced to the whole team?"

" I...I... Come on, you're not serious."

"Of course not. Lyons didn't tell me beforehand what his plan was. He doesn't ask for my advice. And he would never do anything unpredictable like have a financial guy as his vice president." Mac shook his head with disgust, turned his back to R.J., and looked out the window onto Pennsylvania Avenue. The silence lasted over a minute and became oppressive.

"Mac, I'm sorry."

Mac whirled back around. "Do you want to know what I said to him?"

R.J. didn't answer.

Mac leaned forward. "I told him that I couldn't serve my country because R.J. would poop in his pants."

R.J. winced. "You are such an asshole."

"Agreed. But you've been with me so long, you've become almost impossible to punk."

"Do you have anything of value to say?" asked R.J.

"Yes. Lyons was brilliant. The speech was short and powerful, very impactful. No one cares if he bought his way in. It was theater."

"Did Grace see it? How did she react?

"Well. She glared at me and walked upstairs to bed without a word."

"Good."

"That's why I took it out on you. Did you watch *60 Minutes*? I missed it."

"Before I give you my observations on Bill Reynolds's performance, do you think Lyons has something on him?"

Mac thought for a few moments. "It's possible, but I hope not. *The Post* mentioned that he is young enough to run in '20."

"Reynolds did a masterful job," said R.J. "Came out looking like a patriot rather than a quitter. My guess is that with his foreign policy experience, he's maybe the secretary of state if Lyons wins."

"Haven't thought about that. So he had already spent time with Lyons, because he'd been scheduled to be on the show for a while."

"Reynolds stressed the urgent need for action. Mentioned that he and Lyons did not agree on social issues, but both are adamant about a strong defense and fiscal sanity."

"So you don't see him as a possible veep?" Mac asked.

"No. I think Lyons needs a woman to combat Carlyle."

"If Lyons picks Sabine," said Mac, "he'll win in a landslide."

CHAPTER 85

THE LANDSCAPING SURROUNDING THE RED brick church could use some attention. At least the adjoining cemetery still looked like a military graveyard. The pastor had always been adamant about that. It had been a long time since the visitor been here.

In a gray pinstriped suit, vintage 1980, the elderly man took a seat in the last pew on the right. That sign of rebellion should have made him smile; instead, it made him uneasy. Rubbing his hand over the dark-stained wood, he noticed that the high sheen could still reflect hand gestures.

The man kept his eyes straight ahead, fixed on the cross, as the preacher walked down the center aisle. He didn't need to look to know that even walking to the pulpit was an orchestrated production for this man of God. Knoxville, Tennessee, had its share of Bible thumpers and mega-media ministers, but no one would ever convince this congregation that any of them compared to the Reverend Charles Wesley.

"Brothers and sisters," Wesley began, "it is my job, my scared duty, to tell you how to follow the Savior. We have learned how to laugh at temptation. Listen to John 12:35. Then Jesus said unto them, 'Walk while ye have the light, lest darkness come upon you: for he that walketh in darkness knoweth not whither he goeth.'"

Unconsciously, the man in the last row mouthed the words.

"Why is this passage important? Because Jesus is the light! Without him we are wandering aimlessly; we are pawns of Satan." As his continued his message, the preacher's powerful voice, enhanced by practiced movements of his hands, mesmerized his flock.

It wasn't until a few minutes later that Reverend Wesley went on the tangent that drew the man to his church. "I know, my brothers and sisters, that I tell you a lot of things." His smile was apologetic.

"But there is one thing I have never told you, not in the thirty-five years that I have been in the Lord's service. I have never told you how you should vote! Until now." He nodded, drawing out the moment. Even though most of the congregation knew what he was going to say, he liked to act like it would be the first time they'd ever heard it.

"Are our children allowed to pray in schools?"

He was greeted with a chorus of "No!"

"Can we display the holy Ten Commandments in our public buildings?"

The volume of the congregation increased.

"And yet," he said, raising a cautionary finger, "any of the devil's disciples can stand up and shout that GOD IS DEAD!" The people were standing now, including the man in the last row. "How can we put an end to this blasphemy?" Reverend Wesley's eyes rose to the heavens, and his passion-filled voice grew soft.

"We have a true man of God running for president. I don't have to know Jeremy Lyons to know his spirit. He has been saved. And if we are to save our country, then everyone here, everyone you know must vote for him. God has spoken to me. This man can lead us back into the light of Jesus Christ."

His eyes glistened with passion as he raised his arms, rolled his neck back. and looked towards the heavens. The congregation raised their hands in accord. After a moment of silence, the reverend lowered his head and directed, "Let us pray."

A flood of emotion ran through the stranger to this parish. His smile was filled with hope as he hurried out of the church.

As the last of the congregation filed out, the preacher asked, "Who was the old man in the back?"

"I don't know, sir," answered the head usher, "but we want him back."

"Why is that? He didn't even wait to shake my hand."

With wide eyes, the usher opened a thick white envelope. "By my count, reverend, there are fifty one-hundred dollar bills here."

CHAPTER 86

WOULD THE PRESIDENTIAL CAMPAIGN OF 2016 change politics forever? The question was debated by pundits from both sides of the aisle. With his senatorial run as a guide, it was expected that Jeremy Lyons would not attack his opponent. A similar decision by Jean Carlyle was totally unanticipated.

Carlyle had to be persuaded not to attack. After all, the incumbent president's strategy had been flawless. His team had expertly mixed innuendo, misdirection, and false inferences to discredit his opponents. Part of her irritation was attributed to the fact that girls had to play nicer than boys. The overriding factor in her acquiescence was that Gabe Hill had been the architect of both of the incumbent's campaigns.

"You have to appear above the fray," cautioned Hill, "and never be thought of as a shrew." If that had been the sum of his advice, Carlyle would have gone with her instincts and at least covertly slung some serious mud. However, Hill had added, "At the appropriate time, we *will* put the hammer down."

Carlyle was forced to be content with flooding the airwaves with pictures of herself with middle-class Americans and promising to "unstack the deck." As she'd predicted, she did not lack for funding, and her practiced smile assured the public of her experience, capabilities, and caring.

Senator Lyons did not lack exposure. It was simply his unprecedented approach that had the media pontificating on a daily basis. He did not ask for funding and would not accept contributions over one hundred dollars. Ads showing his visage and containing a short message appeared only during those brief periods when he was not being interviewed on a major network.

In addition to network coverage, Lyons was interviewed by every social media site. He was controversial, entrenched in his positions, and unconcerned with the polls. Remarkably, he did not travel to primaries and declined invitations to speak in person other than to the media. Even if Senator Carlyle wouldn't say it, the liberals were shouting that no billionaire could be "a man of the people."

Every question was answered forthrightly, without nuance or equivocation:

FOX NEWS:

Q: "Do you intend to seek the repeal of Obamacare?"

A: "No. It is the law of the land. The president asked congress to suggest ways to make the law better and received silence in reply. Under my administration, if there is no better solution proposed, I shall not entertain discussion."

MSNBC:

Q: "The Supreme Court ruling legitimized same sex marriage. Do you agree?"

A: "Why does it matter if I agree? How does my opinion help our country? Ask me a question that concerns governance. Anything else is a distraction or a search for a controversial sound bite."

ABC NEWS

Q: "What is your position on immigration?"

A: "Secure the borders. No felons should ever enter our country. For those illegal aliens without criminal records, a reasonable path to citizenship should be created."

CNBC:

Q: "You did a wonderful job getting the corporate tax reduction passed. Think you can help with my 1040 (personal tax return)?"

A: "We have studied the economics as well as the lifestyle benefits of creating a simple, fair tax code. With respect to your personal tax return, I will promise that it will be the first return we audit."

CHAPTER 87

It took John Wesley twelve days to summon the courage to make the call. Every Friday night, his father wrote his sermon. Wesley knew he would be home, and when his father was home, he always answered the phone himself. *What is wrong with me? Pick up the phone and punch in the damn number.*

Wesley looked at his hand like it was an alien attached to his wrist. His thumb, suspended over the **Call** button, started to twitch. He closed his eyes and punched his iPhone like it was his worst enemy.

"Charles Wesley," boomed the voice.

His son let out a breath. "Dad?"

The dead silence extended for an eternity. Finally, the reverend spoke. "John? The boy who left our Christian home and has been AWOL for the past eighteen years?"

Wesley knew he didn't want to go there. "Dad, a friend of mine came to your service."

Again a painful silence before his father said, "So?"

The words came out quickly as if it would lessen the pain. "He's an older gentlemen, in his early 80s, always wears a grey suit, and he was very impressed. He's shy, so he probably sat in the back."

"I remember."

"Anyway, he mentioned that you were a big fan of Senator Lyons."

"If you hadn't disappeared off the face of the earth, you'd know that."

Wesley's chest constricted. He'd always felt every sting of his father's barbs, each one chipping off pieces of his self-worth. Yet knowing how painful this conversation would be, how unforgiving and unrelenting his father would be, he had still made the call. *What kind of idiot am I to ever expect this man, who is incapable of ever admitting he is wrong, to miss me or want me back in his life?*

The elder Wesley couldn't see the glass house surrounding him as he hurled stones.

Wesley let out a long breath. "I work for Senator Lyons."

Reverend Wesley drew his words out. "You *work* for him?"

"Yes. sir."

"What do *you* do for a presidential candidate?"

Wesley's voice strengthened. "I'm an integral part of his kitchen cabinet. Sort of a behind-the-scenes-strategist."

"Behind the scenes? That seems convenient." The skepticism in his voice was obvious.

"It's true, Dad. I'm sure he would not be this close without me."

"Come on, John. I don't know what your angle is. I don't hear from you – no one has heard from you in over eighteen years, and now you are the next president's right-hand man? Do you need money? Is that what this is about?"

The iPhone slipped from his hand as Wesley reflexively constricted his hand into a fist in response to his father's doubt. "Fuck!" escaped as his left hand reached to catch the phone and ended up knocking it across the room. When he retrieved it the line was dead.

John Wesley punched in the numbers again and waited . . . two rings . . . three rings . . . a fourth . . .

"I won't tolerate that kind of language. I believe we are done."

"Would you like to meet him?"

Silence from the tiny speaker.

"Would you like to meet Jeremy Lyons?"

"You could do that?"

"Of course, Dad," said Wesley triumphantly.

This time he heard his father's audible exhale. "Well, that would certainly be an honor."

Wesley waited patiently until his father uttered his final word.

"Son."

CHAPTER 88

Senator Elise Franklin was old money. In contrast to that segment of old money that was concerned about appearances and behavior, she preferred to flaunt her inheritance. She wore her wealth like a birthright and displayed condescending disdain for the nouveau riche. But underneath the veneer of the ageless sex siren, Elise Franklin was sneaky smart. She knew which way the wind was blowing.

Her apartment at 1210 Watergate South was a testament to her wealth and impeccable taste. She claimed all the credit for the renovations and design, and thus was regarded as *the* person to consult with any home decorating decisions. Contrary to what should be the case, money can buy beauty.

The large apartment had three bedrooms and a library replete with first editions of the classics. The 260-degree views were accessed through floor-to-ceiling windows. A wide balcony surrounded the perimeter. Walnut-stained oak floors showcased selected Oriental rugs, which somehow melded perfectly with the contemporary feel.

Designer directional lights in gallery areas and throughout the residence highlighted her extensive art collections. Captivating sconces and lighting fixtures were aligned perfectly with the self-venting, large, state-of-the-art linear fireplace. A long rectangular table easily accommodated up to 24 guests.

The twenty invitations to today's event had been hand delivered by two trusted members of Franklin's staff. "CONFIDENTIAL...FOR YOUR EYES ONLY" was emblazoned on the front of each envelope. Inside was a request to each of the female senators to attend an urgent meeting at Elise Franklin's home. The time was 11:00 a.m. *sharp*, and brunch would be served.

Normally, an invitation to brunch at the senior senator's residence would be accompanied by a mouth-watering description of the sumptuous delicacies that would be served. This invitation, however, contained no frills, no enticements; in fact, it was more like a summons. Without a purpose or agenda stated, the recipients were left to wonder. Still, 18 out of the 20 female United States Senators confirmed that they would attend.

At 10:30, Franklin began pacing her spacious halls. With any major decision, she challenged herself. *I can abort. Make up some meaningless shit about why I called this meeting. I'm not meant to be Lyons's bitch. Then what? That cretin spreads the Jacob story on the internet. If I deny it, maybe the bastard has pictures or audio, and I am fucked. I could admit it and say my thinking has evolved; that's why I've done so much for gay rights. Still, it'd be a shit storm.* Head down, ignoring her priceless art on the walls, she walked faster. She was in the zone. *On the other hand, the first convert owns the kingdom.*

Franklin stopped walking and stood in front of a magnificent oil painting depicting Joan of Arc. "What the hell," she said out loud. "I get to pull the strings and have all these women dancing to *my* music."

Fifteen of the guests arrived within five minutes of the specified time. Those women were all greeted personally by Franklin and told to please take a seat where their name cards directed them. Drink orders were taken immediately, as the guests exchanged glances at what felt like a hurry-up offense.

The unfortunate three who arrived outside of the window of acceptability were not greeted by the hostess, but instead ushered summarily to their seats. Elise Franklin ignored them. She sat at the head of the table, a stern look on her face as she silently nodded to the servers to expedite placing plates before the guests.

It was unusual for senators to accept this abrupt, bordering on shabby treatment, but not one of the women present felt like challenging the powerful senator from California.

At precisely 11:30, Elise Franklin addressed the group.

"Ladies," she began in a no-nonsense tone, "we have an opportunity. Too long has the country been run by egomaniacal men. Oh, they are courteous and accepting of us in public, but privately, believe me, they are dismissive." She made eye contact with every woman at the table before she resumed speaking.

"You are thinking, well that's about to change in '16." She shook her head. "You are wrong. Jean Carlyle is *not* going to win. And even if she did, nothing would change. We all know her. She's the leader of *my* party. But a fake smile, an insincere hug doesn't convince me of anything except that she doesn't stand up to piss."

A few frowns were overridden by those listening intently. "Yes," Franklin continued. "We need a female chief executive, but we need one who will lift all women up. It will not happen with the coming election." Franklin placed her elbows on the table, interlocked her fingers, and rested her head on her hands. Buzzard-like, she waited.

"What do you know that we don't know?" asked the South Carolina Republican.

"I know that although we are all members of congress, we are still second-class citizens." She waited for her audience to absorb her words. "Without a unified voice, we are nothing but a footnote in history."

Franklin was pleased that all eyes were squarely on her as she added, "I know that if we make the right decision today, we will be in the inner circle with the first female president, and as an added incentive, we will all benefit individually when fund raising." She smiled, and her smile was cunning.

Heroin to the addict, a bottle to the alcoholic, nothing is more addictive than funding to a politician. "Hell, I'm in. I don't care what I gotta do," quipped the elderly senator from Iowa.

Franklin smiled as the laughter broke the tension. "Our next president will be..." she paused, "Jeremy Lyons." She bulldozed through the collective gasps. "His vice president will be Governor Mary Beth Justice. Lyons will serve for only one term, and then the way is paved for Mary Beth to be elected. She is fully aware of our meeting today and will meet with anyone who wants to get to know her better. She is attractive, smart as hell, and knows how to play the game."

"She's also a damn Republican," snarled one of Franklin's ultra-liberal colleagues.

"Lyons is going to blow through party affiliations like Sherman tore through Atlanta. You can either get on board or lose your next election. Do I like the fact that she is a Republican? Of course not. But she is a moderate, and he is an Independent. Lines will be blurred. Hopefully, a lot of the shit work will be finished and she can come in on his coattails."

"Why do you think Lyons will win?"

"He doesn't lose. The man is rich, ruthless, and driven. He's also a hero, and the common man will eat his shit up. Women think he's sexy. He doesn't equivocate, lie, or mince words."

"This is unprecedented, Elise," said one of her older colleagues. "What is your game plan?"

"Ladies," said Franklin, leaning forward conspiratorially, "We are going to show the world who's in charge."

CHAPTER 89

Jean Carlyle was prepared. In her final conversation about campaign strategy, the ambitious senator stated her position with a summation that would have swayed the Supreme Court. Using her signature starter, she began, "Gabe, hear me out before you pass judgment.

"I agree with your advice that I should not attack Lyons. It is beneath me. But if I keep a muzzle on the media, ask my friends to publish only milquetoast articles about him, then I am trying to control the media. Lyons's past is begging for coverage. This isn't the BS about Romney traveling with his dog on the roof of his car. This is damaging, embarrassing, non-manufactured material. It's a legitimate part of Lyons's history.

"No matter how reluctant I am to pile it on him, even if I can or should discourage the story, it's inevitable that some reporter will publish a blistering expose on the man. Why not manage the media so that we control when and what is published? The Republicans will scream that I am complicit in spite of any denials. If you're going to get accused of the crime . . ."

She quickly added:

"Exhibit 1." She held up the cover of Lyons's book, *Survival of the Fittest.* "The son-of-a-bitch is nude on the cover of his book! This trash is an egotistical, autobiographical primer on how to get rich, screw the system, and break all the rules. You could pick quotes at random, and they could destroy him.

"Exhibit 2. Margo Savino was his first employee and his lover. An experienced swimmer, she dies in a mysterious drowning accident in the Gulf of Mexico, which is like a baby pool. Watching her die is the guy who led the search and destroy mission to get Lyons. Coincidence?

"Exhibit 3. Senator Lyons has had plenty of experience reaching across the aisles. He padded the pockets of crooked legislators in order to get access to inside information from CEOs." She held up a finger. "And yes, I found someone who, for the right price, will go on the record and admit it."

Carlyle spread her hands and bowed. "Okay, Gabe, it's your turn now."

Hill, who never took notes, responded rapidly. "One, to attack his book, even using an anonymous source, makes you vulnerable. Lyons never claimed it was nonfiction. He would claim that it was a self-help book for entrepreneurs. In fact, he'd probably suggest that you read it. The cover is provocative, but if criticized, he might just say he wanted to 'bare it all.'" His smile was apologetic.

"Two, without evidence of his involvement in the Savino woman's death, an insinuating article would look like the reporter was exploiting a tragedy with baseless innuendo. And, yeah, the stink would spread to you.

"Three, and in truth, this could have been the counter argument for any negative reports that could have even the flimsiest connection to you. Do you really want to cast the first stone? Have you forgotten that his people uncovered criminal and terrorist activities that our massive government couldn't find? You're not taking the high road because I think it is the best strategy for you, you're taking the high road because it's the *only* road available for you!"

Carlyle threw up her hands in frustration. "So I've got to fight with *both* hands tied behind my back?"

Hill sighed. "Perhaps it will be more helpful if I discuss a specific strategy."

"Any strategy where I don't have to smile, gush, and curtsy.....I'm a damn street fighter, Gabe."

Hill looked at her curiously. "In a three-debate format, how many do you think you would win?"

"Three," she answered defiantly.

"I disagree. The support you'd receive for being the first woman nominee would be neutralized by a hero in a wheelchair who only wants to reign for a single term."

"That's bullshit!"

"Perhaps," he said, nodding in agreement. "The job does tend to be addictive. Let's examine your primary strength."

"Um, my experience," she said. placing her hands on her hips.

"I agree. It's a major positive for you. What is Lyons's major advantage?"

"He's a hero in a chair," she said quickly.

"No. It is his lack of political baggage. He is unencumbered. No straightjacket of special interests or wealthy donors."

"So?"

"In three debates, he can pound that point unmercifully into the voters' psyche. It's compelling, Jean."

She was surprised to hear her first name, so she was slow to react. Without a pause, his eyes went from sympathetic to intense.

"The people are angry," said Hill. "They've been played for too long. If the snowball of anger becomes an avalanche, a politician will be powerless. And if we allow him to be the anti-politician, he will win."

CHAPTER 90

NICE TRY, CLOONEY, THOUGHT RICK Donovan.   In 2012, Hollywood's liberal elite had gathered in George Clooney's massive mansion for a $40,000-a-plate dinner for the incumbent president. It was up to those who lived in the weekly pages of *People* to show their adoring fans who should lead our country. At the time, the 15 million raised was a record. With Donovan in the house, consider it broken: 22 million and counting.

He laughed. He loved it when the pseudo economic gurus tried to do the math. What they never understood was that people who pledged just the required plate charge for the event were always left out in the cold. This is an auction, baby; fame never comes cheaply.

In truth, Donovan didn't really give a shit about Jean Carlyle. Jeremy Lyons seemed a hell of a lot more interesting and would be better for business. Still, Lyons had a tragic flaw: he couldn't be bought.

In the Hollywood hills, few houses under 40,000 square feet are looked at, much less bought, by stratosphere stars like Rick Donovan. Yet he loved the fact that his home had belonged to a string of glittering stars from generations past. All it took was a little pocket change, 25 million, to make it the most sumptuous home in Hollywood.

Tonight Donovan was hosting a $50,000-a-plate fundraiser for Jean Carlyle and was pleased to have a select 100 guests in his home. They arrived at the 20-foot, dome-topped front entrance after a winding drive past woods on left and right, appearing as if they could have extended for a half mile. No need to worry that paparazzi would snap pictures from the roadside. There was no line of sight from the curb, and the tremendous porte cochere served double duty as protector from the elements and from prying eyes. Donovan had also added an extra thirty security staff to ensure that the privileged were not disturbed.

Once inside the massive wood front door, guests were warmly welcomed, not just by seasoned staff, but also by the interior design. It indeed made visitors feel like they had arrived. Instead of the traditional sweeping staircase, the wall opposite the door was dominated by a two-story stone fireplace that, in colder weather, would make the room glow with light and warmth. Left and right walls contained large, mirror-topped side tables with lavish, fragrant floral arrangements. Archways on the interior sides of the tables leant a peek into endless corridors leading to the east and west wings of the house.

In the center of the foyer a group of overstuffed chairs circled a substantial, but low-rise, coffee table topped with more fresh flowers. Sliding glass doors on either side of the fireplace led out to the expansive center courtyard, one of three such lawns ready to receive guests when the weather cooperated.

It was there, rather than in the pool or tennis pavilions, where Donovan was receiving guests on this night. The size of a soccer pitch, the courtyard was festooned with flowering trees, manicured shrubs, and clusters of a dozen comfortable conversation centers. Strings of large, white party bulbs cast a soft light down on guests and staff, who appeared in about equal numbers. No want or wish was too much for the servers, all of whom were gorgeous starlets or young men who looked like they had just stepped off the set of *Magic Mike*. Yet, they were professional servers who somehow bustled among the gathering with food and drink without ever getting in the way.

Jean Carlyle was only too willing to excuse herself from the white-haired dowager who was way past her prime and probably had to beg her way into the fundraiser. With a smile and a pat on the padded shoulder of the woman's five-year-old dress, she turned to greet an extremely attractive man who dressed and reeked of money. He looked to be in his early 30s, which likely meant not an actor, but a successful tech entrepreneur. *He had me at the Warby Parker glasses*, she thought as he extended his hand.

"I'm Luke Graham, Senator, and I'm a big fan."

"Well, Luke," she said, trying not to be distracted by his liquid brown eyes and self-confident smile, "Thank you so much for attending tonight."

"It is my pleasure, and if I can get a little time with you, I would like to do a lot more to help."

She took his arm and lead him to a remote corner of the patio. "I'm all yours. Tell me about yourself."

"I'm just your garden variety serial entrepreneur, ma'am. Blessed to be where I am."

"I also feel blessed to hopefully have the opportunity to lead this great nation," said Carlyle.

"I've never backed a loser, yet."

She laughed. "Let's hope your track record remains intact."

"How do you have the energy to campaign as hard as you do and answer so many inane questions?" Graham asked.

Carlyle looked around surreptitiously. "God wants me to be president," she whispered. "She gives me energy and a boatload of patience."

"You, too?" Graham whispered back. "May I ask you a serious question?"

"Of course, as long as it's not inane."

He smiled. "What did you think about the way the corporate tax reduction was pushed through?"

The combination of a glass of wine and knowledge that the coffers were full gave her the confidence to let her guard down. "If people start thinking they can tweet whatever legislative changes they want, well, we are doomed."

"Don't you think you could use that power for your crusade against income inequality?" countered Luke.

"Fair point." Carlyle frowned and looked at him with suspicion. "Luke, may I see your cell phone?"

"Of course," he said, obviously flustered as he took it from his blazer pocket and handed it to her.

She looked at the screen and made sure that the power was off.

"Sorry," she said, handing it back to him. "After the Romney gaffe, one can't be too careful."

"I love the fact that you're cautious. It's a good litmus test for the presidency."

"You know as well as I, that income equality is a slogan, not a promise." She leaned closer and whispered into the handsome young man's ear, "There's an old adage in politics: You can lie to the people, but never to the donors."

"Hey, who's hogging our girl?" The loud voice signaled a man's approach from behind Graham.

Carlyle affixed a big smile and extended her arm. "Luke, I want you to meet one of my staunchest supports, the Senate Minority Leader, Everett Leeds."

"Politics does indeed make for strange bedfellows," said Graham as he slowly turned toward Senator Leeds. Seemingly in one motion, he caught the man and kept him from hitting the ground.

* * *

As the valet left to retrieve his car, John Wesley took off his glasses and placed them gently in his pocket. This pair was particularly expensive. Still, he felt confident that the Google Glass camera embedded in the frames had recorded everything he needed.

CHAPTER 91

I⊤ WAS AN UNWRITTEN RULE that Sabine did not like to be disturbed when she was working. While Alegria's role on the team was clearly defined, it was Sabine's responsibility to interpret the computer genius's voluminous data and recommend strategies to optimize the research. Often, she merely added nuance to an idea the Jeremy had, but her instincts and insight were invaluable.

By choice, Sabine's office was a functional cave. There were no windows, and the only furniture in the small room was a black-lacquered standup desk, a straight-back chair, her computer, and a metal crook-necked lamp. She preferred paper to studying a monitor, and when she turned abruptly at the unwelcome door opening, her papers slid off her lap onto the tile floor.

"Did I miss the knock?" Sabine asked as John Wesley walked through the open door. Her terse tone matched the annoyed look on her face.

"Sorry," said Wesley dismissively. "Do you have a minute?"

"If I said no, would you leave?"

"Probably not," he said, adding a quick laugh.

She was tempted to get up and kick the grin off the clueless bastard's face. Instead, she folded her hands, glared disdainfully at him and waited for him to speak.

"I need a favor," he said expectantly and waited for a response.

She remained silent.

"After you hear what I captured with the glasses, you're going to want to give me whatever I want. It's pretty explosive stuff."

His charming smile didn't penetrate her mood, so he forged ahead. "My dad is a big-time preacher in Knoxville, Tennessee. Every week he tells his congregation to vote for Jeremy. I want to fly my dad to Naples or D.C., have him shake Jeremy's hand, and then he'll be on his way. Can you take care of that for me?"

Sabine looked at him like he had two heads. "You interrupted my work to ask if your father could meet Jeremy?"

"No. I got you the smoking gun you were looking for," he said defensively.

"That's your job, a job for which you are highly compensated. I'm speaking about your request to have Jeremy meet your father."

"It's not a big deal. He'll be in and out in five minutes."

She shook her head. "It's not going to happen."

"What!"

"The senator has many supporters. He does not meet with them individually. If he met one and others found out, they would feel slighted."

"But I'm…"

"You're *what*, John?" She rose and got in his face. "You have no connection to him. You work for me. I'm your boss. Tell you what, you want your dad to meet me, I'll give him a thrill. Now leave." Sabine tuned her back to him.

Wesley spread his fingers apart, flexing them and then releasing them. The impulse to grab her by the neck and lift her off the ground was overwhelming. He bit his lip so hard it began to bleed. He didn't trust himself to speak, so he walked to the door and closed it quietly behind him.

CHAPTER 92

J<small>ACKIE</small> M<small>AYFIELD WAS NORMALLY UNFLAPPABLE</small> on camera. But sitting this close to Sabine literally took her breath away. Getting the interview was a terrific coup, but Sabine was so stunning that Jackie directed the camera to stay on the woman. With dark mesmerizing eyes, high cheekbones, and skin the color of warm caramel, it seemed excessive that her beautiful head sat on top of a perfect body. Sabine could make the hottest Hollywood starlet feel like the ugly duckling.

Jackie took a breath and plowed ahead. "Sabine, I can't tell you how pleased we are that you agreed to this interview." The camera panned to Jackie as she continued. "Sabine is an extremely private woman, and we at Fox News respect her privacy. We will not ask intrusive or insensitive questions. However, we are interested in finding out whatever she's willing to share about herself and about her relationship with Senator Jeremy Lyons."

Jackie turned her head, and the camera followed her and went to split screen. "Sabine, what can you tell us about your relationship with the senator?"

Sabine's voice was as smooth as single malt. "For the past five years, we have been in a monogamous relationship."

"You're not married."

"No," she said with a warm smile. "For us, it's not necessary."

"All of the other presidential candidates have spouses. Do either of you feel that not being married is a disadvantage? Would you perform the duties of the first lady?"

"I hope I'm not a disadvantage," she said shyly, "and no, I would not serve in the traditional role as first lady. I would not expect

Jeremy's administration to participate in most of the ceremonial events of the past."

"That's interesting," said Jackie, raising her eyebrows. "How does he expect to escape the considerable protocols that are ingrained into the presidency?"

"What he lacks in pomp and circumstance, he will make up for in effort and progress."

"In other words, you don't know either," Jackie joked.

Sabine laughed. "He doesn't tell me everything," she said.

"Any reason you decided not to get married?"

"Well, if we were married, I probably couldn't get away with passing off the first lady duties."

"Okay, I give up. What else would be different about his presidency?"

"You mean other than he will not lie and he never makes empty promises?"

Now Jackie laughed. "Yes, other than that."

"He won't be golfing or going on lavish vacations. Also, he intends to work some out of our Naples home. Undoubtedly, he will drive the Secret Service crazy."

"So it's safe to say that he'll be an unconventional president?"

"Yes, but the voters will know what they're getting before they vote. Heads of state will know that the vice president will be much more involved in personal meetings, except that Jeremy will always be available in times of crisis."

Shifting gears, Jackie leaned in. "I know you were there for Senator Lyons when he got hit by the car. He told me that you never left his side while he was in a coma. The first time you and I met was right before his election."

Sabine nodded.

"Are you his closest confidant?"

"Yes. Jeremy has a small group of trusted advisers, but I have the longest tenure. In addition, I am in charge of his philanthropic responsibilities."

"Responsibilities?"

"Yes, Jeremy feels that success requires a person to give and give generously."

"Excuse me if I'm being too intrusive, but are you two considering children?"

Sabine winced and answered in a soft voice. "We were, before the incident."

Jackie changed the subject. "Is there anything in your background, family history, or even your last name that you'd like to share with us?"

Sabine laughed again. "No, but I'm afraid you've blown my cover. My history is really not that interesting, and I intend to go back into hibernation after this interview."

"That would be a shame," Jackie said with sincerity. "You are a highly intelligent, articulate young woman who also happens to be extraordinarily beautiful. You are truly fascinating." She paused. "Do you think this interview will help or hurt Senator Lyons's chances?'"

"I certainly can't judge that. Thank you, by the way, for your kind words. It was my decision to appear on your show."

"And why did you want to do this?"

"To speak from a woman's perspective and show the world that Jeremy is a real person. To tell America that Jeremy Lyons is not a politician. He is a brilliant, driven leader, who *will* restore our country's greatness. He is decisive, but compassionate, strong, honest, and trust me, he bleeds red, white, and blue."

Jackie waited a beat, then reached out and patted her arm. "Last question, Sabine. What keeps Jeremy Lyons up at night?"

Sabine's smile went viral, and her one-word response damn near broke the internet. "Me."

* * *

Grace McGregor gave her husband "the look." Every married man is familiar with the look. Often it's accompanied by questions such as "*Where* did you say you were last night?" or "*What* do you want me to do?" In this case, Grace merely pointed to the TV. "*That's* the woman who beat you up?"

Mac shrugged.

"Are you sure that it wasn't a wrestling match, and she pinned you? Don't expect me to feel sorry for you."

"Hey, she jumped me. It was a sneak attack."

"Uh huh, and didn't you also tell me that she later had breakfast with you?"

"Oh sure," said Mac with a practiced whine. "Blame the victim."

*　*　*

Identical lamps were centered on matching night tables on either side of their king-sized bed. Everything in Grace McGregor's world was perfectly placed. When she and Mac sat in a booth in a restaurant, she would slide to the middle and motion for him to sit exactly opposite from her. On the numerous occasions when he wished to annoy her, he would slide three inches off center, and she would impatiently wave him back.

Grace, who always brushed her teeth first, because she didn't want to witness her husband's predictable mess, had turned on the lamp and picked up her Kindle when Mac plopped on the bed and asked her a question.

"I'm unwinding," she said, signaling her reluctance to engage in a lengthy conversation.

"Short conversation," said Mac. "Erase the fact that Sabine obviously wanted to get close to me when she narrowly won a controversial split decision and then tricked me into breakfast as a last gasp to compromise me."

Grace's beautiful blue eyes appeared to roll out of sight.

"Start with a clean slate" Mac went on. "As a discerning woman, what did you think of her?"

Realizing that subtleties would be useless, and she would have to get up and ugly to discourage him, Grace succumbed. "I think she was impressive. Obviously beautiful, but non-threatening, like a gifted athlete who doesn't flaunt it."

Mac, sitting cross legged on the bed, nodded to encourage her to continue.

"I like the fact that she stands by her man and believes in him. I felt she was credible."

"Do you think she helped his candidacy?"

"You're the political junkie. That's your call."

He reached over and hugged her. "Thanks for your thoughts."

"What do you think?" she asked.

Mac released her and thought for a few moments. When he summarized thoughts, he tended to speak in bullet points. "She made him more human. She reinforced the fact that he would be an unconventional president, more concerned with what he thinks is right than what is traditional or expected. I think she came off vulnerable, soft, and playful. I'm sure everyone watching smiled at her last comment."

He hesitated. "In the last election, 90 per cent of African-Americans voted for the incumbent. After tonight, I can't imagine any man wanting Sabine to disappear from view. And," he nodded towards her, " I think she may *finally* be over me."

Her pillow connected with his head at the exact moment of his last word.

CHAPTER 93

CERTAINLY FROM THE TIME OF Lyndon Johnston and probably before, the role of Vice President of the United States has been mostly ceremonial and mostly thankless. Yes, there is the "what if" factor, but the odds are that the veep will be doing everything the president doesn't want to do. Mary Beth Justice was well aware of this, but not the least bit concerned.

She suspected that a number of presidents had promised real input to their seconds in command, but she'd seen no evidence that they delivered. In her case, starting with the campaign, every responsibility, every move was planned, and, in some cases, even choreographed. Justice had agreed to this unprecedented lack of flexibility for a number of reasons:

1. She would be the face of the campaign, traveling to different states, meeting with the press. In other words, she was getting free exposure for her 2020 presidential run.
2. In the event that one of Lyons's agenda items went south, he would state that Justice had disagreed with the proposal.
3. Any action that worked and was well received would have her as an after-the-fact co-author.

In politics, it was unheard of for a vice presidential candidate to be the only one giving on-the-ground interviews and stump speeches to the voters. It was a huge gamble for the ticket. The only thing that prevented the ticket from brutal attacks by the media was, frankly, Senator Lyons's disability. In our politically correct world, there were some places that even the mainstream media didn't go.

Normally, with the vice presidential candidate being a Republican, the party would take an active role. For once, however, there was a consensus. Let the ticket sink or swim on its own. Most of the party faithful had been convinced that the only way to fight the demographics was to pit an outspoken maverick against the Carlyle juggernaut. If Lyons/Justice won, whatever was accomplished could go on their ledger, and if the four years were a disaster, they'd be there to pick up the pieces. Most convincing was the fact that their donors could save their wallets for the congressional elections.

In the televised vice presidential debate, Justice held her own. Her opponent, a moderate Democrat who was a three-time senator from the swing state of Virginia, had been an extremely successful entrepreneur. Justice had worn a navy blue suit over a white silk blouse, while the senator had worn the traditional navy suit, white shirt, and red and white striped tie. Both wore the obligatory American flags on their lapels. They were political cut-outs, perfect in every way.

Although both running mates were judged competent and capable, Justice had an ace up her sleeve. She had "girl power."

For Justice, the best proof of her performance was the positive assessment from her running mate. Still, the quote that made her smile the most was from *The Washington Post*'s Tom Hessell: "The Republicans have finally discovered that it is possible to combine beauty with brains."

CHAPTER 94

THE ONLY INDICATION THAT STEVE Cannon was awake was the cell phone in his hand. His black leather office chair was meant to recline, but Cannon was currently testing the laws of physics. In order to fully stretch out his lanky frame, he was almost parallel to the floor. Bare feet, crossed at the ankles, were slung over his small, battered desk.

"I don't think so," he said, as if it were an effort to respond. He thought about shaking his head, but judiciously decided that the act could result in the chair spinning out from under him.

"All right, I'll bring it up to him, but I'm telling you, not a chance in hell." Cannon clicked off. Gingerly, but reluctantly, he lifted his torso and scooched the chair closer to the desk. This was not his first rodeo.

He sat up and rubbed his hands over his face. "Resting his eyes," he'd tell his wife, who, in reply, tended to roll hers. Not only had the call interrupted his contemplation, but Carlyle's dumb-ass chief of staff wouldn't stop yapping about their stupid proposal until he'd agreed to pass it on. *When your guy is a home run hitter, you don't limit his at bats.*

* * *

The inner circle was in session. Instead of rejecting Carlyle's proposal out of hand, Lyons had asked for discussion. Cannon was adamantly against it. To him the logic was unassailable. Alegria agreed that from a statistical perspective, Lyons would win every debate. Only Sabine seemed on the fence as she studied her lover's reactions to the conversation.

"Alegria," Lyons turned to her, "see if you can get McGregor on the phone."

All clients received the white-glove treatment from Mac McGregor's team, but certain names meant "red alert." Whenever Alegria called, every effort was made to locate first Mac and then R.J., if Mac was not available. Advisors want to be instantly accessible to those rare clients with accounts in the hundreds of millions. Whenever those clients call, whatever else the advisor is doing is put on pause. This time it was easy. Mac was finishing a salad at his desk.

"Hi, Alegria. Good to hear from you. It must be busy in your world."

"It is," she agreed. "Mac, you're on speaker, and Jeremy, Steve, and Sabine are with me. Do you have a few moments to talk?"

"Absolutely. How can I help?"

Jeremy spoke. "Good afternoon, Mac. We have a proposal from Carlyle, and we'd like your opinion on its merits."

A diminishing part of Mac still suspected that Lyons was toying with him, but if so, it would be an elaborate prank.

"As you are aware, since 2000, there have been three televised presidential debates in each election cycle. However, this format is not set in stone. Assuming that the Republican hangers-on fall off, then the two remaining candidates have the ability to determine the number of debates. In the past, a secret memorandum of understanding has been issued. Carlyle's camp would prefer to have only one debate. What are your thoughts?"

Mac closed his eyes, his mind racing.

"Would you rather cogitate and call us back?" asked Jeremy.

Mac let out a breath. "No. I'm paid to think on my feet. Plus, if I go with my first reaction, I won't have to stew on this until I call you back. By the way, I do feel more comfortable opining on strategy than on the issues. Okay." Another breath. "Conventional thinking would be that you are the superior debater, so you should want the three debates. Moreover, the tendency is to not want what is appealing to your opponent." Mac hesitated

"But, you are anything but conventional. Romney won the first debate, took his foot off the gas, and Obama coasted in. You'd never take your foot off the gas, but I could see you come off as the heavy in three debates. She will definitely play the female card.

"You don't equivocate. Certainty is your calling card. That self-assurance can be off putting in extended doses. As laid back as I am, you've even managed to piss *me* off." Mac waited and received the expected chuckles.

"Think of the mantra of entertainers: 'Always leave them wanting more.' Personally, I like the one and done, the Super Bowl of elections. It will get historic ratings and play into the public's limited attention span."

Lyons looked around the room. Alegria was listening attentively, while Cannon was still shaking his head, though not as vigorously. Sabine had caught his slight smile and nodded at him.

"One more thing," said Mac. "I would leak the fact that Carlyle asked for only one debate and that you graciously accepted. Before that, I would want something in writing from them requesting the single debate format. You can't have them claiming later that you requested it because you were too busy or some other nonsense."

"Thanks, Mac. Any other thoughts?" asked Lyons.

"Nope. Hope it helps."

"It has. You missed your calling."

"That's what *all* my clients say," quipped Mac.

CHAPTER 95

J OHN W ESLEY FELT LIKE HE was on a stakeout. Lyons had arrived back in Naples on Friday afternoon, and Wesley had remained in the shadows waiting for an opportunity. He knew if he hadn't controlled himself with Sabine, the bitch would have dropkicked him on the spot, and there would be no opportunity. *Live to fight another day.*

Finally, shortly after dinner on Sunday, Sabine excused herself, claiming a headache, and left the senator alone. Still Wesley waited for the perfect moment. When he saw Lyons wheel himself out onto the porch, he knew it was time. His game plan was simple: Propose his plan to Lyons and then remain calm and under no circumstances interrupt the man.

"Senator, do you have just a moment?"

Lyons looked over his left shoulder as Wesley approached, and nodded.

Fighting the urge to lean down so he would be on eye level, Wesley began. "I know that I didn't articulate this well when I spoke to Sabine, but I wondered if I could have my dad meet you just long enough to shake your hand. He is one of your biggest fans."

Lyons furrowed his brow. "Was Sabine not clear in her decision?"

Wesley gave a shallow smile. "Yes, sir, she was clear; I just thought you might have a different perspective. My father is a well-respected pastor who has over 500 devoted parishioners."

"I reread your file. You've been estranged from your father for a long time. What made you connect with him now?"

"I attended one of his services, and he was telling everyone that they should vote for you."

"Did you speak then?"

"No. I wore a disguise."

Lyons nodded. "So the only reason you reconnected with your father was because you thought you had something that he wanted."

Wesley lowered his head. "I guess that's right, sir. "

"Well, you don't. You have no relationship with me. Whatever you have been doing for Sabine is not my business. I don't know and don't care to know. You have a history of violence that if you and I had any relationship could be damaging to the presidency. Do you realize the importance of that? Nothing else matters. What do you think would happen after I met your father? Would you become the prodigal son? Is that what you want? At what cost? You acted on impulse; and impulsive behavior leads to disaster."

Wesley couldn't breathe. "Is it possible that you're overreacting, sir?"

In a blink, Lyons's pistol was in his hands. Wesley jumped back. "*This* would be overreacting, Mr. Wesley. What do you think your father would do after you arranged a personal meet and greet? He would tell his parishioners what an honor he had, and it was all because of his son. It would become a Hallmark moment. At some point, the truth would come out on you, and the presidency would be irrevocably blemished."

In almost a whisper, he added, "People like Grant, Leeds, Steiner, and Franklin might start making connections that, although erroneous, might lead to me. Your request is denied. Sabine asked me to inform you that as of January 15, your services will no longer be needed."

Wesley's eyes burned a hole through the senator. He saw no logic in Lyons's words, just spite, and refusal. All Wesley felt was loss and rage. Lyons had ripped away his salvation, leaving him with nothing. As he exited the porch, he vowed to reciprocate – "an eye for an eye" as the Bible says.

CHAPTER 96

Every time Senator Lyons appeared on another network, Jackie Mayfield unconsciously ended up giving herself an old-fashioned manicure. Enough reminding from her mom had caused her to stop biting her nails when she entered college, but she assuaged her guilt by telling herself that she didn't know when she was doing it. But tonight the presidential candidate was on her network; mom would be proud of her nails.

"It's a week before the debate, the *only* presidential debate, and you are down in the polls." Jackie's concern was evident, the emotion genuine.

Jeremy Lyons's smile was reassuring, not unlike a father's to his child.

"I have a number of questions," she began, her large emerald eyes alight with excitement and intelligence. "First, it has become standard to have three presidential debates. Since your campaign has virtually ignored your opponent, and I must say, you haven't done a great job of bragging on yourself, I would think that you would want multiple debates. Why would you agree to only one bite of the apple?"

"That's a fair question. I'm of the opinion that oversaturation dulls the senses rather than stimulates them."

"That's a nice sound bite, Senator, but this is still puzzling. I believe having only one debate was your opponent's idea rather than yours."

Lyons nodded. "That is correct, Jackie. But remember, underneath this crusty exterior beats the heart of a gentleman."

She laughed. "You're great at charming me out of a direct answer. Seriously, I hope you know what you're doing."

His smile was confident.

"My second question concerns the consensus of political strategists. They feel that your reluctance to appear personally in battleground states is the primary reason that Senator Carlyle is projected to win. What is your response?"

"It's initially difficult for people to reconcile someone running for office who marches to a different drummer. A leader who refuses to publicly criticize his opponent, a leader who is not making speeches and appearances regurgitating empty promises at every stop." He paused, then asked her a question.

"Do we want a president who will say the right thing or a president who will *do* the right thing?"

Jackie pounced. "Are you saying that Senator Carlyle is strong on rhetoric, but weak on action?"

Lyons laughed. "No, but you just did. Jackie. I can't divine how a person would perform what I consider their 'sacred duties.'"

"Senator, the media has been very critical about your voting record. How do you respond?"

"I believe the complaints center on my lack of a voting record."

"Sorry, that is more accurate. You have been accused of being missing in action on a significant number of senate votes."

Lyons nodded. "The criticism is valid. If you check the record, any vote that I missed, the senators voted straight down party lines. The outcome was predetermined."

"Don't you think that your constituents expected you to be more, uh, at least disruptive?"

He smiled. "I don't believe Florida has suffered under my watch, Jackie," he said modestly. "But there is a larger issue. May I use a stock market reference?"

"Of course," she answered, returning his smile.

"The best indication of future performance of an individual stock is the quality of management. Yet it is impossible to assess the strengths and weaknesses of management without getting to know them. Due diligence is critical in any endeavor where the objective is to create a better outcome."

Cocking his head, he asked, "What do you think I've been doing for the last 15 months?"

Caught off guard, she blinked. "I, I don't know."

"I work. Ten to twelve hours a day, every day except Sundays, I am studying, analyzing, speaking with confidants, scholars, men and women of exceptional insight. We need to fix our country. I don't believe that it can be done without exhaustive research. Frankly, I backed congress into a corner with the bill to lower corporate taxes, but the element of surprise is gone. I need compelling evidence, hard data that the measures I advocate will help our nation."

He raised his hands. "I'm guilty of what would historically be viewed as poor campaigning. But we want to create history, not relive it. I needed to work without distractions; the job is too vital to be approached haphazardly.

"Listen," he said, leaning forward. "In a perfect world, all legislators would serve a single term. It could be four years, six years. The duration is not as important as the finality of service. It would dramatically reduce the influence of special interest groups and the effectiveness of cronyism. Representatives could vote their conscience, not be beholden to those who provide campaign donations."

She raised her perfect eyebrows. "That would be utopia."

"Imagine if a congressperson's legacy were determined by how much better the country was when he or she left."

"If you lose, will you share your research with the new president?"

Lyons seemed to digest the question and then offered a tight smile. "I don't consider failure an option, for me or for America."

She persisted. "So you're not the least bit worried that the election is less than a month away and every poll shows that you will lose?"

Lyons folded his hands and addressed her. "During the darkest days of World War II, there was a cabinet meeting in London. France had just capitulated. Prime Minister Churchill described in dire detail the hopelessness of England's situation. Staring back at him with eyes of despair and thoughts of surrender, his dispirited colleagues awaited his decision. The visionary statesman lit a cigar, showed a hint of a smile, and with a twinkle in his eyes responded. "Gentlemen, I find it rather inspiring."

CHAPTER 97

LESLEY SIMMONS WAS PACING THE floor of the CBS studio. She did not believe that Jeremy Lyons was an Independent. She was deathly afraid that he would pull a rabbit out of a hat and defeat her candidate. The ramifications of having a maverick closet Republican running the country were too dire to imagine. *I did not become the country's most influential news reporter (Jackie Mayfield can kiss my ass; the bitch is probably sleeping with him.) to let some right-wing cowboy destroy everything we've gained.*

Lesley knew that CBS would be all over another interview with Lyons, but if she reached out to him at this stage of the campaign, he would know that he was being set up. She was desperate. She placed a call to Gabe Hill.

"He just had a puff piece with Jackie Mayfield," said Hill. "I would tell him that you were sure he would want to give you equal time. *You* have to make the call. He is more vulnerable to women than men. Be advised; if your intention is to trap him into a losing position that will cost him votes, he is smarter than you."

"It's a good thing you're giving me this advice for free, Gabe," Lesley said evenly. "I guess you'll just have to watch the segment to know who the winner is. If your advice is similar to the strategy you suggested for Jean, I won't get the interview anyway." She disconnected, which might not be smart long term, but sure felt good.

* * *

"Senator Lyons, you are very generous to give us your time. The day of reckoning is almost upon us, and I know there are other things you had to do. We appreciate your fitting us into your busy schedule."

"Always have time for a fan," Lyons said, adding a smile.

"Well, as you know, I promised that I would ask only a limited number of questions."

"You did, Lesley. However, you neglected to tell me the questions."

She smiled. "You're so good on your feet, sir, that our viewers wouldn't have it any other way."

He was silent, so she continued. "Your vice presidential nominee has been very explicit in her views about a number of controversial topics. I am aware that you have chosen to let her represent your ticket, and in fact, you've been on the campaign trail less than any other candidate in modern history. But I'm sure that our viewers would like to hear some answers from the presidential candidate. For instance, how did you, an Independent, persuade the plethora of Republican candidates to step aside and allow you to be the nominee?"

"I'm grateful that they did, because it was a crowded field, and I think America deserves a clear choice. Although they would be better equipped to answer your question, I believe the idea that someone with no political baggage was needed to create real change was part of their reasoning."

"So you don't agree to the claim that it was because you are a Republican in an Independent's clothing."

"Lesley, I don't think keeping our citizens safe both militarily and economically is a Republican platform; it's part of the American dream."

"What are your views on helping the poor and our welfare programs?"

"President Clinton, with the support of the Republicans, passed welfare reform that included welfare-to-work requirements. I will seek to have this reinstated."

"Would you consider that more a Republican or Democrat issue?"

"I would consider the horrendous state of our welfare system a national issue."

Her smile was challenging. "But you're comfortable with all the issues because *God* has chosen you to lead this country."

He looked at her for a long moment. "Lesley, as you may know, many followers of Christ believe that their lives are led by Him. And it's hard to refute from our forefathers forward the contributions made by people of faith. We can attribute such seminal moments in history as the abolition of slavery, women's suffrage, the reform of labor laws, and the civil rights movement to the intervention of people of faith."

"Would you include the Affordable Care Act in those seminal moments?"

Lyons paused. "It was a noble intent. However, the economic premise was faulty, the promises were invalid, and for such a technologically superior country, the implementation was embarrassing."

Lesley changed the subject abruptly. "What are your views on enhanced interrogation techniques, such as waterboarding?"

"The individual rights of a terrorist are secondary to protecting our citizens."

She almost jumped out of her chair. "You know that in 2009, President Obama banned the use of those techniques. So you disagree with his decision?"

He nodded. "Yes."

Lesley did everything but salivate. Her eyes flashed. "Then you think it is *permissible* to torture individuals who have not been given access to an attorney or formally charged?"

"That's not what I said."

"Well, it's what both our audience and I heard."

"Then perhaps we can sharpen your listening skills."

Lesley started to protest, and Lyons raised a cautionary finger. "You asked me if I agreed with the decision to publically declare that enhanced techniques were off limits. I do not. I do not believe that we should give our enemies any information about our tactics or our strategies. If captured enemies of our country know that they can get a lawyer and have their say in court to spout poison, they will be emboldened. Fear is caused by uncertainty. As commander in chief, I want the terrorists who are trying to attack our country to only *imagine* the consequences."

"Okay," she said, holding up her hands. "I may have jumped the gun, but it sounds like you do believe in waterboarding."

His darks eyes glowered. "Lesley, what I believe, and what I will do to protect my country are none of your business or anyone else's outside of my administration."

"The American people have a right…"

"To be safe, and I will keep them safe by any means required."

"That's not acceptable!"

"Really?" he said. "I guess in a few days, we'll know." His gaze challenged her. "Whether or not a policy is acceptable to the media elite is meaningless to me. My responsibility is to American citizens, and telegraphing our intentions to our enemies is bad policy."

She studied him for a quick second, her practiced smile only showing cracks to those looking for them. "So you're not concerned that there has never been a third party candidate who became president in the history of the United States." Her lips opened just enough to allow the words to come out.

To the audience, his smile was confident; to Lesley, it was patronizing. "Lesley, as I have studied our position in the world, I am convinced that our people do not want someone to repeat history. They want someone who will *create* history."

CHAPTER 98

THE PRESUMPTIVE PRESIDENT AGREED WITH Gabe Hill's strategy of limiting the number of debates. Against any of the Republican candidates, if Lyons had not bought or coerced them to drop out, Senator Carlyle would have a major psychological advantage not unlike her predecessor. In his case, in addition to the fact that he was viewed as more likeable than his opponent, a century of guilt could be erased by electing an African-American president.

So, although many would like to see her as the first woman president, and, normally, any aggression from her male opponent would garner instant sympathy, Lyons in a wheelchair automatically made him a tragic hero and, to some, elicited comparisons to FDR.

In a single debate, Carlyle could lull Lyons with kindness and civility, and then......hammer time.

The most difficult discussion had been the choice of venue for the debate. Finally, both sides had agreed to the Daughters of the American Revolution's Constitution Hall in Washington, D.C. The concert hall, built in 1929, is a neoclassical-style structure faced with Alabama limestone. The auditorium has a U-shaped balcony, which provides for an enormous amount of seating while retaining practical sight distances.

Every president since Calvin Coolidge attended at least one event at DAR Constitution Hall. Located at 1776 D Street, NW, the largest auditorium in the nation's capital was actually the perfect place for this historical debate.

In keeping with the unconventional debate forum, both parties had also agreed to hold the debate without live moderators. From all over the country, citizens submitted their questions, and a panel of supposedly nonpartisan experts sorted, filtered, and ultimately chose those that would be asked of the respective candidates.

Senators Carlyle and Lyons received the questions via their teleprompters, while the audience heard and saw them on a giant screen that was behind the candidates.

"Senator Carlyle, what are your specific plans to ameliorate income inequality?"

"Great word," said Carlyle, smiling broadly. "The only way to level the playing field is to make sure that the middle class has the same opportunities that the rich do. When a billionaire," she flashed an apologetic smile at her opponent, "pays taxes at a lower rate than the average American, well, it just takes a strong leader to insist on that change."

"Senator Lyons, how are you qualified to deal with our country's enemies?"

"First," said Lyons, "I would surround myself with men and women of experience and vision. Second, I would listen to my Joint Chiefs of Staff, require them to justify their recommendations, and then act appropriately."

"Senator Carlyle, how do you propose to break the gridlock and get congress working again?"

"How many presidents have said that they would reach across the aisles?" Carlyle asked. "How many of them actually did it? How do we get America working if we can't get Washington working? I have a theory about this..." She whispered the next words. "It's high time for a woman to come in and clean house."

The audience laughed at her delivery, and even Senator Lyons smiled.

"Senator Lyons, how do you intend to fix our nation's fiscal policies?"

"I've spent the majority of my life analyzing the strengths and weaknesses of companies. Our enemies are making critical judgments about our solvency every day. Over the past nine months, with the help of a dozen forensic accountants, we have analyzed our nation's fiscal problems. We will solve them."

Throughout the majority of the debate, both senators stayed true to their roles: Senator Carlyle shined with her foreign policy experience and came across as the sweet grandma that everybody wants. An experienced debater, she did not misstep.

Senator Lyons was precise and unequivocal on his positions, but came across as less personable. All in all, it was civil, answers were expected, and it was boring. Fortunately, for the audience there was a second act.

In Act Two, each candidate had three minutes to express his or her concerns, which could include any misgivings about the other's ability to lead the country. Other than the time constraints, there were no rules. It was must watch television.

* * *

With utter calmness, Jean Carlyle turned and looked directly at Jeremy Lyons. Her eyes were sympathetic, and her face showed her concern. "A man of the people?" She raised her eyebrows. "I don't understand why through the entire campaign, you never spoke *with* the people. Every campaign stop was left to your vice presidential choice. I can't tell you how many people have asked me, 'Is he too good to shake my hand or look me in the eye?' I don't think a president should just speak *to* the people." She shook her head.

"I can't erase the image of Don Quixote chasing windmills," she went on. "Senator Lyons, your certitude is admirable, your conviction inspiring. Though your aspirations are noble, Senator, I'm afraid that they are impossible to achieve.

"Reducing the national debt without closing loopholes and increasing taxes on the wealthy is impossible. Adding to our defense budget without increasing the debt is also impossible. Making money with our country's most powerful and influential people and doing it behind a curtain in the stock market is not the same as balancing a budget. Yes, we need to reduce our debt." She wagged a finger. "But we cannot do it by reducing our compassion.

"You want to slash entitlements: Social Security, Medicare, and our national health plan. I submit that it is *impossible* to do that without hurting the elderly, the poor, the sick.

"You want to drain our treasury to secure our borders, and then *you'll* decide who stays and who will be deported. That is an impossible situation for our immigrants and impossible for Americans to accept.

"You want to lead our allies and contain our enemies." Carlyle raised her eyebrows. "We all want that, sir; it's not a new idea. Do you really think it is possible to accomplish that with a president who does not have a minute's worth of experience in foreign affairs? Maybe you do think it is possible. In your autobiographical book, it sounded like you believed you were Superman.

"Foreign policy requires not only an educated grasp of the situation, but also the flexibility to compromise when required to accomplish your objective. During this entire campaign, I have yet to hear you admit that it is *possible* for you to make a mistake."

The indelible image was of a mother's disappointment in a child when she next spoke. "I'm sorry if I sound harsh." She raised her hands in a placating manner. "But we really can't afford to turn our country over to a man who thinks he's perfect."

Carlyle closed her eyes and shook her head as if she were wrestling with the words. When she slowly raised her head, her eyes were glistening. "It's time, America. It's time for a woman of experience, courage, and integrity to lead this country. Anything else is impossible to consider. Thank you, and God bless America."

Lyons's head went back as he squeezed his eyes shut. Later, what happened next would be described as like watching a volcano erupt. Eyes still closed, he said, "One of the few things my father ever said to me was that it was impossible that I would amount to anything. When I decided not to go to college, the president of my military high school said that without a college education, it is impossible to get ahead."

His eyes flew open, and he glared at Carlyle. "When I left the brokerage firm of Johnston Wellons to go out on my own, the head of the firm said that it's impossible to succeed without financial backing. When the government came after me because I had been too successful, they told me it was impossible to have done what I did without cheating. Yet, they found nothing!

"No one thought it was possible to get a bill passed in less than sixty days. How did it happen? The *people* made the impossible happen."

Veins popped in Lyons's neck, and a red flush rose from his neck to his head like a thermometer under a heat lamp. "It was impossible to uncover a manufacturer of illegal drugs that were killing children, and certainly impossible for one man to stop a terrorist attack on our National Cathedral on Easter Sunday.

"When a cowardly assassin ran over me at a speed in excess of forty miles per hour, the doctors said that it was impossible for me to ever be a United States Senator. And finally," his voice rose to a crescendo, "every doctor swore that I WOULD NEVER WALK AGAIN!"

With that shout, Lyons's arms gripped the sides of his wheelchair, and his body was suspended by his arms. He thrust one leg out and placed it on the ground. Grimacing, he placed his other leg on the ground, and with a mighty shove, he staggered upright. The world gasped. Sweat covered his head. He placed one foot in front of the other, fighting for balance the whole way. His teeth were clenched, his lips contorted as he shuffled towards Carlyle's podium.

Reflexively, she stepped back, a look of horror on her face. Lyons fell forward and grasped her podium for support. He looked into her eyes with the passion of a zealot. "FUCK YOUR IMPOSSIBLE!"

Each station cut immediately from the feed. No tape delay on this live broadcast.

In the massive auditorium, the studio audience sat in stunned silence. Then Charles Whitley, from Beaufort, South Carolina, started to clap. Angie Holloway, from New Brunswick, New Jersey, looked over at Whitley, nodded, and began clapping. Like the wave at a football game, the applause became contagious, and soon the sounds flooded the hall.

Someone from security took Lyons's arm, helped him to his chair, and wheeled him off. Senator Carlyle stood with mouth agape. Finally, she grabbed her notes and left the stage.

* * *

Mac and Grace McGregor were sitting at a 90-degree angle from each other on their sectional sofa watching the debate. Both leaned forward, transfixed, when Jeremy Lyons stood and started to walk. It was impossible to look away. As his last three words echoed, Grace recoiled and repeated them as if she knew she had heard wrong.

"Fuck your impossible?"

Mac nodded, but said nothing.

"Defend him! You're an expert at that!" she challenged.

Mac did not respond, which only fueled her anger.

It did not slow her down. "You're still riddled with guilt over something you did to Jeremy three decades ago. It was wrong. It was selfish. It was reprehensible. You served your time! How much damage did you do? The man will probably be the President of the United States. As he said in his narcissistic book, the end justifies the means."

Grace picked up a couch pillow and threw it at Mac, now furious that he had not reacted. She pointed to the television. "Fuck your impossible." She shook her head. "That's *your* president. I hope you're proud." She looked at Mac as though he had written the words and walked up the stairs to bed.

Mac sat motionless on the couch, holding the remote that he had used to pause the show. He didn't believe for a second that Lyons had been faking not being able to walk. He would never resort to parlor tricks, and if he had, he wouldn't have lost it and told a likely President of the United States to basically "go fuck herself."

Will his explosion scare the hell out of voters? A profanity malfunction for a presidential candidate has to be worse than a wardrobe one. Still, Carlyle really humiliated him, calling him a hopeless dreamer. I think that brief glimpse of her superior smile when he started to go off will hurt her. Yet, you can make a case that if a friendly rival can get him to that level of rage, how certain can we be that he won't push the button whenever somebody pisses him off.

Mac's mind was a jumble of questions that probably would not cease when he went to bed. He started to push the remote to listen to the commentary, then thought about what Grace had said. It had taken every ounce of his self-control not to react. He turned off the television and searched for comfort in the dark, quiet room.

CHAPTER 99

STEPHEN COLBERT, FLASHING HIS PATENTED, full-toothed smile, moved like a cat on a griddle. If he'd ever doubted the wisdom of following in David Letterman's wake, those days were over. For her first interview after the most explosive, controversial presidential debate in history, Senator Jean Carlyle had chosen him!

Leaning towards her, unable to conceal his excitement, he asked, "Do I seem like a little boy who needs to go to the bathroom?" Not allowing her to answer, he added, "I am just so excited to get your reaction as the first survivor of the 'F-bomb' on network TV. Instead of a Janet Jackson wardrobe malfunction, we had a seismic verbal malfunction." He spread his hands, "WTF, Senator?"

Calm, presidential Carlyle smiled at her host. "You tell me, Stephen. I felt assaulted. It appeared to be a total loss of control by my opponent." She gave an apologetic look to the cameras. "I admit it. I provoked him." She cocked her head. "But don't you think that Rouhani, Kim Jung Un, and Putin will provoke a president?"

"So you think that Senator Lyons just lost his cool? You got to him?"

Carlyle paused as if searching for an answer. "I don't think we can ever know what makes people act in certain ways. My intention was not to 'get' to him. It was simply to point out that his positions and proposals could not be accomplished without considerable damage to our economy and the middle class."

"I notice you did not use the word 'impossible.'"

Carlyle laughed politely. "With you I could, Stephen. You're a seasoned professional."

Colbert nodded, biting a smirk. "Okay, Senator. I can't predict what will happen in the election, but you are definitely running away with it tonight. Let's see if we can dissect the pivotal moments of the debate. Senator Lyons seemed to build up rage as he spoke, culminating in what his staff swears were the first unsupported steps he's taken since he was hit by the car. Do you believe that?"

"I would never be so callous as to suggest that his actions were staged. If indeed those were his first steps, then I am happy for him. From what I understand, it is a miracle."

Colbert bowed towards her. "Then that would make you a miracle worker."

Carlyle smiled humbly.

"Last question. The world is stunned. Talking heads are mute. By the way, that is another miracle." He waited until the laughter subsided. "Same question we started with, Senator: WTF?"

CHAPTER 100

BROADCAST FROM ROCKEFELLER CENTER, *The Tonight Show* is the world's longest-running talk show. Jimmy Fallon is the sixth official host, following such legendary hosts at Johnny Carson and Jay Leno. It was the perfect venue for presidential candidate Jeremy Lyons. The fact that it aired after the Colbert interview with his opponent added to the audience appeal and cemented the appearance's strategic value. The last word rarely loses to the first one.

After two years at the helm, Jimmy Fallon was ready for almost anything. Still, he knew that this guest would be a challenge.

"Senator, now that you can walk, I guess I'll have to lighten up my approach with you. I felt like when you were in the wheelchair, I could outrun you."

"I'm really quite harmless."

"You didn't sound harmless in the presidential debate. Finishing with an F-bomb was classic. Do you regret that?"

"We've had a number of profane presidents, Jimmy. Lyndon Johnson comes to mind. But I normally prefer to communicate on a higher level."

"Your response was obviously unscripted, because you had no idea what Senator Carlyle would say. Yet in every other appearance that I've watched, you've kept a cool demeanor. She must have really gotten to you."

Lyons's smile was self-assured. "It's rare that my emotions overcome my self-control when I'm angered. Thankfully, I can't recall an instance where that happened since I became an adult."

He turned to look directly at his host. "Contentious or combative situations would normally cause me to be more serene and controlled."

"Is that because of your training? You've had a considerable amount of martial arts training, haven't you?"

"Yes."

"So why do you think you lost your cool this time, on the world's biggest stage?"

Lyons hesitated. "Jimmy, I'm of the generation where a handshake meant something. "

Fallon nodded.

"At her request, instead of the standard three-debate format, I agreed to only one. We both agreed that the American people were tired of the negative campaigning that has become the hallmark of political campaigns. In the event that Senator Carlyle had attacked me and violated our agreement, I admit, my researchers had a full dossier of negative information for retaliation. But as you know, the campaign itself was clean. During the debate, she violated our understanding. I felt betrayed." His comments were matter of fact, without a trace of emotion. "I apologize to those who were justifiably offended by my words."

"Was your anger the impetus for your standing up, or had you done that earlier?"

"In spite of any inferences to the contrary, that was the first time I stood unassisted. Remember that I promised the American people I would not lie to them."

"So why did it happen?"

"My doctor attributed it to adrenaline and to the fact that I didn't consider the possibility that I could fall."

"I'm sure you realize that Senator Carlyle refused to intimate that the debate was not the first time you actually took steps."

"How very nice of her."

"Do you really feel that charitable towards her? She's pounding the table on the fact that you don't have the emotional discipline to be president."

"Of course not," Lyons said. "What she may not realize is that managing money requires incredible emotional discipline." He raised his eyebrows. "It's one thing to get angry when you feel like a colleague has betrayed you; it's quite another to display unintentional emotion when confronting heads of state, particularly ones that may be enemies of our country." He paused. "On the other hand, we might wish that our current president had been a little more forceful with those who threaten our safety."

Fallon nodded, but did not follow up. "I understand you've been killing yourself ever since the diagnosis trying to prove your doctors wrong. Do you need to continue your strenuous workout routine now that you're ambulatory?"

"Even before the assassination attempt, I worked out constantly. I'll do whatever it takes to remain standing."

"What had you planned to say if Senator Carlyle had stayed on script and simply outlined the reasons that we should vote for her?"

Lyons paused and collected his thoughts. "It's natural for me to look at America like a business. So my charge is how to relate to folks who have not spent their lives in business when I describe the state of our union. I thought it might be easier to think of the financial underpinnings of the United States as the foundation of a house. If our eyes focus only on the furniture, the appliances, or the ceiling, we may feel that all is in order. Imagine that underneath the floors and throughout the walls, termites are destroying the structure. If we close our eyes, the house may remain standing for our lifetime. Yet, without a shadow of a doubt, future generations will stand in rubble.

"Jimmy, my life's work has been in finance, determining which companies will survive and which will fail. No credible financial mind will tell you that the course our country is on is sustainable." Lyons leaned forward and planted his forearms on his thighs. "Here is my promise to America. I *will* strengthen our foundation, *destroy* the insidious enemies of our financial freedoms, and *preserve* our precious liberty."

Fallon grimaced. *If I close here, I'm going to be accused of serving up only softballs.* Making up his mind, he asked, "Okay, final question. Why do you think the studio audience applauded?"

Lyons shrugged. "It may have been that they were happy it was over."

Fallon gave him an exaggerated skeptical look.

"Or," Lyons said more forcefully, "the audience may have been applauding the death of political correctness."

CHAPTER 101

FOR THE THIRD TIME, JEAN Carlyle pounded on the apartment door. Her fist ached from the repeated blows. She looked back at the two Secret Service agents, wondering if they would break down the door at her request. At that moment, she heard a chain being removed, and the door opened.

The man standing in the doorway wore only black nylon running shorts, and his sculpted chest glistened with sweat. With an impassioned face, Gabe Hill stepped aside so she could enter.

"I've texted you, emailed you, and left a dozen messages on your phone. Why didn't you answer me?"

"Our contract clearly states that I am not an on-call consultant." Hill looked at his watch and clicked a button. "You have precisely five minutes."

"Five minutes! My presidency is going up in flames, and Mr. Fucking Know-It-All gives me five minutes!"

With the back of his hand, he calmly wiped her spittle off his cheek.

"Who's in there?" she demanded, gesturing at his closed bedroom door.

"My guest," he said, as his face went cold.

Carlyle shook her head angrily and pointed an accusing finger at him. "You talked me into proposing a single debate. You told me to get him mad. I believe your exact quote was 'If you hit the right spot, you only need to put the hammer down once.' And you told me if Lyons went nuts on me, people would see who he really was and discard him like yesterday's trash."

310

Hill stood like a statue as she ranted. All that did was infuriate her more. Red welts appeared on her neck, and her eyes were crazed.

She turned and walked towards the bedroom door. Hill took two steps toward her, and the silent agents moved protectively forward. It was a feint. She spun around and confronted him. "I really pissed him off, just like you suggested. The cripple got so pissed off that got out of his wheelchair and walked! I, Jean Carlyle, made a paraplegic walk. I'm a miracle worker." She paused and glared at him with laser-like loathing.

"What is my reward for the miracle? He screams 'Fuck your impossible' at me."

With sarcasm coating every word, Carlyle brought her face within six inches of Hill's. "I get him to drop an F-bomb on national television, and do you know what happens, my guru?" She didn't wait for an answer. "I'll tell you what happens while you've been screwing the day away in your love nest. The polls swell in *his* favor!"

She spread her hands. "What do think of that, genius?"

"A best-selling book, unimaginative and poorly written, turns into a trilogy and then an unbearable movie, all because it is about bondage," Hill replied. *The Book of Mormon* is sacrilegious and blasphemous, and yet is considered a brilliant satire. Search the internet. It makes Sodom and Gomorrah look like a church revival."

"Seriously?" she interrupted. "I'm getting a lecture on the mores of our society? Your strategy failed, and you blame it on our deviant nature? Is that something that just occurred and so it couldn't be included in your calculations? Give me a break. You blew it."

"He walked. If he had stumbled, fallen, he would have appeared irrational. You did succeed in angering him. At that moment, the odds were overwhelming in your favor. Strategy is an art, not an exact science. It is impossible to forecast the impossible."

"Fuck *your* impossible!" Carlyle said as she spun on her heel. She grabbed the doorknob and turned back to him. "The election is two weeks away. What do I do now?"

The buzzer on Hill's watch went off. He touched the button, silencing it. He stared at her for a long beat and then gave her a one-word answer: "Pray."

* * *

Hill opened the bedroom door, and the exquisite Asian woman held up her half-filled champagne glass. "I didn't know that Improv theater was part of tonight's activities," she said, her mischievous smile making him automatically reciprocate.

"You are really enough treat by yourself," she teased, "I don't need any extra entertainment."

Hill looked at the diminutive beauty, her saucer-sized dark eyes; pert, perfect breasts; and red, full lips. Smart, interesting, and carefree, she was definitely a keeper. He raised his eyebrows. "Will you think less of me if it was my encounter that aroused me?" He dropped his shorts to illustrate his point.

She laughed deliciously. "Whatever works, my dear."

"Ah, Mia," he said as he slid into the bed. "What would I do without you?"

CHAPTER 102

As she waited for the signal to begin, Jackie Mayfield studied Jeremy Lyons's vice presidential candidate. Perfectly dressed in a gray pin-striped suit, Mary Beth Justice's olive skin, dark hair, and penetrating dark eyes commanded attention. Her robin's egg blue shell matched perfectly with the faint stripe in her suit. Some women wear their beauty as a calling card. With Justice, it was just an accessory.

With a smile on her face, Mary Beth was appraising Jackie. Mary Beth took the lead, leaning in and whispering, "Let's kick some ass, tonight."

"3-2-1."

"I am here tonight with Governor Mary Beth Justice, who as you know, is Senator Jeremy Lyons's vice presidential nominee. Unrehearsed, unedited, just the way we like it. Thanks so much for coming, Mary Beth." Justice had requested that the Fox anchor address her by her first name.

"I am delighted to be here, Jackie."

"So that our viewers don't tweet me about being disrespectful, Governor, could you confirm that you asked me to call you by your first name?" She smiled.

"I did no such thing."

For a split second, Jackie blanched.

"I know I'll pay for that later," said Mary Beth with a smile.

"You'll pay for that right now," said Jackie, quipping right back. "First question: The media has said that Senator Lyons chose you because you're a woman. How have you responded to that?"

"Jackie, I have not needed to respond, because no one in the media has made that accusation to me."

"Okay, I'll ask you the question. Do you think you were chosen to minimize gender criticism?"

"Absolutely not. Senator Lyons does nothing without considerable research. As a two-term governor of New Jersey, every action of my leadership was transparent. In one of our earlier conversations, he told me that his vice president would be like no other in history. That person would not be just a back-up to the president. He said that he needed someone who was a fiscal conservative who would be his partner."

"Why do you think you haven't been asked this before?"

Mary Beth raised her eyebrows. "I'm not sure. It's certainly possible that males in the media might be afraid that the question would sound sexist. In politics, lying has become acceptable, but a political correctness mistake will mark you for life."

"How did we let that happen?" asked Jackie, leaning forward.

"My opinion is that we let the media and the liberals dictate what is right and what is wrong, but I'm running with an Independent so I'm not supposed to say that."

"Don't worry," said Jackie, waving a hand. "No liberals watch my show."

Mary Beth laughed warmly.

"You said that you would be a partner with the president," Jackie continued. "It seems like that means that you are the one assigned to do all the traveling, pressing the flesh in every location. Why do you think Senator Lyons doesn't attend any public rallies? Is it because he thinks he is above them or because of his disability?"

Mary Beth paused. "Jackie, that question is insulting."

Jackie blushed. "I'm sorry. It was improperly phrased. Why does the senator have you attend all of the public events?"

Mary Beth nodded. "Because he is preparing to be President of the United States. From the start, he told me that he had a choice: He could campaign vigorously and increase his chances of being elected, or he could spend the time studying how to help our country." She paused and smiled. "Jackie, I know your question was not to imply that I wasn't up to the task."

"To the contrary," Jackie said quickly. "I love your energy, your forthrightness, your candor, and your intelligence. Senator Lyons hasn't done anything by the book, so I don't know why I should be surprised. And your answer is more than logical. The presidency is the most important responsibility in the world, and even after presidents are elected, how long does it take before they are campaigning again?"

"Has our current president after stopped?" Justice asked with a smile. "Senator Lyons has committed to be a one-term president so that all of his energy and time can be spent on the welfare of the nation. I am the eyes and ears of the administration and am committed to understanding the voters' issues first hand and standing for them in the White House."

"A frequent criticism of Senator Lyons is his limited experience, but as a two-term governor, you cut taxes, employment increased, and you've even met one-on-one with foreign leaders."

"I do believe that my experience is a valuable asset, Jackie. And although I am a Republican, I do think it is time for independent thinking. I'm confident that the country is searching for true objectivity."

Jackie let the sentence linger, then reached for the governor's hand, "Mary Beth, thank you for your time and your candor and for bringing us this Fox exclusive."

Jackie looked through the camera to her audience as the red "Exclusive" banner enveloped the bottom third of their screens. "You are about to see the last Lyons/Justice campaign ad to be released prior to the election. I am required to tell you that airing this during our show does not constitute an endorsement. While I haven't seen the ad, I've been told that it's the most powerful ad in presidential history."

CHAPTER 103

MARY BETH JUSTICE'S FACE FILLED the screen. Her makeup was light. Her eyes were intense and inviting as the camera started its gradual widening of the shot in sync with her words.

"I registered as a Republican when I turned eighteen. I believed in the conservative agenda, the fiscal prudency, and the strength of the American military. There were, of course, parts of the agenda that didn't fit. Issues that are fundamental to my womanhood. In my public service, the more I dug into the issues, the more resistance I felt from the established members of the party. As I looked across the aisle for help, I found a lack of understanding and willingness from many of my colleagues to bend from the dogma that got them elected."

"When Jeremy Lyons approached me to be his vice president, his words resonated in my heart. 'Mary Beth, I don't see you fairly represented as a Republican, and you wouldn't fit as a Democrat. Our two-party system was fabricated hundreds of years ago by white men who lived by completely different rules and a severe lack of information. You and I can see eye to eye on many things, but in one way we will never be the same. I am a man, and you are a woman. In our White House, you will lead as the predominant voice for women. I will never assume to know what it's like to walk a step, let alone a mile, in your shoes. You call the shots. You introduce the policy. And you will have my unwavering support.'"

She paused, and a glaze filled her eyes. "Throughout history, the office of the vice presidency has been one of second chair. In this administration, I will be an equal partner.

"I have been able to reach out to many women in congress and engage them in conversation about a new future that will have us represented not as party members, but rather as women. Women independent of the constructs placed upon us. Women independent of the rules and positions of their party. Women independent and not blocked by ceilings of any kind.

"Today, I stand before you, not as a Republican…"

The frame widened farther and panned to the right to show Senator Elise Franklin standing at Mary Beth's side speaking, "and not as a Democrat."

"I am an independent woman," the two said in unison as the frame continued to grow, revealing two rows of women standing behind them in the hall of the Capitol. Fourteen female legislators, from all sides of the aisle, were holding hands as a unified front, letting the image seal their statement.

CHAPTER 104

The political quagmire that existed in 2016 was abominable. Due in part to an early outspoken entrant into the Republican primaries, the GOP was labeled as rich, racist, and rude. None of those adjectives appeared in the definition of presidential. Thus, the Grand Old Party's chance of winning the Hispanic or African-American vote, or even making progress with those groups, was mired somewhere between slim and none.

The Democrats had captured the high ground. They pledged to give the people more, raise the living standard of the middle class (a constant refrain with as much success as Charlie Brown had with Lucy holding the football), and by raising taxes on the filthy rich, eliminate income inequality. Ironically, after eight years of liberal leadership, the minorities and the middle class were worse off than before. Facts should never get in the way of a good story.

The media, which had attached itself to Jeremy Lyons's wheelchair, loved the candidate who appeared to be without nuance. Of course, Senator Carlyle was still revered by the more liberal reporters, but without Republicans to vilify, Lyons was certainly a more interesting story. And up until the final minutes of the debate, the lack of negative comments by either candidate really challenged the media to create tension.

Now, two days before the election, 26 seconds of video was co-opting every Facebook feed and Twitter stream with comment exchanges that set records for both quantity and profanity. You can't pull the post that instantly replicates across the world.

"God wants me to be president," a woman's voice says in a hushed tone while the camera pans across an extremely well-heeled crowd. "If people start thinking they can tweet whatever legislative changes they want ... we are doomed."

The camera continues its movement through the excessively opulent scene. The top 0.1 per cent are laughing while the grease of miniature lamb chops drips from their fingers. A man waves his hand while enthusiastically making his point and sloshes the olive straight out of his martini. The camera moves to zoom in on a woman standing in the corner, speaking with a white-haired socialite. As she turns toward the camera, there is a brief fade to black...

"You know as well as I do," Jean Carlyle's visage fills the screen as if she were looking directly at the viewer, "that income equality is a slogan, not a promise." Then with incredible familiarity and a slight smile that is exaggerated when replayed in slow motion, she leans in for the punch line: "You can lie to the people, but never to the donors."

Uncharacteristically for any politician, the Lyons camp did not pounce on her disparaging remarks. Their only response was, "No comment."

CHAPTER 105

Election night at the McGregors' was a tense affair. In marriages, the decision to "agree to disagree" never works well in practice. As results poured in, Mac glanced at his wife for a reaction. Any reaction. It wasn't that she was a fan of Jean Carlyle, it was simply her animus towards Carlyle's opponent that permeated the room.

At 10:30, when the highly contested state of Virginia was declared for Senator Lyons, the electoral race was over. Looking straight ahead, Grace stood up and walked out of the room. "Please be quiet when you come to bed," she said over her shoulder.

Mac was angry. He paused the television, got off the couch, and went to the bathroom to relieve himself. He was tempted to yell up the stairs, "I guess sex is out of the question!" Fortunately, he did not always act on his impulses.

* * *

The popular vote wasn't close. Due to excellent management of social media on both sides, voter turnout was up substantially for this election. Nevertheless, the people had spoken: Jeremy Lyons would be the 45th President of the United States.

Once again, the *Post*'s Tom Hessell was credited with the best headline. "Our new president is a bad ass!" His analysis concluded that if the newly elected president could stand up when every doctor decreed that he would never be upright again, then the odds were good that he would stand up for America. It was a particularly bold assessment for a reporter who'd previously been accused of a liberal bias. The country loves underdogs, those who overcome adversity, and bad asses.

* * *

From all appearances, it might have been a victory party, but the newly elected president had a full agenda. Four days after the election, the inner circle was assembled on the mammoth balcony of Lyons's compound. It was hard to hide the smiles, but the host acted like the election process had been a senseless interruption of his work day.

Sabine held up her chilled champagne glass. "To the beginning of a new era." She clinked glasses with Alegria, Steve Cannon, Mia, Vice President Justice, and the newcomer decked out in his casual uniform.

Reluctantly, Lyons held up his glass of fresh-squeezed Florida orange juice for the group clink. Changing the subject quickly, he said, "I want to formally introduce the newest member of our group."

All eyes turned to the attractive man who made Cannon seem like he was overdressed. Black running shorts, gold running shoes, and a white tee shirt that said, "Any school but Ivy League." Swinging his swivel chair from side to side, the man seemed like he had been born in the group.

"Gabe Hill," Lyons announced, and Cannon's eyebrows went up in surprise.

"Pardon my confusion, Mr. Hill," said Cannon, "but didn't you just run Jean Carlyle's campaign? And, I believe she uh, how do I say it, lost."

"So much for your secret identity, Gabe," said Mia.

"Gabe is extremely knowledgeable about Washington." said Lyons. "He is a superb strategist who can also give us good intel on potential cabinet members. And, people, that is our job today. I don't want to be thirty days on the job without having all of our cabinet members on board." Lyons would not let the meeting be distracted by banter; he was a man on a mission.

He directed his question to Hill. "I promised state to Bill Reynolds. Do you concur?"

Hill shook his head. "It needs to be more dramatic. Besides, with the Republicans barely holding the senate, you will need strong leadership there. Make sure he is the majority leader. He'll understand."

"Then who should be secretary of state?" asked Cannon with a little edge. He wasn't sure how the newcomer had become the favorite child so quickly.

"You and I will talk off line, Steve. I want to be sure you agree before I submit the name."

Slightly mollified, Cannon asked. "So how and why did you come over to our side, Gabe?"

Mia gave him a sultry look. "I recruited him, and you're too old to get the details."

Everyone laughed, and Hill raised his hand half way. "I don't know the protocol, but, Steve, I'm here because your boss is the first politician I've met who is not full of shit."

"Enough chit-chat," said Lyons impatiently. "Let's get down to business."

CHAPTER 106

A PERFECT PLAN REQUIRES PATIENCE. Flawless preparation and seamless execution are essential; however, plans often go awry for lack of patience. No such mishap was on the radar screen for John Wesley.

It was the fourth of January. The timing could not have been better. Lyons was in Washington getting briefed by the outgoing president on national security issues and protocols, and the 50-degrees difference in temperatures had prompted Sabine to remain in Naples.

"By the way," said Wesley as he walked out onto the balcony, "you were right."

Confused, Sabine waited for him to elaborate.

"It would have been a mistake for Jeremy to meet with my dad. He would have told all of his friends, and my anonymity would have been history. Also, I never should have approached Jeremy. I let my emotions color my reason, and I'm embarrassed by my actions."

She nodded in response.

"Anyway," his smile was humble, "I really am sorry. I hope you accept my apology."

"Apology accepted," she said.

"I want to make up for being such a jerk. Since I am off the gravy train in less than two weeks, how about I buy you a goodbye dinner?"

She wrinkled her nose and shook her head. "John, ever since the Fox interview, I've been a marked woman. I can't be seen having dinner with another man."

"Dinner tonight at Baleen's. 7:30. You and me." He raised his hands. "Strictly platonic."

"Did you hear what I just said?"

"I have taken that into account, and I can guarantee that no one will recognize you."

Sabine rolled her eyes in exasperation.

Wesley reached behind his back and, with a flourish, held up a mask of a beautiful Asian woman.

In spite of herself, Sabine smiled. "You could just take Mia and save yourself the trouble."

"First, you are the one who needs to get a life. And as you know, the mysterious Mia is already seeing someone."

"I know," she said, her eyes widening, "and he's a good recruit."

"So there should be no impediment to our having some innocent fun." Wesley placed the mask gently on her lap, "This is specially made for you. It's a gift. It's bad luck to refuse a gift. Think about it. You can use it to go shopping, walk the streets without being gawked at. The temperature tonight will only be in the high 60s. You wear slacks and a light sweater. We have reservations in front of the fire pit. Dig your toes in the sand, and we'll eat and giggle. I'll have you home by 9:30."

"John........."

"It's also bad luck to refuse a condemned man his last request. Come on. You know you want to play a role. There's still that wild child hidden behind that cool exterior."

The logical part of her brain wanted to refuse his offer. But, she was bored. Besides, what could it hurt?

PERSUADE

"Should I practice my accent?" Sabine asked as they walked the quarter mile on the beach.

"Mia doesn't have an accent."

"No. I was just kidding. I do feel this will be fun. I feel kind of naughty. Hey!" She held up a warning finger. "Don't take it the wrong way."

"I am the consummate gentleman," he replied with a bow.

Baleen's restaurant is part of the La Playa Beach Resort, which states on its website that it's the only truly beachfront resort in Naples. It boasts white, powder-like sands, premium accommodations, and a pampered stay for hotel guests as well as members of its private beach club.

Above Baleen's is a restaurant that is available only to those definitely one-per-centers who are club members. In addition to the luxurious hotel, the facility has several beachfront cottages that can run a thousand a night in season. The tuxedo-clad waiter showed them to their seats and left after taking their drink orders. "Just so you won't be tempted to try to take advantage of me, I am only ordering a half bottle of wine," said Wesley.

The waiter smiled at Wesley's statement, and then his smile broadened when the beautiful Asian woman made a circling motion with her index finger to indicate that her date was crazy.

"How did you know that Cakebread Chardonnay was my favorite?" asked Sabine.

"I've had nothing to do for the last six months but acquire knowledge. And it is not only the wine. I will order for both of us, and you will love it."

"John, this is starting to feel too much like a date." She picked up her napkin as a precursor to standing. "I'm feeling uncomfortable."

"First, I have too much respect, okay, maybe fear, for Jeremy to hit on you. And second, your ability to resist these rocking abs has been duly noted. Sabine," he turned serious, "I hope you know that you would always be safe with me."

ASSURE

"We'll start with the baby arugula salad, and for the entree we'll both have the molasses key lime glazed halibut." The waiter smiled and hurried away.

"Are you a regular here?" Sabine asked.

"No. I just do my homework. It's called Google. The question is, 'What is the chef's signature dish?'"

Dinner was easy and harmless, filled with light banter. There had been no sexual innuendos, and Sabine relaxed.

"Fun night?" asked Wesley.

"Yes. I must admit that this was a good idea. I feel very clandestine, very spy like."

He took another sip of wine and motioned towards the fire pit. "Look. It's so calming, almost mesmerizing."

As her eyes went to the fire, Wesley's hand covered her half-filled glass of wine. A fine powder quickly dissolved.

DISTRACT

"Last taste?" He poured the last few drops from the bottle into her glass.

"Sure," she said. "Then we should probably head back."

"Of course. I promised that you'd be in bed by ten."

He watched as her head started to weave back and forth.

"I..I'm dizzy."

Wesley raised his hand to get the waiter's attention. He paid the check and helped Sabine rise. Half carrying her, he started walking. At the last beach cottage on the property, he stopped and inserted a room card. The first thing he removed was her mask.

EXECUTE

The waiter's eyes followed the couple. Something wasn't right. Maybe she'd had drinks before coming here, but she'd barely touched her wine. Seemed she went from being fine to loopy in half a heart-beat. He scratched the back of his bald head.

He stared at the three hundred-dollar bills lying under the check. Lots of rich folks in Naples, but not many gave a 100% tip. The only one that had ever been that generous before was.......

Damn. She may have looked Asian, but her voice sure sounded familiar. He wasn't sure if he could get through, but he might score just for trying. He picked up his cell and tried to stop his hands from shaking.

CHAPTER 107

THE TEMPERATURE HOVERED AROUND FREEZING, but it was a cloudless sky, and the sun shone brightly on the anointed. In his two previous opportunities administering the oath of office, Chief Justice Roberts had been a part of less than perfect execution. In 2008, the head of the Supreme Court tripped over his tongue a bit, and in 2012, it was the president who misspoke. This time, however, just like the brisk weather, which had failed to live up to its forecast of cloudy with light rain, fate did not dare to interfere with a perfect performance.

"I do solemnly swear that I will faithfully execute the office of the President of the United States and will to the best of my ability, preserve, protect, and defend the Constitution of the United States."

The 45th president stood, his body erect, and savored the moment. In his dark blue suit, his tie forming a perfect "V," he was the picture of purpose and strength. Oblivious to the roar of the crowd and the presence of Sabine standing just steps away from him, he focused only on the Bible. He closed his eyes for just a moment. "If it is Your will, Father....."

When the president looked up, the crowd had stilled in anticipation. "I have spent my life investing, analyzing companies to determine which will succeed and which will fail," he began. "My only goal was to make money for my clients and myself." His purposeful pause was to allow the reporters and pundits to get their heads around the fact that this would not be like any other inaugural address in history.

"My focus has not changed. The only difference is that I expect all of our citizens to benefit and reap the rewards of my most important investment. As of today, my administration is dedicated to investing in America.

"For too many years we have taken our county's resources, ingenuity, and work ethic for granted. Politicians have pandered to their constituencies, telling them what they wanted to hear, and making empty promises that they could not keep. That ends now.

"What makes a company a good investment? It starts with management. Are the corporate officers and the board of directors competent, and are they committed to making their company grow? Do they have an easily understandable business model like McDonald's or Apple? Are they the best of the breed? Do they have a history of solving problems and enriching their shareholders? To this end, I am today announcing the names of two outstanding Americans who have accepted my offer to join our board of directors and become members of my cabinet.

"Winning my senate seat in Florida was a bittersweet moment. It was a necessary transition to my ultimately winning the presidency, but it resulted in removing an extremely capable legislator and hero from governance. Fortunately, Florida reelected him two years later to serve as their senator. It is with great pride and confidence that I announce today that Alan Smathers will assume the vital position of secretary of defense.

"As an Independent, it is my responsibility to the country to select the best qualified individuals from both sides of the aisle to join my administration. In the past, history has relegated the capable presidential challenger, who typically has almost half of the country's support, to the sidelines. That ends now. Jean Carlyle's extensive foreign policy experience and grace under fire will be invaluable to our administration. She has graciously accepted the role of secretary of state.

"In the near future I intend to name more cabinet appointees, and none will be out of obligation. I will seek only the most qualified individuals for our country's board of directors.

"The United States of America would be the largest company in the world. For the past six months, my team and I have studied the complexities of this mammoth bureaucracy," his smile was humble, "and it is almost indecipherable. But I did not seek this office to tell you what could not be fixed. Instead, with your help, I intend to make America a compelling investment.

"What are our financial problems? We have twenty trillion dollars of debt, and up until now, we have not had the will to address it. We are growing at less than two per cent a year. Our underemployed, which combines those that are seeking work and can't get a job with those that have given up, is close to twenty per cent of our citizens. To a company, that is valuable inventory that is not producing revenue. To our country, it is a national shame.

"How do we invest in America? This is not a new theme; only our pledge to recommit is new. During World War Two, Americans bought U.S. Government Savings Bonds, which not only financed our war effort, but also demonstrated our patriotism and our willingness to sacrifice. In the shock and horror of the tragedy of 9/11, the nation mourned. But there was more: across the country there was a rebirth of nationalism and patriotism. We were united.

"During my campaign, I pledged to increase our military readiness, and within the next hundred days, you will see evidence of that. But as a professional investor, I know that the best defense is a solid balance sheet. We must become financially strong and return our country to Triple A status.

"In 2011, for the first time, a rating agency downgraded the status of the United States of America because of our burgeoning debt and our lack of will to tackle our entitlement problems. Over the next four years, we will regain our Triple A status. To do this, I will need not only help from congress, but also help from you. Remember, both the president and congress are your public servants.

"During my senate term, the people joined me, exercised their will, and the corporate tax was lowered. Since then, no public companies have moved overseas, and more jobs have become available. So the first rule of my administration will be," he held up the forefinger of his right hand, "do not spend more than you earn.

"The second rule will be, don't forget the first rule. We will be transparent to you; however, it is up to you to hold us accountable.

"I ask for your trust, your sacrifice, and your prayers for our nation. Thank you, and God bless the United States of America."

*　*　*

The ceremony had sent a chill down Mac McGregor's spine. President Lyons's booming voice, echoing through the streets of Washington and throughout the world, radiated confidence and patriotism. In a nation starved for leadership, this was the seminal moment when hope was at its highest. Mac prayed that this time the people had elected a selfless leader.

Because of the uncomfortable situation between himself and Grace, Mac had watched the ceremony on television. He had been offered front-row seats, and it would have been the first inauguration ceremony for both of them. Every time he thought of this, he had to swallow resentment. Like any couple, the McGregors ran into roadblocks in their marriage, but they'd always worked together and solved them. Nothing worked this time. And the frightening part of that scenario was that it was about to get worse.

CHAPTER 108

CERTAIN AREAS OF WASHINGTON, D.C., are constant action at night, regardless of the weather. But Pennsylvania Avenue near the White House is not a hub of activity unless the president is on the move.

On this particular night, David Grant was the last to leave the office. It was not because he was overloaded with work; it was because he had nothing else to do. For a single guy, hooking up in D.C. was not overly challenging, but David wasn't ready for a relationship, and anything else ended up being complicated.

Melancholy hung on him like cheap perfume. He ran his fingers through his thinning hair and pondered his most critical decision: pizza or Lean Cuisine. Looking out the window did nothing to upgrade his mood: dark with freezing rain. *Life's a bitch*, he thought as he picked up his briefcase and headed for the elevators.

At 7:30 p.m. traffic was almost nonexistent. David knew that the weather would cause traffic nightmares during rush hour, which was another reason he had delayed his exit. He grimaced as he pulled up the collar of his raincoat and stepped into the revolving door.

The soles of his black wingtips crunched when they hit the thin layer of black ice covering the concrete. The parking garage was only a block away. He lowered his head so that the rain wouldn't blind him.

It crossed David's mind that he had stopped carrying his pistol a while ago. He couldn't get a concealed carry permit in D.C., and while a pistol in plain sight might actually be effective with some clients, the majority would prefer him to be unarmed.

He wasn't sure why he was thinking about a gun at all. Located this close to the White House meant that his office was about as crime free as you could get. In fact, having a firearm in this vicinity could result in about half a dozen Secret Service types landing on top of you. He flexed his biceps, enjoying their new girth. Time in the gym and those private sessions with his martial arts instructor increased his confidence. Just like riding a bike.....

David heard the fall before he heard the cry of pain. He put his hand above his eyes to shield them from the rain. The man in the army-green service uniform was lying on his side with hands outstretched on the pavement. David's eyes immediately went to the black stripes on the outer side of each of the man's trouser legs and the black band just above the sleeve cuff on the green jacket. An officer. The man's right leg was sticking out in an awkward position.

David heard a slight moan. He knelt down and touched the man's shoulder, simultaneously trying to shake the water out of his hair. "Let me help you, sir."

The man whirled around to face him. David's eyes zeroed in on the gun as the man pulled the trigger.

CHAPTER 109

THE TWO FIT MEN IN dark suits, white shirts, and ear buds standing on either side of the hotel room door were expected, yet still a bit intimidating. Mac approached the door of the Presidential Suite in the East Wing of the Four Seasons Hotel with a mixture of awe and trepidation. Cupping his hand around his mouth, he whispered to the two agents, "You're probably wondering why I called you here."

No smiles. He raised his hands as requested, holding his cell in his right hand. Having already taken measure of his audience, he resisted the urge to declare that his weapons were all verbal.

As he walked into the room, his eyes were drawn to the floor-to-ceiling windows that flooded the room with sunlight. The president-elect of the United States gripped his hand with firmness.

"I apologize for the change of venue," said Lyons, "but I wanted absolute privacy for our lunch."

"I'm easy to please," said Mac, adding a lazy smile. What he wanted to say was, "Why am I here, and what do you want?"

"Have a seat," said Lyons as he motioned to the small table covered with a white tablecloth.

Mac sat, Lyons sat across from him, and they picked up menus simultaneously. There was an undercurrent of nervousness in the room, perhaps because of the silent strangers who were assigned to cover the 45th President of the United States. Mac pointed to an entrée on the menu. "This salad looks good to me, and if you could bring the balsamic on the side, that would be great."

"I'll have the same," echoed Lyons, "and bring us two iced teas. The wide-eyed, tuxedo-clad waiter scurried away.

Trying to break the ice, Mac raised an eyebrow and quipped, "Room service? I don't know what you've heard, but I'm not that easy." On offense and defense, Mac's go-to move was always a shot of humor. Wisecracking came as naturally to him as breathing. It wasn't that he was entirely uncomfortable being sequestered in an opulent suite with the king of the world and a gaggle of Secret Service agents, but it did feel surreal.

"A public sighting of the two of us together might have caused tongues to wag," said Lyons by way of explanation.

"Do you have me confused with someone who's famous?"

Lyons shook his head. "No, but you've never been reticent to criticize me."

Mac checked the agents who were playing the parts of see no evil, hear no evil, speak no evil. "You are my commander-in-chief. I would never publically disparage you." He looked at Lyons and added, "Even if I thought you deserved it."

Lyons laughed. "I just hope we can focus on the future rather than the past."

Mac nodded. "Agreed. Mr. President, before you tell me your agenda, may I ask you a few questions?"

"In private, I'd prefer Jeremy. I don't want to start thinking I'm important. And of course, Mac, what would you like to know?"

Not quite expecting that answer, Mac let out a breath as he collected his thoughts. "You plan everything, down to the smallest details. I'm curious about what was planned, what was spontaneous, and what was theater in the debate. Are you willing to discuss that?"

"With you."

"I know what your answer was on Jimmy Fallon's show, but if you give me different answers, I will take them to my grave. Had you taken unsupported steps before that night?"

"No."

Mac thought the answer had the ring of truth. "Are you 100 per cent ambulatory now?"

"I tire more easily than I would like, so I have a cane that I will use some in my Naples home. I would appreciate keeping that between you and me."

"I will. Do the doctors expect a full recovery?"

Lyons's laugh was bitter. "The doctors expect me to be in a wheelchair. They are useless to me. I'm continuing my physical therapy routine, and *I* expect a full recovery."

"That's great to hear." Mac's mind flashed to Blake Stone. "Did you take any drugs that helped you? By the way, if you think that I'm just trying to get inside information on the next miracle drug stock, you are correct."

Lyons smiled. "I took a rather imaginative cocktail of experimental drugs that had a few uncomfortable side effects. I have stopped taking them and would only restart if I regressed."

"The entire country hopes that is not the case." Mac rubbed his chin. "One last none-of-my-business question. Was the F-bomb really unplanned?"

"Yes. I was infuriated that Jean Carlyle violated our tacit agreement of civility. I had acquiesced to her every request concerning format and had refrained from bludgeoning her with facts that could have decimated her support. She crossed the line, and my outburst was stream of consciousness, definitely not scripted. I consider cursing the result of a weak vocabulary. The risk of repulsion over my profanity far outweighed the prospect of acceptance."

"Okay," said Mac, nodding his appreciation. "Now, how can a lowly financial advisor help the most powerful man in the world?"

Smiling at the self-deprecating humor, Lyons asked, "Do you think I can get the country to buy in on investing in America?"

"You want them to buy Treasury bonds?" asked Mac, wrinkling his brow.

"No," said Lyons. "I am seeking a different kind of investment." He steepled his hands. "What I am going to ask of you next goes way beyond our periodic discussions of the economy. In my inaugural address, I asked our citizens for their trust, and their sacrifice." He nodded and spoke quietly. "And of you, I have a similar request."

Other than major concerns over a child, health scares for family or friends, or a terrorist attack, it was really hard to shake up Mac. The remains of a delicious lunch were pushed aside, and Lyons was looking at him intently. Mac's face was white and felt frozen. He felt as if his lips were flapping up and down like a fish. He was in shock.

He tried to speak, but the auto switch on his verbal skills was stuck. He blinked his way back to the real world. "Would, would you repeat what you just said?" he asked in a voice that sounded strange to him.

"Yes," said Lyons firmly. "Would you be willing to serve your country as my treasury secretary?"

* * *

Mac just shook his head to Lyons's offer to have his driver take him back to the office. He was still in a daze, not sure even how he'd responded to the question. Disoriented, he pulled up the collar on his black raincoat and started walking. He felt like he was in a different universe.

No way am I qualified. This was a position held by Alexander Hamilton, Andrew Mellon, and during the financial crisis, Hank Paulson. Sorry. Angus "Mac" McGregor does not compute in this list of luminaries. Maybe if they put an asterisk after my name. Damn him, telling me that his goal was to get the country to invest in America. He knew that would tempt me.

What if a crisis occurred on my watch? My first instinct would be to call all my clients; but I couldn't....not allowed. Sure, there have been treasury secretaries from my industry, but Paulson was the head of Goldman Sachs, not a guy who manages money for his friends. Lyons has really lost it this time. If I accepted, they would seriously question his ability to lead.

Almost every friend is a client, with the exception of my advisor friends, and I often tell them that they should be clients. In the inevitable stock market correction, bear market, or (shudder) market crash, they are used to me helping them through it. To not be able to be there for them would be painful for me. Yes, I have confidence in R.J. and the team, but I'm the old soul with 37 years of experience.

Mac waited at a crosswalk for the light to change. *What if it worked? It would be a rush.* Mac shook his head again, feeling like this conversation with himself was a clear cry for help. He either noticed or imagined every pedestrian looking at him curiously as he trudged down Pennsylvania Avenue with wind billowing his coat. Normally sensitive to the cold, he was immune. *I'm probably muttering to myself.*

It took only a moment for Mac to re-enter his world of hypotheticals. *In the battle between my doubts of inadequacy and the lure of the challenge, doubt is a clear favorite. How could I even consider working for a man I know is ruthless and consumed by the idea that he is the only one to save the country? Am I drawn by a kindred hubris? My group brings in more revenue than any other in the firm, and we have the ultimate flexibility. Why would I give up my freedom for a lower paycheck and a decent chance at infamy?*

Grace. That's a whole other story. I wonder what it will cost when she divorces me. She says I'm a control freak. She's right. A jury of my peers would convict me. Except that like most men I know, I lost control as soon as I said, "I do!"

He stopped to get his bearings. He'd walked half a block past his office. "Ridiculous," he said out loud. *Then why can't I stop thinking about it?*

CHAPTER 110

"THE NEXT THING YOU'RE GOING to tell me is that it's all fun and games until someone gets hurt." Blake Stone was rubbing his sandy brown hair dry with a towel from David Grant's bathroom.

"I did get hurt! Look at these bruises!" David lifted up his shirt. A cluster shot of tiny welts peppered his abdomen. A single remaining plastic pellet that had been trapped in the fabric fell to the floor. "You're an asshole and a child."

Blake's gas-powered semi-automatic pellet pistol was primarily used for military training exercises. Blake had customized his weapon to maximize the feet-per-second velocity to inflict a little extra situational awareness in his trainees. The look in David's eyes showed that he was an unwilling participant in tonight's campaign. "Know your weaponry and you know its capabilities and its weaknesses."

David finished drying himself off and threw his towel at Blake, who ducked easily. "Now you're quoting the special forces handbook. Aren't you special. Did you consider that I might be carrying, or maybe spear you with an umbrella?" asked David.

"You always were more practical than me, but I figured you were out of practice. Besides, the alternative was to zap you with a Taser, and then I was afraid that you'd wet yourself."

"Bite me," said David, who was resigned to the fact that he could not change his friend, and damned if he wasn't glad to see him.

"Speaking of that, I'm hungry, Bro. What say I take you out for drinks and dinner?"

"Don't drink."

"Damn! Then I was lucky that you didn't get the drop on me."

"I'll order a pizza, but first I need some answers."

"How about the pizza first?"

"Nope. It's my only leverage. What are you doing here?"

Blake took it down a notch. "Checking on you."

David nodded. He knew his friend looked after him like a big brother. "After I gave you up, I've had radio silence. There's no reason to further harass or try to intimidate me."

"I prefer a final solution," Blake said somberly.

"And I prefer a real major," David said, pointing to the leaves on Blake's collar, "rather than a fake one. Not only are you not a major, you're not in the marines unless the army finally figured out you were too soft to be one of us."

"That's cold, Bro," said Blake, smiling at the abuse.

"Isn't it a felony to impersonate an officer?"

"Dude," Blake whispered, "I am black ops; there are no rules for me. I can impersonate the president."

"Wishful thinking," quipped David.

Blake got up from the kitchen table, walked over to the sink, and tossed the towel beside it. He took two steps to the refrigerator, opened the door, and then closed it with a frown. "The frigging cupboard is bare, man! Order me some food!"

"Other than baby-sitting me, I need to know why you're in D.C. You've put yourself right in the line of fire."

"It's where I live, baby," said Blake, throwing his arms out.

David folded his hands, lacing his fingers, and waited.

"God, I hate it when you do this." Blake leaned over the table and placed his palms on the surface. "I've got 24 hours. I'm pretty sure I'm up for a shit assignment. I'm meeting my contact at Langley at zero eight twenty. And yes, I was worried about you; you're family."

People who never experience combat have a difficult time understanding the bond that can arise between fellow warriors. David knew that Blake had told him all that he would tell about his mission. He nodded acknowledgement. "Pepperoni work for you?"

CHAPTER 111

"I NEED YOUR HELP."

Mac surmised that this was not a request that Blake Stone made easily, or ever. At Blake's request, he, Mac, and David Grant were eating lunch at one of the District's busiest eateries. Devon and Blakely happened to be one of Mac's favorites, because he could get a fresh, custom-made salad and iced tea in less than ten minutes, regardless of the size of the crowd.

From spring through late fall, the outdoor tables were great for folks enjoying quality soups, salads, or sandwiches. Now it was early February, and they were lucky to have secured an inside table.

When David set up the luncheon and asked Mac to join them for a private conversation, Mac had suggested the lower level of the Army and Navy Club, where there were no dress requirements and the tables were isolated. Adding to the confusion as to why the two friends wanted Mac to be included, David had chosen Devon and Blakely instead.

"This less than private spot was not my choice," said Mac over the cacophony of voices. Both the soup and salad lines had people backed up to the door.

"I've found that privacy is often easier in the midst of a crowd," said Blake. "Everyone strains to hear his own conversation."

"In that case, how can I help?"

"David says that you're on the inside with the president."

Mac shot David a sharp look.

David raised his hands. "It was necessary boss, I promise."

340

His explanation did not sit well, but Mac focused his attention on Blake.

"At 9:00 a.m. tomorrow, I'm supposed to report to the Oval Office."

Mac couldn't hide his surprise. "What for?"

Blake shrugged. "I have no idea, but I've got no desire to spend the rest of my life in Leavenworth."

"What are your options?"

"I could disappear, but I've never run from anything."

Mac nodded, his mind reeling. By silent assent, the three men resumed eating their lunches. It took over five minutes for Mac to make a decision. He reached in his side suit pocket and extracted a business card. He pulled out his pen from his breast pocket and wrote on the card.

"Here's my cell. Call me as soon as the meeting concludes. If I don't hear back from you by two o'clock, I will call the president. He wants something from me. If he charges you or arrests you, I will not be a part of his administration."

Blake grimaced. "You don't owe me. I don't . . . "

"It's nonnegotiable," said Mac with authority.

"But why?" asked Blake.

This time Mac shrugged. "You bought lunch."

CHAPTER 112

GRACE MCGREGOR LOOKED AT THE kitchen clock: 6:20. Mac had been coming home later and later. Conversations had been stilted, casual affection felt forced. The distance that neither had ever antici-pated was like a third person standing between them. Someone or something had let the air out of her husband.

"Hey," Mac said listlessly as he entered the house through the garage. His tie was pulled down, his collar was open, and his right hand held his suit coat over his shoulder. In his left hand he carried his black briefcase, which contained his electronics and various research material. He walked towards her and gave her a perfunctory kiss on the cheek, then headed to his office, where he dropped the briefcase.

She watched him re-enter the kitchen area in order to walk up the back stairway to their bedroom. Part of the evening ritual was for him to change out of his work clothes as soon as possible. The shared silence felt oppressive. He was on the first step when she spoke.

"Mac, after you change your clothes and relax a little, do you have time for a short conversation before dinner?"

His shoulders slumped, but he said, "Sure. I won't be long."

Part of her routine was to have a cold glass of Pinot Grigio while she made dinner. Tonight she wanted nothing to interfere with their talk.

The two chairs in front of the "big ass windows" were the McGre-gors' favorite place to talk. Neither felt like constant eye contact was required for listening or responding, and the view acted as a delay, so

that they could gather their thoughts. Grace had turned on the outside lights, and last night's slight sprinkling of snow was still in evidence.

Wearing his lucky Redskins pajama bottoms and a tee shirt, Mac
gave the illusion of being relaxed, even though he was 180 degrees
from feeling that way. Leaning over and folding his hands, he looked
straight ahead. "What's up?"

Ten seconds, twenty seconds, and then Grace spoke. She
squeezed her eyes shut, and her words were as soft as a prayer. "Are
you seeing someone?"

"What?" He jerked his head and looked at her with alarm.

"We, we can talk about anything."

The pain in her voice was like a razor slicing his insides. *No, we
can't talk about anything, not about this...* "Grace, I'm not seeing anyone. Don't ever think that." He shook his head and let out a long
breath. "Three weeks ago I received an offer and agreed to respond
within thirty days."

"To go with another firm?" she asked tentatively.

"No. That decision would be easy. This decision I can't make
without talking to you, and I know what you'll say."

Her voice rose. "Mac, you're not sleeping well. You pick at your
food. You're miserable. I'm miserable. Talk to me!"

Mac hesitated, frantically thinking how to frame his words. For
what seemed like a long while, they'd been like roommates who tol-
erated each other. "Okay," he said forcefully. "Jeremy Lyons asked me
to be his treasury secretary."

Grace stared at him.

"You're going to say no way, what about your clients, a political
life puts us in a fishbowl, and by the way, I hate the murdering bastard!" He hadn't meant to shout.

She saw it in his eyes. "You want to do this."

"Yeah, I want to serve my country. I think I can make a difference."

"I agree."

"What!" He looked at her like he hadn't heard right.

She reached over and rested her hand on his arm. "I've thought and prayed about my reaction every time you mention his name. I get furious and take it out on you. My guess is that if I got the back story on most of our country's politicians, I'd be repulsed." She rubbed his arm lovingly.

"You're a good man with good instincts about people. You didn't fall into his web easily. You're also a patriot. It's an incredible honor to be asked to be a member of a president's cabinet, and I'll feel better knowing that you won't allow any shenanigans on your watch.

"The questions you assumed I'd ask are valid, but you don't need my approval for what you believe is right. I may not believe in Jeremy Lyons, but I do believe in you." She moved her hand from his arm and wiped the corner of his eye. "Have you spoken to R.J.?"

"Not yet," he said. The stunned look remained on his face.

She touched his arm again. "It's my fault we are where we are." She needed to see a smile. "I don't want to control you, and I'll try not to criticize your decisions unless you do decide to be with another woman. Then I would definitely hurt you."

Mac got out of his chair, walked to her chair, and lifted her up.

"Careful."

He hoisted her onto his lap and wrapped his arms around her. Their lips met, and the wall dissolved.

"Well," she said, catching her breath and grabbing hold of his pajama pants. "These pants weren't lucky enough to get your beloved Skins past the first round of the playoffs, but I'm pretty sure they'll work for you tonight."

CHAPTER 113

YOU COULD SEE YOUR FACE in Blake Stone's black shoes. It was the only sure tell that he was military. The dark blue suit jacket barely stretched across his chest, forcing him to leave the coat unbuttoned. It was David Grant's suit, and he had joked to David that the waist of the pants was too big and the crotch needed to be let out. Classic cemetery humor.

His hair was not short, and there were no white sidewalls. His assignments often required him to look more like a drifter than a soldier. Besides, if today was his last day of freedom, Blake Stone was not going down looking like a new recruit.

He stood at strict attention while the president finished signing some papers. Light from the three windows behind the president's desk seemed to illuminate the man. Anyone who was not intimidated by the Oval Office didn't have a pulse. Absently, Blake checked the room's four exits. He calculated that his only hope was out the east exit through the Rose Garden, and there were way too many serious agents around to make that more than a fantasy.

Finally, Lyons put down his pen and stood up. "Mr. Stone, thank you for coming. At ease." He reached out his hand.

Blake walked briskly over, shook the president's hand, and immediately stepped back.

"Have a seat, Mr. Stone," said Lyons as he motioned to a chair. As the soldier sat, the president sat on the edge of his desk. "Have we met before?"

"I don't believe so," said Blake quickly.

Shaking his head, the president said, "It's strange. Somehow you seem very familiar to me. It's as if we previously had a close encounter."

Blake clenched his jaw and unconsciously held his breath.

Lyons studied him like a cobra preparing to strike. Sweat formed on Blake's forehead. "Ah," said Lyons. "It must have been in another life."

Blake parceled out an exhale.

"Do you know why I asked to see you?"

"No, sir."

"That was a quick reply. Think for a moment. Can you think of any reason that I would single you out?"

Blake held the president's intense gaze. "Perhaps you've heard that I was a discipline problem, sir."

Lyons leaned back and folded his hands. "You really don't have a clue, do you, soldier?"

"I never presume to know what my commander in chief's intentions are, sir."

"Good answer, Stone, even if it is total bullshit."

Blake went quiet. After a lengthy period of silence, he was ready to fall on the sword when Lyons spoke.

"You're the best, Mr. Stone. A sniper who never misses, an assassin who does his duty for his country with no hesitation or remorse. With a lot of enemies who want to kill me, wouldn't it behoove me to meet a man of your skills? A man I could count on to perform any mission I gave him, till death do us part?"

Lyons spread his hands. "Although..." He spoke the word slowly, then reached over and picked up a manila folder on his desk. "All I know is what is in your press clippings. Quite a bit of this was redacted, but I managed to obtain a more complete report. It says here that you have executed over 200 missions. Excuse the word 'executed,' and that is quite impressive." The president closed the folder and held it to his chest.

"Is there any mission in here that you regret?" Lyons asked.

Looking straight ahead, Blake spoke woodenly. "I do not have access to the file, sir."

"It is probably unfair to ask you that question. I understand you are a fellow Christian, and no follower likes to disobey the sixth commandment." He paused. "However, you do take the 'eye for an eye' quote literally." He pointed to Blake's knuckles to emphasize the point.

Blake's eyes did not leave the spot behind the president's head. "Has there ever been an unauthorized mission, Mr. Stone?"

Visible sweat tickled Blake's neck and ran down his back. In a strangled breath he said, "Once, sir."

Lyons walked back behind his desk and slammed the file down. He stood looking out the windows, his hands on his hips.

Blake felt like his head was on the guillotine. The next words the president spoke would send the blade crashing down.

After an interminable delay, Lyons spoke softly still with his back to Blake. "There can be no unauthorized missions on *my* watch, Mr. Stone. I would consider that treason. Do we understand each other?"

"Yes, sir!"

Lyons spun around. "The leader of the free world needs to have a patriot, an infallible soldier who never ducks an assignment and never misses by his side. I need to be sure that whatever mission I assign you will be carried out without question. I need a warrior that I can count on. Are you that man?"

Blake clenched his jaw. "Yes, sir."

"Let us both pray that I have made the right decision."

For what seemed like an eternity, Blake stood at semi attention, his eyes straight ahead. The entire time Lyons's eyes bore into him. Finally, the president spoke. "Approach me."

Blake walked quickly to his desk. Lyons handed him a file and said, "In the past, your missions have been to seek and destroy." He paused. "And your record is almost perfect." He paused again. "This time it is to find and deliver."

Blake maintained eye contact and gave a slight nod.

"Even though we are taught to turn the other cheek, there are times, in those rare instances when someone does something unspeakable to someone you love, when forgiveness is unimaginable. The man I want you to find is two faced," he said angrily. "Actually, he has many faces, but I need you to find him. Until you do, a relentless cancer of recrimination will consume me." Lyons's eyes were hard. "Do you understand the significance of your mission, soldier?"

"YES, SIR!"

Lyons turned and said, "You are dismissed."

CHAPTER 114

"To what do I owe this honor?" asked R.J. as he sat down across from his senior partner.

"Twenty-three other people canceled on me. You were lucky 24."

"That means I've made a quantum leap on your friendship list."

Mac shook his head. "It's not a friendship list. I only know 24 people who don't bore me."

Mac had emailed R.J. the night before asking him to meet for breakfast at eight the next morning. When you've worked in downtown D.C. for 35 years and you're a breakfast creature of habit, the venue is assumed.

The familiar waiter had left after taking their orders, and the Hay Adams had accommodated them by giving them the farthest table to the left as you entered the restaurant. Unless it was insanely busy, that ensured privacy.

"What's up, boss?" asked R.J., unable to control his curiosity.

"A changing of the guard," Mac answered in a low voice.

"Is something wrong with you?"

"Not health wise, but conceivably mentally. I have something that I will discuss with the team, but it's necessary to brief you first." He paused. "I'll be taking a sabbatical."

"What?"

Mac leaned across the table. "Lyons has asked me to be in his cabinet."

"You can't."

Mac raised an eyebrow. "Why not?"

R.J. went into rapid fire mode. "I need you, the team needs you, our clients need you, and Grace will go nuts!"

The waiter walked over with their iced teas, and Mac thought he'd need to drop a fast-acting Valium in R.J.'s drink. "Grace was my first conversation; you are the next. I haven't notified Jeremy of my decision."

"Then don't!" said R.J. adamantly. "Mac, this is a mistake. Have you really thought this through?" His face was contorted with concern.

"When have you known me to be impulsive?"

"You're the face of the franchise. Barron's Hall of Fame. You get more hits on Google than all of the other advisors in the complex combined."

The firm of Johnston Wellons had eight offices in D.C. and the surrounding areas of Maryland and Virginia. R.J.'s assertion could not be fact checked, but Mac didn't call him on it.

"Max term is for four years. Jeremy promised he wouldn't keep me more than two. He knows I love my job. I don't believe that my leaving to serve my country will be a negative with our clients. I see no attrition from that, but your concern that my absence will stymie growth in the short term could be legitimate."

"I think the whole team will be upset. And I'm not sure that I or the team is ready for me to lead."

Honesty and humility — it was why Mac had hired him in the first place. He looked at his partner with affection. "I think you'll be surprised at how our clients react." Mac could see that R.J. wasn't sold, so he added, "If we spin this correctly with them, it will be a positive." He raised his eyebrows up and down. "We politicians are masters at spin." Still nothing.

"What if the country is actually in better shape when I leave office? Imagine being able to say that our practice is run by a former secretary of the treasury," said Mac.

"Wait! You'll come back and demote me?"

"Come to think of it," said Mac, rubbing his chin with his hand, "probably not. Odds are that I'll be offered a ten-figure consulting job, and you clowns will have to flounder on your own."

CHAPTER 115

February 7, 2017, 8:00 p.m.

WITH TEMPERATURES IN THE HIGH fifties and an absence of wind, it was said that the perfect night must have been decreed. It was abnormally mild weather for February, but even without an overcoat, the principal speaker was sweating.

The White House Rose Garden borders the Oval Office and the West Wing. It is approximately 125 feet long and 60 feet wide. Seasonal flowers are interspersed to add nearly year-round color. Focused television lights made the area the spotlight of the nation.

The President of the United States was illuminated by carefully placed lights, which seemed to create a three-dimensional effect for the television audience. In his dark blue suit and cardboard-crisp white shirt, with tanned face and head, he was in their living rooms.

Part actor and part evangelist, Jeremy Lyons spoke with power and conviction not witnessed since Ronald Reagan. "My fellow Americans, I want to introduce you to my treasury secretary. He has spent his life navigating the intricacies and snake pits of the investment world in order to help his clients achieve financial freedom. My charitable foundation was in his capable hands and now resides in a blind trust with his team.

"I assure you," he looked at Mac with a half smile, "that Mac McGregor did not volunteer for this job. When I asked him to serve his country, he told me that many others were more qualified for the job. When I told him that his country needed him...," he paused, " he had the nerve to tell me that *I* was mistaken!" The dignitaries and reporters on the lawn laughed.

"Well, then I had no choice. I had to prove him wrong.

"When I was a senator, I asked for his advice on how to fix our economy. His first recommendation was to lower the corporate income tax rate and encourage our companies to do business here. Tonight I've asked him to discuss an idea that can reduce volatility in our stock markets and, at the same time, raise revenues from some of our wealthiest citizens. Please welcome a man of vision and purpose, my friend, Mac McGregor."

Mac had given hundreds of speeches and television interviews, his speech tonight was on the teleprompter ready to go, and the president had given him a glowing introduction. Dressed in a navy pin-striped suit, crisp white shirt, and red and blue silk tie, he looked ready. But his smile felt fake, painted on to get strangers to like him.

His heart was in his throat. He said his silent prayer: *May the words of my mouth and the meditations of my heart be acceptable in Thy sight, O Lord, my strength and my redeemer.* Now, his smile filled his eyes.

"Mr. President, thank you for your kind introduction. I hope I can live up to your expectations.

"Any attempt to add value to our economy and to the American people requires exhaustive study, endless projections, and legislators with the courage to enact the changes into law. Yet, the effectiveness of the changes can only be measured in the rear view mirror.

"Lowering the corporate tax rate is not an original idea. Congressmen and -women, as well as President Obama, previously advocated lowering the rate to make us more competitive in the global markets. Enough time has passed that we can judge this action to be an unqualified success.

"One of the primary goals of this administration is to create a simpler, more equitable tax code." The audience applauded vigorously. "This cannot be done in a short period of time. In fact, we are convinced that there is no perfect solution. Just the continuing analysis of proposals may take the next twelve months. Pressure from various political factions and special interest groups will be enormous."

Mac spread his arms. "Everyone wants simplicity and fairness; no one wants to give up any tax breaks, and bless their hearts, the tax attorneys and CPAs want to make a living. So not only must we present a better alternative to the burdensome tax forms we have today, it must also be one that the politicians do not tinker with whenever they want to spend money." Again he waited for the applause to diminish.

"Every year our citizens are forced to wade through voluminous papers, to be aware of an encyclopedia of rules, and to fill out barely understandable forms. Why else would almost every successful individual hire someone to file his or her taxes?"

Mac held up four fingers. "We have four years to get this done and, at the same time, reduce the national debt. It is my responsibility to help the president and congress succeed in this mission.

"This evening our task in simpler, to take one step in lessening a problem. For over 35 years, I was joined at the hip with the stock market. I saw its transformative power in helping companies such as Apple, Google, and Microsoft increase the quality of our lives and our standard of living. I also witnessed the gut-wrenching pain of destructive recessions and bear markets as they decimated net worth.

"The stock market was formed so that companies could raise capital, so they could grow. Individuals could own parts of companies and prosper through dividends and price appreciation. Anyone who has invested in the stock market knows that at times it is like being on a roller coaster. We expect stock prices to fluctuate due to factors such as valuation, company earnings reports, and merger or acquisition news. We're also aware that unforeseen events or a crisis can affect the entire stock market."

Mac paused. "A precipitous decline in individual stocks or the market as a whole is disturbing and frightening. But if we can identify a logical reason, a *real* reason for the loss in value, it still hurts, but we can sleep at night.

"In today's stock markets, the majority of the rapid moves have nothing to do with value or events. Markets are dominated by algorithms. Computers, some working in concert, buy and sell millions of shares. The average holding period for these purchases or sales is less than five seconds. High-frequency traders are not investors; it is not their intention to raise capital or help our economy grow. It is their intention to make money…quickly.

"Proponents argue that the computerized trades add liquidity to our markets. Perhaps that is true. It is not this administration's purpose to outlaw any trading or disrupt free markets. However, it is our purpose to reduce market volatility that is created only for instant profit. And it is our purpose to raise revenues to help our economy grow.

"The president has garnered sufficient support in congress such that we expect fast-track legislation that will result in a one per cent tax on any security trade of ten thousand shares or more that are not held for 24 hours. In order not to add administrative burdens to the high-frequency traders, the individual exchanges will immediately extract the tax on each transaction and forward the proceeds to the government."

Mac paused again. "I was there on October 19, 1987, when the stock market crashed 23 per cent in one day. I was there for the flash crash on May 6, 2010, when the Dow Jones dropped over 9 per cent in 36 minutes. It was caused by a trader working from home. In May of 2014, the Commodities Futures Trading Commission determined that high-frequency traders did not cause the flash crash, but they contributed to it by demanding immediacy over other market participants. And I was once again at my desk in August of 2015, when the Dow Jones Average plunged almost 1100 points in the first ten minutes of trading.

"I am now at a different desk, where I will work to create a safer and better functioning stock market. Thank you, and good night."

As the cameras dimmed, the president walked over and embraced Mac. It was a powerful moment, but Mac's thoughts were elsewhere. He searched the crowd until he spotted Grace, her right arm raised and pumping, her ice blue eyes filled with happy tears.

CHAPTER 116

INSIDE THE BLACK LINCOLN TOWN Car, the two post-60 year olds were cuddling like teenagers. Al, being an experienced driver, did not consider glancing in the rear view mirror.

"Your shirt is soaked," said Grace, running her hands up Mac's sides.

"I'm not surprised. That was intense.,"

She tilted her head back and looked up at him. "I'm really proud of you, Mac."

"Thanks, babe. It was hard to forget the enormity of the situation. I'm much more comfortable just punching the **on** button and going with whatever comes out."

"All the kids texted me, congratulating you."

Mac smiled.

"And so did R.J. I think he's afraid to text you."

"What did he say?"

"That you did a great job of presenting his idea."

Mac laughed. "When I get skewered by the press and every investment house in America, I'll be sure to give him credit."

Mac exhaled and lovingly rubbed his hands up and down Grace's back. Their renewed connection made every moment more precious.

"Did you understand it?" he asked softly. He had not asked her to preview his speech so that he would get an unvarnished answer.

"All I got was that some greedy bastards are messing with the stock market and you are going to make them pay!"

He hugged her tighter. "Perfect."

CHAPTER 117

As an inducement to get Mac to accept the appointment to his administration, the president had authorized a two-week sabbatical before he would assume the duties of treasury secretary. This gave Mac the opportunity to talk personally with his clients and discuss the transition, and also the inability to respond to the predictable criticism about the new regulation.

However, it did not prevent Mac from reading the plethora of attack articles on the policy and on his obvious lack of qualifications. It was hard not to take it personally, and he didn't expect the criticism to go away quickly. The collective vitriol from the big banks and traders dismissed Mac's 35-year clean track record. He was now officially a pariah.

* * *

I probably should have called Uber, thought Mac as he cautiously maneuvered down River Road. He loved his 15-year-old Lexus, but the light sprinkling of snow challenged his limited driving skills. Due to school closings, traffic was moderate, which should have eased his anxiety.

Alternating between CNBC and Fox Business on his satellite radio, he found that he remained the topic du jour. CNBC's Joe Carvel, who was a bit of a rival as well as a big Lyons fan, gave him the benefit of the doubt. "How about we give the guy a chance? He may not have the street creds of a Paulson or Lew, but I thought he handled himself well. And I think the move will be great for investors."

The impulse was to take both hands off the wheel and raise his arms in triumph, but, fortunately, Mac squelched that impulse. He turned right on Falls Road, thought about changing the station, but instead decided to continue to bathe in the masochistic rhetoric.

About twenty minutes later he turned right onto the Whitehurst Freeway, joining the gaggle of vehicles moving gingerly over the sand-splashed street. Recalcitrant patches of ice clung to the many pot-holes.

* * *

Although it was only 7:20 in the morning, Mac's phone was ringing off the hook. Even with Lyons's permission, he wasn't sure if he was still allowed to be in his office. In the event that he was challenged, his first defense would be, "the president said so." If that didn't work, he was an expert in begging for forgiveness. Besides, the office was his sanctuary; no press were allowed.

One of the problems with accepting the job was that a certain subset of clients would still expect Mac to be there for them even though he was the treasury secretary. On a brief respite from explaining the situation and answering congratulatory calls, Mac looked up to see Lena Brady watching him.

She cocked her head to one side, studying his desk. "I'll either need to raise the seat on the chair, or, what the heck, I'll order a new one."

Mac smiled, the first genuine one of the day. "So you are ascending to the throne?"

"Who else?" she asked, throwing up her hands like he'd asked the world's dumbest question.

Another call came in that he needed to take, and she rolled her eyes and moved away. *Damn, I'm going to miss her; I'll probably be surrounded by polite, politically correct people.*

He spun his black ergonomic chair 180 degrees and stretched his legs. He half listened to a nearby conversation as he alternated looking at the traffic on Pennsylvania Avenue and the family pictures on his desk that always comforted him. He felt like an athlete being forced out of a game. *A little late to be having buyer's remorse.*

In a few moments of silence, Mac Googled the different print media thoughts. He was gratified that positive comments at least came from Barron's and Tom Hessel. Predictably, there were still scattered articles centered on the theme, "Who the heck is Mac McGregor and how on earth is he qualified for the job?"

He had to admit they had a point.

* * *

Mac had been the treasury secretary for a total of two weeks, and he was big-time homesick for his team. Going from a hard-working family of clowns to an efficient group of government workers was a bit of a culture shock. And God help him, he was forced to be politically correct every minute he was with his staff.

Al, his driver (there were some perks), let him off in front of his garage. Mac had to almost tie the man down to make sure he didn't get out of the car to open the door for him. Grace had gone to dinner with their two daughters, and it gave Mac an opportunity to not be important.

In jeans and a blue, collared, long-sleeved shirt, Mac's temperature was already dropping. Behind the wheel of his silver Lexus, he almost felt human again. Driving down Falls Road, he passed his church on the left. Even there he felt like a celebrity. A Beach Boys song came on the radio, and he butchered the harmonies at the top of his lungs. He pulled into the parking lot at Cabin John Shopping Center. He didn't want to eat in the Potomac area, because even an innocent dinner could be misinterpreted.

Already seated at a table in the Grilled Oyster, R.J. Brooks rose with a big smile. The two friends hugged unabashedly and then sat down across from each other. "Why do I feel like I'm sneaking out for an assignation?" asked Mac.

R.J. raised his hands in a stop sign. "Whoa! We've had this discussion before. I'm not that kind of guy."

Mac laughed. The facial movements were better than the line. "Damn, I miss being with everyone. If I abuse my new team, they tear up on me."

"We miss you too, Mac. It's hard not to feel rudderless."

"So tell me what's going on."

"Our clients are proud of you, although expectations may be a bit unrealistic."

"Meaning?"

"Let's just say that our clients have never *under*estimated your abilities."

Mac nodded. "So I'm responsible for eliminating the national debt and creating a fair, simple tax code."

"Bingo."

"That should be easy. Send me your recommendations by eight o'clock tomorrow morning, and I will expedite implementation."

R.J. laughed. "I wish we could talk some specifics, but there may be a Romney microphone in the restaurant."

Mac reached over and smacked his shoulder. "Nah. Tonight you'll impart all of your inside knowledge of sports."

"Perfect," said R.J. "And for dessert, you can bring me up to date on your encyclopedic knowledge of technology."

CHAPTER 118

THE TREASURY DEPARTMENT'S GYM WAS infested with gym rats, that subhuman species that must work out or die. Tee shirts with cutoff sleeves, running shorts barely containing muscular thighs, these warriors got all kinds of tense when they missed even a day of working out. Secretary McGregor, on the other hand, got tense just thinking about working out.

He had opted to walk the few blocks to the White House gym under the joint rationalization that he did not want to be interrupted with business questions and that he did not want to embarrass the iron addicts with his workout regime. Besides, the walk could legitimately be counted as cardio. Now, as his leather soles skidded on the slick streets, he used his black Johnston Wellons duffle bag for balance and questioned the wisdom of his decision.

Workout aficionados would not be impressed by the pedestrian White House gym. Mac looked at the modest equipment with the same loathing he had when approaching an excessively backed up TSA line at the airport. Alone, he stood with his hands on his hips, dressed in running shorts and an extra-large tee shirt that read, "No one gets to see the wizard, no way, no how."

It was five p.m., normally not too late to leave for home, but a light sheen of snow that turned immediately to ice made the gym seem like the lesser evil. The streets were parking lots, and no matter how good a driver Al was, he wouldn't make it back to Potomac for at least three hours. Mac picked up two 25-pound dumbbells, glared at them, and started doing curls.

Twenty minutes later, as Mac stood deciding if what he had done counted as a workout, the president walked into the gym. Mac wiped his brow with an exaggerated motion. "Give me a few. My two hours are almost finished."

Lyons laughed. "You never promised that telling time was one of your strengths."

"You wanna go?" Mac challenged, puffing out his chest.

"No, no. I know when I'm outclassed."

With the size of your guns, you can probably curl 250 pounds, thought Mac. "What can I do for you, Mr. President?"

"You can have dinner with me."

"Well, Grace is expecting me home," Mac offered lamely.

"I have already called her, and she felt like it would be safer for you to leave later. She said something about texting her when you're close so that she can kick her boyfriend out."

Mac raised his eyebrows and pointed to himself. "Like any dude could compete with this body."

* * *

The old Family Dining Room had been refurbished to serve as a showcase of modern art and design, a far cry from what it looked like when Mr. and Mrs. John Quincy Adams established the room in 1825. A new gray wall color highlighted new gilded metal and glass wall sconces, and new red draperies replaced the more formal ones that had been installed by Jackie Kennedy in 1963. In February of 2015, for the first time in White House history, the old Family Dining

Room on the State floor was opened for public viewing.

"Sabine, who obviously has better sense than I, opted to stay in Naples for the week, so I would have eaten in solitary tonight if not for you," said Lyons.

Mac shrugged. "Okay, I guess it's a positive that I am preferable to eating alone."

Lyons leaned his head back and looked at the ceiling. A few moments later, he resumed eye contact and said, "One of the most wonderful tenets of Christianity is that we have the ability to confess our sins, and when we repent, our God not only forgives us, but wipes the sins from His memory. I admit, when I became born again, the confession part took about a day and a half, and it's likely that I missed more than a few sins."

He paused to look at Mac, and his words revealed a vulnerability. "I enjoy your company tremendously. When you started at Johnston Wellons, I was instantly jealous of you. You were competition.

"It would be impossible for anyone to be more driven than I am, and I had no family, so I could work until I was exhausted. But you were smart, quick witted, and everyone liked you. I was unable to get people to like me, so I ran over them. When you introduced yourself to me, I told you to screw off." He grimaced. "Not a great recipe for likeability."

"You remember that?" asked Mac with surprise.

Lyons nodded. "God has wiped my sins away, but that doesn't mean that I have forgotten them."

Mac waved it off. "Come on. Guys say that to other guys as a sign of affection. And by the way, 'screw' was not the verb you used."

Lyons laughed, then turned serious. "The fact that you are with me now is evidence of your tolerance and your willingness to give me another chance. I regret deeply that I didn't have the self-esteem to befriend you then. You would have been good for me, perhaps saved me from at least some of my multitude of sins, and at the very least, made me laugh."

Mac appreciated Lyons's attempt to lighten his comments at the end. "That's yesterday's news, Jeremy." He shook his head and waved around the room. "You don't get to be President of the United States without being likeable. And you are president for the right reasons. No perfect pasts at this table. I appreciate that you value me enough to have me as a confidant and a friend. Both of us are where we are because of the grace of God."

"Amen." Emotional conversations between men often have a short shelf life, and now Lyons was feeling a bit self-conscious "So, Mac," he said, and then waited while the butler cleared the table and asked, "Will you be wanting any dessert, sirs?"

Mac spoke first, "No, thank you. The meal was magnificent." The butler beamed and left the room.

"You have seen our agenda, our to-do list. What am I missing?" The president folded his hands and leaned towards Mac.

In his best Lyons imitation, Mac rolled his head back and looked at the ceiling as if he were pondering many answers.

Lyons barked out a laugh. "No stalling. You're a political junkie. You've spent your life playing 'If I were king.'"

Mac's head snapped up like it was on a rubber band. "Guilty. You are addressing most of the big concerns." Turning serious, he went on, "No one likes the fact that billionaires can buy elections."

Lyons stiffened.

"You're not the first," Mac said in a matter-of-fact tone. "Bloomberg bought New York, and every dark money PAC is just a shadow billionaire. Regardless of the legitimacy of abiding by the campaign finance rules, money should not be able to buy elections, and the public has a right to know who is funding the candidates." He shrugged. "At least there's no mystery about who funded your campaign."

Lyons waited almost a full minute before responding. "How do I propose changes without looking like a hypocrite?"

Mac shook his head. "We'd have to talk about a salary increase before you get all the answers. It's my job to tell you what's wrong; it's your job to execute."

CHAPTER 119

"I'm surprised you're still in town," said David Grant as he picked up his cup of coffee.

Blake Stone shrugged. They were eating a quick breakfast at Founding Farmers restaurant. David, who was back up to his fighting weight, threatened to go over it with his side order of beignets.

"I think it's because you complete me," said Blake with a smirk.

"Bite me."

"Actually," said Blake, as he looked around to make sure that no one was near their booth, "I need you to look at some pictures." Turning over one at a time, he watched David for a reaction.

On the third picture, David turned white and pointed to it. "That's the son-of-a-bitch...."

"Lower your voice," said Blake, as he scooped up the photos and placed them in his thin, leather carrying bag.

"How did you . . .?"

Blake leaned across the table. "I can't discuss anything with you. I broke all of the rules just showing you the picture, but I had to be sure. Plus, the irony is delicious."

David knew that it was futile to try to get his friend to explain, but he tried an end-around anyway. "Can you at least tell me that the asshole is in trouble?" he asked.

Flashing a wide smile, Blake said, "Oh, yeah...."

CHAPTER 120

THE EAST ROOM OF THE White House is used for large gatherings. During the Obama administration, the East Room served as the site for the signing of the Affordable Care Act in March of 2012. It was also used to celebrate the arts with performances by Paul McCartney, Stevie Wonder, Bob Dylan, and many more. On this late afternoon, there was more combined net worth in the room than at any other time in history. The guests included the CEOs and chairmen of every major commercial bank, every investment bank, and all of the major rating agencies.

The guest list was by invitation only, but when the President of the United States asks you to attend, it is a command performance. The crowd looked up expectantly as Jeremy Lyons strode confidently to the podium. "Ladies and gentlemen, thank you for coming."

None of the attendees knew the precise purpose of this meeting, but speculation ran from an innovative partnership to the issuing of even more draconian rules. Their cell phones had been collected at the door, and all were pleased to note that no one under the rank of CEO had been included

"You all know my treasury secretary, Mac McGregor, a fellow veteran of the financial wars," Lyons said as he gestured towards his friend, who stood about four feet from him and to his right. "I will speak first, then I have asked Mac to add some color to my statements, and then I will conclude. Mac's presence on the dais tonight should reinforce the fact that this is not the first rodeo for either of us."

Lyons continued over nervous, polite laughter. "We have an explicit agenda. We will not waste your valuable time. I will outline what we intend to accomplish and finish with compelling reasons for you to concur with our thinking. We expect you to be willing partners."

Lyons paused for effect. "I regret that I cannot protect future generations from financial Armageddon, nor can you who are with us today. But we can and will create a blueprint for posterity. Here's what we know for certain: Dodd Frank is cumbersome, over-reaching, and a business killer."

Spontaneous applause broke out.

"We intend to analyze every facet of law, eliminating any extraneous regulations, and leaving only the bare minimum necessary to provide transparency and accountability."

The applause grew louder, and Lyons gazed solemnly out at the crowd until it died down. "We also know that you," he pointed an accusatory finger at the crowd, "or your predecessors, came this close," his index and middle fingers were only fractionally apart, "to destroying this country." The president's anger stilled the room. He stepped back, and Mac stepped to the podium.

"Thank you, sir," Mac began. "I was there, a witness to the carnage. So were countless other investment advisors, 12 to 14 hours a day, often performing triage for panicked clients. Only the eternal optimist, or someone not paying attention, could tell his clients, 'Don't worry. Everything is going to be okay.' How frightening is it to have to rely on the government to make sure that America doesn't die? Everyone who was there knows I am not exaggerating. We were a week away from five major brokerage firms going out of business, and General Electric likely would have followed.

"There is plenty of guilt and blame to go around. Bankers with their 'no doc and liars loans,' rating agencies that labeled these bogus loans as triple A credits, the Securities and Exchange Commission that decided to revoke a 70-year-old rule and allow hedge funds to sell stocks short on the 'honor system,' and politicians who thought that everyone should own their own home.

"Our economy was circling the drain, and no one was punished. Trillions in market value lost, and the people saw all the culprits simply bailed out. Not only was it necessary to pass the Troubled Asset Relief Program in order to provide liquidity and restore confidence, but it was actually profitable for the Fed.

"In the light of day, the insane leverage, the dark markets are viewed as incredibly risky and, in some cases, sinister. Investors tend not to have long memories, and if the candidates did not beat the drum, a rising stock market would ease resentment. However, this administration does have a long memory, as well as a mandate."

Mac turned to Lyons. "Mr. President."

"So why are we giving you a history lesson?" asked Lyons. "Most of you are well aware of the facts and, in most cases, you are aware of those who were culpable. For too long, many businesses have put profits before people. If we are to prosper as a nation, that has to stop. So, this is what we expect of you:

"First: We ask that no financial institution donate to politicians. Your personal contributions are your own business.

"Second: Use leverage prudently.

"And third: No financial institution should market products to their customers that they would not purchase themselves.

"I realize that these strongly encouraged recommendations appear unenforceable, and the term 'prudent leverage' sounds like it is open to interpretation." He flashed a tight smile. "Some of you may already be thinking about how to use these guidelines to your advantage, and in your shoes, my thoughts would be similar. But I promised that I would offer compelling reasons for compliance.

"Over the last six months, we have gathered data on each company represented here. When I tell you that your financial operations, to the minutest detail, are an open book to us, I would encourage you to believe that. Our data-mining team is motivated and uniquely talented. Any corporate decisions that we consider excessively risky will be singled out, and in my humble opinion, your shareholders will suffer.

"It was helpful to thoroughly investigate your companies; however, in many cases, it was more helpful to thoroughly investigate each of you." Lyons let the implied threat hang in the air.

"It would cause embarrassment for me to issue an executive order declaring that your companies could no longer donate to political candidates. I realize that the people would applaud, but I do not feel that step is necessary.

"What is prudent leverage? Rather than dictate that, I will leave it to your discretion, but I will be watching. And if you try to screw your customers, well, I'll be watching that also.

"Remember that everything we are proposing would clearly be won in the court of popular opinion. The people are still justifiably outraged over all the malfeasance attached to the crash of 2008 and the fact that no one was incarcerated. That will not be the case in the event that this country ever has a self-inflicted financial crisis again.

"I am offering you the chance to be a part of history, to become men and women who refuse to buy political influence, those patriots who put people before profits. You have the chance to help America restore its fiscal sanity. It begins with your companies and your willingness to do the right thing."

Muted whispers followed until a single hand rose, asking to be acknowledged.

"No disrespect, Mr. President, we are all looking forward to positive change," said the pugnacious chairman of Exxon Mobil, "but I'm not comfortable having you or anyone else dictating behavior. Most of the companies here have endured through countless presidents. While we appreciate any guidance, it sounded to me like you were threatening us."

"Perhaps you misunderstood," said Lyons evenly.

"No, I don't think so, Mr. President, and as for me, if you have any dirt, bring it on. You may be a financial genius, but you're not an oil man. I'll continue to run my company as I see fit."

Lyons nodded and stared at the man. "That is your prerogative. In a free society we can choose to unite for the common good, in this case, your country and your shareholders, or we can choose to pursue our own self-serving agenda."

The chairman's mouth opened in surprise. "I find that insulting, Mr. President!"

"They're a size ten, aren't they, Clarence? If the shoe fits…" Lyons forced a smile.

"I regret that Mac and I have another meeting, but my press secretary, the extremely affable Steve Cannon, will host those who would like to remain for drinks. Again, I thank you for your attendance."

CHAPTER 121

THE TWO MEN ENTERED THE Oval Office. President Lyons removed the pillow from one end of the striped couch and added it to its twin in order to prop up his head. He stretched out, untied his tie, tossed it onto the desk, and kicked off his shoes. "Have a seat," he said waving his arms. "See how it feels."

Trying to ease some of the tension from the previous meeting, Mac ambled to the desk. His walk was somewhere between a caricature of a power walk and a pimp walk. He sat heavily in the chair, leaned back, and gave the president a condescending look. "Bring me Sabine!" he bellowed.

Lyons cracked up. "Be careful what you wish for. You might get another ass whipping."

Before Mac could retort, Lyons's personal secretary poked his head into the office. "Sir, a Martin Gonzala asks if he can speak to you. He says it's urgent."

Lyons grimaced and grabbed at his head like the mere thought of this man caused him pain. Martin Gonzala was the CEO of Global United Bank, the world's largest financial institution, and had been a powerful contributor to Lyons's trading syndicate in another life. "Send him in," said Lyons, not moving from his position.

Mac looked at him curiously and then asked. "Do you want me to leave?"

"No," Lyons said loudly. "Stay exactly where you are."

Although he felt extremely uncomfortable sitting behind the president's desk, Mac was reluctant to challenge him.

"Mr. President," said Gonzala, looking first at the desk and then quickly at the couch.

"Are you confused, Martin?" asked the president, not moving from his supine position.

"Yes, sir, a little," said Gonzala nervously.

"Well, what the fuck is so important that you had to interrupt us?"

Mac started to rise from the desk.

"Sit DOWN!" Lyons said, with a look in his eyes that Mac hadn't seen before. He knew that his best option was to comply.

Lyons focused intensely back to Gonzala, who stammered out a reply. "I, I needed to talk to you about our campaign donations."

"Were we not clear?"

The tone in his voice made Mac want to be anywhere but where he was.

"Yes, uh yes, sir, but we give almost equally, and it's necessary."

"NECESSARY?" Lyons exploded up from the couch and moved to stand over the man who was at least a head shorter. Gonzala, who had turned white, bent over and grabbed his knees.

Mac was afraid the man was going to vomit on the floor.

"STAND UP STRAIGHT WHEN YOU ARE TALKING TO YOUR PRESIDENT."

Mac wanted to intervene, but was at a loss as to what he could do.

Painfully, the CEO struggled to stand up.

Lyons placed a powerful hand on his shoulder.

"Martin, how long have we known each other?"

Gonzala looked nervously at Mac again, unsure of where this conversation was headed and how much he was at liberty to divulge. "Ten years, I believe."

"Ten years. And would you say that our arrangement over the years has been profitable for you and your firm?"

"Yes, Jeremy."

"YES. MR. PRESIDENT. SHOW SOME FUCKING RESPECT, MARTIN!" Lyons's fingers were white as dug them into the man's shoulder.

"I..I'm sorry, Mr. President." Gonzala's body began to shake with pain.

"Better." Lyons let go of his shoulder. "Just because we have a history together does not give you the right to forego formalities. Correct?"

"Yes, Mr. President."

"It is probably best that you drop your request and trust in my vision. Remember: discretion is the better part of valor."

Lyons shook his head at Gonzala's apparent confusion. Leaning in, he whispered, "It would be a shame for the lovely Mrs. Gonzala to learn about your mistress, Marguerite."

Gonzala's eyes rolled back in his head.

"Get out," the president said, waving his right arm in a backhand motion. "And never question me again."

Gonzala hurried out the door as Lyons stared after him without moving. After what seemed an eternity, Mac rose from the chair, and said quietly, "Jeremy, I'm going to see if I can get some work done."

Lyons looked at him like he'd forgotten that Mac was in the room. "Yes, yes....thanks for your work today."

CHAPTER 122

BLAKE STONE HAD MADE AN exception for David Grant, because he trusted him completely. He would work alone and not discuss the operation with anyone else. Never before had a U.S. President personally given him or, to his knowledge, any of his fellow operatives, a mission. Everything was always in layers, ensuring the ultimate requirement of plausible deniability. Yes, this president was different. Blake wondered if Lyons knew that his assignment would also be personal.

It took three days of research to discover the location of the target's mask maker. Another day wasted finding him and gently persuading him to give up John Wesley's last address. When Blake heard the address, he had to smile. Wesley did have balls.

* * *

It was not difficult to be unobtrusive waiting outside of the Ritz Carlton of Georgetown. Originally an industrial building, this boutique hotel is one of the few hotels in the world to feature a soaring brick smokestack.

Even though the Ritz was way above his pay grade, Blake could still appreciate the lofted ceilings and the grandeur of the luxury hotel, which still had the feeling of a cozy, intimate hideaway. Add a roaring fire in a massive fireplace, and he could see where this would be catnip to the beautiful people.

It took three more days before he saw Wesley returning to the hotel. There was nothing covert about his entrance, not even a disguise. Well, hiding in plain sight is not necessarily a bad plan. This time, however, it was.

Dressed in a conservative suit, it was easy for Blake to fit in as he entered the hotel lobby. Wesley went straight to the elevators. Blake headed to the reception desk.

"Can you tell me which one of the five luxury suites is open?" he asked the receptionist, smiling apologetically. "It's for my boss."

"You're in luck," she replied. "The only one that is occupied is the Presidential Suite."

"Thank you so much. I'll check back with him and call you as soon as he decides which one he wants." He rolled his eyes. "Rich people."

She laughed as he walked out.

At 2:00 a.m., Blake returned to the hotel and walked towards the elevator. His shirt collar was open, tie pulled down. He carried his suit coat over his shoulder.

When the elevator door closed, he used a small electronic sensor to bypass the security protocols, and in another thirty seconds, he exited on the penthouse floor.

Picking the lock on the Presidential Suite took another minute, and Blake opened the door slowly, prepared to encounter a security chain. The door opened all the way. Either Wesley was in another room, or the man suffered from tragic overconfidence.

Unfortunately for Wesley, he was sleeping soundly. Lying on his back, snoring like a race horse, he probably wouldn't have heard the security chain break if it had been latched.

Although he had no frame of reference, Blake felt that being awakened by having a Glock shoved in your mouth had to be one of the worst alternatives. Part of him had hoped that the mission parameters would have allowed for more of a scuffle, but his job was merely to deliver the package intact. Simultaneously with the gun insertion, Blake flipped on the bedside lamp.

Wesley gagged and tried to spit out the gun. Blake shook his head, discouraging resistance. When Wesley's wild eyes settled on him, he said, "I understand you've been looking for me."

CHAPTER 123

Mac thought it was ironic that he now had a designated driver. Whenever he and Grace went out to dinner or a gathering, she drove to the destination, and it was his job to drive home. An admitted control freak, Mac never had more than one drink, which left his better half free to have that second glass of wine.

He waved to Al, the driver, and punched in his garage code. He walked between Grace's white van and his Lexus and opened the door.

"Hi honey," said Grace from the living room couch. "How was the president?"

Startled, Mac asked, "And what brings you to the conclusion that I was with the president?"

Not even bothering to pause *Jeopardy!*, she answered, "No briefcase, home early, and you are grinning from ear to ear. You definitely have a bromance."

"Maybe I'm smiling because I've been with my girlfriend."

She shook her head. "Nope. Then you would be all despondent for failure to perform."

"That does it!" He rushed to the couch and grabbed for the remote.

Suspecting the move, she held it aloft, gave it a quick look, and hit **Pause**. He tackled her and gave her a bear hug. "Well, aren't you frisky," she laughed.

Mac sat back on the couch. "Grace, I have to tell you that I'm not sure I believe what I'm saying, but I think I'm making a difference."

She raised an eyebrow. "At least one of us is surprised. I had no doubt that you would."

"I know you don't like Jeremy."

"Stop," she interrupted. "That's over with. Quite frankly, the fact that any man can change is a miracle, but it's hard not to believe in God if you've witnessed the before and after with that man." She gave a half backhand wave of dismissal and then asked her husband, "But underneath the enthusiasm, something else is bothering you."

Mac continued to be amazed at her perception. "Tell you the truth, I'm kind of worried about Jeremy. Every once in a while it seems like he goes off the deep end."

"Mac, it is the most stressful job in the world."

"You're right. I'm probably hypersensitive about it because I think the country really needs him."

He pulled her to him. "I miss my work terribly, but this country was such a mess. I didn't realize how much stress out-of-control spending and a twenty-trillion-dollar budget was causing me. Right or wrong, every move Lyons makes has the right intentions.

"We have two huge financial issues left to wrestle with, and he's saving entitlement reform for next year. Every senator or representative is fully aware that if we don't reconfigure Social Security and Medicare, we will have to default on our promises or truly be a bankrupt nation. Yet everyone is afraid to bring it up, because it's always unpopular to tell people that they will get less."

"It's amazing how involved the public has become."

"They were left out of the conversation for way too long. Not for me, because I would never do this job more than one term at the absolute maximum, but it would be great for the country if Lyons ran for a second term."

Grace smiled an evil smile. "Never say never, Mac. Nothing is stronger than a full-blown bromance."

CHAPTER 124

As EXCITING AS MAC'S NEW job was, it was sometimes hard to find important things to do. It was easy when Lyons gave him direction, or if he had a project he wanted to bring up with the president, but otherwise, way too much down time for a workaholic like Mac. Not that he'd complain. When a financial crisis occurs, the treasury secretary is truly 24/7.

Still, as a wealth advisor, the only question was which job to do next. Down time was an illusion, and if taken, its constant companion was guilt. Mac's eyes rose in reflex to the muted flat screen.

The knock on his half-way-open office door startled him, and he quickly clicked off CNBC as if he'd been watching porn.

With a laugh, Sabine said, "Was that 'Wanda Does Wall Street'?"

"Okay, you caught me," Mac said as he stood up quickly. "Please don't tell Grace about my fantasies."

Sabine laughed again. "I'm sure she knows all of them. I just came to see how you're doing. I would have called, but I thought it would be more fun to surprise you."

"I'm glad you did," said Mac as he walked over and hugged her. "Don't try a takedown. I'm ready for you now," he whispered.

Sabine stepped back. "Will you ever let me live that down?"

"As soon as everyone who knows about it quits reminding me," Mac said, adding a good-natured smile. "Please sit down. I'm lonely controlling America's financial future all by myself."

She took a seat on one of the two guest chairs in his office, and Mac sat in the adjoining chair.

"What do you know that I don't know?" Sabine said pointedly.

Mac hesitated and then leaned closer to her. "Is the boss okay?"

"Why do you ask?"

"This is not something I would tell anyone else, and it may be just an aberration. But after our speech to the major banks, the CEO of Global United Bank came into the Oval Office. Coincidentally, I happened to be there, and much to my chagrin, I was even sitting behind Jeremy's desk."

As Mac continued describing the incident, Sabine's face looked more troubled. When he'd finished, she leaned over and hid her face in her hands. He waited.

When she spoke, Mac felt like a vise was squeezing his heart.

"I don't know, Mac." He watched as a tear ran down her cheek. "He won't tell me."

CHAPTER 125

A FEW YEARS AGO IT would have been inconceivable that a doctor of Adam Pollack's status and celebrity would relocate. As head of orthopedic surgery at the prestigious Mayo Clinic, he was treated like he was a deity. Yet the combination of excessive compensation and notso-subtle moral suasion can move mountains. Now firmly ensconced in a pedestrian office in Georgetown University Hospital, Dr. Pollack was finishing a consultation.

In what he hoped was a covert gesture, he glanced at his watch. It was 9:10 a.m., and he was ten minutes late for a new patient appointment. Anywhere from 45 to 60 minutes was the normal wait time, so his concern was unusual. With unapologetic arrogance, his next appointment had insisted that he be prompt. Even more unsettling was the fact that she had referred to him by his first name.

Pollack did not recognize the name Lisa Granier, but this takeno-prisoners woman had shoehorned her way into his schedule. She had assured the doctor's assistant that she would leave willingly if the doctor decided that he did not want to meet with her.

Curiosity had caused him to accept the appointment. Still, Adam Pollack had a strange sense of foreboding when he opened the exam room door.

"I explicitly requested that you be prompt," said the woman without a hint of levity.

It was 9:15. "Sa..bine," he stuttered. "I, I didn't know…"

"Have a seat, Adam. I'm uncomfortable being here, and I don't have much time." She looked at the nurse. "You can leave."

The nurse frowned and looked to Pollack. "Yes. Please go," he said with resignation. It had taken only an instant for him to completely lose control. He turned back to Sabine. In spite of her extraordinary beauty, her demeanor was intimidating. He wasn't sure whether it was because he saw her as a proxy for Jeremy Lyons or because she reminded him of a guided missile.

After Pollack took a seat in the chair next to Sabine, she leaned close to him. "Can I assume that this meeting is covered by doctor/patient confidentiality?" she asked in a low voice.

"Of course!" he replied emphatically.

"Even if we are discussing Jeremy?"

Pollack sat back, blinking repeatedly. "I..I can't discuss.."

"Gerald Rodgers."

Pollack's body sagged as if someone had opened the release valve on his soul. His face turned pasty white. It did not take a profiler to see that he was a heartbeat away from regurgitating his breakfast. He opened his mouth and then quickly shut it. His mind flashed back. He was in the hospital, sitting by his friend's bedside. Dr. Gerald Rogers was the most brilliant orthopedic scholar that Pollack had ever known

Rogers's hands were shaking as he held a stack of papers out to Pollack. "This is my legacy," he rasped through lips that were caked and dry. "I spent so much time on research. Maybe," he coughed, and his whole body shuddered, "they will forgive me now."

Rogers had reached up and wrapped his cold hands over Pollack's. Looking him in the eye he said, "There is no one else I can trust."

"Breathe," said Sabine, breaking Pollack's reverie. "Now listen carefully. I am Jeremy; he lives because of me. I expect you to answer any question that I ask you about his health with complete candor. It is my job to protect him. I need full, unabridged disclosure."

Sabine paused, and her next words were delivered like a judge issuing a death sentence. "I want to forget that name that haunts your past forever."

Pollack vigorously rubbed his face with his hands as if he could make her disappear. He cleared his throat once and then again. "May I get some water?"

Sabine nodded.

Shakily, Pollack rose and walked over to the sink. He turned on the faucet, bent down, cupped his hands, splashed water on his face, and drank greedily. With water running down his still pallid face, he searched for a paper towel. Finding nothing, he shook the water off his hands and wiped them on his white doctor's coat. With the sleeve, he tried to blot his face. He returned to his chair and sat down heavily. His face was a caricature of resignation and defeat.

"I'm sorry that I didn't have time to convince you that playing the confidentiality card would be unproductive and useless," said Sabine. There was no regret in her voice. Her dark eyes were like lasers when she spoke next. "However, any discussion of our conversation would be considered treasonous."

She paused to see if there was any resistance left in the man. Leaning forward, she squeezed her eyes shut and took a few deep breaths. Her voice broke when she spoke. "Adam, is Jeremy losing his mind?"

Pollack's body sagged. He buried his face in his hands.

"The ostrich act doesn't work with me," Sabine said sharply. "I want answers."

He had the look of a condemned man as he raised his head slowly and then shook it from side to side.

Sabine pounced, her face now inches from his. "Do not fuck with me, Adam."

"Have, have you noticed any violent outbursts?" Pollack asked weakly.

"You mean like when he broke the now vice president's nose with his knee?"

Pollack looked surprised and then nodded. "Yes," he sighed, "like that."

She waited with her hands on her hips.

Pollack exhaled. "All I can say is that the abhorrent behavior, and even violence, will not go away. It may, may even become more frequent." He raised his hands in supplication. "I'm sorry Sabine. Do with me what you must. I cannot tell you more."

CHAPTER 126

THE BOEING 747-8 HAS A tail the height of a six-story building and can carry more that $5 billion in gold bars. Today it carried more than that in net worth. The aircraft served as a state-of-the-art replacement for the pair of planes that transported presidents safely for the past 25 years. The only other manufacturer that could potentially meet the specific military criteria to transport the cargo inside Air Force One was the Airbus 380. Due to the highly classified decisions that go into the structure of the plane, the fact that the Airbus was made in France ruled it out.

Today's agenda and corresponding in-air meetings were put on hold when the president received a message. Due to the recent construction, his office on board was equipped with even more technological advancements than the oval one he normally occupied. His private video conference was crystal clear, encrypted, and secure between the plane and the corresponding unit he had installed in his doctor's office. Jeremy Lyons was studying the screen for any information he could glean from the micro-expressions on the doctor's face.

"Did you tell her?"

There was no lightness in the president's tone. To Adam Pollack, it felt like a death sentence. "No, no sir. I didn't."

Lyons arched an eyebrow. "Sabine can be very convincing."

"She threatened me."

Lyons nodded. "Makes sense. If she wants something, she always comes armed."

Pollack bowed his head.

"Did she pull the trigger?" asked Lyons.

"Not yet, sir."

"So, am I to conclude," said Lyons, "that you are more afraid of me than you are of Sabine?"

Pollack looked up at him with weary eyes. "Yes, sir."

Lyons nodded again. "I concur with your analysis. What is the consensus?" He held his breath as he waited for the answer. Everything else was meaningless.

"All three doctors," Polack said in a faint voice.

"And to them the MRIs were anonymous?" Lyons challenged.

"Yes, sir," Pollack replied. His words were barely audible.

"Unanimous?"

Pollack nodded. He was incapable of uttering a word.

"Well, shit."

CHAPTER 127

THE STERILE, GRAY ROOM LOOKED like it was out of a movie set. The gun metal table had two folding chairs. A crook-necked black lamp rested on the table. There were no windows in the 10′ by 10′ room. Jeremy Lyons stood when he heard the door opening.

John Wesley stumbled as two agents pushed him into the room. "What the fuck is going on?" He looked up and saw the President of the United States standing against the back wall. "What the hell did you have them pick me up for?"

"Please leave us," said Lyons to the agents.

"Sir?"

"You can wait outside the door. If I need you, I will call."

With great reluctance, the agents looked at each other, glared at Wesley, and then left the room.

"Have a seat, John," said the President, pointing to one of the chairs.

'I'd rather stand, if you don't mind, Mr. President."

"I do mind. I won't ask again. Take a seat."

"You know, if you wanted to see me, I would have come. You didn't have to send two goons to muscle me here."

Lyons let out a breath and shook his head. "I should have known that you were too stupid to make this easy."

"FUCK YOU!"

The door opened immediately. "Get out," said Lyons with steel in his voice. The door closed.

Lyons walked towards Wesley, who subtly moved into a defensive position. "Are you going to assault the President of the United States?" asked Lyons in a tired voice.

Wesley relaxed slightly, and, in an instant, Lyons pulled a Taser from behind his back and aimed it at Wesley's groin. "Take a seat, John. Last chance."

"You have got to be shitting me," said Wesley as he walked over, pulled out a chair, and slammed into it.

Lyons slowly walked over and sat down across from him. He interlocked his fingers, placed his elbows on the table, and rested his head on the top of his hands. "I've been trying to figure out why, John. Was it unbridled lust, a way to get back at me for some imagined slight?" He looked at the man with disgust. "Or was it just a death wish."

Wesley's smile was not one of contrition. "How did you find out? It wasn't Sabine. She might have walked a little funny the next day, but she didn't know what hit her. I make up a mean potion."

When Lyons didn't respond, Wesley exclaimed, "I'll bet it was that fucking waiter! And I gave that asshole three bills..."

The edge of the table caught Wesley on the chin. In one move, Lyons had upended the table and propelled it into him. Almost before his body hit the floor, the president was on him, his forearm pressing powerfully across Wesley's throat. Wesley reached to grab his attacker, and Lyons slammed his head on the floor three times in succession. "NO!" shouted Lyons as the door started to open.

Lyons ripped off the duct tape he had secured to the desk and quickly taped the stunned Wesley's mouth. He wrapped the man's two hands together and then his feet. In less than 60 seconds, Wesley was basically immobilized. The prisoner's eyes started to clear, and he stared daggers at Lyons.

As Wesley struggled to sit upright, Lyons snapped a kick into his chest, sending him back to the floor.

The president sat on the floor next to his captive and began to talk. "You could have done anything else. But you chose the one way to hurt me. I love her, something that you would never understand. My first instinct was to kill you with my bare hands, but that would happen too quickly. As a Christian, it is my duty to allow you the time to repent for your sins." He lowered his face to within an inch of Wesley's and pulled off the duct tape.

"Ow," said Wesley turning his head.

"Just one question," whispered Lyons. "How many times did you rape her?"

Wesley's eyes shone in triumph. "One. The next two were at her request."

Lyons nodded and retaped the man's mouth. He picked up the Taser and shot 50,000 volts into the man's groin. He waited for Wesley's eyes to clear. He wanted the man to be fully aware of his circumstances.

Fear had replaced defiance. Lyons leaned closer. once again pressing the Taser to Wesley's groin. "Only two more to go."

CHAPTER 128

THE LEAD AGENT SHOT HIS second-in-command a worried look. The president's eyes were glassy, beads of sweat covered his brow, and his face was pale. Ever since he emerged from the room, he had been sullen, non-communicative. It was unthinkable, almost like the man was in a daze.

Silently, Jeremy Lyons got into the back seat of the armored Suburban and bent over as if he were going to retch. He placed his elbows on his knees and supported his bowed head with his hands. The black Suburban decoys gathered around them as they drove away.

"Sir?" asked the agent tentatively.

"White House," came the strangled reply, which eliminated further conversation.

The president's secretary stood with alarm as he walked past her. "Mr. President?"

Without acknowledging her or turning his head he said, "Cancel everything."

* * *

Lyons sat heavily in his office chair, then closed his eyes and laid his head on his desk. He could not sleep, could not banish the images. *Am I but an animal? Is my faith a joke? A prop? Change was my ultimate challenge, proof that I was "born again." And I failed. A barbarian, a revenge-possessed sadist. And now I leave him in that tiny cell to fester and rot. A perpetual reminder of both my pre-emptive and reactive mistakes.*

He stifled a sob. *I hid myself from Sabine's part in my rise. Shrouded myself in plausible deniability.* His laugh was harsh, bitter. *A modern-day*

Pontius Pilate. Wash my hands of the ugly side of politics. If I don't know specifics, I can still proclaim Christian values. Until today.

For the next two hours, the president's only visitors were self-recrimination and self-pity. Slowly, he raised his head, picked up his phone, and punched in an extension.

"Mr. McGregor?"

Mac frowned at the president's secretary.

"Sorry, sir, I mean Mac. I don't know whether he's sick or not, but he's definitely not himself."

"How quickly can you get a HazMat suit here?"

She blinked twice, and Mac smiled.

"No problem. I'll just avoid excessive hugging," he said as he walked into the Oval Office with a smile.

Lyons nodded, but remained seated.

"You look like shit, boss," Mac said as approached Lyons.

"Have a seat, please, Mac," said Lyons, his face impassive.

Mac sat and looked at him expectantly.

"Have you ever had a serious backslide?" asked Lyons, looking at Mac with tired eyes.

"I need more than that."

"Sorry, I'm not at my best. Have you ever done anything that felt like a betrayal of your faith?"

Mac let out a breath. "I can't count the things I've done that I'm ashamed of later. A day doesn't pass that I don't have regrets; but major, penance-requiring sins? I can't recall anything where my shame consumed me."

Lyons nodded. "And if you did?"

Mac leaned forward and shook his head. "Let's skip the hypotheticals, Jeremy. This isn't about me. What happened?"

"You are aware that before I was saved, I had a history of violence."

Mac remained silent.

"I thought it had been washed from me," Lyons said despondently. "I thought I had risen from the cesspool of my former life, and I'd vowed to never return."

Mac blanched. He opened his mouth, but no words came. Almost under his breath he said, "Did...did you kill someone?"

"No. He was very much alive."

Neither man spoke until Mac said, "Did you enjoy it?"

"What?" asked Lyons.

"When an alcoholic falls off the wagon and takes a drink, it is a glorious feeling. When a heroin addict goes back, it is a phenomenal high. Did you enjoy inflicting physical pain?"

"No!" said Lyons with a look of revulsion.

"Okay," said Mac. "It doesn't sound like you care to return to your previous pattern of violent behavior. So, you're not a junkie. Reverting back to bad behavior once doesn't kick you out of the Christian club. You know the drill. You ask God to forgive and also to help you not sin again." He paused.

"If you don't want to discuss it, I understand. Frankly, I can't imagine what would cause the President of the United States to commit a violent physical act. At least tell me that you had someone else do it."

Lyons looked upward and shook his head slowly. His pained smile was filled with regret. "Nope. Anything worth doing is worth doing yourself."

Mac stood up abruptly. "That is really dumb. You could torpedo all the good you've done!"

"No one else knows, just God, me, and the victim." He looked at Mac. "And now you."

"What do you want from me?" asked Mac as he sat back down.

"What would you do if you found out that someone had drugged and raped Grace?"

Mac felt like a knife had sliced into his heart. He closed his eyes and rubbed his forehead. He was reluctant to speak. Finally, he raised his head and looked into the eyes of the leader of the free world. His eyes were fierce. "I would castrate him."

CHAPTER 129

I̲t̲ ̲w̲a̲s̲ ̲n̲o̲t̲ "ɪꜰ," ɪᴛ was "when." Ever since her frustrating confrontation with the president's physician, aka, that weasel, Pollack, Sabine knew that she needed to talk to Jeremy. It was definitely not pillow talk conversation, and she absolutely was not going to initiate anything after a glass of wine. There were too many ears in the White House, so it had to be done off site.

Sabine looked up at Jeremy as they walked through the wooded paths. "We are in the most protected place in the world. Can the militia back up a little so we can talk?"

Lyons spoke to the agents, and they fanned out ahead of him. "Let's sit down," he said and took Sabine's hand. The rustic bench in the middle of the woods had been there since FDR first started coming to Camp David.

The month of August is not comfortable in either Naples or D.C., and the president and his lady had spent a number of summer weekends in the 62-acre presidential retreat.

"What shall we talk about?" asked Lyons.

"Dr. Pollack."

He stiffened at the name. "Do you have a medical problem that you need him to check?"

"No. I went to see him about you."

She touched his arm as he started to rise, and he sat back down. "There is a doctor/client privilege, especially when the client is the President of the United States," he said. His displeasure was written on his face.

"The little weasel didn't open up," Sabine said begrudgingly, "and I threatened him with exposure."

He nodded. "Then what do we need to discuss?"

She reached for his hands. "Jeremy, I love you more than life itself, but I need you to always tell me everything. When I feel like you're holding back on me, the pain in unrelenting. How can you keep secrets from me if you truly trust me?"

Lyons gently removed his hands from hers and pressed the heels of both on his forehead. Defeated, he asked, "What do you want to know?"

"Everything, damn it! Why when you don't know I'm looking do you look like you are the unhappiest person on the planet? Why are you having outbursts of temper? And why the FUCK aren't you talking to me about it?"

Her outrage caused two agents to move quickly back into the clearing. "LEAVE US!" said the president, venting his frustration.

The agents moved away.

The tears running down Sabine's cheeks belied the defiant look on her face.

Lyons turned back to her, the pain evident on his face. "I will tell you everything," he said softly, "but first you must agree to something."

Sabine didn't understand. She looked at him like he was crazy, but she knew that she would do anything for him.

He reached for her hand, and in one movement went to one knee. "My darling Sabine, will you marry me?"

CHAPTER 130

No matter how close a wealth advisor is to his or her spouse, a true professional will never discuss a client's financial situation outside of the office. Mac had the necessary conversation with Grace early in his career, and as he expected, it was never an issue. Many of his clients became friends, and had the sacrosanct confidentiality ever been breached, it could have made the relationships awkward. Sometimes clients were so concerned with anonymity that Mac wouldn't even tell Grace who he was meeting.

Even though Mac was currently a government employee, today's meeting reminded him of his strictly business clandestine meetings.

It was Columbus Day. The uniform green of the trees had turned to a kaleidoscope of fiery, brilliant gold, yellow, and red. For now, the leaves remained tethered to their branches, patiently waiting for their inevitable descent, when they would float and swing through the air, painting the sky as they fell.

Mac had arrived early for this auspicious occasion. As he waited outside the nondenominational Evergreen Chapel, he couldn't help but feel humbled by the moment. He was in Camp David, one of two people invited to witness a historic event. It was logical that the vice president wasn't invited, as that might have alerted the press, but Mac was surprised that Steve Cannon was not on the list. He breathed in the crisp fall air. He couldn't remember ever feeling more present, and if he allowed himself, more special.

The Evergreen Chapel was a rustic octagonal building made of wood and stunning stained glass. Light wood pews stood on an irregularly shaped gray stone floor. The mesmerizing large stained-glass windows seemed like they were reaching to heaven in the high-ceilinged room. Every week that he stayed at the presidential retreat, Jeremy Lyons attended services in the chapel. Mac stepped inside and bowed his head.

Mac blinked when Alegria entered the chapel. When she saw his momentary confusion, she blushed and lowered her eyes. For perhaps the first time in her life, her dark hair was pulled back and shone in the lighted room, and expertly applied makeup had transformed her. Mac walked over and gave her a hug, then leaned back, nodded appreciatively, and smiled broadly. They turned as Jeremy and Sabine entered the chapel.

Any doubts Mac had about whether Jeremy Lyons was a changed man were completely erased. The president picked him up and squeezed him like a python. He put him down and mouthed, "Thank you." Sabine let go of Alegria's hand and laced her arm into Jeremy's. They walked slowly up the aisle.

The minister smiled at the couple. He had no doubt that they were in love. Sabine held Jeremy's arm in a death grip, and he could not take his eyes off of her. The president looked so young, so healthy, that the age difference was unnoticeable.

Unwiped tears cascaded down his bronze cheeks as the President of the United States said his vows. Sabine was radiant in a short white dress that ended just below her knees. Their love was a palpable energy that suffused the small chapel. It was genuine, and Mac could not remember ever being more moved. He wished that Grace could have shared this with him.

It should have been Camelot revisited, a declaration of love so beautiful that it would inspire the world. Yet no pictures were taken, no announcements would be made. The only witnesses were the minister, Mac, and Alegria. All were sworn to keep the marriage secret until Jeremy Lyons left office. The president had promised never to lie to his constituents; he hadn't promised to tell them everything.

CHAPTER 131

THE SATURDAY AFTER THANKSGIVING IS still family time for many Americans, particularly those where relatives come together from different places to celebrate the holiday. Since their four children lived close enough to almost be considered neighbors, it had not been difficult for the McGregors to extract themselves from the leftover turkey and stuffing.

Although Grace had refused to concur on her husband's first choice of transportation, the private plane that flew them and the Cannons to the Naples airport was impressive. Still, as Mac repeated often, a trip on Air Force One would have been the opportunity of a lifetime.

Grace had met Steve Cannon's wife, Barbara, previously and liked her independent, quirky personality. And if you didn't like the laconic Mr. Cannon, well, then something was wrong with you.

The President of the United States raised his glass of sparkling water and clinked it with five exquisite wine glasses and one specially made 24-ounce glass tankard filled with Mount Gay rum and caffeine-free Diet Coke. Etched on the side of the tankard were the words "Financial Wizard." It had been presented to Mac as one of the many perks of accepting Lyons's offer to be part of his cabinet.

"My appreciation to all of you cannot be measured by mere words." Lyons smiled at his assembled friends and confidants. He turned to Mac, grinning, as Mac hoisted his drink. "Are the proportions satisfactory?"

"Four limes may be overkill," answered Mac in his most serious voice. "Particularly since key limes tend to have more flavor than garden variety limes. In your desperation to please, I sense over-exuberance. However, I took the liberty of checking the bottle, and it was indeed a good year for Mount Gay."

Mac held the tankard up for inspection and took a sniff. "It is crisp, but not dense. The bouquet is tantalizing, and there is sufficient depth." He carefully placed the glass on the white stone circular table and gave the group an imperious look. "All-in-all, quite satisfactory for a rookie."

The table joined in the president's laughter until Steve Cannon interjected his southern drawl. "And here I thought that *I* was the one who was full of shit."

The combination of Sabine's natural warmth and Alegria's unpretentious innocence had assuaged Grace's initial nervousness. She also got to see Alegria at her finest. Her hair was washed and pulled back, and she was wearing a pale blue sundress picked out by Sabine.

In late July, Mac had sent the president half a bushel of Bennett peaches, which are indigenous to Bethany Beach and purported to be the "nectar of the gods."

Mac had promptly received a handwritten note of thanks, but he'd been secretly annoyed not to have heard any superlatives about the succulent taste. Now Mac looked a Grace, whose wide-eyed smile was acknowledgement as she swallowed the first bite of her peach crisp.

"Damn!" exclaimed Steve. "This is the most delicious thing I've ever tasted!" Barbara, with mouth full, nodded her agreement.

Lyons extended his hand. "Dessert is courtesy of the McGregors."

* * *

Sitting in the great room after dinner, Lyons turned to Grace and asked, "Grace, could I entice you to accompany me on a short moon-lit beach walk?"

Perplexed, she looked at Mac.

"I don't know, boss," said Mac. "After a second glass of wine, she's been known to get a little frisky."

It was all Grace needed. She shrugged off the frown she'd given her husband, stood up, and grabbed Lyons's arm. She tossed her head back jauntily. "Don't wait up."

Now that she was outside, Grace's bravado had faded. She felt like she was walking in the middle of a caravan. Secret Service agents bracketed them, their heads on swivels. She concentrated on the cool sand beneath her bare feet.

For the first few minutes, Lyons walked silently beside her. Grace took deep breaths. He spoke softly. "You were right to dislike me, Grace, but I'm ashamed that you were ever afraid of me. I know that my past justifiably makes you uncomfortable. It is unforgivable." He exhaled and seemed to consider his words before he spoke again. "It is only through the grace of God that I can, with a reborn spirit, promise that I want only the best for you and your family."

She turned to look at him, but didn't comment.

"Grace, your trust is more than I have the right ask for, but I love Mac like a brother. I don't think I could run this country without him."

She looked at him skeptically. "Why is my husband so important to you?"

Lyons looked away. "I've led a friendless life. All those who acted like they were my friends were either on my payroll or feared me. Genuine people are hard to find."

Grace walked in silence as she absorbed his words. She watched the moon illuminate a pale ribbon over the blue-green waters. "I didn't trust you, and I realize this has not been an easy conversation for you, Mr. President. You already had my husband's loyalty, so reaching out to me was very generous of you. I hope that I can learn to trust you."

He smiled thinly. "So do I, Grace. So do I."

CHAPTER 132

L IKE MANY PRESIDENTS BEFORE HIM, Jeremy Lyons opted to sleep in the second-floor suite of the White House. The suite consisted of a large bedroom, living room, dressing room, and two smaller bedrooms. The views outside the window were spectacular, out across the Potomac River down to the Jefferson Memorial. On those nights when Sabine joined him, agents kept a cone of silence around them so that there was never any mention in the press. Particularly in comparison to his predecessor, this POTUS was well liked by his staff.

Sabine sat cross legged at the end of the bed as the president fluffed up a second pillow to support his back. When he had settled in, he said, "We have some unfinished business."

"Okay," she said warily, leaning towards him.

"Here's what I know: Although his public rhetoric has been turned down to simmer, Senator Leeds is still making noise."

"In what way?"

"He's using burner phones to persuade his cronies to hold up any action on our tax proposal. "

"How do you know that?"

Lyons smiled. "It seems that one of his brethren is a former client of mine. He is very grateful that I did not expose him."

Wrinkling her brow, she said, "The fat bastard was mildly tortured and then sent a compromising picture. You would think that would keep him in line."

"On the surface, it did; and if I hadn't gotten a call from a happy investor, we'd still be in the dark. I need him 'all in' if we're ever going to get this government to work again."

Sabine thought for a moment and then said, "I think better when I'm in your arms." She scooted up on the bed and lay beside him. They hugged each other, and Lyons felt like he could almost hear her mind working.

"What does Leeds want?" she asked.

"What do you mean?" Lyons pulled his head back to look into her eyes.

"You know that arrogance runs through Leeds's veins. He's been one of the most powerful senators for many years. Maybe the more we push, the more determined he is to sabotage you. What does he want that he can't get himself? Give it to him, and you'll own him."

Lyons's smile spread across his face as he pulled her on top of him. "You're not just a pretty face, Mrs. Lyons."

Placing her arms on both sides of his body, she raised up to look into his eyes. "Would you care to be more specific, Mr. Lyons?"

"I have an assignment for you, my dear. It may be intense, but I believe you will find it invigorating."

Her dark eyes shone with excitement.

"In fact," he added with a devious smile, "we may accomplish the enviable goal of killing two birds with one stone."

CHAPTER 133

THE WHITE HOUSE MESS CONSISTS of three small dining rooms located in the basement of the White House next door to the situation room. Run by the U.S. Navy, it is decorated with polished wood paneling. Nautical themes and paintings of ships are softened by fresh flowers, table linens, and official White House china. Sitting at a table by themselves, the president and his treasury secretary were discussing the economy.

"Did you have any idea that the reduction in the corporate tax rate would generate this much growth?" asked Mac.

"I think it's the combination of two things" said Lyons. "Corporations are now incentivized to bring business back to the U.S., and business knows that we are a pro-growth administration."

"Either that or they realize that I can no longer manage my own assets, so I'm all in on the stock market," quipped Mac.

"If the country is not completely focused on you, then it damn well should be."

Mac's hand massaged his chin. "If that became part of your platform, your popularity would soar."

Lyons smiled and leaned forward to privatize the conversation. "Have you made any more progress on the tax reform package?"

Mac shook his head. "I've read so many proposed plans that the ideas are spinning around in my head." He shrugged. "I don't think there is a perfect plan."

"That means we will have to power through the provisions of our plan that have hair on them. The objective is to benefit the majority and not give the opponents enough voice to override."

"Accomplishing the first part just requires adding logic to my research," said Mac. "When you're ready, we can discuss the changes. I've prioritized them, and I've got no pride of authorship, so you won't hurt my feelings if you discard some or all of the ideas."

Lyons nodded. "We've got a good run going, Mac. I'm not sure I would be here without you."

You don't know how true that statement is, thought Mac. On a number of occasions he'd tried to correct the president's exaggerated opinion of his contributions, but had been rebuffed. *Unfortunately, a positive outcome doesn't excuse a deplorable action. Every anxious moment, every feeling of helplessness I felt as a result of your taunting me, I deserved.*

"Did I say something to offend you?"

The question jarred Mac from his self-flagellation. "Sorry boss. I appreciate the praise, but I'm just a bit player in the play. Your path must have been predetermined, because you had a mountain of shit to overcome."

Lyons's raised eyebrow, coupled with the empty silence, forced an uneasy Mac to fill the void. "I'm in awe of your accomplishments, especially in the face of such adversity." He tried his best not to let his tone reveal his guilt.

Mac's phone vibrated, and uncharacteristically he removed it from his suit coat pocket. "Jeremy, I've been waiting for this. I need to handle it."

Lyons broke his gaze and flicked his hand, waving Mac off and releasing him from what had become an extremely uncomfortable moment.

As Mac walked from the room, he was thankful that he'd set alerts for Redskins news on his phone. Without that excuse, he might have opened a vein and finally told the president the truth.

* * *

The press and the public agreed that the Lyons administration was indeed on a good run. In his first hundred days, the president and his defense secretary, Alan Smathers, met with the Joint Chiefs of Staff and asked them what they needed to be militarily ready. Lyons followed that by meeting with some of the largest defense contractors, including Lockheed Martin, Boeing, General Dynamics, Raytheon, and Northrop Grumman.

Lyons and Smathers challenged the group to present their most advanced weaponry, as well as those weapons that were prototypes. The contractors were told that in order to increase the defense budget, they would need to reduce their profit margins. All orders would be systematized and granted solely on the basis of merit. By the time the administration asked Congress for an increase in the budget, the supportive data was compelling.

Within the first six months, Lyons's army of independent auditors and forensic accountants had uncovered over 200 billion dollars worth of waste and fraud in government agencies. By the end of the year, nonessential government agencies would be eliminated. It appeared that the combination of robust growth and reduced expenses would exceed the president's objective of lowering the 20-trillion-dollar national debt by ten per cent.

Criticism on immigration reform had come from the progressives, because the only action that had occurred was sending more agents to provide border security. Vice President Justice had publicly stated the administration's position to provide a path to citizenship for long-term illegal immigrants with clean records, but so far critics felt that this remained a back-burner item.

The country's enemies had toned down their rhetoric, and Russia had been unusually docile. No one, including U.S. citizens, knew how the president would act if threatened or challenged.

CHAPTER 134

"GOT A MINUTE, BOSS?"

Jeremy Lyons peered over his wire-framed reading glasses at his press secretary. Placing the glasses on his desk, he said, "Of course, Steve. Take a seat."

Steve Cannon plopped his lanky frame onto the couch, immediately slouching into the soft cushions as if he were positioning himself for a nap. He interlocked his fingers behind his head as he leaned against the arm of the couch.

Cannon had been an excellent choice for press secretary. Although his answers did not always please the insistent media, his southern drawl, laconic manner, and penchant for pushing his thick, silver-gray hair off his forehead whenever he had to think about an answer somehow made him endearing.

"Make yourself comfortable," said Lyons with a wry smile. He was tempted to tell the man to sit up straight and be a grownup, but it was enough of a burden to get him to dress appropriately. "What's on your mind?"

"I've just got to ask again. You're sure you're okay with this?"

The president reached up and massaged his brow. It was not the first time he had discussed "this" with Cannon.

"I mean you are definitely feeding your boy to the lions," said Cannon. "I'm used to fighting through an angry swarm of hornets trying to sting me, but I'm a lawyer. And the 'I don't give a shit because I'm getting paid' attitude is part of our DNA."

The president did not respond, realizing that a response would not slow Cannon down.

"Mac is different," Cannon went on. "He's got a legit good reputation. He's even got integrity. And excuse me for saying so, but you're making him the sacrificial lamb. I can see a lot of ways this could so sideways for him."

"I'm sure he would appreciate your concern, Steve, and you know that Mac is my best friend. I assure you I'm fully aware of his attributes, as well as his ability to perform under fire."

Cannon sat up. "There's a fire and there's an inferno. How can you let him get torn to shreds on national TV and then toss him into a pool of piranhas?"

"I once owned piranhas," reflected Lyons with a wistful smile. "They are lovely fish. I see that you have been studying up on your metaphors."

"Come on, boss. I know you're trying to distract me, taking advantage of my ADD. You know you can help him. You don't even have to say anything! Just be there for moral support. All you gotta do is to look stoic and smart."

The president folded his hands and laid them on his desk. Practicing patience, he said slowly, "I wish there were another way."

Cannon shook his head and stood. "Well then, do me one favor, Mr. President."

"What is that?"

"Give him a cyanide pill for when he's captured."

CHAPTER 135

"You want me to pitch this to America?"

"They are your ideas," answered the president with an easy smile.

Mac *still* found it hard to have a serious conversation while sitting in a chair in the Oval Office. *What the hell am I doing here?* Lyons, on the other hand, was unfazed. It was like he was born to be president.

"I thought my job was to do the research, bring you my ideas, and have you step up to the plate. I'm R.J. here, the Chartered Financial Analyst of the team. You, on the other hand, are the King of Charisma, the silver-tongued devil, the people's choice. Let's bring the cabinet in on this and take a vote." He tried to keep the panic out of his voice.

Lyons's smiled broadened, which added to Mac's anxiety.

"You're probably just playing me," Mac said, "which means I will get you back when you least expect it, but let me run this down for you."

Mac went into sales mode. "The president, that would be you, by the way, tells his people to come up with solutions. If he doesn't like the recommendations, he sends his minions back to the drawing board. Finally, in a moment of bliss, his majesty says, 'You have done well, good and faithful servant,' pats said minion on the head, and presents the plan to the adoring public." Mac added a theatrical bow.

The president nodded. "That is a perfect rendition of how things have been done in the past." He folded his hands.

"You are a manipulative son of a bitch."

Lyons's eyebrows raised.

"And yes, I mean that in a flattering way. You want to be the anti-Obama, and the only way you can do that is to give credit to someone other than yourself."

Lyons interrupted. "That's a little harsh."

"Seriously? I forgot, you're an Independent, so you love everybody. The only thing missing from this scenario of throwing me into the Lyons den is that I have no desire for a verbal ménage a trois with two barracudas."

Lyons laughed. "Both Jackie and Lesley are lovely ladies, and I have no doubt that you will dazzle them with your charms."

"They'll probably pepper me with every chauvinistic remark I've ever made," Mac groused.

"Sounds like acquiescence, my friend." Lyons turned serious. "Mac, if you believe nothing else about me, believe this. Whatever happens, I will always have your back."

CHAPTER 136

"DO YOU HAVE A MINUTE?" asked the president as he entered the vice president's office in the West Wing.

"Of course, sir," Mary Beth Justice said as she instinctively stood.

"Please sit, Mary Beth," said Lyons as he took the seat across from her. He steepled his long fingers before he spoke again. "There is evil in all of us. Some wear it like a badge, proud of the power it gives them. Others hide it, try to tamp it down. If they can compartmentalize their demons, they believe they can control them."

Justice's face remained impassive. She had no idea where Lyons was going.

Lyons leaned forward. "If we know this, if we can truly understand human nature, we may not be able to control it, but we can survive."

"Mr. President, have I disappointed you in some way?"

Startled by her question, he quickly answered. "No. I was merely soul searching. In this case, trying to discover if I have one."

"Can I help?" she asked uneasily.

"Yes. In due time, Senator Leeds will approach you. Ostensibly, he will be looking for me, but it is essential that you be my intermediary.

"What does he want?"

"Revenge, and he will go to any lengths to achieve it."

"On you?"

"No. He has a specific target that in time he will reveal to you. He is desperate, and desperate men make mistakes."

"So what is our purpose in this?"

"To give him what he wants."

"I'm sorry, but I'm still confused. Can't you give more details?

"It's better for you not to know. One of us must have plausible deniability." A sad smile followed his statement. "Have him come to you at your residence, and I will activate a live feed to your laptop. Make sure he knows that after this, we own him."

CHAPTER 137

THE OFFICE OF THE VICE president is housed primarily in the Eisenhower Executive Office Building. Because of her actual duties, Mary Beth Justice held court in additional offices in the West Wing or, in Lyons's absence, in the Oval Office. That was definitely disconcerting for some visitors, particularly males. For this particular visitor, only the office of the president would do.

Looking around the office like he thought Justice was hiding Lyons, Everett Leeds demanded, "Where's the president?"

Justice did not like Everett Leeds. He was a manipulative, bloviating bully. Alegria had dug up enough dirt on him to bury him, but Lyons had cautioned, "Better the devil you know..."

"I assure you, Senator, he's not under the desk." She had not risen from her chair, thereby ceding him the higher ground, but he wasn't worth the effort.

"I need to speak to him," said Leeds, taking three steps closer to the desk.

Normally, the oily bastard dressed up well, but today his tie was twisted and rose above his collar. The left lapel of his custom-made suit had a smudge of toothpaste or something even more odious to imagine. His white hair looked like it had been combed with a towel, and his bulbous, red-veined nose glowed like Rudolph's. Even from a distance, Justice could smell his pathetic attempt at covering his breath with mouthwash.

"Have you been drinking, Senator?" she asked.

"Listen, lady..."

"It's Madam Vice President to you," she said as she stood.

"Yeah, sorry." He waved his hand as if she were a pesky fly. "I need to talk to him. He's gonna want to talk to me. I've got a deal to offer him that he can't refuse."

Curiosity overcame repulsion. "I know you are aware that I act as his proxy."

"Yeah, yeah." Leeds looked desperate as he rubbed his hands over his puffy face. "Okay. Tell him that anything he wants in tackling entitlements, I will propose it. That way, he doesn't take the heat."

Her heartbeat quickened. "AARP, the unions, your constituents, they'll run you out of town."

"Let me worry about that."

"You do know," said Justice, "that the president doesn't horse trade. You obviously want something big..."

"This one's easy." Leeds reached into his pocket and pulled out a crumpled piece of paper. He shoved it at her. "This man. I want Lyons to find him for me, and I want his balls!"

CHAPTER 138

No matter how many times he practiced before a mirror, no matter how many speeches he had given before, Mac McGregor was scared shitless. Compared to this, speaking in front of 500 of his peers at a Barron's conference was a piece of cake. In that case, he might get ribbed by his friends, but there was little chance he'd be hanged in effigy. One misstep, one slip of temper, and his reputation would not need Drano to flush it down the toilet.

The president believed in him and assured Mac that his solo flight was the best way to introduce their plan. Easy for him to say. Lyons was Teflon; Mac was tissue paper. Friends, family, all had confidence in him and told him he'd nail it. Mac was unflappable; he would slow dance these two professionals into submission. If only Mac shared their confidence.

As a wealth advisor, Mac was trained to analyze every investment and every situation. He had analyzed his live national television appearance equally as thoroughly. Fox's Jackie Mayfield was one of the interviewers. He and she were surface friendly, and she thought the president walked on water. A positive, except that her journalistic training and professional instincts wouldn't let her hold back.

No barrier such as friendship or respect would deter CBS's Lesley Simmons from taking him to task. She was not a fan of the president, and, by proxy, that meant she was not a member of the Mac McGregor fan club.

Underneath his dark blue suit, Mac felt like every ounce of courage was leaking out of his body.

"3-2-1."

"Ladies and gentlemen," began Lesley Simmons with a broad smile. "It is April 15th. Welcome to our tax day conversation with Treasury Secretary Mac McGregor."

At the president's request, the setting was like a fireside chat. Mac sat between the two women, and all three were in comfortable chairs, a bottle of cold water resting on each of three identical dark wood tables.

Flying solo. Welcome to target practice. The commentary running through Mac's mind at warp speed stopped when both women turned to look at him expectantly. He hoped his fake smile wasn't too transparent.

"Mr. McGregor," Lesley said with a deceptive smile, "normally both Jackie and I would have received copies of your tax proposal." She gave him a mock scolding look. "Not being able to read the proposal ahead of time makes it difficult to ask provocative questions."

This was a predictable first statement, and it relieved some of the pressure in Mac's chest. "Lesley, it's probably not the first time you've seen the president detour from protocol. I have every confidence that you and Jackie, along with an army of pundits, will have every opportunity to dissect our proposal before it is enacted into law."

Lesley raised an eyebrow. "You're not hiding behind the president are you, Mr. Secretary?"

"Please call me Mac, and if I intended to hide, I would have asked President Lyons to present this tax proposal to the people himself." A tic appeared in his jaw. He wanted to grab the water bottle and take a swig.

Lesley shrugged.

"Mac, who is the author of this plan? Is it the president's plan, your plan, or a collaboration?" asked Jackie.

"The president asked me to study all of the different tax proposals and visit with anyone who I felt might contribute to the process. My team and I were responsible for the analysis and the underpinnings of the plan. I had numerous meetings with President Lyons, batting ideas back and forth."

He smiled. "That's a long answer to your question. It was a collaboration. However," he pointed both of his thumbs at his chest, "the attacks stop here."

"So do you expect a lot of pushback?" asked Jackie.

"It's a mortal lock. Our plan is radioactive to special interests and influence peddlers."

"Ooh," cooed Lesley. "Now I'm interested. Tell me more."

"Let's start with some acknowledged facts," said Mac. "My guess is that neither of you prepares your own tax returns." (It was not a guess.) "Everyone knows our tax system is an abomination. It is way too complicated." He looked into the camera. "Raise your hand if you've read all 73,000 pages of the tax code.

"So we know that we have a seriously flawed system. Yet, every time anyone proposes a new tax plan, those adversely affected start a media blitz, which often turns into a smear campaign. Regardless of the merits of the plan, it is dead on arrival."

"What makes you think that your plan will survive?" asked Jackie.

"Americans want and deserve a simple and fair tax plan. And," he smiled sheepishly, "the president has no sense of humor about losing."

He paused. "After studying options for the last twelve months, I don't believe there is a perfect plan. But I do believe that almost any plan is better than our current plan." He turned to look at each woman individually. "I believe *the people* will really like this plan."

"It will be interesting to see how you can devise a plan the does not exacerbate income inequality," challenged Lesley.

Mac blew out a breath. "It's time to stop vilifying those who have become part of the American dream. According to the IRS, the top three per cent of wage earners pay over half of all income taxes collected. It stands to reason that a fair tax will benefit the wealthy, because they are already carrying most of the load."

Lesley rolled her eyes and cupped her ear. "I'm starting to hear the cheers of the Republican party."

Mac ignored her and continued. "The majority of tax loopholes benefit the rich. How many of our citizens can take advantage of an interest rate deduction on their homes? The mortgage deduction on homes can go as high as $1,100,000."

He raised his hands. "The average American can't relate to that amount of money. It is fine to encourage home ownership, but not logical to incentivize leverage. One of the key contributors to the stock market crash in 2008 was excessive leverage, which was *encouraged* by politicians."

"You're prepared for the claims that you will kill the real estate market?" asked Jackie as she leaned closer to Mac.

"President Lyons is always prepared. There are *no* deductions in our tax plan."

"None!" The women voiced surprise in unison.

"The logic is that if you allow any deductions, you open the door for additional deductions. Also, if you're going to infuriate one special interest group, you might as well upset them all."

"You seem very cavalier about wiping out deductions that have not only been beneficial to our economy, but in the case of the charitable deduction, have certainly saved lives," said Lesley, who tried to remain civil, but the edge in her voice was evident.

Mac gave her a hard look. He reached down, removed the cap from his water bottle and took a sip. He replaced the cap and spoke forcefully. "Proposing a tax reform package without assiduously evaluating all the ramifications would be cavalier. We have faith that the removal of a tax deduction will not remove the compassionate nature of the American people.

"As with the mortgage deduction, the charitable deduction is primarily advantageous to the wealthy. Good folks will still put cash in the collection plate at church. Our plan will put more money into every citizen's pocket, and it is our contention that generosity will ultimately be increased because of that. Let me expand that thought, if you will."

Both women nodded. "How many hours are freed up by eliminating the death tax? The wealthy use every loophole in the tax law to leave the most money they can to their heirs. To do this, they often have to transfer assets while their beneficiaries are young. We only need to examine the number of professional athletes who go broke to know that money without experienced guidance can be a burden rather than a blessing."

Jackie smiled. "Mac, is that an advertisement for when you go back to managing money?"

He looked at her sternly. "You delivered that line without the smirk in rehearsal."

Both women laughed, and a bit of the tension ebbed.

"I know," Mac continued, "we'll get blasted by the tax attorneys as well as the life insurance industry. Who will need second-to-die life insurance if no taxes are paid on death? So, at least conceptually, putting more money into people's pockets could make them feel more generous and want to leave a legacy of giving."

"Mac, give us a few minutes to digest the fact that the administration's tax plan will offer no deductions. Can you give us the details of how Americans will be taxed?" Jackie was assuming the role of peacemaker.

"Of course. Remember, the objective is simplicity and fairness, a tax code that our citizens can understand. If you Google how many different taxes Americans pay, the answer is 97. That's a mandate for change. We will repeal the alternative minimum tax; it will longer be necessary. As I mentioned, the estate or death tax is an especially punitive form of double taxation. It will be eliminated. You pay taxes all your life. It doesn't seem fair to continue paying taxes after you die.

"We want to encourage ownership of our corporations. In my career I've seen ordinary citizens save and invest in the stock market and then be able to retire in comfort. If the tax on dividends and capital gains is too high, it discourages individual investment."

He reached into his breast pocket and pulled out his iPhone. "Without investments in the stock market, this doesn't happen. Technological breakthroughs are a direct result of innovative companies having the capital to invest in research. Upon approval of our tax proposal, all dividends and capital gains will be taxed at fifteen per cent.

"There will be two tax brackets. For single tax filers who make less than $50,000 and joint filers who earn less than $75,000, five per cent of their earnings will be taxed. All income above those levels will be taxed at fifteen per cent." Mac stopped and looked to each woman.

"That's it?" said Lesley.

"I'm sure that you forecasted the revenue shortfall from this plan," said Jackie.

"We did," said Mac. "But in the past, projections have not been very accurate. It is imperative that the tax proposal is ultimately revenue neutral. For example, the growth projections from lowering the corporate income tax were woefully understated. We believe that the combination of letting the people keep more of their money and the lessening of stress that is associated with tax filing will energize the economy."

"We will obviously need to have our people run the numbers, but what do you do if there is a major shortfall?" asked Lesley.

"Because this is not an exact science, we have a list of possible stopgap proposals that would equitably add revenue. With your permission, I'd prefer to defer listing those alternatives to a later time."

"Sounds like a 'trust me' scenario," said Lesley. With undisguised rancor she added, "The one per centers are going to love you guys."

Mac leaped on the shot. He was well prepared. "The majority of the so-called one per centers are our employers. I agree. They will love us. Envision what a boon this will be to entrepreneurs, the next Steve Jobs, or Bill Gates, or Elon Musk. This legislation will dramatically increase employment and productivity.

"Our most precious assets are our health and our time. How much stress will be relieved by filing a short, uncomplicated tax return? The biggest deterrent today to small business owners is the incentive-killing burden of paperwork and regulations."

"We appreciate your promo," said Lesley, "but...

Jackie interrupted. "Mac, I can certainly applaud the simplicity of the administration's plan. I'm still stuck on the fact that eliminating all deductions is going to cause enormous pressure from those that are affected. We've already discussed charitable organizations and the real estate industry. But every state issues tax-free bonds. They will not go quietly into that good night."

Mac nodded. "Jackie, both you and Lesley have bosses. Due to your successes, and popularity, you have considerable latitude in your professions. Yet ultimately, you are accountable to the corporations that employ you.

"We understand and sympathize with the difficulty that our congressmen and women will have resisting the persuasive powers of those trying to sabotage our plan. But those forces are not their bosses. They did not hire them, and they cannot fire them. Our representatives are elected by the people. We will ask them to do the right thing and pass a logical, simple, fair tax code that the average American can understand. Isn't it time that we returned our country to the people?"

CHAPTER 139

APRIL 15, 2018 WAS ON a Sunday. As usual, everything seemed to fall in place for Jeremy Lyons. He knew he wanted the tax plan presented on April 15, no matter what, so it was just typical serendipity that the fifteenth landed on a Sunday. More people watch television Sunday evening than any other night.

The next morning Grace was surprised to see her husband eating his cereal and fruit while wearing his suit pants and undershirt. He looked up from reading his daily meditations. "Hi, babe. Good morning."

"Didn't your boss suggest that you take a week or two off from work?"

"Um, maybe."

She walked over to him and gave him the stink eye. "I believe he was explicit, particularly since he personally emailed me. He said that you would be hammered by reporters and criticized in the press. You did very well last night, and you should be proud. But the *president* wants you to disappear until this dies down. What am I missing?"

Mac sensed that Grace was not in the mood for jocularity. "I read the papers this morning, and I got a few subtle digs, but nothing I can't handle. The *Post* and the *Times* questioned the feasibility of the plan and the odds of congressional approval, but no one has called me a dumb ass yet."

"Do you think that might be because they want to wait and see if the president weighs in? If they go ugly early and he chastises them from the bully pulpit, they've already used up their ammo."

Mac put down his spoon and looked at her. "I didn't even consider that. Where did you come up with that analysis? I'm very impressed."

She glared at him. "Do you think I'm incapable of astute observations?"

It was spinning out of control. "No. I'm just surprised you put that much thought into it."

"Someone has to look out for you." She put her arms around his neck. "It will be more fun if you stay here with me," she whispered.

With a pained expression, he answered. "My driver will be here in twenty minutes."

"You're an idiot," she said as she pulled away.

"Grace, there are only two ways to go through life."

"You're an idiot and a dumb ass. See, it's started already. And the only two ways to go through life are with faith and with fear, as you've spouted to the children for over 30 years. Have a good day."

The only positive from the morning exchange was that he was able to watch her cute backside as she walked up the stairs.

CHAPTER 140

TOLD YOU SO   SETH GOLDFARB

"The people" have elected the worst kind of Republican: The charlatan who professed that he was beholden to no one, the poster boy for fiscal responsibility sent his stockbroker to fix our tax code. He wants to simplify taxes by making sure that the rich don't pay any. It only took three days for studies to estimate that this revenue-neutral plan will actually add three trillion to the national debt over the next decade.

Before President "I'm an Independent" Lyons steamrolled the Republican candidates for president like a Humvee rolling over a snowball, every single one of the aspiring commanders-in-chief, proposed his very own tax reform plan. Guess what? They all looked alike. Coincidence? I don't think so.

I would have to write a novella instead of my column to list all the parties who would be injured by this reverse Robin Hood plan. These are the only ones you need to know: every state government; every home owner who has a mortgage; and the unkindest cut of all, every deserving charity.

Let's examine how we, the people, learned of this attempt to further fatten the fat cats. Two highly professional interviewers were shut out, given no prior notice about any of the particulars of the plan. Why? Because if they had studied the plan, they could have attacked it like hungry wolves. Lyons's rookie treasury secretary would have been flailing around, desperately seeking his hero president to save him.

But that's another curiosity. Why wouldn't the president stand shoulder to shoulder with his cherished stockbroker?

For those looking for a typical Jeremy Lyons sneak attack, the hope was that Mac McGregor was a sacrificial lamb, a trial balloon floated to appease the president's Republican comrades in arms. Regardless, congress has a moral imperative to ensure that this tax proposal suffers the inevitable fate of all balloons. Let it deflate, drop to the ground, then be thrown in the trash.

Mac's intention had been to read the *New York Times* column three times before reacting. He made it through two. "I'd like to speak to the president, please," he said through clenched teeth.

In less than two minutes he was connected. "Mac, good morning."

"I'm giving you the courtesy of telling you that I'm going off the reservation. I'm either writing a rebuttal editorial or asking Jackie to give me five minutes on air with or without that fat asshole, Goldfarb."

Lyons waited a long beat before responding. "I wish you wouldn't, Mac," he said softly.

"Damn." Mac squeezed his eyes shut and vigorously massaged his forehead. He could feel a headache coming on. "You're too damn smart to tell me I can't respond."

"Then it would be you rolling over me like a steamroller," said Lyons. "I know it's in every fiber of your being to take Goldfarb on. I also know you would win the battle. But we might lose the war. This bill will pass, I promise you. I also know that right now you feel like you are unfairly criticized and your professionalism and intellect are being maligned."

"Jeremy, I don't need therapy. I need revenge."

"The best revenge will be your place in history. And that, my friend, I can guarantee."

CHAPTER 141

THE WHITE, 19TH CENTURY HOUSE at Number One Observatory Circle in northwest Washington, D.C., serves as a home for the vice president. The Naval Observatory continues to operate on the grounds, even when foreign leaders and dignitaries are visiting the home. Today, although the Democrats and history would argue with her, Vice President Justice didn't believe that her guest qualified as a leader, and certainly not as a dignitary. Still, her home was considerably less public than the White House.

Justice watched Everett Leeds crouched over, fixated on the screen, and would have bet that he watched porn with the same enthusiasm. Fortunately, his hands were on the edge of his chair.

"Nooo, please."

The voice was higher than he remembered, but that was understandable, due to the circumstances. The man Leeds knew as Luke Graham was tethered to a piece of plywood. His wrists and ankles were fastened to cuffs, which were attached to the board. To Leeds's delight, the man's body formed a perfect "X."

Purple bruises covered the man's ribs and abdomen. His only coverings were light-colored running shorts and a blindfold. Leeds smiled at the yellowish stain on the front of Graham's shorts.

"Where am I? Why am I here? I've done nothing wrong!"

The plaintive cries were not answered for at least five minutes. Leeds shot a look at the vice president, who gave him an uncomfortable shrug.

Leeds's eyes flashed back onto the screen as he heard a disembodied voice. "You are in a secure location. You committed a crime. You kidnapped and tortured a United States Senator."

"No! That's not how it happened. It, it was consensual. I swear."

"Consensual?"

"Yes! I have pictures to prove it."

Leeds frowned at the next words.

"We are aware that the victim has a history of liaisons outside of marriage. Curiously, none has ever involved another male. Is it your contention that you turned him?"

"No. I mean yes. We met at a bar and..."

Crack! A whip lashed across Graham's thighs, leaving a trail of blood and angry welts. His anguished cry was cut off by questions.

"Who sent you to compromise the senator?"

"No one. Please don't hit me again," he begged.

"This is your last chance to tell the truth."

The confession sounded like a run-on sentence. "Leeds could have ruined Senator Lyons's chances. I thought that he had to be brought in line. He couldn't see the greatness in the man. I planned everything and thought I had helped the cause."

His response was again greeted by silence, and when the unseen voice spoke, the prisoner heard the sound of a cell door closing. "Your cowboy act almost cost Lyons the presidency. You are not a hero; you are an abomination."

Graham began to weep, his sobs echoing off the walls. "How, how long do I have to stay here?"

"That is up to Senator Leeds."

Leeds looked at the vice president, expectant.

"This is a live feed, senator, as we discussed. If you press the button and speak, the prisoner will hear you."

Justice had to look away. Leeds's body was shaking with excitement.

"Can you tell him I'm sorry?" the prisoner pleaded. "I'll do anything to make it right. Please. My cell isn't even big enough to lie down, there is no light, and I'm wallowing in my own waste. For God's sake, can you at least put me in a real prison?"

"It is not for me to determine," said the cold voice. The only sound in the room was the weeping of the broken man.

Leeds's twitching finger, which had been hovering over the button, pressed down. "KICK HIM IN THE BALLS!"

Leeds watched in fascination as a vicious snap kick connected with Graham's groin. The screen went black.

In a strangled voice, Justice reminded Leeds of the rules. "Because of the individual involved, the video is now destroyed. The president thanks you for your cooperation."

Her lips were curled in disgust. Leeds understood that this exercise went against her protests. That made it all the sweeter. He had new respect for the president. Turning to the vice president, and knowing that his reaction could conceivably be recorded, he said. "I see no reason to hold the man. I merely wanted him located." Leeds paused and spoke with the gravitas of a man who actually believed he called the shots: "Release him."

Justice barely held her revulsion. Leeds had loved every minute of the video. The fact that a woman had administered the beating had caused him to rise up from his seat in delight. Still, the old pro's survival instinct had caused him to cover his ample posterior by making sure she heard his politically correct answer.

Not wanting to touch the man, the vice president simply gestured towards the door.

CHAPTER 142

JOHN WESLEY FELL IN AND out of consciousness as the white panel van drove over the rough roads. With each bump, he hissed through his teeth, feeling the bumps as if they were individually designed to punish his broken body. Although he lacked the energy to examine his lacerations, he could feel the blood seep from under the bandages. For not the first time, he wondered whether his battered testicles would heal.

Mercifully, the van stopped. He heard the two Secret Service agents, who had uttered not a word, open their doors. *Have they already dug a grave? Will they just dump me in and bury me alive? Oh God, please no.*

The back hatch of the van opened, and Wesley sucked in a breath. Roughly, the agents pulled the stretcher out. He tried to move, but he was belted to the stretcher. He cried out in pain, "Please!"

A wave of dizziness assaulted him as the men carried him up a flight of stairs feet first. His eyes were closed, so he heard, rather than saw, a screen door open.

"Bring him in here," said a male voice. The agents laid him on a makeshift hospital bed. Wesley opened his eyes to see a gray-haired man with a thick salt-and-pepper mustache leaning over him. Blinking away tears, he saw a stethoscope hanging around the man's neck.

"You can leave now," Wesley heard the man say. Footsteps echoed on the wooden floor, and Wesley let out a breath. The man poked and prodded, and each touch felt like a new wound. Finally, the man stepped back and left Wesley alone. He heard water running and surmised that the man was washing the blood off his hands.

Wesley waited for the man's return, but he heard nothing. His eyes grew heavy, and he succumbed to sleep.

Some time later, a bottle of water was thrust into Wesley's hands. He realized that his restraints had been removed while he slept. He opened his eyes and looked up. The man with the stethoscope was standing over him. The man's gray eyes showed no emotion. "You pissed off some pretty important people, son. I'm not here to be your friend; I'm here to make sure you don't die. When you're well enough to walk, we'll drop you off somewhere."

Wesley smiled weakly.

The man raised a meaty finger. "I'll just give you one piece of advice. Secret Service agents are sworn to protect the President of the United States. Instinctively, they will jump in front of a bullet for him." He paused. "But this president is different. Those two fellows who brought you here, they wouldn't just take a bullet for President Lyons, they would kill for him."

CHAPTER 143

I shouldn't be here. Grace was right. It was a lot easier thinking that thought than it would be making that statement in front of her. Even though Mac had surprised his staff by showing up for work and had instructed them to tell all callers he was not available, somehow the senior senator from California had not only found out he was working today, but she had bullied her way into his office. Elise Franklin was used to getting her way.

When she announced her arrival, Senator Franklin had told Mac's assistant that he had three options: lunch at Marcel's, dinner at her apartment served by her personal chef, or right now. Flustered, the assistant called Mac on the intercom with Franklin standing next to her.

Mac sensed Franklin hovering and replied, "As attractive at the first two options are, I wouldn't want to waste a minute delaying a visit with Senator Franklin. Please send her in."

Feeling not an ounce of embarrassment for her rude intrusion, she gave him a buss on the cheek and asked, "Where do you want me?"

Mac's first thought was that the woman dressed like she expected a photographer to always be around a corner. His second thought was that he now knew what the kids meant when they said, "I just threw up in my mouth." He kept his smile in place and motioned to the black leather office chair opposite his desk.

Franklin nodded, then pulled the chair so that it was alongside his desk. She plopped into the chair in a half-lounge position and stretched out her long legs. "Mac," she asked in a sultry voice that implied previous intimacy, "haven't I been a good soldier?"

Refusing to back away from her obvious attempt to unsettle him, Mac leaned forward. "I'm sure you're good at all you do, Elise."

"Yet you're afraid to have lunch with me and petrified to come to my place for a fabulous dinner." She put on a pouty face. "You do know that I am one of your boss's most *pliable* Democratic allies."

"I didn't think I could get a permission slip signed by my wife."

"And I thought you were your own man," she teased.

"Elise, I'm sorry but I have a tight schedule today. Could you tell me why you're here?"

The rebuke made her sit up straight. "You have no schedule, Mr. Secretary. You're not even supposed to be here. Your boss wants you to lay low for the next two weeks." She paused, enjoying Mac's concerned look. "I want to know why you and your boss shit all over me with your tax reform proposal."

Mac gave her the party line. "We believe it's the best thing for the country."

Her face reddened. "Don't give me that bullshit! I've been in politics all my life. If you had given me a few weeks' notice, I could have at least laid a little groundwork. My base is furious."

"Shouldn't you be speaking to the president? "

"I helped get him elected." She cocked her head and looked at Mac. "You poor putz. You think because the shitstorm hasn't arrived that it's not coming. The snowball has just started rolling down the slope. By this time next week, *you*, not the president, will be buried. You think you'll be able to skate back into your life managing money? You will be the laughing stock of the country." She shook her head and glared at him.

"Thank you for the career advice," Mac said evenly. "Should I relay your message to the president, or do you prefer to treat him with the same disrespect in person?"

"You know that bastard has me by the short hairs," she snarled.

"Actually, I know nothing of the sort. Nor do I want to know."

Franklin started to speak, but Mac held up his hand to let her know he wasn't finished. "I also can end this meeting right now. If your entire purpose was to malign me and insult my intelligence, you've succeeded."

Franklin blew out a breath. "You have no idea the pressure I'm under."

Mac's look was hard and unsympathetic. "If you weren't running for reelection, would you approve of this plan?" he asked.

Franklin considered the question. "Yes. It's good for me, but I'm rich." She shrugged. "I wouldn't mind not spending three months gathering information and hassling with my CPA."

Mac nodded. "The impossible dream is for all legislators to vote like they weren't running for reelection."

She barked out a laugh. "Fat fucking chance."

Mac stared her down. "Unless I heard you incorrectly, the president, as you so inelegantly put it, has you by the short hairs. So you had no realistic hope of making any progress with me. Do I have that right?"

Franklin didn't give him the satisfaction of a response.

"Or perhaps you hoped that if you continued to play on our team, the president would help you get reelected."

Her dark look served as affirmation.

"Elise, I've heard you speak. You're a master communicator. I'm obviously not a politician, but I've spent my career in sales. What if you waited a few weeks before commenting on the proposal? Then you tweet that you were originally opposed to the tax reform package, but you have met with several tax experts and spent some one-on-one time with the president.

"Although you still have some reservations, and the bill may need to be tweaked, it is an improvement over current law. That's just an amateur's take. You will be able to craft something much better, especially if you add a dash of humility."

"Can you get the president to help fund my campaign in 2020?"

"Ah, the real purpose sticks its greedy little head out." He sighed. "I can't write any checks for him, but he does help those who are helpful to him." Mac stood up, out of patience now.

Franklin shrugged, knowing the meeting was over. She leaned over and gave him a soft kiss on the check, her makeup scarring his white shirt. "Oops," she said, returning to the seductress role. "I hope your wife is understanding."

"No problem," said Mac with a confident smile. "I videotaped our meeting."

CHAPTER 144

If he was going to be called "Benedict Leeds," he sure as hell wasn't going to give them any forewarning. The fact that Bill Reynolds was also on the firing line might blunt the party loyalists' attacks, but Reynolds was only there to appear presidential.

Leeds took a deep breath. Even with a Republican sharing the dais with him, Leeds knew it was his pecker in the guillotine. One of the strongest constituencies of the Democrats was the seniors. And led by AARP and every other seniors lobbyist, they would be on the warpath. Messing with Social Security is a sure way to flush your career down the toilet. Still, one of the only rules of politics that still was sacrosanct was that you pay your debts.

Without a doubt, the most amazing facet of this shotgun wedding between the political parties was that neither Leeds nor Reynolds had discussed his role in this initiative with anyone in his party or their staffs. An unleaked story in Washington, D.C., was as rare as finding a liberal at a gun show.

Ever since Jeremy Lyons became president, the public's interest in matters of state had soared. To those who followed and predicted public opinion, it was a mystery. The consensus was that without the entertainment of outrageous proposals or bickering politicians, the only emotion that the public would show when their primetime shows were interrupted would be annoyance.

The concept that substance sells was still hard to swallow. On the other hand, tonight's primetime address, in which Treasury Secretary Mac McGregor would discuss entitlement reform, had gotten significant play in the media. Partly because the content was shrouded in secrecy and partly because the lobbyists had been burning up the phones and the internet to make sure that the proper responses would be immediate, the ratings were assured.

Senator Leeds, dressed in a dark blue suit that expertly hid his bulk, stood proudly before the large American flag waving behind him. "Whenever entitlement reform is mentioned in political circles, politicians turn their heads," he began. For emphasis, he turned his head away from the cameras. "It's a hard subject to broach, because any changes that we make require sacrifice; some constituencies are worse off than they were before the changes. Your senators and representatives are hard wired to protect our citizens at all cost.

"There is no perfect plan to fix Social Security, but it is unfair to leave this problem to future leaders and future generations. Let's examine the facts. The most important thing to understand is that any changes in Social Security will never affect current recipients." He paused to stare resolutely into the camera.

"Senator Bill Reynolds and I have met privately with financial analysts, President Lyons, and Secretary McGregor in order to propose what we consider to be the best opportunity to accomplish our goal. You, the people, will hear it first, and then we will present the Reynolds/Leeds bill to congress.

"The reason this is necessary is that within sixteen years, without reform, Social Security will not be able to fully pay its obligations to its recipients." Again he paused to let the message sink in.

"Americans are living longer. That's a fact. A number of years ago, we raised the eligibility age for benefits, and that helped erase some of the shortfall. It is necessary to do that again. Consequently, over the next 20 years, we will raise the age limit for full retirement from 67 to 69. This is step one in our plan to responsibly fund Social Security.

"Step two is a logical progression concerning the Social Security tax on earned income. As you are aware, our Social Security payments are tied to inflation, and they increase with the cost of living. Currently, the tax on earnings is 6.2 per cent. That rate is based on the first $118,500 of income. We are proposing that the same inflation factor used in calculating payments be used to slowly increase the income limit."

Leeds turned to his left. "And now, Senator Bill Reynolds will discuss the third step in the plan to fund Social Security."

Reynolds reached over, patted Leeds on the shoulder, and began to speak. "One of the solutions that was debated was means testing. In other words, the government determines how much money is enough for you and then breaks the contract it had with you to pay you your full Social Security benefits. We have a plan that we think will be much more appealing to our more fortunate seniors. With this bill we are creating a "Protect America" fund. Every dollar donated to this fund will be used to help our active-duty soldiers and our veterans. Every distribution from the fund will be transparent and available on line.

"We anticipate that initial funding will come from those who do not need Social Security for their lifestyles. The program is completely voluntary, and any seniors who pledge their lifetime Social Security payments to the Protect America fund will receive a one-year tax credit for half of their annual gift. In addition, we hope that this fund will be used in charitable and estate planning."

Reynolds paused, and his smile was warm and encouraging. "I am pleased to announce tonight that President Jeremy Lyons's will leaves one billion dollars to the Protect America fund.

"On a personal note, my family and I have spent considerable time visiting at Walter Reed National Military Medical Center. We've sat beside heroes, our wounded veterans. We've prayed with them, we've cried with them. With the passage of this bill, we have a chance to show them how much their sacrifice means to us."

His eyes glistened as he concluded. "May God bless our soldiers and all Americans."

* * *

With each public appearance, Mac gained more confidence. After years of speaking without notes and eschewing Power Point presentations, having a teleprompter spit out your speech was pretty sweet. "Senators," he began, acknowledging the previous speakers, "we appreciate your help in our country's efforts to get our financial house in order. In addition, the president and I appreciate your leadership, and we are confident that with your help, our efforts will be successful.

"It is not enough just to address Social Security. The remaining entitlements — Medicare, welfare, and Obamacare — are public services, and it is this administration's intention to run them like public companies. In President Lyons's inaugural address, he spoke of sacrifice. It is my pleasure to announce tonight an amazing gesture of sacrifice and patriotism.

"Four accounting firms: Price Waterhouse Coopers, Deloitte. Ernst and Young, and KPMG, have offered their services to our nation. For a twelve-month period, these firms will send forensic accountants to examine every facet of our entitlement programs. The cost to the U.S. Government for the countless hours these audits will take," he paused and raised his right hand, thumb, and forefinger touching to form a zero.

"Not only does the administration appreciate the generosity and sacrifice of these firms, but your country also thanks you.

"Even before he was elected, President Lyons and his financial team spent considerable time analyzing our entitlement programs. Regardless of whether he became your president or not, he knew that this was an area that could not be ignored. As Senator Leeds said earlier, there are no easy solutions, but the problems must be solved. Finding out where waste, inefficiencies, or even fraud have added to our national debt is the essential first step. However, it is not enough.

"After all the data from our forensic accountants is compiled and analyzed, we have to ensure not only that the deficiencies are fixed, but also that the programs provide the necessary benefits required by our citizens. So while the accountants are doing their work, the administration will be evaluating leaders, men and woman of exceptional corporate experience, among a pool of former CEOs, CFOs, and COOs. These former leaders of public companies will be responsible for making sure that our government works like a successful business."

Mac smiled. "Nothing happens in politics without critics. Legislation is rarely passed without contention. But if the people are informed, if the people believe in what we are doing, then reason prevails. Tonight, once again, the president and I ask for your support. If we all invest in America, we are unstoppable. Thank you, and good night."

CHAPTER 145

MAC CLOSED HIS EYES AS he slowly chewed a bite of his homemade granola with nuts, covered with plump, delicious raspberries. It was 8:20 on Monday morning, and he wondered how many other lucky stiffs had eaten a specialty breakfast in the Oval Office.

"No wonder you are successful," said the president, holding up a similar spoonful, "if your stock picking is this good."

Mac pulled his iPhone out of his breast pocket and aimed it at the president. "Please repeat that so that I can use it when I return to my real job."

Lyons laughed and then asked, "Are you sure you wouldn't want to leave the investment business on a high note and stay right where you are?"

Mac answered thoughtfully. "It's a heady feeling to at least imagine that you might be able to make a difference in your country's future. For me, it was hard not to have the direction of the stock market affect my enthusiasm for driving to work. When the stock market futures were in the toilet, I felt tired before I got to the office. As you remember, in prolonged bear markets, that is when you have to prove your worth. Just like what you are trying to do as president, it is necessary to be proactive in order to comfort clients and remind them of the logic of their investment plans. If they sell at the bottom of the markets, then I've failed."

Lyons didn't respond, so Mac continued. "Working with you, I feel like every day offers possibilities."

"Is it because of our relationship, or because of the strategic plan for the country?"

"Both," said Mac. "But not talking every day with my clients is really painful for me."

"Absent the lack of communication with your clients, I do think you would do your duty with or without me."

Mac gave him a strange look.

"And even though my tenure was short, and I didn't have the connectivity you had with clients, I do understand."

Mac opted for a subject change. "So how do you plan to break this gridlock in congress? It seems to me like they are acting like rival gangs in jail."

"An apt comparison. Do you mind if I use it?"

"As long as you don't attribute it to me! By the way, my question does not indicate a lack of confidence. Anyone who can get Leeds and Reynolds on the same dais can do anything. So what's next?"

Lyons took another bite of his cereal as he considered his answer. "It starts with the cabinet. We've assembled a diverse group of Democrats, Republicans, and Independents to help us govern. It's a highly qualified potpourri of gender and race. As far as I can tell, my Supreme Court nominee does not have a party bias."

"Not after you threatened her," interjected Mac.

"A classic case of hyperbole," said Lyons in mild protest.

"Did you forget that I was in the room?"

"Absolutely not. I wanted you to share a piece of history."

"Well," said Mac, conceding his point, "you did ask her about a dozen times if she was a strict constitutionalist."

"I contend that is a made-up word."

Mac laughed. "You may be right. I am occasionally guilty of listening to Mark Levin. And the bottom line is that it looks like she will be confirmed, so whatever you did worked."

Lyons held up his last raspberry in triumph. "So I guess the end justified the means."

Mac hoped the president's mantra worked for him, as well.

CHAPTER 146

THE VICE PRESIDENT STARTED TO stand, but Lyons motioned her back to her seat. Noting the serious look on his face, she waited for him to speak. When he remained silent for an uncomfortable period, she said, "To what do I owe this honor, Mr. President?"

Even with that opening he seemed to search for words. "I'm gauging your level of preparation."

"I, I'm sorry, sir, for what?"

"To lead our country, Mary Beth."

She relaxed. "By the time you are done kicking ass and taking names, I will be ready and able," she said with a smile.

Lyons's eyes closed for a moment, and when he opened them, there was a sadness. "I will not complete my term, Mary Beth."

Her face paled. Instantly her throat constricted. Her lips parted, but no sounds emerged. Her head shook from side to side as if the action itself could deny the words he'd spoken.

She raised her hands in a beseeching manner, silently pleading for reason. She blinked away tears. A gurgling sound rose from her throat, and she managed to form words. "You can't. I, I won't let you. I don't want it this way!"

His smile was sad, and he looked at her with genuine affection. "You had to know," he said simply.

She continued to shake her head in denial.

He explained further. "I have been experiencing occasional episodes..." He moved his hands trying to find the words. "Unplanned outbursts of anger.. ."

"The job would drive anyone crazy."

His face clouded.

"I'm sorry, Jeremy, but you're not crazy. I would let you know if I saw anything that affected your leadership."

"I know," he said, "and I may well be premature in my fatalism."

With a tenderness she had never witnessed, he walked to her desk, grasped her hand, and squeezed it gently. After a short moment, he turned and walked out of her office, leaving her alone.

CHAPTER 147

THE SOLDIER'S JAW WAS CLENCHED to the extent that it appeared to be wired shut. His eyes burned into his superior's.

"You do realize that my decision is not debatable," said the president in a purposely condescending tone.

The soldier, frozen with anger, remained immobile.

"Perhaps you could consider it delayed gratification."

"Sir," the soldier said for the third time, "I cannot comply."

Moving within an inch of the man's face, Lyons sadistically continued his peppering. "Are you incapable of following my orders? Are there physical maladies that I am not aware of? Or are you just a traitor who refuses to comply with a direct order from your commander in chief?"

The soldier's face was beet red. "Sir!" he said in desperation. "There must be another way."

"Perhaps you are not aware that it is *my* job to assess the situation, consider every available option, and then make the fucking decision!" The president backed off and walked over to look through the stained glass window. Having this conversation in the sanctity of an empty church guarded by his agents was sacrilege. Yet to him, only here would God give him a sign if he were wrong.

Lyons's voice was metered. "I have examined every possible scenario, soldier, and I assure you that the alternative to your mission is chaos. In the absence of strength, there is only weakness. Your mission must be executed precisely as outlined in order ensure the continued cooperation and prosperity of the nation."

The soldier's head lowered, and he shook it from side to side.

"You were there during 9/11," Lyons went on. "You remember how our nation came together. For too long, we had lost that feeling of unity, that commitment of purpose. It is likely that you will not survive your mission. But because of it, America will."

The silence in the room enveloped their breath. Lyons stood before his charge and they squared off, each man at full attention, their eyes locked. Clouds moved across the sun, causing the light through the window to dance colors across the president's face. Lyons's eyes were moist, yet determined. His last words were unequivocal. "I command you to complete this mission."

The soldier's inbred sense of duty wrapped him as tightly as the coffin that was surely his reward. His conscious mind had no control over the words that escaped his lips. "Yes, sir."

CHAPTER 148

"I'LL BET YOU'RE LOOKING FORWARD to your July Fourth week at the beach."

Mac marveled at the fact that he was sitting in the Oval Office and shooting the breeze with the leader of the free world, and it felt normal. "It's my favorite time of the year."

"Do you stay for one week or two?"

"In the past, Grace and I have stayed for two. Because the kids do honest work, they can only stay for a week."

"And you have two grandkids."

Mac smiled. "Look at you, getting all domestic on me. There is nothing better."

"So when do you leave for the holiday?"

"Well, this year, I will leave the day after the 4th because of your speech."

Lyons shook his head. "Absolutely not. No one from the administration will be there. I insist that you go early and stay late."

"Wow, who died and made you king?"

The president's face went pale.

"Sorry, boss," said Mac. "That was flip. I want to be here to support you. The kids will be at the beach, and we'll get most of the time with them. This is a pretty big speech you're giving."

Lyons folded his hands and then said, "Was I there to support you when you proposed the tax reform plan?"

"No, but I figured you had your reasons. Maybe it was to see if I could be seduced by Elise Franklin."

Lyons laughed and faked a shudder. "She can't hold a candle to Grace."

"I'll pass that on." Mac wanted to change the subject so he that didn't get hung up disobeying a direct order from the president. "Did you ever think about having kids?"

Lyons's smile was wistful. "I was afraid to bring a child into the world."

"Why?"

Lyons's eyes rose to the wall behind Mac. "My father was an emotionless, cruel man. My mother was weak and helpless. And there is a lot of anger and ruthlessness in my past. Regretfully, my gene pool is damaged."

Mac started to speak, but the president's eyes now focused on him. "Ambition left unchecked becomes an insatiable addiction to power, a roaring hunger for success that devours people like a lion devours its prey, leaving behind the skeletal remains of relationships. You saved me from that, Mac."

Mac's eyes widened. "How do you figure that?"

"If you hadn't tracked me down, I'd still be running my hedge fund, winning at all costs."

"Most people would think that was a pretty good life."

"It was immoral and without purpose, Mac." His smile did not change the fact that his eyes were filled with regret.

Mac could sense the president mentally wrestling to push those feelings back.

"Were you close to your parents?" asked Lyons.

Mac hesitated. "It feels like I spent my whole life struggling to get a compliment from my dad. It may have been generational, but..."

"Have you been different with your children?"

"Oh, yeah," said Mac, "I've told them from day one how fabulous they are and likely smothered them with affection."

Lyons nodded. "And your relationship with your mom?"

Mac broke into a big smile. "The woman was a saint. She was my biggest fan."

"You are a blessed man."

"I am the poster child for someone with an attitude of gratitude."

"I know that for me, you have been a Godsend. Because of you, I found my real purpose."

Mac looked behind him to be sure no Secret Service agents were within earshot. "If you really thought that totally by accident, I did you a favor, then your subsequent actions were even more baffling. There may be a thread of logic in your connecting with me when you were being hunted by the authorities, but you threatened me and coerced me into a weekly conference call. That's a hell of a way to say thanks."

"The reason is humiliating, Mac."

"All the more reason to give it up." He had gotten this off his chest, and he was not going to leave without an answer.

Lyons gave him a weak smile. "You were my only option."

Mac threw up his hands. "What does that mean?"

Lyons sighed. "First, the threat was empty. I had no desire and no motivation to hurt you or your family. In fact, it was just the opposite. I don't think you'll ever understand. I can't expect you to understand. You make friends easily." His expression was pained, vulnerable. "I knew you wouldn't talk to me voluntarily. I hoped that if you got to know me, just possibly, we might someday become friends."

The silence was awkward. Mac finally broke it. "For a guy who is a financial genius and an incredible leader, you suck at 'friendly persuasion.'"

Lyons smiled.

And I continue deflecting. Humor is my armor. The President of the United States has me on a pedestal. But it's made of clay. Mac squeezed his eyes shut as a familiar pang of guilt knifed through his gut.

"Are you all right, Mac?" asked Lyons with concern.

Mac blew out a breath. "Not really." His gaze was steady, but pained. "I'm not the man you think I am."

"I feel confident that I know almost everything about you, Mac."

"Why did you leave Johnston Wellons?"

"Because they chose you to be the head of the brokers advisory council. You know that."

"I knew that at the time; in fact," he let out a long breath, "even before you resigned."

"How would you know that?" Lyons prompted.

"Because I orchestrated it."

"That's absurd. You didn't have that kind of power. I was the firm's largest producer."

"Oh, I was well aware of that!" Mac's words rushed out like water from a broken fire hydrant. "It haunted me. I was laid back, while you were aggressive, relentless. You went after new accounts with a vengeance. You were unstoppable, unbeatable. Plus," he knew it would sound petty, childish, but he plunged ahead, "you ignored me.

"The head of the advisory group got all the press. I was, and still am, a media whore. I was so jealous of you that it turned into righteous indignation." Mac's smile was sad. "That's the first step in rationalizing your actions. I was married, had kids, needed to support a family. You were single, a loner." He held out his hands as if that explained everything.

Then, Mac bit the bullet. "I told management that if they chose you over me, I would go to another firm."

In a dismissive tone, Lyons said, "That doesn't make sense. The decision would have to have been economically based. I produced twice the revenue you did. There had to be something more."

Mac shook his head. "There was. I knew if it was a me or you decision, I would lose. Do you remember Ellison, Armas, or Gottschalk?"

"Actually, I remember all three of them."

"Well, I had talked them into leaving with me, a regular palace coup."

"And were they in on your plan to sabotage me?"

Mac's head went back as if he'd been struck. "No," he said wearily. "I was the pied piper selling them a bill of goods. I was the only one who betrayed you. Jeremy, I am so sorry. I hope you can forgive me."

The silence felt heavy to Mac. It was like waiting for the jury's verdict.

"Anything else?" asked Lyons with an edge in his voice.

Mac hesitated, then looked him straight in the eye. "Yeah. I told management that you were a compliance risk, pushing clients into inappropriate investments and possibly using inside information. You could destroy the firm, and I wasn't willing to go down with you."

Lyons raised his eyebrow. "That is harsh. You had no basis for that accusation, and yet you sold it to management."

"It's the single worst thing I have ever done to anyone. God help me, I am sorry."

Lyons let the apology marinate for a moment and then spoke. "We may be more alike than you imagined. It was not your finest hour. Perhaps now you can understand better why I have, as you so eloquently stated, tortured you in the past."

"But you had no idea…"

"You really thought that none of your co-conspirators would confide in me?"

Mac's mouth hung open in shock. "You *knew* what I had done and still wanted to be my friend?"

"That has now become a rhetorical question," said Lyons. "Three more salient points, and then we can forget ancient history. First, you could have still been the face of the press. At the time I abhorred attention. Second, I did not want to hear your confession before you accepted my offer to be in my cabinet. Guilt is always a good motivator. And finally, I wanted to go out on my own. You not only gave me the excuse, you stoked my competitive fires, and I was able to give an exit performance that became legendary in the firm." Lyons's smile filled his face.

Mac sat both stunned and depleted. How long had this cancer of remorse feasted on him?

"Feel better?" asked Lyons as he grasped Mac's hand.

"I would have felt better a lot sooner if you'd told me that you knew I was responsible for your leaving the firm."

"Sorry. It was your penance. It had to come from you."

"Yeah, I know." Mac pulled the president in for a hug. The barriers had evaporated. "Now I need you to do me a favor."

"Anything."

"Reconsider having a family. God wiped the slate clean for you, and you are a genuinely good man. Your DNA is not poisoned, my friend, it's blessed."

CHAPTER 149

THE CAPITOL POLICE WERE NOT happy. It was a hot, sticky night in Washington, D.C., and they had double the patrol officers on duty. At the Lincoln Memorial, there are 58 steps from the chamber to the plaza level. For a president to address a crowd from the chamber is dangerous; for him to erect a stage halfway up, or 26 steps from the people, is a security nightmare.

President Jeremy Lyons had insisted that no dignitaries were to be placed in front row seats; it was first come, first served, and all people were equal. The result was that people were packed together at the bottom of the steps like fanatics at a rock concert.

People had started coming six hours before dark. Without question, the sea of humanity would constitute a record crowd. Spread out on blankets and folding chairs, they brought their kids, grills, and enough food to feed multitudes. It might have been the largest tailgate in history.

The police needn't have worried. The enormous crowd was not filled with malcontents or angry people. These were Jeremy Lyons's people; they came to be a part of history. This Fourth of July speech was not a surprise; it was covered by every media outlet.

It was a good five minutes before the president could speak over the noise of the screaming crowd. After about three minutes, he raised his hands to quiet the applause, but they were all standing, and not finished.

President Lyons was not accompanied by any staff tonight, only supported by his phalanx of Secret Service agents. "My fellow Americans," he began. "I come to you tonight with a grateful heart. Two years ago on this day I announced my candidacy for president. I asked you to believe in me. I asked you to trust me. You did and you have. Thank you.

"Two hundred and forty-two years ago on this day, fifty-six men signed the *Declaration of Independence*. Listen to the famous words of that document, which defined our country: 'We hold these truths to be self-evident, that all men are created equal, that they are endowed by their Creator with certain unalienable rights, that among those are life, liberty, and the pursuit of happiness.' He paused. "I became your president to prove that these words, those truths still matter." APPLAUSE

"Thirteen years later, our forefathers signed our constitution. I ask your indulgence once more as I cite the preamble. 'We the people,' *not* the president, *not* congress, 'we the people of the United States, in order to form a more perfect union, establish justice, ensure domestic tranquility, provide for the common defense, promote the general welfare, and secure the blessings of liberty to ourselves and our posterity.' I became your president to prove that these ideals, these words still matter." APPLAUSE

"Two hundred forty-two years ago, it was all about the people. Legislators would be elected, serve, and go back to their jobs. It was public service. Their only goals were to protect the republic and make better lives for the people. Can you imagine where our country would be if every elected official focused only on protecting you and improving your lives?" APPLAUSE

"Every president must make choices. In a perfect world the only question would be what is best for America. Under our current system, eliminating self-interest is almost impossible, unless you are unconcerned about a second term or your legacy. Your safety is my first priority. But you must realize that requires me to make your privacy concerns secondary."

Lyons extended his arms with his palms raised upward. "Do I choose to focus more on our civil rights," he turned his left hand over, "or to protect our citizens?"

His right hand turned over. He made a fist and raised it in the air. "*Nothing* is more important than protecting you and your families!" APPLAUSE

"And you have rewarded our singular focus. Every initiative that we have proposed, you the people have supported. While I was a senator, your voices echoed throughout the chambers of congress, and *you* enabled us to lower the corporate income tax. As a result, the growth rate of our economy has gone from an anemic two per cent when I entered office to four per cent now. That represents a 100 per cent increase in productivity. This could not have happened without you.

"Corporations have relocated overseas plants to cities all over the nation. Over twenty million more Americans are at work this year, and middle class wages increased more than five per cent in the last six months." APPLAUSE

Lyons waited, letting the applause cover him like a warm blanket. "By the end of this year, we will have reduced our national debt by two trillion dollars. How did that happen? The majority of the savings came from just paying attention. Why wasn't this done before? No one wanted to mess with the government. Special interest groups had a chokehold on our legislators. If elected officials wanted to be reelected, they had to play ball." He smiled, and it was like a mirror: the crowd smiled with him. "I confess. I never played well in the sandbox." LAUGHTER

"When you are not running for a second term, it's easy to be a maverick. Independent auditors found example after example of waste and inefficiency. It had been estimated that there was 40 million dollars of wrongful welfare payments each year. Our auditors found more than twice that much, and those erroneous payments have been eliminated. You deserve to have your tax dollars allocated correctly." APPLAUSE

Lyons raised his hands. "Our government must be run like the world's best corporation. Any individuals who are not doing their jobs should be replaced. If any agency is non-essential, it needs to be closed. The culture has become one in which every department spends every dollar allocated to it, because if it doesn't, its allocations will decrease the following year. We must create a culture where merit is rewarded and failure is not excused." APPLAUSE

"We have more to do. We have not had the opportunity to address the immigration issue. In the next two years, we will ask for your input, and *you the people* will help our leaders decide. During my presidency, we have seen a level of bipartisan compromise that had long been absent in our country. We are on the right track.

"Look what happens when the people's representatives work together. Two exceptional public servants, Senator Bill Reynolds and Senator Everett Leeds, put aside their differences and ushered the Reynolds/Leeds bill through congress. As a result, Social Security is funded through the end of this century!" APPLAUSE

His next words were spoken in reverence. "In addition, this bipartisan compromise enabled our more fortunate citizens to join an elite group. They can choose to participate in our Protect America program, which means that every dollar they pledge supports those who protect our freedoms. Today I am proud to announce that over 100,000 patriotic Americans have pledged their lifetime Social Security payments to help our military and its veterans." APPLAUSE

* * *

He began again, his voice calm and reasoned. "Two hundred forty-two years ago, our leaders were prepared to give up everything for the sake of our country. One of the things that makes America great is that we were formed on sacrifice. If short-term pain produces long-term gain and we can protect future generations, we are duty-bound to find a solution.

"On April 15th, I asked my treasury secretary, Mac McGregor, to submit to the people our solution to fix the tax code. He did this at my request, knowing that any change not authorized or promoted by special interests would make him a target. As a result of serving his president, he was vilified and insulted, and the media hassled him for over a month. What would any of you do if you were unfairly criticized? You would fight back with the truth! But I asked him, I implored him to turn the other cheek. It was the most difficult thing he ever had to do. One of the malignancies of our society is that when the opposition hates the idea but has no valid arguments against it, they attack the person." He shook his head.

"What are we trying to accomplish? Get rid of the loopholes that mainly benefit the rich. Lower tax rates for individuals, and dramatically simplify paying taxes. For almost three months, Congress has been trying to tweak the bill, there have been negative articles from the media, and it is stalled." Lyons hesitated, and his face scrunched up like he'd forgotten what came next.

After a moment, he continued. "I need your support. Your voices matter. Tell your representatives to get off the pot and pass this bill as it was submitted! You see what happens when we give them too much of our money! They waste two trillion dollars!" Those not already standing struggled to their feet for a standing ovation, and the president gratefully waited until the applause diminished.

He spoke quietly. "I stand before you humbled by your support. You have taken up the challenge to invest in America. But I must add a warning. Future leaders will try to change what we have done." He shook his head. "Don't let them. They will tell you they need to increase your taxes." He shook his head again. "Don't let them. They will try to divide you with partisan arguments. Don't let them. We are the *United States*. This is *your* country, not just mine, not just theirs. This country was built on free speech. Do not be silent."

Lyons paused, and an involuntary shiver coursed through his body. In response, he clenched his fists. "To create our America will require courage. To create our America will require sacrifice. To create a new America will require faith." He smiled. "Before the fireworks once again ignite our skies in celebration, let us reflect on what we are celebrating. Our independence was gained through courage, through sacrifice, and through faith." He opened his palms, and like an evangelical preacher, slowly raised them upwards. Closing his eyes, he tilted his head back and said, "United we stand...United we stand."

One by one the people stood and joined in his chant. The massive audience spoke as one, their discordant voices forming a harmony of hope. "United we stand . . . United we stand..."

Abruptly, the stage lights were extinguished, and the ghost-like silhouette of the 45th President of the United States faded into the night. The skies filled with the sounds and colors of fireworks.

CHAPTER 150

"No!" SHOUTED MAC AS HE slapped both his hands down on his living room coffee table. Grace, whose eyes had been closed, opened them with alarm. She clutched her husband's arm and looked at the television.

The president moved quickly down the steps toward the crowd. He spun away from the Secret Service agent's frantic grasp. The people closest to the stage pulsed forward in order to touch the president. It was as if a multi-celled organism of humanity were reaching out tendrils to engulf and swallow the man.

"That's why we weren't invited. That's why!" Mac shook his fists as he screamed at the TV in futile protest. He and Grace watched in horror as the scene played out in strobe light stop motion animation: Secret Service agents plunged into the crowd, trying desperately to protect their charge as fireworks sounding like gunfire lit the skies.

Blake Stone had been in hundreds of perilous situations, but never in a human swarm. As he forced his way towards his predetermined destination, his heartbeat accelerated. Suddenly his body was pinned by two grossly overweight men who reeked of sweat and stale beer. A young girl stared at his clerical collar with wonder, and he gently reached down and touched her cheek with his palm. At the same time, he turned her slightly so that she couldn't see him drive his elbow into the closest man's sternum.

"Keep those spoilsports away from me," said the president as two Secret Service agents closed in on him. The crowd responded instantly, purposefully getting in the agents' way. Jeremy Lyons's people had become soldiers for their leader.

Stone marched through the crowd. He knew the exact trajectory his target would take.

As the president pushed through the well-wishers, his eyes swiveled, searching for a prearranged sign. He stumbled, and was held up by adoring fans. Every human instinct told him to stop, to welcome his bodyguards. Then a light flashed and he saw the silver cross.

Standing and shouting, Mac asked, "Where the hell are the agents? Where did Lyons go? Why is he doing this?"

The president stopped in front of the priest. Stone's eyes begged for a reprieve, but none came. Lyons's eyes closed once, and he whispered, "Forgive me, Father."

Hugging the man he once despised, Stone gained the leverage he needed, and with all his strength, thrust the ceramic spike under the president's rib cage and upward towards his heart. Pressing a button on the bottom of the weapon caused the tip to extend in four directions like a claw.

The president shuddered, and his eyes flickered.

Stone lowered his head and slowly wove his way through the crowd, away from Lyons. His face was contorted in anger, and his body shook with grief.

No one around them could sense that history had been altered forever. The crowd continued to carry President Jeremy Lyons, even as his chest cavity filled with blood.

CHAPTER 151

Time stopped. For almost a full minute after the life drained from President Lyons, he was held up by adoring fans. The first one to notice was Sophia Kennedy, a freshman at Vanderbilt University. "He's bleeding!" she cried. Ironically, this young journalism major became the picture of the tragedy. The anguish in her face was all that was needed to tell the story.

Two Secret Service agents immediately pushed her aside, grabbed their charge, and cradled him in their arms. In unison the crowd pulled back, creating a circle of concern. Camera phones added their collective insults to the tragedy.

At 9:52 p.m., at Georgetown University Hospital, the 45th President of the United States was declared dead. At 9:55 p.m., Mary Beth Justice was given the oath of office. At 10:05, Grace McGregor handed the phone to her husband. He had not moved from the couch; his elbows rested on his thighs, and his interlocked fingers rested under his chin. His eyes were closed as if in prayer.

As if in a trance, Mac unfolded, stood, and took the phone from Grace. "Yes, Madam President," he said, his voice hollow and broken.

"Mac, it is important for the country to have confidence in me. I know that Jeremy wanted you to join your family at your beach house, and I want to make the same request of you."

As if he had just been awakened from a deep sleep, Mac wrinkled his brow, trying to understand what she was saying. She had not even acknowledged the tragedy. "What?" He didn't try to hide his confusion.

Justice sighed audibly. "You were Jeremy Lyons's best friend. The press will be all over your reactions to this horrible event. Why did he charge into the crowd? How could the Secret Service let this happen? We both know the answer to that. The service can't protect a president who goes rogue."

Mac felt like a knife was cutting into his brain. He vigorously rubbed his forehead. "Someone killed the president! Do you think I want to be the spokesman for the administration?" His tone was challenging and disrespectful.

Justice hesitated before answering. "You do know that I am your president, your commander in chief?"

Mac winced. "Yes. I apologize, Madam President."

"A few days or even a few weeks from now, I will need your help desperately," said Justice. "We still have much to do to carry out Jeremy's dreams. I cannot do this without you." She paused. "But today I need you to mourn in private, surrounded by your loving family."

As if Mac had telegraphed his need, Grace came up behind him and hugged him tightly. His knees sagged. His mouth opened, but no words came out. Finally, in a voice he didn't recognize he said, "We will leave tonight."

EPILOGUE

SOME OF THOSE WHO SPEND the July 4th week at Bethany Beach have trouble counting. Although fireworks reach a crescendo on the actual Fourth, in the days leading up to Independence Day and for at least a week afterwards, the sounds and sky-illuminating lights of pyrotechnics extend the celebration. Except this year.

The respectful quiet on the night of July 5th only added to the weight on the McGregor family. Mac and Grace had left their Potomac home at two o'clock in the morning after the tragedy of the night before. Mac knew he wouldn't be able to sleep, so like a zombie, he climbed into their van with Grace and drove to the beach to join their children. Mac drove in silence as Grace slept fitfully.

It was unlike any vacation in family history. The joking, the exuberance, the hilarity, all were missing. Instead of constant chatter, the somber family simply exchanged long hugs. Mac picked at his food and spent most of the day just walking on the warm sand, engrossed in his own thoughts.

President Justice had texted him her comments when reporters asked where Mac was. She handled it very gracefully, telling them she had asked him to mourn in private, but that he would be available for comment in the near future. He didn't really care.

At eight o'clock the next morning, Grace answered the phone and handed it to her husband. He listened, a confused look on his face. "Yes," was the only word he spoke.

"I have to go out for a while," he said, offering no further explanation. He slapped a ball cap on his head and hurried down the stairs. He walked out of the house and got into the car that was wait-ing in the driveway.

"Where can we go where we won't be disturbed?" Sabine asked.

Mac shrugged and nodded toward the beach. She opened the car door, kicked off her sandals, and headed for the wooden walkway to the beach. Mac followed her and watched as she continued walk-ing until she waded into the surf. She stopped, and her shoulders slumped. She began to weep silently.

Mac kicked angrily, and first one and then the other flip-flop cartwheeled into the air and landed harmlessly on the sand. He walked into the surf beside her and reached over, putting his arm around her shoulder. "Sabine," he asked softly, "How can I help?"

Without looking at him, she handed him an envelope from the pocket of her windbreaker. "Read it," she said, her voice husky, "and then you must return it to me."

Mac looked at her, then opened the envelope and withdrew the letter. The handwriting was unmistakable. Mac dropped to the sand as if all the air had left his body. His hands began to shake as he read.

Dear Mac,

If the contents of this letter ever became public, it would be extremely harmful to our country. I pray that you will carry its contents to your grave.

I have few regrets. However, a major one is that I was not able to dis-cuss my decision with you. As a Christian, you would have been obligated to try to dissuade me.

In contrast to everything you will read and hear, I was not assassi-nated. Acting upon my orders as commander in chief, a patriot assisted me in committing suicide. After exhaustive tests by renowned physicians, who were sworn to secrecy, I was diagnosed with inoperable brain cancer. Not only was it terminal, but the unanimous prognosis was that I would not see the end of this month.

Before you judge me, consider this question. "If you knew the time of your death, wouldn't you want to determine how you would die?" The prog-nosis of wasting away while a nation mourned would have been unbearable to me.

It is a valid criticism to suggest that I want to be legendary, forever remembered like Lincoln or JFK. If I am correct in my assumptions, then the outrage over my death will propel our tax reform bill and unite our country. In addition, it should open the door for entitlement reform. Future politicians will be tempted to undo the progress we've made, and I am hopeful that an engaged electorate will deter them.

Mac, what you and I have done together in such a short time is incredible. I could not be more proud of our accomplishments. Because of the work that we have done, Mary Beth will have a clear runway to carry out the remainder of my agenda. You had no reason to trust me, to be my friend, yet you did everything I asked of you and more.

My final request is that you use your gifts of eloquence and persuasion and ensure that the tax reform legislation is passed before you return to your friends and clients. I was never the man you are, but I tried.

With respect and admiration,

Jeremy

* * *

Sabine watched Mac's head hit his chest. She leaned down and plucked the letter from his hand. Wordlessly, she left him there, sitting in the sand, his eyes on the ocean. It was too hard for her to be with him.

Sabine sat on the double chaise, bent over, giving in to the pain. Her hands pressed fiercely against her temples. The beauty of the Florida morning seemed to mock her. She had not showered, her hair was in tangles. She had done her job; now she mourned.

Her head shot up as she heard the doorbell ring. There was no further ringing and no knocking on the door. She ignored it. Time passed. Finally, she stood. She walked to the door, saw no one. She looked down and saw a FedEx envelope. She picked it up and tore it open. Inside was a cream-colored envelope. Just like Mac's letter, the handwriting was Jeremy's. *No! It can't be!*

Sabine grabbed the edge of a table for support. The letter hung limply in her fingers. She stayed there, not moving, taking deep breaths. Her heart was pounding as she walked slowly outside and sat heavily on the chaise.

My love,

I know that you did not expect a letter. In time you will understand my decision, even though it cost us precious moments we could have shared together. Every fiber of my body yearned to lie with you until this life drained from me. Yet, because of our sacrifice, with God's grace, we may have saved our country.

I know you will be strong, a symbol to all that forgiveness is divine and that the American spirit cannot be extinguished. I believe that what we have accomplished with be viewed in history as courageous, and hopefully act as a blueprint for the future.

Yet, I know that without you by my side, I would have accomplished nothing. You nursed me back to health, excused my weaknesses, and encouraged me to be a better man. I regret every moment when foolish pride kept me from your arms.

Know that I am in the warm sun, the gentle breeze, and the bright colors of the rainbow. My heart has always been with you and will never leave you. You are my love and God's greatest gift to me.

Jeremy

Sabine's thumb and forefinger went to the corners of her eyes as if the pressure could stop the flow of tears. Her hands went to the small swell in her belly, and she caressed it gently. Inside her was her husband's greatest gift.

Acknowledgements

I MUST FIRST THANK GOD for filling my heart with joy every time I put pen to paper. It is also by His grace that I had the opportunity to work with my son in writing the final book of the Mac McGregor trilogy. For those who might expect that my son deferred to me in all literary areas of contention, you have yet to meet Jamie.

My sister, Kay Krug, who is our tireless editor, has been a critical component in all three books. Through endless rewrites, she is quick to point out when the financial jargon becomes too obtuse or the political speeches too boring.

Mary Perry has once again accepted the job of my "humble researcher." She graciously added some description to scenes that were wanting, and she took charge of the organizational aspects of getting a book to market.

I'm blessed to have a cadre of friends who are gifted with financial, economic, and political acumen. Bill Miller, legendary investment guru, Ed Feulner, the founder of The Heritage Foundation, and Bob Levy, the chairman of the Cato Institute, all showed remarkable patience in answering my multitude of questions.

I need to give a shout out to one of my Citadel friends, Lynn Foltz, who presented me with a lovely, glass-enclosed case in which were displayed the covers of my first two novels. Pointedly, he left a space open for this, my third and final book of the trilogy. I asked my friend Father Ray O'Brien for a description of a private place where a presidential hopeful might hold a clandestine meeting. His encyclopedic knowledge of Washington, D.C, is unequaled. I especially want to thank Pam and Hugh Hill for their generous contribution to the Cure Alzheimer's Fund in order to have their son Gabe as a character in our book.

We are excited that the dynamic duo of Julie Melnick and Jennie Kuperstein, the principals of Standout Public Relations, are enthusiastically helping us promote our novel. And thanks also to Katherine Wynne, who promised that my author's picture would not show every facet of my senior status.

When it takes three years to complete a book, it is a certainty that many people who have helped will regretfully not be acknowledged. Knowing my friends, those who were missed will remind me of it more than once. Still, it is always Faith, Family, and Friends with me. I tell everyone that I have the world's greatest family at home and the most extraordinary family of professionals at work. We feel like every single one of our clients is our extended family, and I am grateful for your trust.

—Marvin McIntyre

It started many years ago when I prodded my dad to "write that novel" he kept talking about. I couldn't have been prouder when he finished *Insiders*. He continues to blaze the path of what's possible in my life. I had the chance to plug some plot holes and help invent his world with *Inside Out*, and I got hooked. I am honored and humbled that I had the opportunity to help him bring the third book home. It is beyond a tremendous gift to work on a project like this with your father – remember that, Jackson.

One of my goals in this book was to strengthen the female characters to align with the powerful women that surround my life. My mom, who continues to raise her husband as well as me and my awesome trio of siblings. My daughter, who continues to be more fearless than I can ever aspire to be. And my wife, who dives into new challenges while continuing to do it all – I am blessed to be your partner.

—Jamie McIntyre

About the Authors

Marvin McIntyre is an acclaimed investment professional with over 45 years of experience. Since being featured in the book *The Winners Circle*, by R.J. Shook, he has been ranked as the top financial advisor in Washington, D.C. by Barron's magazine. In addition, his consistently high ranking as one of the country's best investment advisors made him a member of the coveted Barron's Hall of Fame. In 2016, Forbes magazine began ranking all financial advisors, and McIntyre was predictably near the top of the list.

Throughout his celebrated career, McIntyre has been recognized as one of the industry's most innovative and forward-thinking professionals. He is known as "The Financial Wizard," and his quick wit and affection for his clients are hallmarks of his success. His energy and humor color both his business and personal lives. The grateful father is blessed with a very tolerant wife, four semi-perfect children, and seven perfect grandchildren.

With offices a few blocks from the White House, McIntyre has merged his financial expertise with a keen awareness of Washington's political community. *The Outsider* is the final installment of his well-received trilogy of financial/political thrillers. All profits from his books are donated to charity.

Jamie McIntyre is a passionate entrepreneur.   Over the last twenty years, he has been on a mission with a band of fellow entre-preneurs, software developers, researchers, and agile contributors to define what is next in wealth management. During that time, he co-founded four companies in the wealth management and technology industries.   He has also followed in his father's footsteps to write songs that remind people of what matters most. (Search "Don't Grow Up on Me" on YouTube.) Jamie lives with his wife, son, and daughter in Darnestown, Maryland.

More on Jamie: http://www.rewirecapital.com/jamie